The Fallen

Ravek Hunter

<u>info@WorldsOfAtlantis.com</u>

For Mrs. Wife,
who gave me two incredible boys
that I hope will be proud to read their father's work one day.

FANTASY NOVELS BY RAVEK HUNTER

Red Wizard of Atlantis

The Fallen

Saving Eridu

The Imaziyen Druid

Shadows of Lyonesse

Beasts of Courth

Ys (Coming 2022)

If you enjoy reading books by this author, please remember to leave a review at your favorite bookseller!

To learn more about the backstory, mythology, and character development in these stories or to view world maps visit us at:

https://www.WorldsOfAtlantis.com!

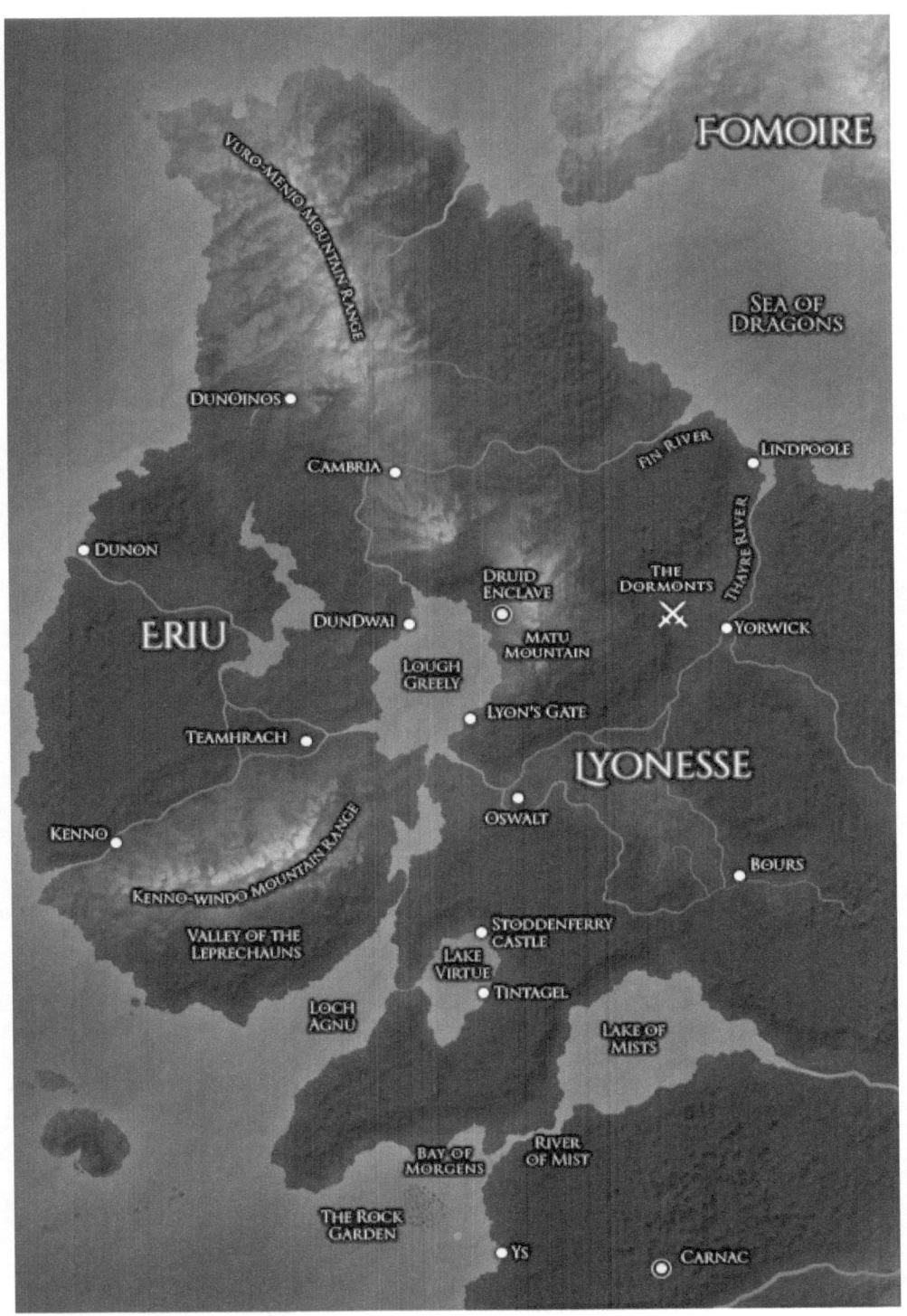

TABLE OF CONTENTS

CHILDREN OF ATLAS

It was from the stars they came, out of the vast darkness of the Primeval Cosmos, plunging from the sky in a great wingless beast consumed by smoke and fire. It fell with a thunderous crash upon the earth plowing a long black rift across the open plain before it came to rest in a final shudder of sparks and lightning. The smoking shell of the massive creature lay shattered, yet from its broken maw came hundreds of odd-looking figures that crawled through the acrid haze and stumbled disoriented onto the lush green grass of a new world.

The Sylvan watched the arrival of the newcomers from the quiet repose of the forest. They scrutinized these strange bi-pedal aliens with blue-tinted skin and elongated heads and large almond-shaped eyes that had come uninvited to their tranquil isle, until now isolate and protected from intrusion by the vast expanse of the Primal Sea. They observed how the slender forms worked as a collective to remove the shiny scales of their battered host piece by piece to make shelters, how they buried their dead, how they mourned their passing.

When that was done, they brought red glowing crystals that shown bright even in daylight from the metallic frame of the silver beast's remains. The crystals they handled with great care and reverence, depositing them in caverns deep in the earth near an inlet on the coast. It was there too, that they began to build with stones.

These were a people with no hope of return or rescue, determined to survive and resolute in their struggle to make a place for themselves. A permanent place that would bring irrevocable change the Isle. To the land, to nature, to a way of life that had existed since time began.

Still the Sylvan watched.

The prophesies spoke of events such as these that would herald the beginning of the Fourth Age, the Age of the Golden Aspen, the Age when the winds from the north would bring an icy chill even in the summertime. And end the elves isolation from the rest of the world forever.

In time the Sylvan learned that the unusual blue-tinted people called themselves the followers of Atlas, the one who had risen among them and offered up hope for a new future. They would name the spine of the island in his honor and build a shining city on the sea that would become known as Atlantis.

And they thrived.

Recorded in the Fourth Age of the Golden Aspen
by Watcher CrellianRafkarSil of Avalon

CHAPTER 1

The Proposal
Sylvan Year (SY) 5489

The Descant of Eriu as I performed it so long ago ne'er made a distinction between the Goddess and the Land—for both were one and the same. The Druids knew this truth dogmatic and lived well with nature and her blessings. Her name defined a promise of "abundance," and it was so. An abundance of life, abundance of prosperity and abundance of terrors to be sure, and it was my fortune to experience every part of that asseveration. Of all the lands I have lived and wandered, over more years than I care to remember, I miss her very nearly most of all.

Wodanaz the Wanderer

Eselt's nerves were frayed almost to their tortured ends, and, impossibly, she was charged with excitement at the same time. It was a maddening sensation with no proper outlet for relief, and she found herself regrettably following her mother's practical advice. She expelled a long sigh, a hollow sound that even to her own ears sounded tired and pathetic. "What will Father say, Mother?" The needlework her mother had given her as the task to distract her mind from the only thing she could think about was only frustrating her. She had never been very good at it, certainly not as good as any of her older sisters, and as far as she was concerned, it was a tedious waste of time anyway.

"He will say what he will say, child. Be patient." Her mother lifted her eyebrow at the needlework Eselt had put aside. "Lord Maruk is the first suitor of any genuine potential that has asked for your hand in marriage, and your father, as the High King of Eriu, must take his appeal seriously."

Her suitor, Lord Maruk, had gone to see her father that afternoon to ask for her hand in marriage. That was several hours ago, and still he had not returned. At only sixteen years of age, Eselt had rarely thought about getting married, except, of course, that her friends, her lady-in-waiting, and especially her sisters teased her about it excessively. But it was not until she had met the duke that she felt what she could only interpret as love. And right now, love was nearly driving her to insanity.

She recalled when Lord Maruk first arrived at the Court of Teamhrach. Eselt was in attendance with the rest of her family to formally greet him and his entourage. They received the duke in their grand capital as a guest of honor, and her father officially recognized him as the principal diplomat of the delegation from the Kingdom of Lyonesse. She had assumed it would be just another boring trade mission between the two countries during which she was required to go through the motions of hospitality: curtsying and smiling and entertaining their guests with witty conversation. Eselt was glad the trade mission occurred only once a year, because the entire royal family was expected to cast themselves as part of the entertainment. Although she did not follow world politics very closely, she knew enough to realize that although Lyonesse and Eriu were traditionally strong trade partners and allies, her father would still complain that there were always laborious details to be negotiated or grievances to be ironed out to ensure the continuation of the kingdoms' amicable relationship.

Reluctantly Eselt resumed her mother's project, sticking her finger with the first thrust of the needle. "What about all the others? There have been at least twenty since I came of age."

Her mother laughed. It was the kind of laugh that had always set Eselt's teeth on edge, and she would have grimaced if she wasn't busy sucking on her punctured finger-tip. "Those . . . Boys were little more than young nobles looking to upgrade their family breeding by marriage. None of them would have enhanced your father's position in the least."

"Lord Maruk is a duke," Eselt countered hopefully. "The Duke of Tintagel, the greatest duchy in all of Lyonesse! Surely father can't say no to a man like that, even if he doesn't know him well."

Her mother repositioned her layered skirts on the divan where she sat. "They know each other quite well, I think."

"What?" This was news to Eselt. Every year there was a different diplomat from Lyonesse, something about the King of Lyonesse keeping all of his dukes and counts engaged in the process of government, so she had never had the opportunity to meet Duke Maruk on a previous occasion, and as far as she knew, he had never been a guest. Eselt considered it a sign from Eriu, the Moon Goddess after which their fair Kingdom was named, that he should be the one to come at just the time when she was eligible to marry.

"Your father and Lord Maruk have known each other for decades."

Her mother was so matter-of-fact as she spoke. She never even lifted her eyes from her needlework as if what she said was as common as observing the sky was blue. "When they were young they fought wars together, went hunting together and Eriu knows what else together when away from their families."

"Mother!" Eselt was shocked at the insinuation.

"Men will be men, dear. You might as well learn that lesson right now."

Eselt regarded marriages between the royals of Eriu and Lyonesse as nothing unusual. They were merely another bond that kept their two peoples united. Fortunately, she was the youngest of her four sisters, and all of them had already been married off to wealthy nobles of influence within Eriu. That left her to get all of the attention when a potential suitor came calling, and they came in droves beginning the day she turned sixteen. So far, her father had not pressured her in any way to choose one of the young men who lined the corridors to solicit their charms. Eselt found them all silly and immature, or far too melodramatic in their "love" for her that she laughed them off, shattering hearts by the dozen.

Her mother's words had given her hope. "If they are such good friends, then father must approve of our marriage, don't you think?"

"We shall see. You know very well that your father has his own agenda and will seek the best advantage from any match he selects for you, just like he did with your sisters."

Eselt adjusted the locks of her long, golden hair and wondered at how striking it was against her fair skin. None of her sisters had hair like hers. They all had brown hair that made them look far too pale in the sunlight. She giggled to herself—she was being cruel to sisters she loved so dearly. All of her sisters were renowned as natural beauties by everyone in Eriu, and she was pleased that Duke Maruk's eyes never strayed to any of them, that Eselt had noticed. From the start, the duke's gaze lingered upon her far longer than was considered appropriate, and it filled her with excitement. He was not like the boys that courted her; he was a man, old enough to be her father, for sure, but that maturity was part of what attracted her to him.

Events had moved quickly after they were formally introduced, she thought fondly. She found herself next to the duke at banquets, engaged in unexpected meetings in the hallways and answering requests for supervised walks in the gardens. She never denied him her time; she actually looked forward to it.

After only ten days in Teamhrach, he told her he wanted to ask her father to allow them to marry. She had been elated, but what would her father think about the match? Would he approve because Lord Maruk was the Duke of Tintagel or deny their intentions because he had another in mind for her? She tried to think like her father. The duke was powerful and carried significant political weight in Lyonesse, and the union of his last eligible daughter with the Duke of Tintagel would serve to strengthen the High King's influence in future trade negotiations and the security of his eastern borders. High King Cadeyrn was, after all, a pragmatic man, wasn't he? She desperately needed him to be.

Eselt loved being with Duke Maruk, she loved his personality and humor, and she loved how respected and admired he was. It was so simple in her mind. If she loved so much about this Duke Maruk, then she must be in love with him. And if her father allowed the marriage, then she would move to Valiant Keep in Tintagel, one of the most glorious cities in the Western Kingdoms. She had been there once as a child and adored the beauty of its towers rising over the precarious rocky outcroppings above the sapphire-blue waves of Lake Virtue. She also knew that Lord Maruk was close to King Praeter Eldorath and Queen Penelope of Lyonesse, which meant that she would be going to some of the most fabulous balls of any kingdom. Yes, she was in love with Lord Maruk—at least, she believed in her heart that she was.

"Your father will keep the duke out all night drinking and reliving the old days. And knowing your father, he will withhold his answer until they are both nearly blind from drink." Her mother put down her needlework and walked over to where Eselt was sitting.

Eselt just scowled at her mother's remark.

"It's getting late, child, and there is nothing good that can come of your worrying." She kissed Eselt on the forehead. "Get some sleep if you can, and dream about a joyful tomorrow."

Then she was alone.

Eselt felt more alone than she ever had before in her young life. Even though her mother was often an annoyance, she kept her company and was someone to talk to, no matter that Eselt didn't like everything she had to say.

It was getting late, she brooded. Too late in the evening for a gentleman to call on a lady. Eselt began to pace. Would he tell her the news first thing in the morning, or would she have to wait until later in the day? It was the waiting that was intolerable. Her father must know how anxious she was for an answer, yet he would keep her duke into the morning hours drinking and trading stories no matter what his decision. She wanted to punch him in the nose! Didn't he care how nervous and on pins she would be? Probably not, she conceded to herself. He knew nothing of his little girl's dreams. She stopped pacing and sternly corrected herself—the dreams of a young woman! She might as well just go to bed and sulk.

And so she did.

The next morning, Eselt was pleased to receive word that Lord Maruk would join her for breakfast. She was nervously anticipating his arrival and the news that would travel with him and worried that her father's response was not favorable. Could she live with the shame? Could the poor duke?

Lord Maruk entered the breakfast chamber. He was dashing in his dark green riding cloak—fastened under his graying beard by an emerald encrusted clasp—a black silk tunic, long brown wool stockings, and high, fashionable black riding boots turned down at the top. But what she noted more than any of that was the serious, almost sorrowful expression that he bore upon his face. A sinking feeling grew inside of Eselt, and she worried about the words he had come to impart, words only moments away that could leave her devastated for the rest of her life.

He strode toward her, forgetting to remove his feathered hat as would be the custom of a gentleman in the presence of a lady. Did he intend to escape so quickly that he couldn't trouble with replacing his hat upon exit? Her heart raced. Something was horribly wrong.

"Good morning, dearest." Lord Maruk kissed her cheek and knelt before her chair. His tone was somber and betrayed the grief in his usually jovial nature. Eselt felt light-headed and feared she might swoon. She had seen it happen a few times before to ladies under stress and considered it a ridiculous ploy for attention and sympathy, yet here it was, about to happen to her.

Ever so tenderly, the duke took her hand and drew it to his lips. His features hid beneath the wide brim of his hat and its downward-facing angle. His whiskers tickled her fingers as if he trembled, and his shoulders quietly shook, although he tried to hide it. Poor man, could he be weeping? The news must be dreadful, and she wasn't sure if she could bear hearing the words aloud.

"I am so sorry, my love." His voice was thick and restrained as if trying to deny her ears the feeling in his sad message. "I have spoken to your father."

He coughed then and sputtered a little, trying to constrain his grief. This was so awful that Eselt wanted to weep not just for herself, but for this sorrowful creature who struggled to say the words neither of them wanted to hear and darken the room with their heartbreak.

"Your father," he whispered as if he held his breath. His last breath.

She held hers.

"Your father said that whether you like it or not, we must be undivided in our love for the remainder of our lives." His shoulders shook violently as he barely released the words.

Eselt was stunned. What did he say? Was he laughing?

"You!" she shouted, falling to her knees in front of him.

Taking his head in her hands, she lifted his face to hers. He had a devilish smile and tears of mirth running down his face.

"Are you trying to bury your bride before you marry her?" She was ecstatic, hugging and kissing him until they both laughed so much they could hardly breathe.

Eselt's mood at breakfast changed quite suddenly while she enjoyed the company of her betrothed, her duke. Her duke! And before he departed, she produced a lock of her long golden hair and placed it in his hand.

"To keep me near to your heart until the day we meet to become man and wife," she told him.

Eselt had mixed feelings about their parting. She hated the idea that it would be almost two months before she would see him again but rejoiced in the delight that when she did, it would be in Tintagel on their wedding day.

~~~

The hooves of Purin's warhorse echoed off the uneven cobblestones that glistened damply in the early morning fog. There were fewer and fewer people in the streets as he rode his massive sable steed deeper into the darkest district of Lower Tintagel. Those few he passed at that hour were beggars, thieves, and prostitutes. Those were considered the undesirables and shunned by the respectable and elite of proper society. There were few prostitutes in Tintagel except on this street, the only street they were tolerated to ply their trade, but he never cared to engage in their business. His taste tended to the more refined edges of dark entertainment, despite his having to find satisfaction among the unclean derelicts and the lowest of the low.

Purin detested this district, the poorest of them all, where the thieves' guilds held sway, although in truth they were an invisible presence in every district. Even in upper Tintagel, where the lights were bright and there were no dark streets at night. Purin accepted it as a necessary trade-off to keep the crime there at an "acceptable" level and the depravity contained to lower Tintagel. Not that Tintagel was any different from any other city in the Western Kingdoms, but His Majesty, King Praeter of Lyonesse, preferred to keep the trash in his kingdom out of sight, presenting higher virtue as the open reality with corruption and misconduct safely swept away into the darkest corners. That was where Purin rode now. It was a beautiful balance, in a way, he thought. He considered it a suitable harmony of good and . . . Less good, particularly since he enjoyed the benefits of both sides of the scale.

He rode without fear, knowing that a lone man in the dark district this late, showing wealth in the breed of his horse and the finery of his clothes, would generally be an easy target for the gangs and cutthroats that prowled the streets looking for any advantage. Not Purin. No one would try to harm him. And not just because he was an exceptional swordsman who would likely kill anyone that attempted assault anyway, but also because of who he did business with. The word in the street was that he was untouchable, and no one had ever dared challenge that decree.

Purin guided his horse to the back of a loud tavern he knew as the Gallant Leper, and there a boy took his mount and disappeared into the attached stables. Almost immediately, a latch released, and the back door of the tavern opened, flooding amber light onto the expensive leather boots he wore.

"Come in, my lord." An old man with a raspy voice beckoned him forward. "Everything is set in your usual room downstairs."

"Good. Send down the wine now, and make sure it's well chilled this time."

"Yes, my lord. I will bring it right away."

Purin walked through the kitchens teaming with cooks and servers loading trays with drink and bowls of stew. None of them so much as glanced at him as he made his way across the crowded room and down the stairs into the storerooms below. There, he went into a small room loaded with barrels of wine and opened another door on the far side. Beyond it, a dark stairway led him down to a landing in front of yet another door, where a small table with a single lit candle stood next to a small plate. Removing his riding gloves, he placed a gold coin on the dish and went through the door.

"On your knees, dog," growled a woman's voice in the dimly lit room.

Purin fell to his knees submissively. The crack of a whip sounded above his head.

"Did you bring me a gift?"

"Yes . . ." Another crack of the whip, this time on his shoulder, tearing the fabric and drawing a trickle of blood.

"Did I say speak?"

Purin remained silent.

"Good, let's try this again. Did you bring me a gift?"

He made no reply.

"Speak."

"Yes, mistress," he said meekly. "I left the gift atop a plate on the table outside."

"Very good dog. Now remove those threads, and let's get started."

The punishment went on for over an hour, and Purin enjoyed every moment of it. This was not his first time, but it was his first time with her. They were all different in the beginning and then all the same in the end. And that's what all this was working up to and why he couldn't stop. He needed the satisfaction of that end.

"Our time is up," the woman said, putting away the rod in a rack on the wall.

Purin slowly looked up to regard his pain mistress. She wore a long black leather skirt split to her waist up both sides and a loose, sheer black blouse with nothing underneath. The room was designed for their purpose with all the restraints, tables, whips, rockers, cords, and strap devices to bring about the desired pleasure from pain. A light cedar incense drifted through the air, disguising the more offensive odors brought on by the exertions of the evening.

He stood from his kneeling position displaying welts, bruises, and cuts all over the parts of his body that would be hidden by clothing. He was not wearing clothes now, and his lean muscled physique glistened with blood and sweat.

"Look at me," he said, and she hesitantly turned to face him.

"Was everything as you wish, my lord? I did my best to follow the instructions that were given to me." Her demeanor had changed completely, and now she assumed the submissive role between the two.

"We are not done yet."

She glanced down at his state of arousal, and he could sense the panic begin to rise within her. It excited him further.

"What do you mean? Surely they told you this is all I do. Nothing more. That was the agreement."

"Things have changed." Purin took a step toward her.

The woman immediately ran to the door of the room, but it was locked from the outside. Purin grabbed her by the back of the hair and dragged her screaming to the center of the room.

"Please, please don't hurt me. They told me to punish you for an hour, and that was it. Please!" Her eyes bulged wildly with fear from the awkward position in which he held her neck, twisted, so she looked up at him. "I don't want to do this."

He shoved her onto the ground and crouched with his face close to hers. "This can go hard for you, or it can go extremely hard. First, I am going to do to you everything you did to me and more. You are going to beg me to stop, but I won't. When I am ready, I will bend you over that table there, and only when I am fully drained of my lust will I allow you to leave. And when you leave here, you will never speak to anyone about this, or you will be found, and it will go worse for you." He let go of her hair and stood. "You are welcome to scream as much as you like."

He walked over to the rack and picked out a sturdy rod with several lengths of leather tied to the end, then stood over the sobbing woman.

"Now remove those threads, and let's get started."

Before dawn, Purin walked out of the storeroom and through the back of the bustling tavern. He had never been here during the day, and he wondered absently if there was ever a time it wasn't so lively.

The old man was waiting for him. "Was everything to your satisfaction this evening, my lord?"

Purin took the reins of his horse from the nervous stable boy, nodded, and flipped him a gold coin. "That was a spirited one. She screamed the whole time." His subjects had rarely been so satisfying. "Have a fresh one for me in three days."

Purin hated the return ride through lower Tintagel. It was almost completely devoid of humanity, except for the few here and there who slouched against a wall, passed out or dead. It didn't matter to him which. And it smelled of vomit and urine. Not even the prostitutes stayed on the street this late.

The first light of the day spread its golden wings over upper Tintagel by the time Purin arrived at Valiant Keep. He left his horse in the stables and walked briskly through the Foregate. The guards snapped to attention as he passed with his long black cloak, emblazoned with the profile of a boar, flapping behind him.

Another man dressed in the uniform of the Duke's Guard walked down the hall toward him from the opposite direction. He was tall and powerfully built, and he planted himself firmly in the center of the hallway, impeding Purin's way forward. When he was close, Purin stopped directly in front of the guard and looked him in the eye.

"Report, Sergeant," he ordered.

The sergeant came to attention. "All was well during the night. No incidents."

"Very good, Sergeant, dismissed."

"Captain Purin, one other thing. There is a message from our man in Teamhrach. It arrived this morning by pigeon," the sergeant hastened.

"What is it?" he asked.

"The duke is getting married."

CHAPTER 2

Departure

Dutiful in spirit, chivalrous to a fault, virtue and honor define this land called Lyonesse. Rife with ballads and tales of good deeds, power, faith, and love, a vision and bloodline would be the lasting vestige of its legacy. Concerning this account, I defer to Myrllin, for my time in such fabled acreage has been fleeting. The lack of corruption and brutal intrigue so certainly would have bored me to my death, until I found the greatest tragedy I would ever tell would be born from it.

Wodanaz the Wanderer

Drystan walked quickly through the broad stone corridors of Valiant Keep, his white cloak, fringed with gold and emblazoned with the symbol of Sun Goddess Sunna, billowed behind him in his haste. His uncle, Duke Maruk, had returned from Teamhrach in Eriu, and there were rumors of news that traveled with him, news that would bring wonderful change to the dreary halls they called home. Drystan said a quick prayer to Sunna that his uncle had not gotten drunk and promised Drystan's hand to one of the many Eriu princesses that always seemed available in abundance. They were, for the most part, very beautiful, but the last thing he wanted was to settle down and raise a family.

His two older cousins, whom he thought of as brothers, were already married by his age, and Duke Maruk had been hinting lately that it was time for him to bring another advantageous match to the family. Indeed, the duke, as Drystan's legal guardian, had the right to negotiate a union with anyone he saw fit, but Drystan never believed that he would actually do it. The duke's own sons had on their own found wives that brought benefit to the family, and he expected it would be the same for himself.

Eventually.

He thought back to those innocent days when he ran down these same corridors without a care in the world. He always felt fortunate to grow up with cousins who treated him like their natural brother, and as they grew older, squired, trained, and became knights of the realm, Drystan was determined to follow in their path. He did well as a student and proved to be highly skilled in his combat, hunting, horsemanship, and tactical military training. By adolescence, he was squired to a reputable knight and began to travel the kingdom and nearby foreign lands while in his service. Those were hard years, he recalled, not being used to serving a lord. He deserved every beating he earned with his mischief.

That knight did his job well, however, and years later when he came of age, Drystan was more than qualified to represent Tintagel as a knight of the realm and found himself wandering the Western Kingdoms as a Silver Cloak, a knight initiate. Now those were some good times, Drystan thought with an internal chuckle. Less than a year after that, he was responsible for saving the lives of several villagers near the Arges River from a giant reptile that had crept into Lyonesse from Fomoire to find vulnerable prey. It had the unfortunate luck of finding Drystan instead. Yet despite Drystan's prowess, the lizard had been a harrowing experience that nearly cost him his life. One of those villagers happened to be a cousin of Queen Penelope Eldorath, and when the word got out about his deed, Drystan was awarded the honor of the Royal Act of Heroism and knighted by the king himself. Duke Maruk and his family could not have been more proud.

So far, he had enjoyed a good life. Why ruin it by strapping him with a wife?

Drystan's attention snapped back to the present when he strode out of the main gatehouse of Valiant Keep and into the inner ward, where the duke's caravan of carriages and cavalry had just arrived. Drystan adjusted his girdle, smoothed his long tan cloak, and polished his gold Knight's Emblem of Sunna with his sleeve. He was here not only to greet the duke but also to represent his family, and he never embarrassed the family.

As soon as the carriages came to a halt, a small army of servants descended upon them, helping the nobles step out, providing mugs of wine for refreshment and removing trunks filled with personal belongings. The lead carriage, the largest and most elaborate of them all, stood with the double doors open on one side with a line of servants waiting patiently for the occupants to exit. From his angle, Drystan could not see inside, so he also waited, only mildly concerned at the delay. Except that whatever was happening in his uncle's carriage went on and on.

While the other carriages emptied and departed, the duke's remained where it was, and the servants stood idle. Finally, he broke protocol and walked over to see if there was something they needed help with. There was a murmur of voices from inside the carriage. Excited, fast exchanges were taking place. Not an argument, more of a debate. Inside he could see the duke in animated conversation with his closest advisor, Sir Wilhem, and his scribe. They were trying to work something out, but he couldn't understand what it was.

"Uncle . . ." Drystan cautiously queried.

The duke turned and squinted through the open doors into the bright daylight only partially obscured by Drystan's form.

"Drystan, my boy!" he exclaimed with unusual excitement. "Tell me, what rhymes with this verse, 'For there resides an ocean of words that pour from my heart'? I must complete this poem before I step onto Tintagel."

Drystan was taken aback. What was this about?

He stuttered for a moment then said, "How about, 'and that ocean I'll sail that we will never be apart.'"

Duke Maruk's eyes lit up. "Yes, that's it! Write it down. Sir Wilhem, tell him to write it down." The duke was blindly waving toward the scribe in the darkened carriage.

"He's writing it down," the knight assured him, a hint of humor in his voice.

"Fabulous, send it right away!"

The duke hoped out of the carriage and embraced Drystan in a tight bear hug.

"I have so much to tell you. To tell everyone. Have your brothers gathered everyone in the dining room?"

"Yes, Uncle, they await you there now." He had not seen his uncle so energized and happy since before his adopted mother died. It was a welcome change from the gloom and melancholy that had gripped Maruk's soul and demeanor for years afterward.

The duke kissed Drystan on his temple roughly and mussed up his long blond hair, before putting his arm around Drystan's shoulders and walking down the corridor. "Then I will get dressed for dinner and see you there!" Releasing Drystan, the duke called loudly for his servants and walked into Valiant Keep in the direction of his apartments.

Shaking his head, Drystan had no idea what had gotten into the duke, but he was glad to see it. It had to be love, he mused, and he made his way to the dining room to inform the duke's guests that he had arrived and would be joining them soon.

Drystan felt a twinge of regret that he had never known his real father. The man had died near Cambria fighting a resurgence group trying to revive old sentiments of the Atiod-bherto, the ancient Cult of Earth Druids who believed in the blasphemous ritual of animal and human sacrifice. The cult was defeated during the Oak War by combined forces from Lyonesse and Eriu that supported the Nature Druids of the Sun and Moon Goddesses, Sunna and Eriu, which ended some five centuries previous.

As for Drystan's mother, she had tragically died shortly after his third birthday from a coughing illness, leaving Drystan an orphan. His uncle, Duke Maruk, took Drystan in and set him among the ducal family to be educated and trained alongside Maruk's other sons. Drystan found it difficult to feel bad about his past. Of course he would have preferred his parents to live and raise him themselves, but he had no memory of who they were or what they were like. They were just stories told by his uncle, whom he thought of as his father because he was the only father he had ever known, and the duke's wife, who had died tragically a few years ago, had been as good a mother as anyone could ask for.

He kicked up his step in anticipation of the night ahead and felt the excitement building as if his limbs were infused with lightning. If his uncle's announcement was what he expected, then it would be not only good fortune for the duke, but also for his family and the city itself. And especially for Drystan.

~~~

Drystan waited with his brothers, their wives, and various nobles assembled in the dining room. Fifty of the duke's closest friends and family had been invited, and fifty were in attendance. No one was going to miss this mysterious gathering. Already the wine was flowing, and everyone was speculating about the news the duke was planning to announce.

When the duke arrived, he nearly danced into the room in a mood bursting with exuberance. For just a moment, he paused regally in the dining room's double-wide doorway and just smiled. Truly he could have been a king standing there, dressed in his finest burgundy overcoat and black silk stockings and completing the ensemble with gold buckled small boots and his thick gold chain of office.

If there was a reaction from those he faced, it was stunned silence. *Who was this man that paraded around in the duke's likeness?* thought Drystan, and based on the faces around him, they must have all been thinking the same thing. In truth, it was a pleasing sight to see him like this.

The duke spoke then, breaking the spell that held them all inanimate.

"I return from Teamhrach with happy news. Not only have we negotiated a continuation of the strong trade relationship between Lyonesse and Eriu, but I have returned with something more. In less than two months from today, I will marry the youngest daughter of High King Cadeyrn!"

At first, the duke's announcement was met with stunned silence, as if those present were unsure if the words they heard were real or fantasy, and then almost as one the room erupted in cheers. Until this moment, it was popular opinion that the duke would die a widower. Even Drystan's brothers received the news happily for their father who had been in a state of despondency for so long. Not only would it be an advantageous political alliance, but he appeared genuinely infatuated with his intended bride.

"Her name is Princess Eselt, the youngest and most beautiful daughter of the High King. She will be brought here for the happy occasion, and we must make sure she feels welcome and loved! This wedding will rival the splendor and elegance of any king's!"

More cheers rose from the dinner guests. Drystan cheered too—partly for his uncle and partly that it wasn't him getting married. He briefly wondered how long he could successfully dodge that arrow. For now, anyway, he was safe and would join the duke in celebrating what many in the duchy might consider a miracle for the old fellow.

Rounds of wine and poetic salutes followed before dinner was served, and by the end of the night, the duke's daughters-in-law had volunteered to organize a massive celebration and ceremony. They promised an event of such beauty that it would be remembered by the kingdom for generations and be the envy of every future bride. Then there was a general discussion at the table regarding the guest list, and Drystan couldn't help but shudder. There would be hundreds from all over the Western Kingdoms, and every princess looking to land a handsome noble of Lyonesse would be casting their greedy gaze upon him. Maybe his cheering was a bit premature after all.

~~~

Within a few days, invitations were sent by horse, pigeon, and magical means all through the realm, into Eriu, Courth, the four cities of the Tuatha De, and the city-state of Ys. Royals, nobles, ambassadors, wealthy tradesmen, and military officers from those nations would likely be present, which made for a vastly inclusive guest list. Valiant Keep and the upper ward would be a beehive of activity preparing for the arrival of all those important personages for the next few weeks.

Drystan had never seen excitement of this scale in Tintagel, and he was doing his best to stay out of the way when a golden opportunity presented itself that would allow him to escape the chaos of Valiant Keep before the wedding.

"I will be sending an honor guard to Teamhrach in a few days to escort Princess Eselt and the royal family, their nobles, and their attendants back to Tintagel for the wedding," the duke was saying. "Your brothers have other responsibilities I need them to attend to, so I thought maybe you would be willing to lead . . ."

"I'll do it!" Drystan jumped at the chance to be away from Valiant Keep, which was already jammed with hordes of workmen and servants preparing for the massive influx of guests.

The duke chuckled. "Very well, my boy, assemble a hundred knights and plan to depart in no more than two days' time."

Drystan nodded smartly to his uncle. "It would be my honor to escort the future duchess to her new home." He was excited about going to Teamhrach, and although he had been there once before as a squire, he looked forward to seeing the city again. It was a ruggedly beautiful city that sat within the two forks of a wide river against the background of the snow-capped Kenno-windo Mountain Range. More than that, the women there were among the most beautiful he had ever seen.

The duke patted his shoulder and turned to leave, then hesitated. "One other thing. Take Knight Commander Blevin to lead the company. He knows many of the Eriu knights in Teamhrach and Commander Teutjorīk of the Fianna well."

Drystan knew of the Fianna. They were an elite group of the best knights selected from all over Eriu that formed the core of the Royal Guard for the High King and his family. Competitions and tournaments were held every four years for those who wished to serve as a Fiann, and it was considered one of the highest honors for an Eriu knight to join their ranks. Sir Blevin, whose mother had been from Eriu, had many relatives in that country, some of whom had served with the Fianna in the past.

"Of course, Uncle," Drystan agreed. "Sir Blevin would be my choice as well."

The duke smiled, then went on his way, leaving Drystan eager to get on with the business of arranging a company for the journey ahead. The cities of Tintagel and Teamhrach were about one hundred leagues apart, or seven days on horseback. With so much distance between them and less than a month to prepare, time was running short. He could only hope that the entourage preparing in Teamhrach would be ready to go very soon after he arrived.

The morning of their departure, the Temple Knights, in full battle armor under the colorful pennants of their houses carried by their squires, were marshaled in tight formation awaiting the arrival of the duke. Drystan was at their head next to Knight Commander Blevin. Drystan's metal armor gleamed brightly in the morning light, and like the others, he wore the white cloak fringed with gold and the Sun Emblem of Sunna affixed to his right shoulder. Mounted in rows five across, the knights were the perfect spectacle of the most exquisite parade lined up on the east side of the inner ward.

Sir Blevin was an older man with a well-kept gray beard and bushy gray eyebrows over steel-blue eyes. He had risen to the rank of knight commander when Drystan was only a young boy after an envious career in service to the duke. Tales were still told of Tintagel's most famous knight, the majority of which were surprisingly true, despite the embellishment of the bards and minstrels.

The duke emerged from the shadowed entry of Valiant Keep flanked by Sir Wilhem, his scribe, and both of Drystan's older brothers. None were armored, nor should they have needed to be, and they wore their usual wool tunics and stockings. Although it was summer, there was always a cool breeze that blew off the glaciers less than three hundred leagues to the north and chilled the early and late hours of the day.

Duke Maruk was carrying something in his arms that appeared to be folded fabric, and as he approached the mounted Temple Knights, he unfolded it and held it high for all to see. It was a white surcoat fringed with gold typical of every Temple Knight and worn casually or for ceremony. What made it remarkable was the beautifully sewn image of the duke's coat of arms on the front of it. The field of the arms divided with the left half tincture argent and the right half tincture sable and a counterchanged profile of a tusked boar—black where it lay on the white field and white where it lay on the black field. Most remarkable was the addition of golden thread that seemed to shine brightly with a light of its own and outlined the boar's profile.

Drystan dismounted at the duke's approach and carefully accepted the surcoat offered by his lord.

The duke spoke loud enough for all in the ward to hear, "This is for my Eselt, my love and my light. She will know that you, Drystan, are my true representative sent to fetch my betrothed to me, as evidenced by her golden hair, which has been magically woven into my house arms. Bring her to me swiftly, Prince of Tintagel, and guard her with your very life and soul. I happily wait upon your return."

It was a rare occasion that Duke Maruk spoke in this fashion, and Drystan could feel the weight of responsibility that passed from the duke's hands to his own when he was given the surcoat. He also knew that his uncle meant every word he said about guarding her life, and saying them meant that there would be no return for him without her safely delivered.

With all the proper etiquette of ritual, Drystan slowly bowed and carefully packed the surcoat in his saddlebag. There were hundreds gathered in the ward, standing on the ramparts of the inner curtain wall and open towers. He could hear the criers describing the scene from the walls to the thousands massed in the outer ward and the description carried down the lined, broad boulevard that led from the front gates of Valiant Keep to the outer gates of the city wall. It was a moment that approached a spiritual experience for him, rivaling the occasion he was knighted by the king.

Drystan mounted his big spotted bay and with a salute to the duke signaled to Sir Blevin to move his company of knights through the gates of the ward at a stately pace. The throngs that received them as they traveled out of the city were exuberant, and Drystan found himself smiling and waving as if leading a fanciful parade. The other knights couldn't help but join in the pleasure, and soon they were all laughing and calling to patrons and family members they knew on the street. When they finally exited the city, Drystan followed Sir Blevin's lead and kicked his horse into an energy-conserving travel pace, and the knights who followed quickly restored their discipline and kept up in proper formation.

It was early summer, and the chill of spring had nearly given way to the cool days of the warmer months. It never got very hot in Lyonesse, not even at the height of summer, and traveling was comfortable if one was not in a hurry. Except that Drystan was in a hurry. He worried that he would not return on time with the princess and her extended retinue, causing a delay of the wedding that so many had worked so hard to plan. It was especially frustrating considering that the return trip, when they would be riding encumbered with baggage trains and carriages, would be much slower. Emboldened by haste, he pressed his men and horses to their limits in the hope of gaining as much time as possible before they reached their destination.

~~~

"Mairwen? How old is your husband? Isn't he the oldest of all of ours, dear?"

"You know he is, Braith, but Gwynn's husband is very nearly as old, and she is ten years younger than I."

"Our age doesn't really seem to matter I think, as long as we've started bleeding." Braith was doing something adventurous with Eselt's hair. "I wonder why the age of the man is of no consequence. Surely the match would be better if younger gentlemen were paired with younger ladies."

The other women in the room laughed as if Braith had told a funny. For her part, Braith's face reddened several shades, and she looked around abashed.

"Well, why not?" she demanded, stamping her petite foot on the floor.

Mairwen fixed her with a look that they had all seen on their mother more than a few times. "Because the older men don't want the older ladies and because the older men have titles and wealth."

"That is true," Gwynn chimed in, "especially if the older men don't have children from previous marriages."

"Legitimate children!" Braith giggled.

Eselt had heard all of this before. Her oldest sister, Mairwen, had married a man twenty years her elder, Gwynn had married one thirty years her elder, and Braith had married one only twelve years her elder. Now Eselt was set to wed Duke Maruk, and he was forty-eight years her elder.

"What's wrong with an older husband?" she asked to no one in particular.

They all laughed again, but it was Gwynn who answered. "Nothing, if you are simply waiting for them to die so you can inherit an income. Unless you have a male child with them, and then the entire estate is yours until your son comes of age."

"And what about love?" she asked.

Mairwen fielded that question. "You love them like you love our father. Except in the bedroom, of course, and then you must be the greatest actress ever to recite the scurrilous works of Auvray!"

"We have all heard your performance, Mairwen," said Braith. "Father never allowed another wedding night spent in the Tower House after that! What a scandal!"

That brought mischievous giggles and applause from her sisters, causing Mairwen to return an unapologetic bow.

Eselt was only a little girl at the time, but she remembered it well. "I thought our home was haunted for years afterward and never slept again without a lit candle in my chamber!"

The room erupted with shrieks and snorts of laughter. For some reason, her sisters had always thought her funnier than she really was. And they loved her dearly, just as she loved them. She would miss them all when she went to live in Tintagel.

Gwynn walked over and took Eselt's face in her hands. "Don't worry, little one. The duke will be so taken with you he won't last a minute in bed, and then you can roll him off of you, and he will sleep the rest of the night with no bother."

Mairwen agreed. "The older they are, the less stamina they have for it. Save your passion for your next husband. That one will be your own choice and hopefully a young stallion who will make up in exuberance what he lacks in experience."

Her sisters laughed at that, but Eselt was a little disturbed by the thought of taking the duke as a husband only to sit waiting for him to die to have real passion and love in her life. It was not at all like the stories her mother used to read to her as a child. Was there no dashing prince to sweep her away to his castle far away to live happily ever after? Had she deluded herself into believing that the duke could play that role in her life? Did he even truly love her, or did he love her youth and beauty?

Eselt felt as if the naiveté had been knocked from her by a terrible blow of reality. To her father, she was a chip to bargain, and to her husband, she would be a plaything. She wanted a knight in shining armor, she wanted a handsome young prince who would run in the fields with her and put flowers in her hair and sing to her, she wanted someone to love her as much as she loved him, she wanted . . .

For the first time in her life, Eselt realized that it didn't really matter what she wanted.

CHAPTER 3

Challenge

Drystan and Sir Blevin's company of Temple Knights arrived at Castle Teamhrach two days early. The weather held, and the men expertly paced their horses to cover the distance expeditiously. Fast as it was, they rode long days to grind down the leagues to their destination, leaving at dawn and not stopping until there was no light to see by. None complained. None would have dared. They, as much as he, considered the journey a mark of pride and honor.

The news of their arrival preceded them, and the bride's father, High King Cadeyrn himself, greeted them when they rode through the gates of the inner ward and onto the driveway where the massive ivy-covered Tower House rose high above them. This was the center of power in Eriu and where the royal family lived and entertained. Drystan was in awe of the scale and beauty of it.

"Greetings, Sir Drystan, Sir Blevin! We are pleased with your early arrival!"

"Thank you, Your Majesty." Drystan dismounted and made a deep, flourishing bow. "It will be my honor to escort the Princess to Tintagel at her convenience."

He presented the coat of arms sewn with Eselt's golden hair to the High King. "Here is the evidence that I am the true representative of Duke Maruk, sent to bring his betrothed to Tintagel to be wed!"

"I see you are eager to return to Tintagel with my daughter. Do you think your uncle would allow the celebrations to begin without the bride? Put that thing away until it's time to give it to her." The High King's voice cracked with humor at Drystan's impatience to return.

Drystan's faced reddened with embarrassment. "No, no, of course not, Your Majesty. Please forgive my excessive desire to keep my part on schedule."

"Fear not, Sir Knight, Maruk is a pragmatic man. He already knows the princess will be several days late. It's just the way of women—call it tradition. If we depended on them to fight our wars, they would never manage to get armies on the field of battle at the same time!" He laughed. "Maybe we should leave it up to women after all! Come in and have a drink—you too, Sir Blevin—while the servants get your personal effects and your knights situated."

Drystan and Sir Blevin walked with the High King to where the wine was.

The rest of the day slipped by quickly before Drystan, resting in his quarters, received an invitation to the feast hall for the next evening. He still had no idea how long he would be in Teamhrach and resigned himself to be patient and prepared to leave when the princess was ready. The invitation stated that the evening would be a formal occasion with the High King, his family, and the entirety of the nobles and guests that would be traveling to Tintagel for the forthcoming nuptials. He hoped that the gathering signaled their intention to leave the day after, but he tried not to set lofty expectations.

The next day, Drystan spent the morning seeing to his horse and chatting with the Temple Knights who accompanied him to Teamhrach. He knew most of them from the time he was a boy. Everyone was a decade or more older than he, and they frequently sparred and drank together back home. He enjoyed being around these goodly fellows and considered them all brothers who he would trust his life to without hesitation.

The Temple Knights erected several lanes of large, colorful circle tents just off the inner ward where the training grounds were located, and not far from the stables. There was no room in the Tower House for them to stay, and only Drystan, a noble by right if not by birth, was afforded a chamber. It was from this camp that Drystan first caught sight of who he presumed was his charge for the return trip.

Too far up on a tower balcony to see any detail, a young woman with long golden hair stood facing in the direction of Lough Greely. Her locks were unbraided and flew freely in the steady breeze. She shook her head occasionally and sometimes reversed direction to allow the wind to press her hair against the back of her head and across her face. He thought the whole display odd and wondered if it was some kind of Eriu ritual.

"One of the High King's Fiann told us she does this every morning." It was Sir Blevin standing next to him who spoke.

"To what end?" Drystan asked.

"To dry her hair." He chuckled. "I wonder if she is beautiful—everyone says she is, but you know these Eriu. They think warts on a frog's backside are attractive."

Drystan stared hard at the young woman far above but could see no better for it. Something in his heart knew that she was beautiful. The way she moved and tossed her hair. There was a gentle grace and elegance . . .

"Drystan?"

He was startled from his rumination. "Yes, yes, Sir Blevin. I am certain that she is."

Later that afternoon, Drystan and Sir Blevin climbed the steps to the highest point on the inner curtain wall that surrounded the inner ward and Tower House. Drystan marveled at the view from these heights. The so often overcast sky gave way to brief periods of bright sunlight. Castle Teamhrach was built on a high hill that sloped gently down to its base, where the fortifications formed a ring that connected to an offset smaller ring of fortifications, where Drystan and Sir Blevin stood. The impressive gray stone Tower House, at the highest point on the hill, loomed over their shoulders like a gloomy sentinel. Below them, they could see the outer curtain wall of Castle Teamhrach's defenses and the thousands of dwellings of the city beyond that. The two forked rivers that separated from one and flowed around Teamhrach were not only a natural defense, but were, more importantly, vital waterways that ferried trade into Lough Greely and from which every major city in Eriu and Lyonesse except Tintagel could be reached. The only way to get to Tintagel was by wheel, hoof, or foot. The narrows and shallows that hindered the flows from Lake Virtue into Loch Angu were far too hazardous to navigate safely in a trade ship.

Drystan turned and allowed his gaze to follow the lines of the Tower House that rose high above them into many towers that nearly reached the clouds. One tower stood out more than any and was among the highest. It was narrower than the rest, and although it was constructed of gray sandstone like the others, it appeared far more ancient. It was very difficult to imagine which had been built first: the tower or the Tower House. It wasn't the tower's architecture or age that drew attention, rather, it was the red glowing crystal in the shape of a small four-sided pyramid that rotated slowly at its apex. Its illumination reflected off the clouds, it was so near them, and seemed to stretch to the horizon in every direction. There were similar constructs in Tintagel, Lyonesse City, and every city he had the fortune to visit over his lifetime. He knew they had something to do with the Exceptional Ones from Atlantis, but not much beyond that.

Drystan had only been to Eriu a few times and just once before to Castle Teamhrach, when he squired for a knight who competed in the tourneys. His most recent venture was to the port city of Dunon just a few years ago, but that had not ended well for him. Despite that experience. He loved the wild and unrestrained nature of the country that was as beautiful as it was dangerous.

Drystan grew up hearing stories about Eriu. It was considered a magical land by most, and it was said that in Eriu men stayed to the roads, cities, and lands they farmed and left nature's untamed wilderness to the Trolls, Leprechauns, Sprites, and Fairies of legend. Although he had never seen any of them, he never met anyone from Eriu who hadn't claimed to.

Returning his attention to the city below, Drystan realized that there always seemed to be a misty fog and low clouds covering anywhere he had ever been in Eriu, and today was turning out to be no exception the closer the sun fled toward the horizon. The smell of smoke from the chimneys of cooking fires drifted upward on the shallow draft that flicked at the pinions lining the crenellations. Otherwise, the air was still.

Drystan noticed that people here did not seem to move at the same busy pace that they did in Lyonesse. It was refreshing to watch them go about their business at a more leisurely stride than the rush of strict purpose that was always the norm back home. Drystan wondered if he could ever get used to it if he lived here and suspected that he could if he managed to settle down with one of Eriu's fabled beauties. One day, perhaps.

"It's a beautiful land, this is," Sir Blevin commented.

"It is at that." Drystan could stand there all day watching the world go by, but he had to clean himself and change for the formal that evening.

"I wish it were you going rather than me, Sir Blevin. These formal feasts at a king's court with the poetry and platitudes delivered from scrolls that go on and on and the quiet intrigues expressed with winks and smiles. I like you, Sir Blevin, but you are far better suited to it than I."

Sir Blevin smiled and rolled the long ends of his mustache. "It's the curse of your station, young man. Listen more than you speak. Speak not at all if you can, and you will stay above it all. Soon you will be an expert diplomat!"

"Now that would be a proper folly!" Drystan laughed, and Sir Blevin laughed with him.

~~~

Dressed in his best silks and finery, Drystan took his place at one of the twenty long tables indicated by a servant in the massive great hall. It was almost as large as the court in Lyonesse City, and far larger than the one in Tintagel. He held the surcoat that his uncle had given him folded under his arm. Drystan expected to present it to Princess Eselt at some point during the celebration that evening. A pit formed in his stomach when he looked over the crowd. He estimated that there must have been over two hundred guests in attendance. If all of these people were traveling with him back to Tintagel, then it might take another fortnight before they arrived!

He felt himself sinking into a brood and decided to indulge in the wine that was flowing freely by the time all the guests arrived and were seated. Then finally, with a blare of trumpets, the royal family was announced to the room. There were loud cheers when the High King led his queen, followed by his sons, their wives, and then his daughters with their husbands into the room. The very last in line entered alone and without an escort.

Drystan was paralyzed by her beauty.

It must be Princess Eselt. She had long, straight golden-blonde hair that hung to her waist; her eyes were blue and clear like the summer sky; her cheeks were slightly blushed and her lips perfectly red. Her dress was pale blue and typical for her age, with a gold lunula on her silky-smooth neck. So innocent she seemed, almost as if she would transform into a woman once she married, like a caterpillar to a butterfly, or in her case a beautiful butterfly into another beautiful butterfly, considering he had never seen a beautiful caterpillar . . . *What was wrong with him?* His mind was wandering like some lovestruck little girl's.

All of High King Cadeyrn's daughters were beautiful. Still, there was something about Princess Eselt that was different than the others. Perhaps her youth, but more than that, an exuberance or glow that lit up the room when she entered. Drystan wondered why his uncle, easily four decades older than she, would want a wife so young. But after looking at her, he could readily understand the spell that Duke Maruk had fallen under. To have her warming the cold dark halls of his home would be a welcome wonder. They had not enjoyed the benefit of such light in so long . . .

The High King and his family arrived at the head table. Everyone stood while High King Cadeyrn said a few words about the upcoming wedding and how fortunate his family and the kingdom were for the union and his appreciation to his nobles and people for their support. It went on and on. Drystan was hardly listening. His attention was fully upon Princess Eselt. She was smiling and nodding in response to whatever her father was saying as if it were the most interesting thing in the world.

Drystan stood midway down the length of one of the long tables when, for just a moment, their eyes locked. A ripple of emotion crossed Eselt's face, but he could not comprehend what it was. Then she looked away quickly, making an effort not to look in his direction again. He hoped that he had not offended her with his bold gaze. His uncle would flay him alive if the bride forbade his attendance even before they left Teamhrach.

When the High King finished speaking, he sat, and everyone in the room followed. Except for one. Only Drystan and a spare few noticed him still standing until he spoke loudly and boldly across the room to the head table.

"High King Cadeyrn! I claim right of challenge for the princess's hand in marriage!"

The entire room gasped in shock. The man was tall and muscular, not particularly handsome, but he wore the colors of a noble house and gold headband of an Eriu knight.

"What is your name, Sir Knight, and by what right do you make this claim?" shouted the High King in return.

"I am Sir Murhalt of House Biswaldt. My father is Baron Rubart, and my sister is Queen Gwyr of DunDwai. You have no other daughters of marriageable age to trade for Princess Eselt. Therefore, I claim my right of challenge for her hand," he finished with a smug smile.

The High King's face was red with rage now, but his voice stayed even. "Does anyone stand by this claim?"

An older man stood up next to Sir Murhalt. "I am Baron Rubart, and I stand with my son. I also have the blessing of Queen Gwyr to press this claim."

Standing, the High King lowered his voice and stated deliberately, almost dangerously, "You could have made this claim at any time before now. Instead, you wait until this moment to not only press a ridiculous claim, but to do so in the most public and embarrassing way for my family. I will not forget this insult. It will take several days to inform Duke Maruk of your challenge and several days more for him to send a champion or come himself to accept your challenge. For my part, I hope he comes himself to remove that insolent smile from your face."

"I will accept the challenge!" Drystan could not believe he had spoken. Something inside him could not help but defend the beautiful princess who was crying in her mother's arms inconsolably.

"Who are you to accept my challenge?" Sir Murhalt demanded.

"I am Sir Drystan. Duke Maruk is my uncle by birth and father by adoption. He has charged me to bring Princess Eselt to him for their wedding day, and he has commanded that I speak for him in all things while I carry out this duty!"

"Are you sure you wish to accept this challenge, Sir Drystan?"

cautioned the High King. "You do not need to decide now without further consideration."

"I am sure, Your Majesty." Drystan bowed deeply.

Princess Eselt stopped crying and watched him intently now. Was it curiosity, like looking at a strange bug, or something else?

"The right of challenge will take place in two days' time at dawn on Marwo Isle," the king declared before he stormed out of the great hall, quickly followed by his family.

"Enjoy your last two days on this earth, boy." Sir Murhalt spat the insult as he and Baron Rubert also exited the feast hall.

The entire room of two hundred guests and nobles sat in awkward silence. What did they do now? Stay and eat or leave? Drystan decided to leave, he no longer held an appetite.

~~~

Drystan sat in a small chamber to which he was summoned near the royal apartments. High King Cadeyrn sat in a chair on the other side of a wooden table, pouring them both a goblet of wine. They were alone, and the High King had a long head start on the wine.

"Are you familiar with the political system inside Eriu?" the High King asked.

Drystan searched his memory. He was sure the tutors had covered it. "I know it is somewhat similar to what we have in Lyonesse, although I am not an expert of our own system by any means."

The High King poured himself more wine. "Eriu is divided up into five kingdoms: DunOinos, Kenno, Dunon, DunDwai, and Teamhrach as the current capital. Each is ruled by a king or queen and their royal family. There are duchies, baronies, and counties within each, and they operate as independent kingdoms with sovereign powers and autonomy. From among them, a High King is elected to negotiate trade deals, peace agreements, and so forth on the kingdoms' collective behalf. It's a sort of confederation, and I am currently that man. It is also my duty to ensure fair and beneficial laws and pass judgment when there is a dispute between kingdoms. I will have this position until I die, relinquish the crown, or fall out of favor with the other rulers. There's much more to it, of course, but that is the short version."

The High King paused to drink from his goblet. Drystan remained silent.

Once his thirst was assuaged, Cadeyrn continued. "I am embarrassed by what has occurred. It is a custom and law in Eriu that suitors of the greater noble families have the right to challenge the marriage of a ruler's daughter to a foreign nobleman, with the only exception being a king. Since Maruk is a duke and not a king, the challenge is legal. This Sir Murhalt has a sour reputation as a bully, with the skills to back up his loud talk. If you do not wish to go through with this challenge, I can still get you out of it without it becoming an embarrassment for you."

Drystan shook his head. "I welcome this challenge in that it means I will put an end to this controversy and end the career of a dishonorable knight."

"It is my wish that it is so. I trust your skills are as refined as your uncle's? I will not have my daughter in the hands of that lout. She requires a proper defense by a nobleman up to the task."

"I have confidence that I will emerge the victor. If not, then I will have given my life to a good cause."

High King Cadeyrn stood suddenly and a little off-balance. He patted Drystan on the shoulder. "You sound like Maruk. A good man. There was never better. Perhaps you will live up to his reputation." The High King of Eriu drained what remained of the wine from his cup and stumbled out of the room to find his bedchamber.

Drystan left the meeting room a moment later and walked through the quiet halls of the royal quarters. As he passed a door niche, he noticed that it was slightly open and a shadow blocked the light beyond from escaping. Suddenly a slender hand shot out and took hold of the silk folds of his shirt. Just as quickly, he had that hand in his own and squeezed tightly. A squeak erupted from behind the door, and the hand shot back in.

A soft, feminine, youthful voice spoke. "You are not gentle, sir."

Peering into the crack of the door, Drystan could not identify who spoke to him. "I am unaccustomed to being clutched at by unseen persons in hallways."

"I was not clutching!" the voice cried back with effrontery.

"My shirt states otherwise." He nodded to the mussed creases on his shoulder. "To whom is it that I speak?"

"It is Eselt, and I know you were just speaking with my father."

"Princess." Drystan immediately fell to one knee.

"Get up, you fool!" Princess Eselt implored in an urgent whisper. "I don't want anyone to know I speak to you now."

Drystan rose quickly and glanced down the hallway. "How can I be of service, Princess?"

"I need you to kill that horrible Murhalt," she sobbed.

"That is my intent, my lady."

"Listen to me! He is much quicker with his sword than his size would suggest, and he will not fight you honorably. You need to know this."

"Well noted, Princess."

"He was a good man once, you know, and considered among the best and most honorable of knights of Eriu. I would have been proud to marry the man he was before, but something changed not long ago that no one can explain. He just changed. Do not let him suffer if you prevail, good knight. He deserves a quick end for the noble soul he was once."

"I will do what I can to see to it if the fortune of Sunna smiles upon me in this contest."

"And one other thing, Sir Drystan. My life is tied to yours now. If you die, then I will follow. I will throw myself off the tower before I allow that beast to have me. I swear it!"

Before he could speak further, the door slammed shut. Was that weeping he heard at the end? Sadness filled him. He had to defeat this Sir Murhalt. Otherwise, he would not only lose his own life, but the young life of a princess would stain his soul for all eternity.

He had only two days to prepare for this battle, and he knew the perfect man to find out everything there was to know about the knight he would face in mortal combat. It was still early evening, and there was no need to waste a moment. He headed for the tent of Sir Blevin.

CHAPTER 4

The Liafal Stone

To almost everyone, even the most learned, the Tuatha De are an enigma. To visit their homeland, if one were permitted, would mean finding a strange and extraordinary place filled with magic and wonder and people not so unlike any other. But their past is dark, and their future is driven by those they name the Blood, the few left pure and unadulterated. Sometimes I wish the Tuatha De were an enigma to me as well so I would not have to think too hard on what they have done. To everyone else in this grand world, beware of gifts from the Tuatha De, for they are not always what they seem.

Wodanaz the Wanderer

"Why have you brought me here, Your Majesty?"

"Do you know what this is?"

"A monument to Eriu? Something of the druids?"

"It is the most sacred artifact in all of Eriu. A gift from the Tuatha De at the dawning of our people's rise from savage to civilization, this is the Liafal, Stone of Destiny. Every High King from the first has been coroneted on this spot, myself included."

Drystan stared at the monolith. There were no markings, no carvings or drawings upon it of any sort. It was as plain as any stone he had ever seen, except that this one stood upright, half again as tall and twice as wide as he was. He reached his hand toward it, but the High King stopped him before he could touch it.

"Be careful, young knight. There is power unimaginable in this stone. If your heart is not true, the consequences of contacting the stone could be unfavorable. If your heart is true, then the consequences could be even more dire than you could ever envisage." His smile was as disconcerting as was his cryptic warning.

Drystan retracted his hand.

"Let me give you a sample of the power. It will aid you in your contest today." The High King glanced around for anyone else in the vicinity.

They were alone.

"What I am about to do is forbidden, but my daughter's life and well-being are at stake. Thus, I must take the chance."

Drystan thought to protest, but what could he say? This wasn't the deed of a High King. It was the deed of a father deeply concerned for his daughter's welfare. Drystan was skeptical about any benefit he could derive from a stone, even massive as this was, but still, if it gave the High King comfort, what harm could there be in it?

The High King stretched out his arm and placed his hand on the stone. A small convulsion seemed to move him briefly, but he shrugged it off quickly.

"Take my hand, Drystan, and taste the power of the Liafal through a royal body."

Drystan reached for the High King's hand and then hesitated. He felt something from the stone or the High King, he didn't know which, causing him to question if he should proceed. He looked into the High King's eyes, and the intensity there was nothing short of euphoric, and in that moment, he believed. With firm resolve, he clasped the High King's hand.

With a gasp, Drystan felt waves of energy course through his body, forcing his spine straight and his body to lift onto his toes. He wanted to release the High King's hand, but he didn't have the control or the strength to do so. Drystan's mouth opened, but he could not scream. His body shuddered so violently that he was sure he might break into pieces, and then he realized there was no pain, and the initial shock of the power began to wear off. His body relaxed, and the startling effects of the energy that hummed within every fiber of his being left him feeling . . . exuberant.

Except, there was something else.

Drystan could also feel the exuberance within the High King and within the stone as well. Then suddenly it was over, and he realized the High King had released his hand, and the two stood staring at each another. Drystan wanted to reach for the stone himself, reluctant to release the ecstasy he felt, but he resisted the temptation, not knowing how touching it directly might affect him. Even without touching the stone, the effects still lingered, leaving him feeling stronger and more energized than he ever felt in his life.

He never wanted it to end.

"What you are feeling will subside in a few days, although it will never cease completely. Your body has been imbued with the power of the stone, giving you strength and durability beyond most men that walk the earth, as well as a long natural life. If there is a price, it is that our souls are now connected, and so long as we both live, we can point in the direction of the other, no matter the distance apart. We will also know the moment of the other's passing from this world. I think it is worth the price."

Drystan nodded. The price seemed trivial indeed for the way he felt right now.

"Why could I feel the same emotion from the stone as I could from you? Is it a living thing?"

The High King did not smile or laugh at what sounded like a ridiculous question. "The essence of all the High Kings from the past resides in the stone after they die. They are the source of the power you felt and feel now. Someday I will join them, and over time the stone will grow stronger."

"Can you do that with anyone?"

"Only one of true heart and nobility. I took a chance with you. To be honest, it might have worked out very badly if I had misjudged your character. Each time it takes a piece from me. Now only you and my sons have benefited from the experience. I doubt I have enough to give to any other. That's how important you are to my youngest child's future, starting today."

He gestured to a group of Fianna casually walking in their direction. Sir Blevin was with them. To a man, they were armed and armored with the stern look of men who were ready to go into battle. Fortunately, the day would require the bloodshed of only one, not many, and it was up to Drystan to make sure it wasn't him.

Sir Blevin provided him with a detailed picture of what he could expect from Sir Murhalt through sources who once fought beside the knight against the Vikja raids in the west or had sparred with him for practice and in the tourneys. He had a nasty reputation as a cruel man and a lack of compassion, for acts verging on what could be considered dishonorable for a knight, but none would accuse or challenge him, as he was an exceedingly gifted combatant. Knowing this, Drystan did not fear him. He never felt fear in combat, not anymore. Not after the months he was held captive as a hostage by the Vikja not so many years before.

"Everything is ready and in order, High King," a Fiann announced when they came near enough to speak to.

"Very well. Sir Blevin, Sir Drystan, shall we make our way to the boats?"

"I am ready," Drystan replied, and he was.

~~~

Drystan was stunned by the throngs of nobility gathered at the edge of the mountain lake near the southern fork of the river that flowed into it and around Teamhrach. There were nobles from the wedding party, the entire royal family, a large contingent of the Fianna, the Temple Knights, and hundreds of ordinary citizens in attendance to watch the nobles resolve their differences.

And then there was lovely Princess Eselt.

The spectators on this occasion would have rivaled those at any tourney he had ever been to in Lyonesse. They were all there to watch him and Sir Murhalt fight to the death on the small island they called Marwo in the shadow of the high peaks of the Kenno-windo Mountain Range.

Drystan stood between the High King and Sir Blevin. His gaze shifted to Princess Eselt often, and curiously, it seemed hers often shifted to him as well. He told himself it was nothing. He was nervous, and so was she. If things turned out badly, neither of them would see another sunrise. The thought of it made him anxious, not for him but for her. The image of beautiful Princess Eselt casting herself off the side of a tower brought heat to his cheeks and fire to his belly. It angered him that this Sir Murhalt would bring travesty upon this noble family with so little regard for their lives. Especially the innocent lives.

Why should this young woman, so new to life, have such despair presented to her so callously? Fight a champion, a king, or even a High King for power and prestige, but leave unmarked in body and soul those without defense and protection of their own. The heat and rage rose high within, fueled by his recent experience at the Liafal Stone. It felt beautiful, the anger coursing through his veins, the fury that powered his limbs, the disregard for the life of his opponent that he was so eager to take. It was not a different feeling than what he always felt before a battle, but this time it was far more intense.

Sir Murhalt appeared through the crowd flanked by Baron Rubert and their retainers. Drystan started forward, determined in his fury to drop the vile knight right then and there, but he was restrained by the High King and Sir Blevin, one on each shoulder. Somehow the two veterans sensed his mood and held him back. *Let him live,* he thought, *breathe the sweet air just a little longer before there is no more breath to take, monster!*

Sir Murhalt sneered at Drystan. "Ready to die, dog? It may not be quick and painless. In fact, it will likely be just the opposite."

Drystan growled and began to reply, but the High King interrupted, "Save your banter for impressing the whores you frequent so often. It is not honorable to taunt another gentleman of station. You should know that." He turned his back on the knight and shouted for the crowd to hear, "Knights! To your boats! May Eriu bring strength and courage to the victor!" The assembled crowd roared their approval. Drystan was surprised to hear his name cheered by so many, far more than for Sir Murhalt.

Two small boats were bouncing a wide span apart against the wood-and-stone constructed dock, each with a rower ready to cast off. Drystan no longer heard the crowd—the blood rushing through his veins drowned them out—yet his eyes couldn't help but linger on Princess Eselt. She was beautiful and serene and awaiting a fate that only he would decide. How noble of this young woman to give herself so fully over to his grace and command of his blade that she would entrust her very life to him. Words were said in his ear first by the High King and then by Sir Blevin, but what they said was lost in the rush of blood and adrenaline. There was nothing they could tell him now that he didn't already know, anyway.

Drystan took to his assigned craft, and with a shudder he felt the boat leave the dock. It was a quarter of a league to the small island, too far for the crowd to see the outcome of the contest from where they stood at the dock with the mist of the lake rising. Once he and Sir Murhalt were let off on the island, only one empty boat would remain, and the victor would have to row himself back on his own or die trying. From the stories he had heard, it was no unusual thing to find the small boat of the champion days later down the river, rowed by a corpse after a contest such as this. Sometimes there was no real victor.

Drystan watched the form of Princess Eselt until he could no longer see her in the crowd, and then he imagined he could see her a little longer. Sir Murhalt was a stone's throw away, traveling on a parallel course to the island. Inexplicably, he was making lewd motions with his hands, apparently in reference to the princess. Drystan wished he could walk on water and separate the foul knight's head from his neck. Since that wasn't an option, he refused to give his adversary the satisfaction and showed no outward reaction. Instead, he studied in every detail the man he intended to kill. He was surprised that Sir Murhalt's armor was dented and unattended to, as if it was an obligatory thing he had to wear for appearances. Some of the metal pieces were even been replaced with leather. Didn't he have a proper squire to attend his equipment? Supposing he didn't, what kind of knight would not take pride in the condition of his armor, even if just for the sake of appearances? Drystan's mind registered, almost without thought, every vulnerable point for him to exploit while he continued to stoke the fires of rage that burned inside.

Sir Murhalt stared back at him. He had the blackest eyes, dead eyes, soulless eyes. Drystan had never seen eyes so black. They reminded him of the eyes of the giant reptile from Fomoire rampaging villages along the Arges River that he killed years ago. It seemed crazed and full of bloodlust. Drystan later described the odd behavior of the beast to a druid who thought it sounded like the animal had become deranged for some reason, which was not that uncommon for unnatural creatures created by the Tuatha De. Even so, most of the time, beasts of that sort avoided human settlements. Was there something unnatural about Sir Murhalt as well? Perhaps a touch of madness that drove his aggression and vulgarity? He could hope for it. Insane people were easy to kill, since they had no method or thought in their combat strategy.

With a grinding shudder, they were on the beach. Drystan stood and jumped into the knee-high water before wading ashore, never taking his eyes from the other knight. He felt energized, strong, and determined, ready to carve up this man who would dare to call himself a knight.

As suddenly as the boats arrived, one departed with the two oarsmen who brought them. Drystan barely noted their departure as he took in his surroundings. The island was treeless and devoid of anything but sand, massive rocks, bones, and remnants of armor. The smell of the place was a strange mixture of rotting shellfish and rust. He supposed no one ever came to the island to clear the debris of fallen heroes and villains. He vaguely noted that the island was little more than a sandbar and couldn't have been more than a hundred paces wide or long.

Sir Murhalt was wearing his open-face helmet, and Drystan could see his lips moving below those dead, black eyes. He was shouting insults or taunts, Drystan wasn't sure. The sound of blood and adrenaline in his head had not lessened any since they left the dock, and that left him almost deaf to the sounds around him. Absently he noted the sheer size of the knight not ten paces away, but Drystan had never seen this as a distinct advantage. He had killed men nearly Sir Murhalt's size in the past.

His mind was in his work ahead, invaded by fleeting thoughts of Eselt that he couldn't seem to shake. Where was his helmet? He must have left it in the boat. It didn't matter. Sir Murhalt was screaming at him now, asking a question he had apparently asked more than once already.

Back in the moment, Drystan strained to hear what Sir Murhalt was saying. "You don't want to tell me where to send your head? Then I will throw it into the sea!" Then the giant knight was charging toward him.

There was no thought, only instinct. Drystan quickly sidestepped the charge and circled around while Sir Murhalt regained his direction. Approaching more cautiously this time, the knights traded strikes on shield and blade while they circled. Drystan was impressed by the strength of Sir Murhalt's attacks, and he knew he would tire quickly if he continued swapping blows with him. Sir Blevin had assessed his opponent well. This knight's strategy was to batter his opponent with brute strength, just as Sir Blevin expected. Drystan had fought men like this and knew how predictable they were. No imagination.

Well, enough of this, he thought.

Spinning around his opponent, Drystan landed a blow behind Sir Murhalt's thigh, breaking the straps on his greaves. Clanking against Murhalt's leg as he moved, the loose armor distracted the Eriu knight, and he paused in his assault. Knowing that was his moment, Drystan pushed forward on the other knight's shield, spun to his left, and connected his blade with his opponent's forcefully. A sharp *ping* echoed from the force of the blow, and to Drystan's dismay, the top third of his sword broke away and bounced off into the sand.

Sir Murhalt responded with a triumphant shout and pushed forward on his own shield. Spinning back in the opposite direction, Drystan caught the inside edge of Murhalt's shield with his own, and he flung it outward just enough to thrust his damaged sword through the expected opening. Betting the sword was still long enough, he crowded dangerously close to the larger knight. The broken tip of the sword just made it through the opening in Sir Murhalt's helmet and plunged into his left eye socket.

The knight violently reeled backward screaming in pain and jerked the hilt of the damaged sword from Drystan's grip. Sir Murhalt dropped his own sword and flung away his shield to grasp the blade protruding from his skull. The broken end of the sword lodged in the bone of his eye socket must have been a hair shy of penetrating his brain. Still, the wound was bleeding profusely. Had the blade not been broken, the kill would have been clean, Drystan thought. This one might take a while.

He stood back and casually watched Sir Murhalt struggle to remove the sword. The other knight was trying to say something between screams. The words came out in unintelligible gurgles with the blood and spittle, so much of it was running down his face. Drystan pulled out his long knife, then reconsidered and thrust it back into the sheath on his belt. Instead, he nonchalantly walked over and picked up Sir Murhalt's sword, leaned on it like a cane, and remarked to the dying knight in the most casually mundane tone he could manage, "I'm going to remove your head with your own sword as soon as you die."

Somehow the remark must have registered with Sir Murhalt through the pain and loss of blood. Becoming very still, Sir Murhalt stopped struggling with the sword still lodged in his eye and charged Drystan with everything he had left. Sidestepping once more, Drystan tripped the flailing knight, sending him facedown onto the ground. His head bounced from the impact of the pommel of the still-lodged sword. The force was enough to push the blade far enough to finally skewer his brain. Then Sir Murhalt lay still in the sand, except for a few last twitches and spasms, Drystan's sword propping up his head in an awkward and gruesome display.

Not one to renege on his promise, Drystan severed Sir Murhalt's head from his neck with the knight's sword and then dropped it to take the pommel of his own sword, still impaled through the dead man's right orb. Just as he lifted it from the blood-stained sand, a dark shadow seemed to crawl reluctantly from the severed head and evaporate into the air like wisps of smoke. A stark chill of evil cut through his adrenaline and euphoria, replacing it with inexplicable fear. Immediately he dropped the severed head back to the ground. Then the apparition was gone.

Drystan stared at the head of the dead knight while he brought his emotions back under control. He wasn't convinced that what he just witnessed was real. The fear was real; that he could not deny. Whatever it was or wasn't, the black void was gone, and Drystan began to feel foolish. Finally, he grabbed the pommel of his sword and retreated toward the lone boat that quietly waited for him.

CHAPTER 5

Return to Tintagel

The crowd at the dock was silent in a tradition of respect for the fallen as Drystan rowed his small boat to the mooring. He had not been gone long, and it didn't appear that anyone departed. If anything, the crowd apparently grew larger. Looking over the hundreds of faces, he felt no emotion. He was still in the heightened state from his experience with the stone, but the rage was gone, and the adrenaline had subsided. Oddly, he felt calm and content.

He walked to stand before the High King, who was flanked by Sir Wilhem and Sir Blevin. Their expressions were solemn, but their eyes were bright with relief and satisfaction. His gaze quickly fluttered across the others around him, yet there was no sign of the face that he most wanted to see—Princess Eselt's. She was saved, and because she was, so was he.

Drystan knelt before the High King, absently holding Sir Murhalt's head by the pommel of the broken sword still impaled on it. The entire crowd remained utterly mute. Despite what they saw, he would not be declared the victor until the High King pronounced it. Drystan took a deep breath to clear his head. His thoughts were so consumed with the princess that he nearly forgot why he was there and then held the blood-drenched pommel up to the High King.

The High King took the blade and held the head high above his head, heedless that he sprayed himself and everyone around him with Sir Murhalt's blood.

"We have a champion!" he announced. "Sir Drystan of Tintagel!"

The crowd roared with approval. Although Sir Murhalt was their countryman, there were few who did not secretly wish him dead, and this display was more than satisfying.

Not even bothering to walk over to Baron Rubert, who was understandably distressed by what had happened, the High King tossed the head at his feet. "Bury your son," he said, and without a word of condolence, he strode over to his waiting carriage.

~~~

The morning passed while Drystan tried to rest in his quarters, but he was not tired in the least, so full of energy from the events of the day. He paced the room, contemplating all the new feelings brought on by his interaction with the Liafal, considering how it helped him in his contest with Sir Murhalt and the permanent effects that would stay with him the rest of his life. Even now he could determine, with little effort, in which direction the High King was located and his general state of wellness. It was disconcerting, to say the least. Especially since he knew the High King could say the same about him. But that was nothing compared to the strength and awareness that had been enhanced in his person. So many more things seemed possible, and the world around him seemed more vibrant and beautiful. The High King said that some of what he felt would wane over time, but Drystan hoped that it would not diminish too quickly. There was a furtive knock at his door, rousing him from his internal deliberations. He caught his breath when he opened the entrance. "Princess Eselt," he greeted her, and his heart picked up by a few more beats.

She curtsied where she stood. "Just Eselt, if you please. May I enter?"

"Yes, of course!" He moved aside as she glided through the door and into his room.

"It is not proper for me to be here," she said, "in the room of a man who is not my husband."

Drystan closed the door quickly. "I would have been very pleased to meet you in a more public setting."

"I wish to speak with you about something I want not to be so public." She sat in one of the two wooden chairs next to a small table.

Drystan took a seat across from her. "Please go on."

Eselt nodded. "I was impressed by the loyalty you displayed toward your family and your care for my own life. Just looking at the physical size and fierce personality of Sir Murhalt would have turned most men's blood cold. You did not hesitate, even without knowing anything about your adversary."

"I have always been a pretty good judge of character, and I could tell right away that he was a bully. A bully with some skill, I admit, but a bully nonetheless. And just as importantly, I could not allow the insult to my father's honor . . . or yours."

He swallowed hard, feeling emboldened by her presence.

Eselt responded with her pretty smile. "Well, you certainly proved that today, very convincingly, I might add. Clearly you are very skilled with that blade of yours and the true honor of a knight. And it is precisely because of the way that you conducted yourself that I wish for you to be my knight."

"Your knight?" Drystan was confused.

"Yes, Drystan, my knight, my protector and my champion."

"It would be an honor, Princess Eselt, but what would that mean?"

"Eselt, just Eselt, my good knight. It would mean you would always be near to protect my person from injury and champion my virtue against any insult. It is a tradition here in Eriu for a queen or duchess to have her own personal knight.

Drystan fell to his knees before her. "It would be my privilege and my honor to be your knight, Eselt." He kissed her hand.

The moment was frozen in time as they looked into each other's eyes, then slowly Eselt retrieved her hand and stood before him, smiling. "I am pleased, Drystan. I will inform my father this evening. Good night."

She exited his room, taking all the light with her, yet her lily-blossom fragrance lingered to remind him that she really had been there. Drystan wondered if he was playing at a dangerous game that could end in tragedy for both of them. It was impossible for him to avoid the feelings that welled up in him every time she was near. What could he do? Was this attraction also part of the power he had received from the Liafal Stone? No, he had been instantly smitten when he first saw her in the great hall. This was nothing more than a youthful infatuation that would soon pass, most likely when he gazed upon another brown-eyed Eriu beauty. The duke expected his bride to be brought to Tintagel safe and unharmed, and Drystan was determined not to be the most harmful thing near her and the danger he was supposed to guard against. He resolved to suppress his feelings. He had no choice, and he would admire and love her as a member of his family and nothing more.

Later in the evening, Drystan was taking his dinner in the great hall among the Temple Knights and Eriu nobility when a messenger announced that the wedding party would leave for Tintagel the next morning. He was relieved that they would finally be returning and immediately sought out the roost to send a pigeon informing his uncle of the news.

The next morning, Drystan was amazed and dismayed at the

organized chaos taking place in Castle Teamhrach's courtyard. Servants were running everywhere, nobles were arguing and complaining about their position in the entourage, and supply wagons and livestock were being shuffled about without regard to their cargo.

Eventually, the High King's Fianna jostled into the inner ward, mounted and wearing their metal armor and gold-fringed surcoats with the High King's coat of arms. Drystan admired the way the knight commander of the company, Teutjorīk, quickly took charge of the situation and within an hour had the caravan of carriages and wagons properly ordered and ready to depart. Not a single noble dared to argue with the scar-faced veteran as he roughly ordered them into positions before the High King and the royal family, including Princess Eselt, emerged from the Tower House to take their places in the royal carriages. The sight of her took his breath away. She was so graceful and beautiful in the way that she walked and how the sun reflected off her golden locks and her delicate manner when she took the hand of the carriage driver assisting her into the carriage . . . Drystan wanted to beat himself over the head with a stick. Refocusing on the journey ahead, it was just as he feared. There were at least five hundred men, women, and children traveling to Tintagel for the wedding.

With an inward groan, Drystan realized that he would have to send another pigeon. It would easily take double the travel time he expected before they were in sight of Tintagel. Racing as fast as he could back to the roost where the pigeons were housed, he gave a note to the Keeper of the Loft and returned just as the tail end of the caravan was departing the Castle Teamhrach's grounds. Without delay, he located Eselt's carriage and moved his mount into position immediately behind it. Sir Blevin and his Temple Knights would travel behind the Fianna while in Eriu and then reverse positions when they entered Lyonesse.

Drystan calculated that it would take twelve to fifteen days to reach Tintagel given the speed that they crawled along the eastward road. And that was assuming the weather held and the roads didn't turn to mud in the rain. He was impatient to move more quickly, except that would be impossible, so he just accepted the inevitable delay and made the best of it. Even knowing Eselt was so close, just inside the carriage in front of him, so close he could sometimes taste the fragrance she wore, the travel was tedious.

Until the princess left her carriage to ride beside him.

Drystan's heart leaped at those occasions, and suddenly the leagues of travel were no longer a burden. When she was there, they spoke of everything from philosophy and poetry to the king's court in Lyonesse. Sometimes she rode in her carriage with her attendants, and other times she rode beside him on her chestnut mare. Those were always the best times of the day, and his heart sank when she returned to her carriage or was summoned to ride with her mother. Even then he thought too much about her, and he reminded himself over and over that no good would come of getting too friendly with the princess. When they arrived in Tintagel, they would whisk her away, and the next time he would see her would be when he bowed to the new duchess.

When they stopped in the evenings at a wayside inn or to set up camp, he sang for her and played his travel harp, telling stories of mythology, adventure, and love. There were always others around, especially Lady Fedelmid, her rigid lady-in-waiting; the attendants; and the unmarried daughters and sisters of the nobility who traveled with them. Often those unmarried women made doe eyes and attempted to draw his attention to themselves with clever conversation, and on more than one occasion he was sure Eselt's cheeks colored when he spoke to one of them. After two nights of that, she had her ladies shoo them off to no end of protests and feigned distress. Even with her own attendants, she found trivial tasks to occupy them so that she and he could talk and laugh together in private. These were the moments when Drystan began to know Eselt as more than just a princess, and he found himself opening up his most private feelings and experiences despite his reservations. Perhaps they would become good friends, yet he knew when he thought the words that they were hollow assurances.

"How did you get that scar?" She stroked the blemish that ran down his right forearm below his rolled-up sleeve.

"That is quite a story to tell, Princess."

"We have time." She smiled. "My ladies will be busy gabbing and mending my dresses for a while. So, it is just the two of us and the stars."

She lay upon his lap, staring up into the clear night sky, with his bare arm entwined with hers and resting on her waist while he leaned back on a fallen log. They were near enough to the main camp to hear the noise of cooking and conversation and far enough to feel alone at the edge of the tree line in the clearing where he had set a small fire.

"Very well, Princess, I will deliver this sad tale, but I beg that you spare your judgment of me. It was a difficult time."

Eselt took his hand in hers and pressed it to her chest. "You have my promise, lov—" She nearly choked trying to stop the word. "My good knight," she corrected.

Drystan smiled in the darkness. He knew her cheeks were red even though he couldn't see the color in the dim firelight. He continued as if he hadn't noticed her slip, but inside he felt wonderful and afraid.

"The year after I was first knighted, a group of young nobles from the city of Dunon extended an invitation to me. Have you been to that city? I understand it is the only major port in all of Eriu."

"I have not. Father never allowed my sisters and me to travel much," she confessed.

"It is a beautiful city high upon the cliffs overlooking the Primal Sea, with a winding roadway down to its fortified port. It is the most northern port in all the Western Kingdoms. If it weren't for the dangerous ice floes and frequent raids by the Vikja, I'm sure it would undoubtedly be the wealthiest port on the west coast, to the unhappiness of Ys, so much farther south."

Eselt nodded in agreement. "Those Vikja are a blight upon our fair land."

"The invitation I received was to join these nobles in a great hunt south of Dunon in the thick coastal forests where the giant boar, deer, and elk are abundant. I was quick to find glory and adventure at the time, and the opportunity to hunt those mythical forests was an invitation I eagerly accepted. When I arrived in Dunon, I was surprised that none of the three nobles had been knighted, nor had they any interest in becoming knights. They were a jolly bunch about my age that loved to drink and carouse, but what I did not know at the time was that they were living off their families' expenses and had sent invitations to over one hundred knights in Eriu and Lyonesse connected to any family with a prominent name. It turned out that I was the only one foolish enough to accept."

"You were young, good knight, and had been a sheltered squire for years. How could you be expected to know the turbid ways of the world yet?"

Drystan grunted at that and continued. "Yes, well I blithely joined their company and the intrepid expedition they promised. We left Dunon with thirty men-at-arms borrowed from their families' holdings, a string of Hydruntin Asses that carried our supplies, and twenty terrified servants who had never taken as much as a step into the dark Eriu forests. I should have known it was doomed from the start."

He shifted to a more comfortable position, careful not to disturb Eselt who was by now nestled in his arms, listening intently, her beautiful eyes glittering in the warm firelight.

"The first few days were exactly what I hoped the excursion would be. We hunted down an elk the size of a carriage and killed three giant boars and at least three dozen rabbits. We ate well and sang drunken ballads in the camp at night. Even the servants were relaxed and enjoying the adventure. The three young nobles reveled in the success of the hunt as much as anyone, although they never actually participated in a kill. Come to think of it, I don't remember ever seeing one of them with a bow or spear the entire time. It was also very peculiar that they seemed restless and impatient, as if expecting to find something else, and they kept pushing to stay close to the coast. No one questioned the route we took, least of all I, who knew nothing of their land."

"My land," Eselt yawned, "is a mystery even to we who have lived our whole lives here."

"On about the eighth day out, one of the scouts spotted a trio of Vikja longboats traveling on a parallel course to the coast. The Eriu nobles were wild with excitement and spoke of nothing else the entire night. On the afternoon of the next day, the same scout reported that they had landed and set up camp a league farther south. Again, the nobles were ecstatic and expressed their desire to take home a few Vikja heads as trophies. They would be hailed as heroes in Dunon, they said, perhaps all of Eriu. Of course, none of them thought to remove the Vikja's heads themselves: that's why they had the men-at-arms and a knight from Lyonesse. I thought it to be sheer madness. Even I knew three Vikja ships carried at least sixty warriors, and man for man they would tear through the lot we had with us, even if we outnumbered them."

"Wouldn't they listen to reason? Surely even they could see the folly in attacking the Vikja with a smaller force."

Drystan was surprised. "You impress me with your expert tactical advice, Princess."

She nudged him playfully in the ribs. "I am my father's daughter after all."

"You are at that. And it didn't matter anyway. The decision was taken out of our hands when we were ambushed that night."

Eselt snuggled closer and dramatically clutched tightly at his tunic. "What happened?"

"The men-at-arms and I fought as best we could. I killed three Vikja before my sword was ripped from my hand by a grapple and I was knocked unconscious. That's how I received the scar on my arm."

She gently traced the jagged scar with her finger. It tickled.

"How did you survive?" she asked fearfully.

"Oh, you wish to know the rest? I got to the part about the scar. Wasn't that all you wished to know?" he teased.

She lifted up on one arm, her face level with his and close. So close. He could feel her sweet breath on his beardless face and see the reflection of moisture on her lips. Too close.

"I wish to know everything," she breathed, then collapsed in his lap giggling.

Relief and regret flooded through his body. He might have kissed her. He would have. Shaking the fog from his mind, he focused again on his story.

Drystan took a deep breath. He was about to tell her things that he wished he could forget. Things he never wanted to remember again, but she wanted to know, and he would lay bare his soul for her if she asked.

"When I awoke, it was daylight, my hands and feet were tied together, and it seemed that every part of my body was in pain. Through the haze of my vision, I could see the camp, and it was in shambles. The supplies were stacked in a pile, the tents were burned, smoke was everywhere, and debris littered the ground in every direction. But worse were the bodies, and not just the two dozen or so soldiers and servants who were piled together in a grotesque funeral pyre with their boots and armor stripped from them, along with anything else the Vikja found useful. There were bodies that had been nailed to the trees. Their sagging corpses also stripped of anything useful, they clutched at the spears and spikes that hung them with rigid hands, some with their mouths still wide with silent screams. They had been suspended from the trees alive."

Drystan had to pause at the memory. He had not thought about that in a long time.

"That is horrible and terrifying." Eselt spoke through tears that glittered like diamonds on her face. "Do not speak of it further if it brings you pain."

"I have to get through this Eselt. I have to get it out."

He felt her nod against his ribcage and cherished the wetness he felt from her tears for him.

"It was only me and the three Eriu nobles who were allowed to live. They took us to their ships, where I learned that we had been spared because of our nobility and would be ransomed back to our families if we did not break their laws. One of their ships they loaded with the supplies we had brought, including the boots and sandals that the men in our expedition wore, plus what appeared to be plunder from any number of other locations. They put us on that boat and sent it back to their frozen island homeland in the north, where I would spend the next year of my life."

Eselt stayed quiet and let him speak. She seemed to understand the weight that his experience had placed on his shoulders. Would she understand the guilt as well?

"The Vikja lived a harsh life in a cold, unforgiving environment. There is very little that grows, and their diet is dependent on what they can trade, steal, and keep alive long enough to feed themselves. Since the Eriu nobles and I were considered valuable property, they made sure that we were fed enough to keep us alive and warm enough that we didn't freeze. We were made to work for the little comfort we received, and I learned to do a great many things with very few resources. Eventually, I earned my freedom to move about the village, carry a weapon, and even go out to hunt without supervision."

"Why didn't you run away or try to escape?"

Drystan had to laugh, though it held little mirth. "Where would I go? Without the Vikja, I would die quickly on my own, with no idea what direction to run or how to leave the island. I was lucky. I grew up working hard at my training and developed a solid endurance. The three Eriu nobles captured with me hardly worked a day in their lives. The first month one escaped and was found a day later frozen solid less than a league from the village. Another lasted three months before he died of disease, and the third was killed with unimaginable brutality when he struck one of the clan chief's daughters. I can still hear his screams. They went on for so long that in the end, he had no voice to make a sound."

"What did they do to the poor man?" Eselt asked.

She was so innocent. What a cruel man he would be to tell her how they held the man down, split the ribs from his spine, pulled them back and laid his lungs upon them. The torture was drawn out so slowly that he lived until the last of it. She must never know that men were capable of such atrocities toward one other.

"It is too horrible for me to relive the details, Princess. I am sorry."

She reached up from where she lay curled in his lap and held his face in her hands. "We will not speak of that, then."

"It took several weeks for ransom demands to be sent to Eriu and Lyonesse, then several more for a search party to locate the remains of our expedition south of Dunon and confirm that we were not among them. By then the winter had set in, and travel was far more difficult. I have never been so cold in my life, and it was all I could do to stay warm enough to keep from freezing to death. I distracted myself by learning their language and the symbols they used in their writing. For good or ill, I am sure that I am stronger for that experience."

"You are the strongest and bravest man that I have ever known, and I respect you even more knowing how you suffered." Drystan would have laughed at that, but she seemed so serious that he might have insulted her.

Instead, he smiled his appreciation and went on without comment. "Negotiations commenced again in the late spring, and by then the King of Lyonesse was putting immense pressure on the Dvergr Dwarfs, who had a trade alliance with the Vikja, to intervene on my behalf. I was later told that it was one thing for the sons of a few minor nobles to be held for ransom by the Vikja, it happened more than you would think, yet quite another for the adopted son of the most powerful duke in Lyonesse."

"You must have felt proud that the King of Lyonesse himself was demanding your safe return."

"I felt foolish," Drystan scoffed. "I never should have allowed myself to be deceived by those young nobles looking to gain fame on the backs of others. I embarrassed myself, my country, and worst of all, my family."

"Is that why you were so quick to defend your uncle's right to marry me?"

"Partly, I owe him everything."

"How did you finally get back home?"

"It's not clear to me what exactly happened behind the scenes, but one day a group of Dwarfs showed up in the village. There was shouting and maybe a scuffle, I'm not sure, then they came and took me with them to their ship."

Eselt became excited. "Tell me about the Dwarfs!"

Drystan chuckled. "They are the ugliest little men I have ever set eyes upon. They all had big bushy beards and eyebrows, giant bulbous noses, thick cheeks, and larger-than-normal heads. And by little, I mean short, not small. While the tallest of them came to the height of my chest, they were far thicker and wider than any man. Their hands were easily three times the size of my own, with matching muscular arms and legs and chests the size of fish barrels. When they spoke, it was like they were gargling rocks, and they tended to yell at one another rather than speak."

"I would love to see a dwarf one day!"

"You will, Princess. Their ambassadors often appear at the Court of the King in Lyonesse."

"So, they rescued you, then?"

"Not really. The Dwarfs tend to stay out of the affairs of men except for trade. Even then they use the Vikja as a surrogate to move their goods under the Dvergr flag of trade. The Dwarfs reluctantly agreed to get involved so as not to risk their trade revenue. Lyonesse was threatening to burn every Vikja ship no matter what flag they flew and suspend trade with the Dwarfs indefinitely. Fed up with it all, they retrieved me from the Vikja and delivered me safely to Lindpoole, where my uncle and cousins were waiting."

"A happy reunion for you!" She clapped happily for him. "What a beautiful ending."

Sadly, Drystan spoke softly, "Not so happy as one might think. During my captivity, the duchess died in a riding accident. She was like a mother to me, at least the only one I can remember. My uncle was a changed man because of it. The stress aged him considerably in that year, and he has never completely recovered."

"And what about you, Drystan? Have you completely recovered? Do you still carry around ghosts?"

"Always, Eselt."

She was sitting again at his eye level, and without warning, she pressed her lips to his. She kissed him deeply and aggressively; he eagerly accepted each kiss and pulled her in for more.

Then she pulled back suddenly and whispered, "Now we share a ghost," and ran into the darkness toward her own tents.

CHAPTER 6

Potions

Drystan looked over the wedding entourage camped outside the small village of Sundy on the eastern border of Eriu. The next day Sir Blevin and the company of Temple Knights would lead the assemblage into Lyonesse, where better roads and open terrain provided for accelerated travel, at least until they entered the dense forests around Lake Virtue and Stoddenferry Castle. Now Drystan was no longer concerned with arriving in Tintagel quickly, the opposite in fact, and he secretly longed to travel the roads forever with Eselt.

It had been raining periodically, and the weather was a little on the chilly side the past few days since they left Teamhrach. The progress was slow, and nobody enjoyed traveling through the mud. That afternoon the royal family took refuge at the only inn the village had to offer; it was quaint, warm, and served good food. As far as Drystan was concerned, the best part about the inn was that it was not a tent.

Eselt was in her room that she shared with her attendants, laughing and joking about marriage, men, and the usual intrigues of court. It was late in the evening, and Drystan had already been to her room four times to check on her, each time leaving the attendants giggling when he departed. Not that he needed to be concerned, as the inn was full of guards inside and out, but he was taking his new duty to the princess seriously, although he really just wanted to see her.

Standing at her bedside, Drystan realized that Eselt had not been feeling her best all day, and another fit of sneezing sent her attendants running for warm blankets, hot tea, and silk kerchiefs. The chilly wind and wet conditions were often accompanied by colds, sniffles, and sneezes that rarely became serious or lasted more than a few days. No one expected this occasion to be any different, but she was the princess after all, and Drystan thought precautions would be sensible.

"Shall I go to the camp and retrieve a druid, my lady?" he asked.

Even though they had grown very close to each other over the past days and the pretense of formality was no longer present when they were alone, it was necessary when others were around. Especially the ones who gossiped. Rumors that started so easily were often times very hard to squash.

Eselt responded through her kerchiefs, "No, no, good knight. It would be cruel of me to send you out in this weather. Perhaps the innkeeper has a tonic. I'm sure this is nothing more than a cold. Lady Fedelmid, would you kindly inquire?"

"Yes, my lady. I will go right away." Lady Fedelmid jumped up from Eselt's bedside and started toward the door.

"I will accompany her lady and bring hot water," Drystan volunteered and followed her out the door.

Drystan walked with Lady Fedelmid downstairs to the modest common room that was crowded with nobles, several Fiann, and a few locals drinking warm mead while enjoying the talents of a minstrel. The lady quickly captured the attention of a serving maid and asked for the innkeeper. A few moments later a slim man, balding and with gray at the tips of what little hair he retained, rushed up to the princess's attendant.

"How can I be of service, my lady?" he asked with a slight bow.

"Princess Eselt has a cold and would inquire if you have a tonic that might help her sleep and pass the illness," she replied.

"I can do better than that." The innkeeper smiled. "We have a healer in the room tonight. Shall I send her to the princess's chamber?"

"Yes, that would be wonderful, thank you. Also, would you prepare hot water for the princess to steam?" She gestured to Drystan. "This is Sir Drystan, and he will bring it up."

"No need to bother, Sir Drystan. It will take a few minutes to heat the water, and then I will have it brought up to you with a few clean linens."

Drystan thanked the innkeeper and accompanied Lady Fedelmid back to the princess's room.

"I would still prefer a druid to come. We don't know this healer, and she may not have the required skill . . ."

Eselt cut Drystan off. "Let's give her a chance. If she is not helpful, I will allow you to retrieve a druid for me," she chided.

A few moments later, a stout old lady with loose gray robes, a cloak barely better than rags, and a steady gait supported by a sturdy walking stick entered the room. No more impressive than any vagabond on the lonely country roads. Drystan moved to send the beggar out, but Eselt held his arm to stay his motion.

The woman was looking directly at Eselt and ignoring everyone else in the room as if they didn't exist. Drystan thought her steady gaze would have been offensive had it not also been mesmerizing in some way, and her black eyes held a strange depth of knowledge that was disconcerting. Her black eyes and arrogant scrutiny reminded him a lot of Sir Murhalt.

"Hello, child, I am Healer Aja. I understand you are feeling under the weather?" Her voice was even and without emotion.

Eselt smiled despite her swollen nose and eyes. "I'm sure it is just a minor cold, good woman. Thank you for coming so late in the evening."

Aja confidently strode over to the princess's bedside. "Let's take a look at you, then. I am sure your family would like to have you bright-eyed and full of energy by tomorrow morning."

She planted her heavy forearm on Eselt's forehead for a moment, looked at her throat, and checked for swelling in her neck. "Well, dear, what you have is a cold. Nothing serious, and fortunately I have the perfect remedy."

Aja rummaged through her bag and then produced a small red vial.

"Drink this," she told Eselt.

"Just a moment." Drystan was on the other side of the bed and snatched the vial before Eselt could take it.

"And who are you, young man?" Aja asked with reproach.

Eselt responded for him, "He is my knight and champion. Please do not be offended. He is just overly protective."

"I see," she muttered thoughtfully.

Aja looked closer at him and then again at Eselt, as if seeing them for the first time. Then she smiled a discerning smile that made Drystan feel like somehow she knew their secret. Something about her dark eyes . . .

He took a small sip of the liquid from the red vial and waited.

Suddenly Drystan clutched at his throat and made strangled, croaking sounds as he sank to his knees. The attendants in the room squealed in fear and backed toward the far walls, and Lady Fedelmid rushed over to Eselt's side protectively.

"Drystan!" Eselt screamed. Pure fear stained her reaction.

He looked at Eselt, desperation in his eyes, his last breath parting his lips and . . . winked. "Not bad, actually. My stuffed nose is clearing already, and I am feeling warmth throughout my body. I believe it is safe, Princess."

"Drystan, you are horrible!" Eselt laughed, and the other ladies in the room laughed nervously with her.

Aja stood, her features unchanged, betraying no emotion, and her hands firmly planted on her hips. She was apparently not amused by the display. "The tonic will make you tired." Her penetrating gaze was leveled squarely on Drystan. It made him feel vulnerable and revealed. Still, he didn't look away. "I suggest that you retire to your chamber soon."

Eselt drank the remaining portion of the potion and soon reported the same results. "Thank you so much for your help. I am already feeling better. My attendant here, Lady Fedelmid, will make sure you are properly compensated."

"Thank you child, but it has been my pleasure to serve a princess of our happy land. I heard you are going to be married soon." Aja leaned in close to Eselt and smiled. "I wish you only what your heart desires."

"Thank you, good woman." Eselt yawned sleepily.

Lady Fedelmid escorted the healer out of the room before Drystan, groggy now as well, bid Eselt a good night. He barely made it back to his own bed before falling upon it fully clothed. That night, he slept fitfully and experienced vivid dreams of Eselt, her soft lips and easy touch, which brought excitement to his heart and longing in his soul.

~~~

Drystan joined Eselt for breakfast in a small room attached to her bedchamber. Lady Fedelmid was there, brushing the princess's hair while her other attendants brought in bowls of fruits and porridge. As usual, he kissed her hand when he greeted her, lingering longer than usual with her fingers to his lips. She made no effort to pull away.

"How are you feeling today, Princess?" he asked.

She looked different today, and not because she was no longer swollen and sneezing. There was a glow about her barely sun-touched skin so smooth and silky in the filtered morning light. One of her hands lay upon the table, and Drystan marveled at how delicate and soft it seemed, he wondered at its touch and wanted to brush it again with his. How had he never noticed the depth of blue oceans in her eyes, the slight blush on her cheeks, and the moist, full lips that she licked so innocently while seeming so seductive? Her long golden hair fell in waves down the front of her dark blue riding dress and rose and fell with the heaving of her perfectly proportioned breasts . . .

Drystan was sure that she had answered that she was feeling

remarkably well and something else. Did she ask him a question? She stared back at him, but there was no look of expectation in her expression. She seemed to study him in the same way he was studying her. He wanted to look away so not to be caught staring, but he couldn't.

Someone was speaking.

"Princess? Are you unwell?" asked Lady Fedelmid.

"What? Oh, yes, I am fine, thank you."

Drystan took a seat at the small table across from Eselt.

"If you are not feeling well, I can fetch the druid now," the lady offered.

Eselt smiled the most beautiful smile Drystan had ever seen, and her eyes were locked on his own while she spoke.

"I feel wonderful."

"Well, that's excellent news. You look much better, and I'm sure you'll be in perfect health by the time we reach Tintagel in a few days." She made a quick curtsy. "Unless there is anything else you need, I will pack away all your personals in your travel chest. No doubt they will be banging down the door for it soon."

Absently, Eselt answered, "Yes, Lady Fedelmid, that will be all for now. Thank you."

They were alone.

Drystan's heart was racing. He wanted to say something, but he had no words. Instead, he stood from his chair and quickly walked to kneel where she sat. There was nothing that needed saying. Placing his hands on the sides of her head, he pulled her to his lips and kissed her passionately. She did not resist. Her lips pressed hard against his of their own accord. She placed her hands lightly yet firmly on his hands, and she drew her body in closer to him. He wanted her right then, all of her.

There was the click of a latch on the door handle, and he drew back quickly, still holding one of her hands.

"Princess, would you prefer the red or—" Lady Fedelmid had stopped in shock.

Trying to recover quickly, Drystan kissed Eselt's hand and stood straight and formal.

"I enjoyed our breakfast conversation, and I am especially pleased that you have recovered from your illness. Good morning."

"Good morning, sir knight," she replied as if nothing unusual in all the world had occurred.

Drystan nodded to Lady Fedelmid, who was peering at him through squinting eyes as he hastily exited the room. Standing outside in the empty hall, he put his back against the wall and breathed heavily. How close had they come to an undeniably disastrous picture of deceit and betrayal? He could not allow the princess to be burdened with such shame! How could he live with himself, and what future could there be for either of them if they were found in that situation? He could not allow that to happen again.

They would have to be much more careful in the future.

~~~

Eselt was restless inside her carriage. Her lady-in-waiting and attendants were gossiping and laughing and making the most of the slow journey to Tintagel, but not her. All she could think about was riding beside Drystan. He was so close, just outside the carriage, riding behind them. She couldn't see him, but she knew he was there. She could feel him there. If she could spend all day beside him, she would, and the gossip would no doubt start, so she would bide her time until it was appropriate. She felt so desperate.

She thought about the last two days since they left the village. So much had happened, so much had changed, and now they shared a dark secret together, one that could never be undone. It all started so innocently, giddy and childlike. They rode together closer than before, spoke softer, and laughed quietly with each other. Their hands began to touch often, and Drystan would look into her eyes longer. No one appeared to take notice, no one could suspect, except for Lady Fedelmid. She was looking at Eselt now from across the carriage with a look of disapproval and uncertainty. She was the only one who watched them closely. Eselt didn't think she knew anything for certain, and even if she did, she would never tell. An accusation against the princess, true or not, would cause a stain upon the noble lady that would likely leave her disgraced and unable to find service to another noblewoman.

Every night since leaving the village of Sundy, Drystan took charge of Eselt's camp. He set his tent next to hers and the one for her ladies and attendants farther away. He said it was so that he could better protect her from dangers in the night. Eselt surprised herself by dismissing them all to their own tent at night with the excuse that she needed to get used to sleeping alone and that the quiet would allow her to pray and contemplate the role she would be assuming soon. Of course, they protested, but they did as they were told. Even Lady Fedelmid quietly accepted and never said a word about it.

Drystan came to her that first night—somehow she knew that he would—and they ran into the woods together without anyone the wiser. He had not prepared a shelter for the two of them, but it did not matter. Drystan took her virginity that night, under the stars on a bed of soft moss and leaves. He returned to her the next night and this time prepared a shelter in advance so she wouldn't have to explain the thistles and twigs in her hair the following day. She was sure he would do the same later that night.

Eselt knew what they were doing was wrong and very risky. If they were caught, both of their families would be shamed. Her father might marry her off to a farmer or send her to serve the druids, and she didn't want to think about what might happen to her lover.

They hadn't yet spoken about what would happen when they reached Tintagel either. It was an inevitability they silently agreed to avoid for the moment. Their destination was still days away, and so it was like they were living in a wonderful dream in the meantime. They passed the time telling each other stories about their lives and reading poetry to each another. Penhallow was Drystan's favorite, and so it was hers. It wasn't really, but she loved the poet's prose because he did. Soon the caravan would pause, and she would bring him lunch, and they would spend the afternoon riding together. How impossible life seemed when she was in love and wanted to sing praises of her lover to the world only to realize the harsh reality that doing so would destroy them. She wondered if there would ever be a time when it wouldn't matter.

There must be a way out, she thought. Certainly, she could go to her father and tell him she had changed her mind about the duke and had decided to wait a while longer before she was married. Would he be sympathetic to her plea? Didn't he want what was best for her? No. Her father would never see it that way. Already a man had died because of her decision to marry the duke. A vile, evil man, to be sure, but he hadn't always been that way. And his family loved him. What affront would they take at a silly girl changing her mind about her marriage after their son had been killed in a challenge for her hand? And what about the duke? He would be embarrassed in front of his family and considered a foolish old man by the whole of the Western Kingdoms. Her father would find himself in a very precarious position both at home and abroad. Yes, he would see it much differently. Her path was set no matter what she wanted anymore. She had no choice but to see it through to the end.

Despite all of that, she couldn't help how much she loved Drystan. She knew he loved her too. It was pure and real, with no guilt or regret, and even if she wanted to stop the affair, she knew she could not. Their lives would be in constant danger every day for as long as they loved each other, and she accepted the risk, even if it meant her doom.

CHAPTER 7

Thieves

"The wedding is only ten days from now. I can't have these burglaries unchecked with all the nobles arriving. For Sunna's sake, there will be two of the most powerful kings in the Western Kingdoms here! I need more, Firolin, and fast."

Captain Purin was annoyed with the powerful Dvergr dwarf wizard Firolin, once an apprentice to the infamous Mad Wizard of Tintagel, who was driven into the Wilds several decades ago. Purin was a child at the time, but he remembered how Duke Maruk's father feared that the Mad Wizard's unfettered use of power would bring destruction to the city and injury or death to the population of Tintagel. The dwarf spent many years in the wizard's service until he found his master's murdered and mutilated body in the wilderness tower they called home. Now he used the talents he had developed to help Captain Purin track down criminals who committed crimes against the nobility of Tintagel. Today he was on the trail of a repeat offender who was burglarizing, of all places, Valiant Keep.

How the cunning thief had managed to get onto the grounds, much less into the private chambers, was baffling, and that's why he was standing in front of Firolin. He needed answers; he needed an identity. So far, Duke Maruk had not been well informed about the incidents, and Purin preferred to keep it that way until he had the culprit waiting in a cell to be hung by the neck.

"Turn dat glove inside out, an' we see if-ta somtin' else-ta find," said the knobby dwarf.

Purin turned the glove inside out, pulling each finger one by one, stopping at the thumb when he noticed a small red dot that appeared to be blood.

"How about this?" He showed the mark to Firolin.

Taking the glove, the dwarf sniffed at the spot. "Dat be gud if it-ta be blood."

Firolin could see things about people if he had a personal item to examine, and so far the glove only told him that the thief was from a powerful guild in the lower city and not much else.

"I'm going to step out front for some fresh air. Let me know what you find."

The dwarf grunted and disappeared through a door in the back. Usually, Purin would sit in Firolin's workroom and observe the ritual, but on this occasion, the dwarf had been working on something earlier that left his entire house smelling like pungent mushrooms, and the lingering fumes burned Purin's eyes. It didn't seem to bother the dwarf one bit. Maybe it was his lunch.

Outside the air was clean and fresh. Even with the droppings of horses and livestock in the streets, it was like standing in a field of daisies compared to Firolin's house. Purin hoped the dwarf would come up with something that would help him. The sooner he had the thief, the better. So far, there were five burglaries that he was aware of, and each time there was no one in the chamber that was burgled, and no one saw anyone unusual come or go. He worried that if it happened again and someone came upon the thief unexpectedly, there could be violence. The last thing he needed was to be in the position of trying to explain to the duke why someone in the Valiant Keep had been injured or killed by an intruder.

Worse than that, this thief was very talented, and he could imagine a scenario in which something valuable was stolen from the King or Queen of Lyonesse or the High King or Queen of Eriu while they were in town for the wedding. Not only would that be a massive embarrassment for the duke, but it would also spell certain doom for him since he was in charge of the security in Valiant Keep and all who dwelt there, resident or guest. It infuriated him that his guards had not seen a thing, even when he doubled the patrols after the second robbery was reported.

The front door opened, and Firolin poked his head out. "I has somtin'," he said, and Purin followed him inside.

Back in the workroom, the dwarf held up the glove. "Dis person is young, black hair, brown eyes, short an' thin. An' it-sa woman."

Purin was genuinely surprised: a woman in this line of work? It could also explain why no one noticed her if she was dressed like an attendant or chambermaid.

"Anything else?" Purin demanded.

"Jus' da gold."

"I paid you a gold already."

"Dat was jus' fer da glove, not-ta blood inside."

Reluctantly, Purin flipped Firolin another gold coin and walked out the door. He wondered who the bigger thief was: the one he was after or the dwarf. At least he had a description of who he was after now, and with his contacts in the lower city, it shouldn't be too hard to track her down. A woman thief. The idea intrigued him, and he allowed his mind to wander as he rode toward the district where the thieves plied their trade unhindered. He hoped she was pretty.

The Gallant Leper was busy as usual, but Purin never entered through the front. At the back door where the stables stood, the same old man greeted him.

"I was not expecting you this afternoon, my lord. I may need a little time to find a sufficient companion for you this evening."

"I'm not here for that tonight, Lewys," Purin replied. "I need to see Tudful about a job. Is he here?"

"I believe he is, my lord. Please follow me." The old man turned and didn't look back to see if Purin followed.

He did, and soon they stood in front of a set of double doors that Purin guessed led to a parlor or lounge. The old man tapped twice and waited. A few moments later, a stout man with a large cudgel on his belt approached them from the opposite end of the hallway where they stood waiting.

"What is it?" he asked gruffly.

Lewys bowed to him and then gestured to Purin. "His Lordship would like a word with Tudful."

"He's busy. Come back later." The big man began to turn and walk away, but Purin put a hand on his shoulder.

"I am busy as well. Tell Tudful to see me now. Tell him it's Purin, and I have a job."

The man completed his turn, brushing off Purin's hand and continued down the hall and around the corner. Purin was grinding his teeth hard. If Tudful didn't see him now, he was going to stick his dagger in that man's eye. A second later, the doors opened.

The old man gestured for him to enter before he turned back down the hall the way they had come. Inside, the room was large and full of comfortable chairs and plush divans, with a fireplace in one corner that kept the chamber warm. Floating in the air near the ceiling were several light globes for illumination and sitting smugly in one of the chairs was Tudful. There was no one else in the room that he could see, but he was confident that he was being watched carefully.

"Greetings, old friend," Tudful said, rising. "It is good to see you again. Can I get you a glass of Courth's finest?"

"Have you ever known me to refuse?" Purin said smiling as he took a glass.

Purin had known Tudful for several years. He was something of a facilitator between the guilds of Tintagel and everyone else. Whenever Purin was looking for somebody and had a good description of their crime or appearance, Tudful was usually very capable of helping him locate them, even if they were in another city.

"You have a job, I hear? Someone that you need found, I would guess?" He spoke smoothly, like a diplomat and dressed just as finely.

"The usual," Purin stated nonchalantly.

He didn't want Tudful to know how important it was for him to capture this person, otherwise the price would go up exponentially.

Tudful waved to the writing table. "Write down what you know, and I'll see what I can do."

Purin stood over the writing table and wrote with ink and quill on a small parchment the description that Firolin had given to him. Then he handed the paper to Tudful.

Glancing over it quickly, he looked up at Purin. "This woman, what did she do?"

Purin shrugged. "Theft, burglary, the usual. The duke wants an example made of someone before the wedding to deter similar activities that might sour the celebrations next week."

"It's interesting that you chose a woman to make an example of. Surely some brutish cutthroat would do better for appearances?"

Tudful was probing for an angle to give him an excuse to charge more. They always played this game, and as long as Purin didn't give anything away, Tudful would have to honor their standing agreement.

"Usually that would be true, but given the special nature of the coming event, the duke thought it might create more of an impression to hang a woman. We hang brutish cutthroats every week."

Seemingly satisfied with his exclamation, Tudful nodded. "Very well. This one is an easy one, anyway."

"You know her?"

"Not really, but she is in this tavern at this very moment."

Purin put five gold coins on the writing table. "Why don't you have her brought to my room downstairs?"

Tudful swept up the gold coins and deposited them in the inner pocket of his jacket. "Certainly. I will let Lewys know you will be entertaining for a while this evening."

Purin left Tudful's room and made his way down through the kitchen storerooms and into his private pleasure chamber. At least that is how he thought of it. Although he was sure those that he entertained there thought of it as more of a torture chamber.

He didn't have to wait long before two very large thugs walked in dragging the unconscious form of a woman clad all in black leather.

"Will she be OK?" he asked the men.

One answered, "She struggled a bit, didn't want to go with us, so I thumped her. She'll be fine when she wakes up, maybe a headache."

They dropped the woman on the floor and left.

Lewys popped his head in as soon as the big men where clear. "May I fetch your usual wine tonight, my lord?"

Purin was looking at the woman on the ground and waved him off distractedly. "Yes, yes."

He dragged her over to the middle of the chamber and pulled down shackles hanging from the ceiling that he clasped to each of her wrists. Then he carefully removed any weapons he could find on her. To his surprise, she carried nine daggers of various shapes and sizes. She was pretty in a rough way, with straight black hair that fell to her shoulders, the lithe body of an acrobat, and attractive features despite a few scars that ran across her face and neck. He was sure this one would have a lot of spunk.

He took a pail of water from the corner and dumped it on her head. She coughed and sputtered before she opened her eyes, revealing intense dark orbs inside. She looked around in a panic before she focused on Purin sitting in a chair in front of her.

"Who are you?" she growled.

Purin stood to address her. "I am Captain Purin, and you have been placed in my detention for crimes committed against the duke."

"I have not done anything to the duke." She pulled angrily at the chains holding her wrists above her head.

"But you have, my dear, by pilfering personal property from private chambers in Valiant Keep. Any crime in Valiant Keep, whether to resident or guest, is considered a crime against the duke himself."

"I've never been in Valiant Keep! You have the wrong person!"

Purin pulled the glove from behind his belt and matched it with the one found among the loose items and knives he had taken off her earlier. "A perfect match wouldn't you say?"

She stared in disbelief for a moment before she lowered her head and whispered. "What are you going to do with me?"

He walked to a rack on the wall and removed a stiff rod with several long leather straps that protruded from the top. When he walked back to her with it, he ran the straps down one of her arms and then the other before slapping her hard in the center of her back with it. She let out an angry yelp and arched her back.

"We are going to have fun tonight, and in the morning I am going to take you to Valiant Keep, where you will be hung for your crimes."

She stood, much quicker than he expected, and barely missed kicking him in the chest with a sharp heel. He would have to be careful with this one.

He smiled. "We can do this the hard way or the extremely hard—"

The door opened behind him, and without turning, he pointed to a small table. "Put the wine there."

"Wine?" an unexpected voice answered. "Yes, I should have brought wine."

Purin spun around. It was not Lewys standing there, but some other, and his sword was hanging from a rack on the other side of the room. He should have locked the damn door!

"This is a private room! Get out!" Purin demanded.

"Oh, but I must join this party. You seem to be having so much fun!"

The woman looked at the newcomer and rolled her eyes. "What are you doing here?"

The man just shrugged and continued to smile innocently.

Purin looked him over carefully. He was not young, but not old either. He was probably in his thirties with a slight, muscular build. He wore all black leather, like the girl, and had several knives strapped in strategic places that Purin could see and probably more that he could not. The way he stood was confident and assured in his control of the situation, and not a bead of sweat had formed to dampen the edges of his short brown hair.

"Do you know who I am?" Purin asked.

"Of course, Captain Purin. Tudful was very clear about your position and influence. That is why you are still standing there breathing, unlike those two louts that thumped Sione there."

"And who are you?"

"My name is Reskalin, from Arre, and the FatMan would like this little bird returned to him unharmed."

Purin almost took a step back. The FatMan. He was purported to be the Master of the Seven Stars Brotherhood and notorious for murdering those that complicated his world.

"I have a duty to bring her before the duke for justice," Purin spat.

Reskalin spread his hands and looked around the room. "Is this also a part of your duty?"

Purin felt his face turning red. "She has been inside Valiant Keep five times, robbing nobles and their families under the protection of the duke! That cannot go unpunished!"

"Nine." Sione rattled her chains to get his attention.

"What?" Purin asked irritably.

Smiling sweetly, she said, "I have been inside Valiant Keep nine times, not five."

"Let's not get too caught up in the details," Reskalin quickly interjected before Purin could respond. "Do you have a list of what was stolen?"

Purin calculated his odds against Reskalin without his sword, and they weren't very good. "I do," he responded.

"Good. Give it to me, and I will make sure everything on it is returned, plus a handsome reward for your trouble."

"The duke is going to expect a body."

Reskalin smiled. "Well, you are in luck, Captain, there are two conveniently just outside this room!"

Purin realized right away this was a deal he couldn't refuse and handed Reskalin the inventory list of stolen items from his pouch.

"You have been busy, Sione," the man told her.

She responded with an innocent giggle, "Don't tell, Father."

Purin looked over at her and realized to his shock that the woman called Sione was no longer in the shackles he had bound her in. Had he forgotten to lock them? With a sinking feeling in the pit of his stomach, he realized that this woman, Sione, daughter of the FatMan, could have killed him at any moment she pleased.

CHAPTER 8

Stoddenferry

Late in the afternoon, the wedding convoy arrived at Stoddenferry Castle, where they would stay the night. Drystan came here once as a young squire and spent a few nights in its stables. The black stone fortress was not huge, and its high walls did not encompass a city as did Teamhrach or Tintagel. However, it was well positioned on the shale cliffs above Lake Virtue, and its purpose was to guard the northern approaches to Tintagel and protect the villages in the surrounding territory. From the many stories he heard about Stoddenferry Castle, Drystan knew that it had played a prominent role during the Oak War and had never seen adverse action since.

Leading the column of Temple knights alongside Sir Blevin and High King Cadeyrn, they were met outside the gatehouse in the courtyard by the Lord of Stoddenferry Castle, Earl Fineas Eckert, and his two sons. The earl was a man of fine reputation whose family had maintained a vigilant watch over this territory for many generations. He waited in an exquisite long brown cloak lined with white miniver fur over a silk brocade coat brought in close at the waist by a thick gold belt, tight brown trousers, and low-cut buckled shoes. His sons stood next to him similarly attired, with nearly one hundred knights in full metal armor lining the perimeter of the inner bailey.

It was an impressive reception reserved for the king or a visiting monarch that Drystan witnessed only on rare occasions in Tintagel. The royals and nobles of Lyonesse where known for their unparalleled pageantry and celebration; this short overnight visit would apparently be no exception. He could only imagine what his uncle had in store for their arrival in Tintagel.

Dismounting a short distance from where the earl and his sons waited, Drystan led the High King and Sir Blevin to greet them.

"Your Highnesses," Drystan addressed the High King and queen, "I am pleased to introduce your host for the evening, Earl Fineas Eckert, Lord of Stoddenferry Castle, and his wife, Lady Rhoswen."

"It is our greatest pleasure to see you once again, Earl Eckert and Lady Rhoswen," the High King announced. "I anticipate that the fabled game we used to hunt together hereabouts is still plentiful?"

The earl bowed slightly and replied, "It is, Your Majesty, and we are honored by your visit, as short as it may be. Our congratulations on the joyous occasion we shall be attending for your youngest daughter's marriage to our beloved Duke Maruk."

"Ah yes, a grand occasion it shall be, and more so by your presence! I thank you for your hospitality, Earl, I truly wish there was more time for us take to the field together."

Gesturing to his two sons flanking him, the Earl continued the introductions, "I am sure you remember my eldest son, Sir Reginald? He has added yet another girl to his family since you were last here."

"Well met, Sir Reginald, and congratulations on your greater family. No doubt there will be a line of courters to fend off from both Lyonesse and Eriu when they are of age to marry!"

Sir Reginald smiled and made a quick bow before his father introduced his younger brother.

"And this is my youngest son, Perault, a squire to the legendary Sir Aldeman. He is expected to complete his service by the next tourney and receive his silver-fringed cloak."

"That is excellent news, Perault!" the High King exclaimed. "You should know that even in Teamhrach, your prowess in the squires' tourneys is well-known. My knights already dread the day you graduate to the knights' tourneys and compete with them."

"Your Majesty." Perault bowed, smiling.

The High King had a storied charisma with everyone he met, thought Drystan, especially the women.

"And of course, you know Knight Commander Blevin," Drystan completed the introductions to the earl.

"Please come out of the weather, Your Majesty. I will show you to your rooms myself, and Lady Rhoswen will happily attend the queen, and then we will find refreshments," said the Earl.

The High King followed the earl through the gatehouse and into Stoddenferry Castle while Lady Rhoswen followed with the queen. Their voices echoed back to where Drystan stood with Sir Blevin. He could hear the High King, now speaking informally, say, "Fineas, you've become skinny. We need to fatten you up with a regular diet of good Eriu mead . . ."

Sir Reginald and Perault greeted Drystan and Sir Blevin, and after a bit of banter, Sir Reginald departed with Sir Blevin to settle the rest of the royal family into their chambers while Perault was left alone with Drystan to organize the settlement of the remaining nobles.

"I have heard of your skills as well, Perault," Drystan commented while they walked back toward the carriages and wagons. "Perhaps you will quiet the calls for knight's fodder next tourney."

"Knight's fodder?"

Drystan smiled at the young man. "That's what the veterans call the newly elevated knights who enter the knights' tourney for the first time. You may have also heard the term 'easy points'? Basically, the same thing."

"I will endeavor to bring honor to my family and glory to my country, Sir Drystan. Whatever name that I earn among my peers will be the one that I deserve."

"You are a formal one, young squire," Drystan teased. "How is Sir Aldeman? There was a time that he was considered the best swordsman in the whole of the Western Kingdoms. I doubt there are many who could best him now, even at his advanced age."

"He is doing very well and in good health. Although he no longer competes, he does work out every day and has lost only a few steps. Sometimes when we spar, I win only by a squeak."

Drystan laughed at that. "You sound too modest, squire; keep him exercised as long as you might. He is a good man who is loved by everyone."

The two men arrived at the first of the carriages, and with Perault's direction, they began sending the nobles and their small army of servants to their respective grounds to set up camp.

~~~

Drystan did not remember Stoddenferry Castle well enough to know the secluded areas where lovers might meet for a private moment, and he began to despair that he would be unable to see Eselt that evening. They had been together every night since leaving the village and much of the days, so much so that Eselt had become like air to him, and he physically felt it hard to breathe at the thought of a night without her. Of course, he missed her during the day as well, except that there were always so many distractions that he was still able to focus. It was the night that made him feel desperate, when his heart ached, with thoughts of her and the need to be with her as if he was under some cruel spell. Eselt told him she felt exactly the same way.

Before the celebration that evening, Perault was good enough to show him around Stoddenferry Castle grounds. He quickly surmised that Perault had no lover, but he sensed that there was someone special that he thought of. Turning down a hallway, Perault led him into a sizable room with many comfortable chairs that were filled with local knights and nobles from Stoddenferry and the wedding party intermingling in conversation while enjoying a selection of fine wines served before the feast. He greeted many as he walked through the room, taking a mug of wine offered by a server and admiring the variety of preserved animals that adorned the walls.

"Quite an impressive display you have here," he commented to his host.

Perault spread his arms wide, taking in the room. "They are all the result of many generations of my family's hunts. It was even rumored that my great grandfather captured a Leprechaun once, though sadly, there is no evidence of it."

"That would be incredible. They are storied to provide three wishes to anyone who captures them."

"They are vile and ignoble creatures," Perault almost spat with disgust. "Why would Sunna allow the little beasts to have that kind of power? It sounds like a story for children."

"I'm sure you are correct." Drystan didn't want to upset Perault by disagreeing with him about Leprechauns.

He did have a point though: they were disgusting little things, and he didn't care much about them anyway, but he thought they had as much a right to exist as anything. They exited the trophy room and headed down a quiet hallway.

Drystan was going to have to take a small chance if there was going to be any possibility of tasting Eselt's lips that night. "Tell me, squire, where is the most beautiful place in Stoddenferry Castle, somewhere you might take a lover?"

Perault looked at him sideways as they walked. "I know a place. I'll show you if you don't mind a few stairs."

Drystan followed him through a series of hallways, one passing through where he stayed in a guest chamber, then onto a broad stairway leading up to the wall on the cliffside of Stoddenferry Castle and into a tower. The stairs here were very narrow, and they seemed to spiral up forever. At the top, there was a ladder that connected to the ceiling of the tower where a trap door opened onto the roof and a doorway below it. It was the doorway they went through to find a wide landing that connected to another tower on the opposite side.

The landing held several cushioned chairs and tables with potted trees that served as anchors for broad white canopies of linen that fluttered in the afternoon breeze. The view of Lake Virtue was astounding, and with the additional height of the cliffs, the beach where the waves lapped against its rocky shore seemed impossibly far away. Not a soul was there to enjoy it besides the two of them.

"This is the most beautiful venue in the castle," Perault stated simply.

"Absolutely wondrous. Why is there not a crowd of onlookers? I would think this should also be the most popular spot in the castle as well!"

Perault laughed. "I would agree, except there are far too many stairs for those with weak constitutions or physical infirmities. As for the lovers, I have heard that most gentlemen prefer not to tire their ladies out with a long climb up the stairs, as it hinders their opportunity for romance."

Drystan could appreciate the logic and laughed with him.

At the dinner held in Princess Eselt's honor, the night went long with feasting and accolades. To Drystan's delight, he was fortunate enough to be seated next to Eselt as the personal representative of Duke Maruk. The High King and queen sat at her other arm while the earl, Lady Rhoswen, and their sons sat to Drystan's left. The splendor and formality of the occasion also worked to his advantage, as linens were placed on the head table that were long enough to conceal that he held Eselt's hand through the entire evening. It was quite a feat for him, and anyone that might have taken note would think he was left-handed, which he wasn't, causing him to take no little care while dining. Eselt appeared to take particular amusement in his private struggle and even jostled him a few times, inducing him to drop food or utensil more than once. He thoroughly enjoyed every moment of it.

Later that evening, when the formalities had been dispensed with and the drinking began, Eselt excused herself, feigning exhaustion from the day's events, and retired to her room. They had a plan, and before long, Drystan stood holding Eselt in the very spot he and Perault had been standing earlier. He put his arms around her from behind, and they both stared out into the blackness where dim lights could be seen here and there along the visible coastline, indicating villages in the distance and merchant ships at anchor. The moon was only a quarter full and positioned to the west, casting its light onto the never-ending movement of water below. He could smell the scent of the beach on the light breeze that blew through her lightly perfumed hair, giving him the impression of wildflowers growing on a sandy shore.

It was perfect.

He pressed his face further into her hair and tightened his embrace around her waist. She snuggled back into the folds of his ermine-lined cloak and shuddered with a brief chill. This is what he wanted forever, the perfection of beauty in the woman that he loved in a place that reflected who they were at the core of their souls.

A lie.

Drystan amended that terrible thought. They were truth; their love was true. The goal of their journey was the lie. Her life with his uncle would be the lie. Calming his thoughts, he cast his gaze up to the luminous stars. The constellation of Sunna was there, and that of the goddess Eriu. They were sisters in the cosmos, and many believed them Sister Goddesses. There were other constellations, to be sure, but those were the ones he knew.

A slight sound called his attention to the door in the opposite tower, and he thought he caught a shadow of movement. He watched for a while before deciding that it must be his imagination or a guard peeking in on his rounds only to see two lovers on the landing. Perault had told him earlier that the other tower led down into the private apartments of the Eckert family, and the door was usually locked.

Eselt turned suddenly and kissed him, wiping all thoughts of anything else away with the wind. Quickly she unfastened his belt, dropping his trousers, and forced his tunic up to bunch under his arms. She was wearing a nightdress under her long cloak, which split up the front, and she pushed her warm flesh in against his and then pulled the front of his cloak around behind her. There they stood, lips together, then apart, and together again, clutched to each another in the chilly summer night.

Eselt stopped and looked at him more seriously than he had ever seen in her before. "Never forget: you are my love."

With no hesitation, he replied, "My love is you."

~~~

Morning came too quickly, and Drystan was back in his own bed alone. It was dawn, and he wondered what it would have been like to wake up with his lover on the landing high above him. He lay in bed longer these days thinking about such things before finally washing his teeth and preparing his personals to leave.

He knew that Eselt would be breaking the fast with her parents and the earl and lady this morning. Drystan had not received an invitation. He regretted that but knew it would only be awkward for them both to endure being so close and unable to touch. Instead, he would seek out Sir Blevin and help prepare the throng of wedding travelers for departure. If they were lucky, they would finally leave by midday. That was fine with him, considering that meant it wouldn't be long until they struck camp and he could spend more of his time with Eselt again.

From Stoddenferry Castle, Drystan estimated that they would arrive in Tintagel in another three days. Just three short days before his world was turned upside down. Drystan wondered how he would face his uncle knowing what he knew now and the betrayal that lingered in his heart, renewed with every second he held Eselt in his arms. He had deflowered his uncle's bride, an act considered so vile that it ranked with treason and carried the same sentence if discovered: death. Even with the guilt and the threat of death, he knew he would betray his uncle, again and again, doing so happily as long as he had Eselt.

The next several hours he spent organizing the train of carriages and wagons under the experienced leadership of Sir Blevin. The nobles were slow to move and continuously gave their servants contradicting orders, all well-meaning, no doubt, but the old knight handled them deftly. In the end, they did exactly as he wanted. *I could learn the art of diplomacy from this man,* he thought for the thousandth time. And it was already true. Sir Blevin was one of his mentors growing up and the reason he was so well educated and could use his sword skillfully.

He saw Perault on two occasions throughout the day; however, both times the squire was deliberate about not looking his way. Drystan got the feeling he was being avoided for some reason. Hopefully, he had not unwittingly insulted Perault the day before. He certainly seemed to have a very rigid moral compass for one so young.

Finally, at about noon, as he predicted, the High King and his family emerged from the gatehouse and exchanged formal farewells with the earl, Lady Rhoswen, and their sons before entering the carriages. Drystan and Sir Blevin walked over and added their thanks while the cavalcade began their slow crawl toward Tintagel. The formalities dispatched, Drystan made his way to his mount. Unexpectedly, Perault was suddenly in step beside him.

Drystan stopped, and the squire stopped with him. "Perault, I look forward to seeing you at Tintagel. I would like to return the favor of your company and give you a proper tour of Valiant Keep."

Perault had a very serious look on his face, and he seemed not to hear anything that Drystan just said. Then he leaned forward and whispered in Drystan's ear, "I know your sins."

A bolt of ice immediately shot down Drystan's spine and by the time he recovered Perault had walked away. *How could he know? What did he know? Was he in danger? Was Eselt in danger?* For the first time in his life, he considered committing murder.

CHAPTER 9

End of a Dream

It was the last night before the caravan was scheduled to arrive in Tintagel, Eselt lay quietly in the safety of Drystan's arms. Their warm bodies clutched together under covers of thick furs on the side of a grassy hill to ward off the night's chill breeze. She was anxious, with her thoughts returning again and again to what they would do after tomorrow. As soon as they arrived in Tintagel, she would be taken to her new chambers, and neither of them could hazard a guess as to when they would be able to see each other privately again.

She cuddled up next to him more tightly, feeling his warmth. She knew he was awake, staring up at the stars and probably thinking about the same thing.

"Will you miss me?" she asked quietly.

"Desperately."

"You must find me quickly. I don't know if I can stand to be apart from you a single day."

"It is all I can think of, my dear. When you are not next to me, thoughts of you will consume me entirely."

"And you me, love."

Drystan turned to her then and kissed her tenderly. His kisses were euphoric and made her think of nothing in those moments except for the pleasure of it, which she drank in deeply.

He pulled back just a little, still close enough that she could touch his lips with her own and spoke. "We both know why we are going to Tintagel. You will be my uncle's bride. I have accepted that and all that goes with it. Do not feel guilty for what you are expected to do. I will not fault you for it.

My pleasure will be in our company when we can manage it, even if it means my displeasure every second you are not with me."

Eselt wanted to cry, but she held it in. That was not the way she desired to remember their last night together on this journey. "We must find a way to be together forever, Drystan. We will go mad leading a charade that never ends. We must think of a way."

He turned, and they both looked up into the sky. "The stars will guide us, my love. They must."

~~~

Drystan and Eselt were riding together when the first glimpse of the polished gray stone of Tintagel's highest towers and curtain walls became visible on the coastal island that split Tintagel Castle from the headland where Valiant Keep was located. Between the two, a massive stone bridge topped by crenellations, like the walls, spanned the chasm between the sheer cliffs to bring congruency to the awe-inspiring site. They traveled along the coastal road with the expanse of Lake Virtue on their right and the endless forests and fields on their left. Once they broke through the trees south of Tintagel, the full splendor of the city would be in view, and it would only be a matter of hours before they were parading through the city gates.

The playful conversation between the lovers trailed off with the first sight of their destination. Until this moment Drystan had always taken joy in seeing his home; now a pervasive gloom seemed to weigh on his heart and smother his enthusiasm. Glancing over at Eselt, he saw she had the look of one condemned and facing a life confined in prison.

"I almost forgot." Drystan pulled from his pack the surcoat with the duke's coat of arms and Eselt's hair magically woven into it. "I should have given this to you before, but the time was never right."

"What is it?" she asked taking the folded garment.

"A gift from the duke, and my pillow for the last several days." He smiled.

"Well, I am glad it served a good purpose." She stuffed it into a pack on her horse without looking at it and blew him a kiss.

Soon the forest was upon them, and Eselt was compelled to return to her carriage. This would be the last time they rode together on this journey, and already the separation left a cold stone in the pit of his stomach. He wished she could have stayed with him all the way to Tintagel, but it was a tradition for royalty to travel under cover in the forest for fear of assassination. Drystan scoffed at the thought. No royal had been murdered in the last hundred years as far as he knew. The tradition was outdated.

Exiting the forest, he was startled to see hundreds of Temple Knights from Tintagel mounted in full metal armor with their gold-fringed cloaks flicking in the breeze behind them. Each carried a long fluttering pennant with the duke's coat of arms, and as the column of carriages emerged into the open field, the knights formed up in two columns on each side of the road, snaking parallel to the convoy in a slow parade gait until they spanned the entire length of the wedding cortege.

Drystan was riding next to Knight Commander Blevin at the front of the column. "I've never seen anything like this before," he commented. "Not even for the King of Lyonesse."

"It is quite impressive." Sir Blevin agreed. "The duke must be trying to inspire his young love with the grandeur of Lyonesse. And the show is probably just as much for the High King and his nobles. Imagine what he must have planned for the wedding."

Drystan's heart sank again at the thought of it. He had no choice but to bear through and hope that they could find a way to be together after the ceremonies were over and life began to settle into a regular routine. Could he persevere that long?

Just before the city gates, the Temple Knights flanking the column turned their mounts and stood in salute. The broad thoroughfare beyond was lined with thousands of people from every class and privilege, even along the walls and towers that surrounded the inner city. They cheered and waved, calling well wishes to the princess, who smiled and waved back from the open window of her carriage. Soldiers in the duke's livery were spaced evenly along the route that marked their direction and held the crowds back from the road while the convoy of mounted men and carriages passed by. In a show of solidarity, the duke's initial show of force was softened by the thousands of onlookers waving small pennants of the High King of Eriu's household. Drystan had to admit it was a brilliant move that would impress upon the foreign monarch Maruk's military power and, at the same time, his embrace of friendship—all before the royal family left their carriages.

The fanfare continued through the turns and bends as they ascended the high hill where Valiant Keep stood like a protective giant over the city. The lower ward was far less crowded, excluding the remarkable formation of at least one hundred servants waiting in an expansive courtyard next to a fork in the road. It was here that Sir Blevin separated the High King and royal family from the rest of the cavalcade, sending the royalty with Drystan along the final ascent toward the upper ward, escorted by the Temple Knights and the Fianna. The duke and his sons would be waiting to greet them in the broad arc of a driveway in front of the high foregate.

The nerves that ran through Drystan left him wondering if he could face his uncle. To look in the eyes the man who was his de facto father, the man who saved him from a mundane life and done everything possible to make him feel accepted in the duke's family, the man whose loyalty he had forsaken. His face reddened in shame and then despair when he thought about Eselt and the new world she was about to enter on her own.

They rode through the gates of the upper ward. Drystan was in the front of the column, leading the carriage of the High King and queen, with Eselt's carriage following and the remaining family bringing up the rear. In a show of solidarity, the whole procession was flanked alternately by Temple Knights and the knights of the Fianna. Finally, they turned the final bend, and there stood the stark reality of his future. Duke Maruk and his sons, Sir Wilhem, the scribe, and various other lords and ladies of court all stood waving and smiling at their approach.

The duke was dressed smartly in his black ermine-fringed short cloak, matching black coat with silver thread embroidery, black stockings, and low-cut buckled shoes. He wore no cap on his thinning gray head of hair, which matched his short-cut beard and mustache. His joyful, slate-gray eyes were on Drystan the whole time as the procession approached, and he immediately embraced his nephew in a great bear hug almost before Drystan had stopped the carriages and dismounted.

"Cadeyrn sent me the details of your heroic defense of my honor and that of the future duchess against the vile Sir Murhalt. I am so proud of you." There were tears in his uncle's eyes. "After the wedding, you will be properly honored." The duke pulled Drystan close again and whispered in his ear, "I love you, boy. I can't even imagine how I could have managed if I had lost you and my bride in Eriu to a twist of fate."

Drystan almost broke down and told his uncle everything right then, but the duke released him and moved to embrace High King Cadeyrn, who stepped from his carriage with his queen. Then Eselt hesitantly came into the light from her conveyance. Somehow she had managed to change from her riding clothes and now wore an open surcoat with a black bodice threaded with silver embroidery, to match the duke, and a long emerald-green skirt that hung to the ground. Her ears were decorated with emerald earrings, but her long, delicately curving neck was oddly bare.

She was beautiful.

Drystan, in the process of greeting his brothers, nearly went to her but had to stop himself. He could tell that Eselt was struggling to keep her eyes from finding him, so he backed behind others to make it easier for her not to be distracted. The duke was kneeling before her, kissing her hand, and then presenting her with a stunning necklace of emerald teardrops that he placed around her neck. *Well planned,* thought Drystan begrudgingly.

Then she was gone, hastened away to her chambers to rest and refresh along with the Queen of Eriu and the other ladies of the royal family. The duke, one arm over the High King's shoulders, was laughing while they walked into Valiant Keep, no doubt in search of a lounge with lots of wine. His brothers took the High King's sons in hand and followed behind them while the rest of the reception went about their business. For his part, he wanted nothing more than to retreat to his own room in seclusion. If he couldn't be with Eselt right then, he would spend his time thinking of ways by which he could.

~~~

Drystan was in a good mood, considering his perpetual misery. To his surprise, Princess Eselt had been situated in the chambers reserved for the duchess. Although she would have been properly moved there after the wedding anyway, it was a slip in decorum that he did not expect. He could only guess that Valiant Keep had grown short of rooms accommodating the unusual number of royal guests that the duke was hosting for his grand event.

It wasn't the guest accommodations that Drystan cared about at the moment. When he was little, the duchess would take a secret passage that ran behind the royal suite of bedchambers and led them to the garden, where they read stories together. She told him he needed to know about the passage in case a time came that he would need to escape danger or move in secret without anyone knowing. This secret passage would be the key to his design for a secret affair with his lover. Now he just had to figure a way to get to her when no one else was present in the room.

Late that evening, after another agonizing reception dinner was over and everyone retired to their beds or lounges for drinks, Drystan quietly walked through the secret passage to the door behind which he knew Eselt would be sleeping. He had to be careful. If he startled her or Lady Fedelmid, assuming she was there, a scream would wake the entire household, and the guards would be upon them quickly. He had to take the chance. He was going mad sitting in his room pining for her.

Earlier at the banquet, he felt tortured. He didn't have the satisfaction of sitting next to Eselt as he had at Stoddenferry Castle. His uncle was in that envious position now, and Drystan was removed five spaces away as the youngest of the duke's children. He couldn't help but feel a flash of jealousy even though he loved his uncle dearly. The wedding was scheduled to take place in three days, and every night until then he would have to endure this misery, and then for a lifetime afterward unless he contrived an escape that would take them far away.

Drystan didn't eat and felt no enthusiasm for the endless tributes that were poured upon the couple. He was sure he could smell Eselt's wispy fragrance even with the aromas of the food trays that passed around him. Out of the corner of his eye, he watched her, and from the outside, she appeared happy and appreciative of all the accolades, but every once in a while her eyes would shift to where he sat, and they looked as haunted as his own.

Standing in the darkened passage outside the concealed door to the duchess's chambers, Drystan hoped it was not locked from the inside. The light globe he carried was dim and illuminated only a small circle of light around him, but it was enough light for him to crouch and insert his finger into a hole just above knee height. Through touch and memory, his finger searched blindly for the latch that would release the lock. When he found it, he pressed in and up on it and was relieved to hear a tiny *click* inside. The door released and swung smoothly, but instead of pushing it open, he moved it just a crack to listen. No sound.

Taking no chances, Drystan covered his light globe with the small leather bag he carried it in and peaked inside the room. The door encountered resistance, and he immediately stopped. His heart froze. *What was that?* Carefully extending his hand behind the door, he felt what had to be a thickly woven tapestry concealing the door from the other side. *Good,* he thought. If he could squeeze in behind it, he could listen and observe from inside the room. Then he realized the door swung both ways, and he sighed. It had been a few years since he entered the chamber in this fashion.

Drystan peeked around the side of the tapestry. The room was in darkness. If he remembered correctly, this was the dressing room, and the bedchamber would be around the corner, with no door in between. There was just enough light from a candle, likely in the privy around another corner, that he could navigate his way around the wire-framed dress stands and a small table lined with hair brushes and perfumes without knocking anything over. Unfortunately, he missed the shoes lining the wall and stumbled, nearly falling flat, but he recovered quickly enough without making too much noise. Drystan cursed himself silently for forgetting about women and their shoes. A little farther and he was in the arched doorframe where the bedchamber began, and he crouched low, discreetly looking inside.

There she was.

Eselt lay quietly in her bed, breathing in the slow, regular rhythm of sleep. She was so beautiful and at peace, he didn't want to wake her. Instead, he watched for a while and imagined a time when he would be lying next to her, if ever that time could come. She stirred a little, dreaming, and he thought he heard her utter his name. He decided he must wake her then and tell her his plan.

Creeping slowly closer, he was sure there was no one else in the room, but he didn't want to startle her and risk alerting the guards. He placed a hand gingerly on her mouth and with the other gently shook her, then again. Suddenly there was an explosion of air through his fingers, and he put his head close to Eselt's and held her body down.

"Eselt," he whispered urgently in her ear, "it is Drystan. Be still."

She quieted immediately and relaxed her struggles. Drystan removed his hand from her mouth and kissed her cheek.

"Drystan! I knew you would come!" Lifting herself to a sitting position, she hugged him tightly and quietly sobbed. "Today has been awful without you. I have smiled and curtsied and laughed all day and felt none of it. Inside, my body is like a desert thirsting for your touch, my lips dry with the absence of your kiss. How can I go on like this?"

"Eselt, listen to me." He took her face in his hands and kissed her quickly. "I have found a way for us to be together until we figure out a path out of this purgatory that we suffer."

"How Drystan? I see you are here, but I fear it is just a dream."

"Come with me."

He led her to the tapestry hiding the secret door. When closed, the seams were so perfectly intact that it looked exactly like the rest of the wall. A small release, concealed in the mount that held the tapestry, unlocked the little door, and it swung out and into the secret passage beyond.

Drystan removed the light globe from his pouch and, holding her hand, brought her into the narrow corridor.

"If you take a left, it will bring you to the gardens, and if you take a right, you will find a passage leading out of Valiant Keep and another that takes you to the kitchens. That's where I usually enter, since the servants have gone to bed and there are few guards to avoid."

"This is wonderful, Drystan. But what if we come across someone? Where shall we hide?"

Drystan laughed. "These passages have not been used since I was a small child. No one uses them, even those that know they are here, and there are few living who know this secret. I doubt even the duke himself would remember without reminding."

He placed the light globe close to the ground and drew their initials in the thick dust that coated the floor.

"See, my boots are the only ones that have come this way in decades. You can always come to me if you are afraid or in need, but be careful, since there are guard patrols and servants who may see you. Otherwise, it is better for me to come to you, as I would be less noticed walking the halls in the night."

Eselt nodded and held his arm tight next to her, shivering. He noticed she had forgotten her slippers and left her small footprints in the dust next to the larger ones from his boots. He smiled.

"Let's go back to your chamber. It is chilly out here, and I don't want you to get a cold."

After returning to her room, she lit another candle and locked the door.

"I sent Lady Fedelmid away for the night in case you found a way to come to me. And you did!" She hugged him again. "She protested, of course, but I let her know that I needed my privacy to pray and meditate."

"Will she insist every night?"

Eselt smiled wickedly. "I won't allow it!"

Drystan turned serious. "Eselt, there may be a time when my presence is not convenient."

He pulled a small pine twig full of green needles from his pouch and handed it to her.

"When you are alone and it is safe for me to enter, put this outside the secret door. It is from a tree in the garden that I used to climb as a child. When this one has crumbled, have Lady Fedelmid bring you more. Tell her you enjoy the fragrance."

"I do like the fragrance. It reminds me of you."

She stretched up to kiss him on the neck, and he hugged her tight.

"Also, light a candle in your dressing room as a second precaution, since it might not always be easy to retrieve the branch if you receive an unexpected visitor. If it is out, then I will not enter."

"Sounds sensible." She continued to kiss his neck while loosening his shirt.

"Finally, it will be possible to see each other only at night. Your attendants would find it highly suspicious if you locked yourself away during the day, and inevitably gossip would follow."

"Scandalous." He no longer had his shirt on, and she was working on his trousers.

"I hope you don't mind sleeping in late from now on." He winked and put out the candle.

CHAPTER 10

Wedding Day

The wedding of Duke Maruk to Princess Eselt was expected to be one of the most astounding affairs in the kingdom's history and the most miserable day of Drystan's life. He sat with hundreds of others in the great hall—which was elevated above the lake on the island side of Valiant Keep—facing a polished black altar covered by a tabard with the duke's coat of arms that had Eselt's hair woven into it. Above the altar, mounted on the wall, stood an enormous sun symbol of Sunna sparkling gold in the morning sunlight and radiating faith to those who worshiped the goddess. Beside the first altar was another covered by a tabard with the High King of Eriu's coat of arms and lay under the full disk of an equally sizeable yellow moon representing the Goddess Eriu.

The Arch-Druid of Sunna, Filberzh the Risen, wore long white robes fringed in gold with the sun symbol, suspended from a long gold chain, prominent upon his chest, and he stood behind the Altar of the Sun. Beside him, a man Drystan had never seen before, nor had many others, was the mysterious Arch-Druid of Eriu, Caomh the Enlightened. He wore long earth-brown and forest-green hooded robes with a thick belt of gold vines buckled around his waist by a large medallion of the moon. Around his neck hung a smooth, odd-looking, multicolored stone with a hole in the middle that hung from a gold vine thong. His hood was up, and it was hard to see his face, but flecks of long white hair thrust out near the bottom of his face and gave a clue to his advanced age. Ancient, it was said.

Drystan cast his gaze around the room. The entire southern wall of the hall was lined with Temple Knights wearing polished, shining metal armor with the duke's tabard under a white cloak fringed with silver or gold. Each was holding on a long pole a pennant displaying the duke's colors. Opposite the Temple Knights, against the northern wall, stood the ranks of

Fianna wearing intricately inscribed leather armor in earth tones of brown and green. They also held long poles with their High King's colors. Between the knights and the Fianna, rows of seating lined the entire length of the hall to accommodate the multitude of guests. The rows were split in the center by a wide aisle thick with leaves and flower petals from the spacious entry of the hall all the way up to the dual altars.

Scanning the hall, Drystan put a rough count on the total guests at a little over a thousand in attendance, a veritable who's who of the Western Kingdoms. There were dukes, barons, and counts from Eriu, Lyonesse, and Ys scattered all about. Then there was the wedding party from Eriu, which included the High King, his queen, and his daughters with their husbands and children. Sitting next to them was King Praeter Eldorath and Queen Penelope of Lyonesse—they had no children yet. There was the spectacle of a small cluster of druids wearing their earthy cloaks adorned with feathers and their strange luminescent Druid stones that hung about their necks and a small delegation of the Tuatha De who dressed and acted like anyone else in the hall except that they had a strange luminescent aura about them. Finally, and oddest of them all, were the Enlightened Ones from the Emerald Isle. It was the ambassador and her husband, to be specific, and they were easily the most beautiful people in the room. The ambassador wore a long flowing gown with layers of sea-green gossamer and light blue silks trimmed with what appeared to be beautifully cut orichalcum crystals and a gold medallion carved with the symbolic likeness of the sea that hung from her neck on a thick chain of blue glass. In contrast, her husband was dressed in a sharply tailored light blue tunic under a dark blue coat and trousers that appeared very conservative. Taller than anyone else around them, they were striking in their physical appearance. They each presented elongated skulls with long, flowing dark hair—the Ambassador's went well below her shoulders—and large brown almond-shaped eyes and a blue tint to the whole of their skin. The couple was the definition of elegance in the smooth way that they moved and the poetic distinction of their speech. He had heard that they called themselves Atlanteans, and they were the keepers of the towers and pyramids with the floating crystals at their apexes that pervaded every part of the Western Kingdoms. The duke met with the ambassador regularly and spoke of the Atlanteans as if they were demigods.

When he was a young boy, Drystan asked why they were called the Enlightened Ones. The duke replied in a matter-of-fact tone that they "knew the truth of the world" and declined to explain further. Drystan decided right then that he would someday go to their Emerald Isle and discover the truth for himself.

There were two others in the hall who seemed out of place nearly as much as the Enlightened Ones. They were both verging on middle-aged, and their similar complexions and other resemblances made Drystan think they might be related. One was tall and wiry and wore layers of flowing gray robes with sturdy travel boots, a few simple metal bands on several of his fingers and a gold triskele hanging from a leather strap around his neck. Long raven-black hair and a beard to match framed his lightly wrinkled features, and he had piercing eyes the color of the deepest blue of any ocean. The other—shorter, with a muscular build and a hard face seasoned by the weather—bore a medium-length black beard, less-than-elegant oversized dull-blue robes cinched at the waist by a thick gold chain, and a grayish-brown cloak.

Drystan nudged his oldest brother, who was sitting next to him. "Who are the two men over there?"

"Don't you know, brother? The shorter one is the Wandering Poet, Wodanaz, with his brother Myrllin. There is some debate as to which is the older one."

"Myrllin." Drystan tried to remember the name. The wizard did tricks or magic in the court of King Praetor Eldorath; that was what Drystan heard. Or maybe it was that he was a wise man, an advisor to the king? He couldn't remember. He did know of Wodanaz. He was often referred to as the Wanderer or the Wandering Poet, sometimes the Minstrel. Once, when Drystan was still a boy, Wodanaz performed for his family and other nobles when the tourney was in Tintagel. He remembered how the poet's stories came to life so vividly with color and description that it was like watching rather than listening to the stories unfold. He hoped Wodanaz would perform during the celebrations after the ceremony.

Gazing farther down the aisles, his vision settled on the Earl of Stoddenferry and his family. Perault was with them, of course, and Drystan resolved that he would do his best to avoid the man. Whatever Perault's intention was in letting Drystan know that he knew about the affair with Eselt was still a mystery. Drystan certainly didn't need another awkward meeting with the squire who knew more than he should.

Trumpets blared, and everyone stood. Duke Maruk walked from an area off to the side and stood in front of the Altar of the Sun. He was smiling broadly and shifting nervously from foot to foot. So much so that Drystan hardly recognized his uncle in such a state. It was as if he had lost thirty years from his age and was facing the prospect of a wife for the first time. He tried to feel happy for the duke, and he surely would, had the bride been any other.

Trumpets blared a second time, and everyone turned to face down the long aisle and out onto the other side of the bridge that connected the island to the headland. Drystan's heart sank to his stomach. There was Eselt, looking tiny and alone in the distance. Irrationally, he somehow hoped she would not appear, but that was impossible. He watched with everyone else as she strode the long length of the bridge in step with a single drum that beat time from somewhere unseen.

When she drew closer, he could see her in more detail. The perfect white wedding dress she wore had a high neckline decorated with a string of diamonds and long sleeves that complemented a softer-style silhouette and high waistline. It couldn't have looked more elegant on a goddess, with her golden hair pulled up in the front and encircled by a delicate band of flowers before flowing down her back in soft open curls. Behind her followed Lady Fedelmid and two attendants dressed in yellow gowns who looked after her long train and carried posies of flowers. Eselt was a vision of beauty, and lost in the moment, Drystan almost forgot she was walking to another man.

Her eyes were cast down as she walked, and only once did their gaze meet. There was a flash of joy in her eyes, then sadness before she looked away again. Drystan stood in awe at the emotional strength she must have had to hold back her tears when he knew all she wanted to do was run away and cry. If he could have grabbed her right then and taken her far away from that place, he surely would have.

When Eselt came near, he glanced up to watch her pass and found his gaze locked with another's far across the room, with the man his brother named Myrllin. The old man had a look of profound sadness in his eyes, as if he understood every emotion Drystan was experiencing in his perdition. There was comfort in that gaze as well, as if Drystan found a kindred spirit. After what seemed like an eternity, Lady Fedelmid passed between them, trailing Eselt, and broke the connection, leaving Drystan feeling ashamed. When he looked up again, Myrllin no longer looked his way, and Eselt had reached the front of the aisle, where Duke Maruk stood.

Drystan watched with a range of emotions playing through him. Rage at his old uncle's greed in taking a pretty young woman who was meant for a younger man, despair at the promises he and Eselt made to each other that he knew she couldn't keep, fear that he would never find a way to rescue her. It went on and on until the ceremony ended and his lover was declared the wife of another.

~~~

Drystan sat drunk in the great hall at a table where he had been chatting with some noble from somewhere he couldn't remember. After the ceremony, an army of servants descended on the massive room and rapidly put their mastery of organization and décor to use while the guests enjoyed fine wine from Courth and Eriu honey mead on the grass of the open terrace within the inner ward. An hour later, they were all allowed back in to witness the great hall's spectacular transformation into a wonderland of abundance.

Blue-tinted light globes shed their illumination on tree-lined walls in the darkened hall while three rows of long tables faced the center of the room around a long open space for dance and entertainment. There, a dozen minstrels played a festive tune on reed pipes, cymbals, gitterns, and tabors while jugglers juggled multicolored light globes, fire-throwers spat flames, and painted acrobats danced to the rapid beat in circles around the center of the room. Even the air was alive with the twinkling of tens of thousands of enchanted light bugs that drifted around the room like tiny stars.

It was the hours of endless accolades, tributes, and commemorations broken by short sessions of entertainment that had started Drystan drinking heavily. And not because the celebration was a bore. To the contrary, it was likely the most exciting and entertaining evening anyone in the room ever experienced. No, his problem was the inability to keep his eyes off the newly inaugurated Duchess of Tintagel.

In truth, he was proud of her performance and the titan constitution it must have required to keep it up for so long. He knew he played a large part in the deception and thus kept out of her sight. If their eyes were to meet in the heightened emotion of the night, their careful duplicity might crumble and reveal them for what they really were. He could only hope that no one would remember his odd behavior and lack of decorum. The two of them barely made it through the brief moment they met in the receiving line after the ceremony. He paused long enough to kiss her hand and offer his felicitations to the couple before hurrying off at the slightest tremble of her lip.

He knew this night would be difficult, but he never imagined it would be like this. Happily, the drink dulled his senses enough to block out much of the raw desire and even allow him to forget for a moment where he was. He wondered if Eselt had found comfort in her wine as well. He hoped so, for her night was long from over.

"Is this the heralded Sir Drystan who slew Sir Murhalt and dropped the terrible knight's head at the feet of the High King of Eriu?"

Bleary-eyed, Drystan looked up to see who spoke. The shape of Perault, second son of Stoddenferry Castle and squire, came into focus before him. He felt like throwing up on the man's perfectly shined buckled shoes.

Drystan waved him away. "Go find some armor to polish, squire."

Perault sat next to him on the bench as if he had not heard a word Drystan said. *The arrogance!* Drystan thought. He had just been dismissed by a knight. Why wasn't he running away?

"I look forward to the tourneys next spring. Will you be competing?"

Drystan's head felt so heavy, he thought he might lay it on his arm for a moment. "I don't do the tourneys."

"Pity, I thought all the great knights joined the tourneys."

"What do you want with me, Perault? Are you an assassin here to strike at me when I'm most vulnerable? Shall I show you my back?"

The squire appeared genuinely insulted by Drystan's statement and leaned in close. "If I were to ever strike at you, there would be no deception in it," he said angrily. "I only wondered which method you would choose to destroy yourself considering the enormous weight of guilt you must carry. I think I have found my answer."

Perault stood from the table, then leaned back in once more. "Who's the terrible knight now, Sir Drystan? Do you think yourself any better than Sir Murhalt? Beware the good knight who comes for your head one day."

Drystan started to say something, he didn't know what, hopefully something witty and cruel, but Perault had already walked away. He didn't care. His mind was on Eselt and how much drink it would take before he passed out in sweet relief from the thoughts raging in his head.

The revelers suddenly went loud with cheers, and Drystan looked up from his stoup to see Wodanaz entering the clearing in the center of the dim room.

He spoke with the quiet drama of a professional minstrel, the minstrel that all others aspired to emulate, and Drystan, having now been present twice for his oration, held a special appreciation for his skills as a performer. "Before I take you on a journey of celebration for the nuptials we are here to commemorate tonight, I wish to start with a melody of sadness for love found less pure in origin than we have before us tonight." He made a deep flourishing bow to Duke Maruk and Duchess Eselt at the head table. "I present to you an inspiration from one of my brother's legendary visions."

There was a single stool on which he sat, and he began to play what appeared to be a solid gold flute. Barely able to hold his own head up and on the verge of passing out, Drystan found the paradox of a disheveled wandering poet who had a flute worth enough to by a small estate highly amusing.

He laughed out loud, drawing the attention of a few nearby, then laid his head on the table, closed his eyes and listened to the tranquil, haunting sound of the flute. Had he not known better, he would have thought he was alone in the hall by the complete silence of over a thousand people enthralled by the enchanting tune.

Wodanaz began to sing in a baritone with soft timbre that was easy on the ear, and oddly, the flute continued to play. Appreciative applause rippled through the onlookers. Drystan wanted to look up and see what magic allowed the poet to sing and play at the same time, but his head felt too heavy, and his eyes refused to open, so he listened.

"Bitter spice for the one in need, in royal vestige and courtly manner.

Taken to the golden maiden so innocent,

And one who seeks the love of another.

The spell speaks strongly for earthly desire,

Makes true what was before only a dream.

Only a dream.

Beware the bearer that makes the promises and is too eager to serve.

Drink deeply of the cure, and the curse it brings everlasting.

And one who seeks the love of another.

It brings everlasting.

Only a dream, it is only a dream.

For eternal love and embrace, that seeks truth but cannot be truthful.

And in the end will only succeed in the corruption.

For the heart to seek the lie unseen.

Of love everlasting.

Only a dream, it is only a dream."

Curious, Drystan thought, and then he fell across the table unconscious, never hearing the last of the song.

~~~

"She has been known throughout the most remote areas of the Western Kingdoms for decades, but very little is known about her. She shows up in a village, attends to those in need, and then departs just as mysteriously. The locals have spoken well of her and benefited from her strange appearances until recently. Traditionally, the villagers call her the Spirit Healer because of her sudden comings and goings."

It was the Arch-Druid of Eriu, Caomh, who addressed the other men in the room from the depths of a hood that revealed only a hint of his features. He sat in a chair between High King Cadeyrn and King Praeter Eldorath on one side of a long table, facing Duke Maruk, the Arch-Druid Filberzh, Wodanaz and Myrllin on the other. Drystan sat in a chair against the wall behind his uncle with Sir Wilhem and a host of other advisors around the council chamber.

Drystan attended meetings such as these before, but never with the pedigree of bloodlines that were in the room now. His uncle asked him to participate while announcing an intention to involve him in more of the family business of ruling. Drystan worried that he was being groomed as a representative of the duke or ambassador of Lyonesse, which would take him far from Tintagel. He also wondered why Wodanaz and his brother Myrllin had places at the table equal to kings and the Arch-Druids.

"What is her method of curing the ailments of the villagers she helps?" asked King Eldorath.

The Arch-Druid Caomh spread his hands apart. "She has an aptitude for herbs, roots, and remedies that she enhances with enchantments. There has only been one occasion when a pair of our druids has had incidental contact and noted her ability to weave spells. They didn't think much of it and considered her harmless since the people she helped were better off for her efforts, so they let her be."

"What does she charge for her services?" High King Cadeyrn asked.

"Apparently not very much, based on her appearance. Her clothing is threadbare and dirty from sleeping in hedges and ditches. She has not horse or wagon and travels from village to village on foot. In fact, her only luxury is said to be the soft walking boots she wears until they fall apart," replied the Arch-Druid.

"And now the people she treats are dying soon after she departs." It was Myrllin who spoke in a strong, gravelly voice that immediately commanded attention in the room.

"Yes, wizard," agreed the Arch-Druid Caomh, "and we have no idea where she will show up next."

There was a deep respect in the Arch-Druid's voice that was unexpected. What kind of man commanded the respect of the most powerful kings in the world and the revered Arch-Druid of Eriu? thought Drystan.

Wodanaz cleared his throat. "How are they dying?"

"Terribly." Caomh shook his head. "It seems they initially get better and then degrade quickly a few days after her departure. They suffer in agony before they finally succumb to a contrived illness, and the symptoms are not always the same. We have inspected a few of the deceased and found that their original illnesses were never life-threatening and that they all died from a very well-crafted poisonous mixture that she usually administers as a potion. A new reputation now follows her. The villagers refer to her as the

Witch of Death."

"Strange, that after so many years of healing those in need she suddenly starts killing them. It hints at madness, or something else. Do you have her name?" Myrllin inquired.

The old Druid smiled. "That seems to be one of the few consistent things we hear about her. Her name is Aja."

A cold bolt of lightning shot up Drystan's spine. He knew that woman. She was the one who gave Eselt a potion to treat her cold the night before they crossed the border into Lyonesse.

The Arch-Druid continued, "I have Druids looking for her, but who knows in which direction she is traveling now. It is said that she even travels into the Wilds. So far the best we have done is follow a trail of bodies."

"I know where she was a week ago." Drystan thought his voice sounded meek and unsure in the presence of so many great men.

The duke turned in his seat. "Drystan?"

Everyone in the room was looking at him.

"Y-yes. The village at the border, Sundy. Eselt was ill with a cold, and the innkeeper where she stayed sent a healer to see about her. She said her name was Aja."

The duke became alarmed. "Did the witch give her anything or cast a spell?"

"She gave her a potion that she said would make her feel better." Drystan shrugged. "In the morning she was her normal self again."

Near panic, Duke Maruk asked Caomh, "Could she still fall ill?"

The Arch-Druid tried to calm the duke. "She would be dead by now if it were poison, but I will check her with your permission."

"Of course," the duke replied.

"I will attend as well, in case our conjoined healing is required," Arch-Druid Filberzh offered.

"Yes," the duke agreed. "That would be appreciated."

Myrllin had that strange look on his face again as he studied Drystan. "My brother and I will find this witch. There may be more to her than a mad old woman mixing bad medicine."

Wodanaz nodded in agreement, and the two brothers rose to leave.

"Let's go see the duchess then," Arch-Druid Filberzh said to the duke.

"Yes, thank you." Then he turned to Drystan. "Come with us. There may be questions."

"I will attend my daughter as well," the High King requested, concern coating the words he spoke.

"Of course, old friend. Let us hasten to her chambers so the Druids may do a proper examination," Duke Maruk agreed.

The five of them hurried to the duchess's room, and when they arrived, Drystan stayed in the hallway outside while his uncle, the High King, and the Arch-Druids went inside. After only a short while, the duke and the High King came out and waited with him.

"I am astonished that this mad woman happened to be at the inn the very night Eselt was ill." Duke Maruk paced the hallway, nervous as if he were awaiting a babe.

"Truly," the High King gave Drystan a firm look, "why wasn't one of the Druids summoned to attend her illness?"

Drystan was concerned with Eselt's well-being, but he had spent so much time with her since that night that he felt sure she was fine. "You are right, High King. I should have insisted upon a druid attending to her." Then he thought to mention, "I tasted the potion before I allowed Eselt to take it, and I have suffered no ill effects either. Perhaps there was another Aja who happens to be a healer. Her name is not completely unique in Eriu."

The duke stopped his pacing. "You took the potion as well?"

"Yes, Uncle."

He grabbed Drystan fiercely and hugged him tightly. "That is twice that you have put your life before hers in my service. You are a good man, son."

The High King patted him hard on the shoulder. "A noble deed worthy of the best of knights. It will not be forgotten."

The Arch-Druids came through the door from Eselt's chamber and walked out.

"She is perfectly fine," Filberzh smiled.

"Thank Sunna," the duke exhaled and then added quickly, "and Eriu, of course."

Arch-Druid Caomh chuckled. "Don't worry. Eriu loves Sunna, and they both love the people of Eriu and Lyonesse!"

Drystan excused himself, leaving the men to discuss matters further, and returned to his own chamber. The past two nights since the ceremony were difficult for him. Eselt had not left the pine in the secret hallway, and he knew better than to expect that she could. Tonight would be the same as every night until he was alone with her again. When the hour drew later he would experience the bone-deep chill of his lover lying with another man, and unable to accept the knowledge of her nights being consumed by the passions of her new husband, Drystan would flee Valiant Keep to stay alone in the forest until dawn. Getting inebriated in the solitude of the melancholy was the only abatement to stave off his own variety of madness.

CHAPTER 11

Suspicions

"Your father, the king, and I will be going on a hunting trip. I expect we will be gone for a few days." Duke Maruk smiled at his young wife. "It's not often old bears get together and act like young bears, and you make me feel like a young bear again."

Eselt smiled back, but not for the reason he thought. "That is a wonderful idea, dear. My father has not enjoyed your company—or that of King Praeter, of course—for many years. And it will give me a chance to explore the city while you are away."

"Then we will both enjoy a few days of adventure, even though we are apart." The duke kissed her on the cheek. "And, dear, be sure to find a proper guide, and maybe a guard or two. Our city is safe, but some enterprising young footpad might take your unfamiliarity as an opportunity to make a name for himself."

"Do you think Drystan would be willing to look after me until you return?" She knew he would.

"He is your knight and honor bound to do so. Shall I speak to him?"

"No, no dear, I will inquire when I have a moment."

Eselt's heart was racing with excitement. Her husband would be away for several days, far away in a hunting lodge, doing bear things or whatever he said. It didn't matter to her what he did. All she cared was that she had the perfect excuse, with her husband's blessing, to be with her lover as much as she wanted. She intended to make the most of it and couldn't wait to tell Drystan the news that evening.

She spent the rest of her day entertaining ladies of nobility and influence who came with their husbands to attend her wedding. She used to enjoy the gossip and games of her father's court before she left Teamhrach. Then it became tedious after she met Drystan. Lady Fedelmid had the audacity to suggest that she take care not to display her melancholy behavior outside of her private chambers and especially around the duke. Initially, Eselt was furious at her lady-in-waiting and then fearful that she knew the truth about her and Drystan. In time, she realized Lady Fedelmid was right, and she put on a happy face whenever she went out or the duke came to visit.

That afternoon was different. Eselt was her old self again, playful and funny with the other ladies and enthusiastically engaged in their activities. She was happy because of the news she had for Drystan and secretly prepared a mental list of all the things they would do together. It was going to be a fantastic week. Her only concern was keeping Lady Fedelmid from becoming more suspicious than she already was concerning her relationship with her knight. During the journey from Teamhrach, it was impossible to avoid her eyes during the day and difficult to put her off at night. Since they arrived in Tintagel, things had been different, and her rendezvous with Drystan were less visible, mainly due to the secret passageways he used at night. The most her lady-in-waiting could be suspicious of at this point was innocent flirtations and furtive glances. Eselt had even "proven" her fidelity with the elaborate ruse on her wedding night of bloodying the sheets by pricking a vein while her husband slept. She had no doubt Lady Fedelmid inspected the silk linens the next morning when they were collected for the wash. Maruk was too drunk to remember anything and just assumed they consummated the marriage.

Eselt didn't believe that Lady Fedelmid would ever betray her if she did find out about Drystan. Unless someone else found out and she was questioned—then she might use what information she gained to protect herself. Regardless, they would have to be very careful, especially now she was the wife of the duke. One thing she was sure about above all else: ending the affair was unthinkable.

The duke was leaving the next morning, and Eselt was relieved that her husband did not call upon her that night. He was probably drinking and entertaining the "old bears." An hour earlier she put out the pine twig in the secret corridor and lit the candle in her dressing room and waited. She wanted to scream with excitement and run to his chamber rather than wait for him to check the hallway, maybe hours from then, but it was safer for her to stick with their agreed-upon signals and try to be patient.

An hour later she heard a noise from the dressing room and, just like that, he was standing there with a wide grin on his face. How handsome he was wearing his long dark brown coat over a perfectly white silk tunic and pine-green trousers. And that smile! It framed so well with his deep brown eyes and the sharp facial features of his suntanned skin. Then there was his shoulder-length, sandy-blond hair that she craved to clutch roughly in her tiny fists while he sucked the kisses from her lips . . . Eselt jumped up from her chair and ran to hug him. "My love! You will never believe what fortune we have!"

He stood with his arms around her and his face in her hair. "I already know! My uncle, your father, and the king will be going on a hunt. But what about your mother and sisters and Queen Penelope? Won't you be obligated to entertain them while their husbands are gone?"

"No!" She laughed. "They have made excuses and plan to return to their homes tomorrow morning. I made sure their attendants told them that I was planning a number of 'girlish' activities while the men were away to help them reach that decision."

"You are as artful as a silver-breasted sparrow and even more beautiful." He kissed her deeply, then paused. "What about Lady Fedelmid? Will she be a tiresome diversion?"

"Not in the least." She flashed a wicked smile that always made him squint funny at her. It was so cute. "I have her on a very tedious project this week. As the new duchess, I will need a new wardrobe, so I have put her to the task of recommending proper styles, colors, and patterns for my review next week. She will be spending every day with the dressmakers and seamstresses putting together my closet!"

"Artful and industrious, I see." He kissed her neck in a way that made her want to melt. "However, let us not become too complacent. We must still be cautious. Quickly! Lock the door."

"Yes, I mustn't forget that." She pranced over to the door and threw home the bolt, turned and tossed her long golden hair playfully, and pulled the wide edge of her night robe down just enough to reveal her bare shoulder. "Now we can do as we please."

And they did.

~~~

Eselt was walking with Drystan down the long hallway that led toward the stables at the rear of Valiant Keep. It was well lit but drafty, which caused the candles to flicker ceaselessly against the line of portraits of past royalty that hung on the walls. In the direction they strolled, a man strode confidently toward them, and Eselt groaned inwardly. It was Captain Purin of the Duke's Guard. His stern features on a slender, shaved face under short-cut light brown hair complemented his impeccably appointed uniform. Somehow, he managed to appear every time they were about to leave Valiant Keep, and she knew what was coming next.

"Good morning, Duchess." The captain stopped and bowed to her, then nodded to Drystan. "Will you be taking the duchess riding again, Sir

Drystan?"

Drystan smiled at the captain. "Yes, Purin. The duchess would like to see the cliffs today, and I expect we will picnic as well."

"Ah, I see," the captain replied. "Then I shall prepare an honor guard to accompany you."

"No need, Captain. Just as yesterday, we are not going far. I'm sure my protection will be sufficient."

Captain Purin was insistent. "Surely the duke would require extra guards for the duchess when she travels outside the walls. I worry for her safety, even with a protector as stalwart as yourself."

Eselt knew that she better step in before the situation became confrontational. "I will be fine, Captain. Thank you for your concern. I assure you, we won't be too long."

The captain's stern features somehow became even more rigid around the edges of his face before he bowed. "As you wish, Duchess." With another nod to Drystan, he continued on his way.

Once he was out of sight, Eselt whispered, "Do you think he is suspicious of us? That's the third time this week he has tried to collar us with an 'honor guard,' even just going into the city!"

Drystan laughed. "I have known Purin since I was a child. He is always suspicious, but I don't think he is worried about any unscrupulous behavior. He is more worried about his skin if something tragic were to befall us—mostly you—while the duke is away."

Eselt always enjoyed recreational riding, and she was looking forward to seeing the land around Tintagel, in particular the view of Lake Virtue from the slate cliffs. More than anything, she wanted to lounge on the lush green grass in her lover's arms out of sight of prying eyes. The beautifully sunny day and the warm breeze would make for a romantic setting to enjoy an intimate picnic together.

Their mounts were ready when they arrived at the stables, and Lady Fedelmid had seen to it that the kitchen packed an ample lunch for them to take along. Then Drystan led her out through the upper ward, into the lower, and then out the north gate of the city. Along the way, the citizenry waved and cheered her. She still had not gotten used to being the duchess and was so pleased with how gracious and kind the people of Tintagel had been to her considering that she was a foreign bride, even if she was from just across the border in Eriu. It was entirely different from being the youngest princess of the High King in Teamhrach. Surely, she was respected and loved by the people there, but in Eriu she was just another highborn lady. As the duchess,

Eselt almost felt like she had power, much like her mother, she supposed. How she could use that to her advantage, Eselt did not know yet. At least there was no expectation of her producing an heir. The duke had already chosen his eldest son as his successor and didn't need any more children.

A cold streak ran down her spine at the sudden thought of it. What if Maruk made her pregnant? What if Drystan made her pregnant? She must be careful with the duke. A child with him would make it nearly impossible for her to ever consider running away with Drystan. She put those thoughts aside. Nothing was going to ruin the little time she had with her lover.

Almost immediately they left the road and kicked their horses into a trot on the open fields that spread out for leagues in every direction except toward the lake, which was their destination. Eselt's gossamer blue silk scarves, received as a gift from Queen Penelope, trailed behind her in the breeze while they rode, and she couldn't help but laugh out loud for the pure joy of it. She felt so free out here with Drystan that she wanted to just keep riding and never turn back.

They rode a league northwest of the city along a desolate area where the slate cliffs overlooked Lake Virtue. The grassy hills to the east shielded them from the eyes of travelers along the coastal road that led north to Stoddenferry Castle and the farmlands nearby. Eselt could see Tintagel in the distance, shrouded in a misty haze brought forth by the waves crashing on the cliffs below. It portrayed an almost surreal visage. The Lake was choppy due to a strong wind coming in off the Primal Sea far to the west, and even Eselt could recognize the first signs of a storm approaching.

"Looks like we will have a bit of a drizzle tonight, love," Drystan remarked.

Eselt smiled and snuggled up next to him on the grass where they sat. "I love when it storms and you are with me under the sheets. I don't know why. Maybe it's because you are near, keeping me safe while the wind and the rain, lightning, and thunder rage around us."

"I will always keep you safe." Drystan squeezed her tight. "No matter if the storm is real or imagined."

"This has been a good week, Drystan, the best I can remember. I have enjoyed the long rides in the country, shopping in the city, the intimate picnics, the plays we have seen that made us laugh and cry. Mostly I have enjoyed having you with me at night, even though you leave me at dawn before Lady Fedelmid is about. What will we do when the duke returns?"

"What we must Eselt. What we must."

"We can't go on like this forever, Drystan. Sooner or later we will be found out, and only Eriu knows what fate would await us then. And I can never tell you to stop coming to me, I would rather die! But I am already dying, Drystan, every moment that I am without you, playing the part of a duchess with no real love or passion for your good uncle. We made a terrible mistake. Not in what we do now so much as what we should have done. Looking back, it seems so clear. It would have been better for us if we had run away before I was married."

"You are right, Eselt. I can't deny the truth of your words, and my heart aches for them and the things we should have done. None of that matters now. What's done is done. We need to determine our own future together for the best possible outcome." He gave her a squeeze she knew was meant to reassure her. "I have lands and items of value that I will quietly sell, but it will take a little time so that my uncle does not find out. Then we will have enough gold to live on no matter where we decide to go. We will run away, Eselt. Please try to bear it just a little while longer."

"I don't care about gold, love. All I want is to be with you no matter the state of our affairs."

Drystan kissed her tenderly on the forehead. "Just a little while longer. It pains me deeply to think I could give you only the life of a pauper if we just up and left. Keep your jewels nearby and wait for me to bring the news of the day we leave this place forever."

Eselt was surprised that she felt no fear of leaving Lyonesse and Eriu behind or even remorse that she would never see her family again, no matter that they would think of her as a betrayer and fugitive. The only thoughts that gave her comfort where those of Drystan, and she honestly didn't care if they lived as vagabonds as long as they were together. Drystan was right, however. It would be better to plan carefully and leave when he was ready and felt confident that he could care for her. Men needed that kind of assurance.

For reasons she could not explain, it mattered less if her family, whom she loved so much, thought of her as an unfaithful betrayer if Drystan did. She actually felt pain in her chest at the thought of it. Yet she felt precisely that every time the duke came to her at night. So far, he had always been drunk and sleepy, and it didn't take much to lull him to sleep without sacrificing her virtue. But what would happen when he came to her not so drunk? She would have to play the part and do as he pleased, although it would undoubtedly tear her emotionally to pieces. She feared that betrayal more than any she could think of. How could Drystan forgiver her then? Would he run away and leave her broken and alone? She did not think she could bear to live a second in a world without the assurance of his love. Please Eriu, please Sunna, may it never come to that.

She could hear his rhythmic breathing, the slow rise and fall of his chest where she laid her head, and the strong beat of his heart. Such a good heart pledged to her and her alone. She didn't deserve it and accepted it anyway. She wept quietly at the thought of it all, careful not to disturb her lover's peaceful rest. *What did he dream?* she wondered and slipped into comfortable darkness, knowing how much she was loved.

Eselt woke to the first droplets of rain on her forehead and roused Drystan, who held her tightly under the blankets. The morning had stretched into the afternoon, and the storm clouds had begun to roll in from beyond the horizon, where the waters of the lake converged with the sky. The temperature plummeted with the arrival of the clouds, and the mildly chilly wind that was so pleasant before began to blow colder. Quickly, they dressed and packed away their picnic and blankets before urging their horses into a fast canter back to the city.

By the time they reached the gates of the upper ward, the rain was torrential, and they were in full gallop and drenched to the bone. Eselt was laughing with delight when they finally dismounted under cover of the stables where the grooms took the reins and brought dry blankets. Drystan placed one over her shoulders and delicately wiped the wet hair from her face.

"It appears you were gone much longer than you anticipated." Captain Purin walked to stand just out of the shadows of the corridor that led into Valiant Keep and bowed to Eselt.

She was surprised by his sudden appearance, but Drystan handled it smoothly. "You know how it goes, Purin. One gets to enjoying the scenery, and time flies away from you."

"I suggest you get the duchess dry quickly. It wouldn't do for the duke to return from his hunt and find his wife sick."

There was an unmistakable look of disapproval on the captain's face, and Eselt worried that he was beginning to suspect something. Drystan had the groom bring him a heavy cloak that he wrapped around Eselt replacing the damp blankets.

"Thank you for your concern, Captain," Eselt said sweetly as she and Drystan strode by him and into the corridor. She didn't wait for his reply or the expected bow.

Once they were out of earshot, Eselt began to giggle, and Drystan laughed quietly with her. Lady Fedelmid was not laughing, and further, became alarmed at the sight of Eselt as soon as she entered her chamber. She worked quickly to strip Eselt of her wet clothing and warm her with blankets before dressing her again, all the while chiding her for letting herself out in the weather to get another cold like the one she had in Sundy. Eselt was barely listening. She had other things on her mind. Drystan had left her to go to his own room and change before they found each other again later that night.

~~~

Drystan returned to his room after eating dinner in the feast hall. With the duke still away, the atmosphere was very casual, and the ladies who still lingered after the wedding clustered around the head table where Eselt sat. The queen returned home to Lyonesse City the same day her husband left on the hunt as had most of the older nobles including Eselt's mother and sisters. Even though he could not openly be with her, he felt no stress watching her in the feast hall enjoying the company of women her age. Neither of them stayed very long, and they both departed separately. Now he would just need to wait until she shooed away Lady Fedelmid for the night and placed the pine twig in the hallway.

Opening the door to his private chamber, he was shocked to see a figure sitting in a chair that faced the door twirling a chain around his finger. It was Captain Purin.

"What are you doing in here?" Drystan demanded.

"I came to talk. Is this for someone special?" He stopped twirling the chain and held it up for him to see.

It was a gold necklace with small sapphires mounted along its length. Drystan had bought it as a present for Eselt that he planned to give her later since it was their last free night before the duke returned the next day. He must have carelessly left it on his writing desk for anyone to find that came into his room. Now the captain held it with contempt that seemed to infect the beautiful piece of jewelry just with his touch.

With a growl, Drystan grabbed the necklace away from him and stuffed it in the pocket of his light cloak. Purin just sneered back at him.

"You have no right to invade my privacy! Now get out before I throw you out!" Drystan felt rage flooding through him.

Captain Purin slowly stood from his chair, and his face changed from the mocking grin to one of dead certainty. "I know about you and the duchess."

Drystan felt as if a huge weight came crashing down on him. He knew Purin well, and there was no way to convince this man everything he had seen or guessed was a misunderstanding. However, the idea triggered in his head, he had likely been following them and keeping them under close observation before he came to this conclusion.

Drystan didn't bother to deny it. "What are you going to do?"

"That is what I came to discuss." The captain and Drystan had never been friends, but they always had casual respect for each another.

"Go on," replied Drystan.

"I considered going to the duke when he returned, except that would destroy too many lives, including his. He is the happiest he has been since the former duchess died, and I would rather it not be me who takes that away from him."

"So, you have a better solution?"

"Yes. You stop seeing the duchess and allow them to live their lives together."

Drystan felt physical pain in his chest at the thought. "And if I don't?"

"Then I will be compelled to go to the duke. It would probably end my career whether or not I was believed."

"Who else knows of this?"

"Just me, although it has become a common rumor, the way the two of you carry on in public together."

Drystan felt a flash of rage and began to draw his sword. "So, if you die here tonight, my problem is solved as well."

"Drystan, what are you thinking? Even if you managed to kill me, your secret would come out sooner or later anyway. Besides, how much more attention will be on everyone if my corpse is found in some dark corner of Valiant Keep?"

Slamming his sword back into his scabbard, Drystan was horrified by his own actions. "I'm sorry, Captain. I don't know what I was thinking. My head hasn't been clear for weeks now."

"You are young and in love with a woman you can never truly have, and if you did, it would devastate your uncle and bring disgrace upon your family. You of all people don't want that. End it with her. End it with her now and go out into the world and do what you have always done."

"I don't know if I can." Drystan felt profoundly sullen.

"Figure it out, Drystan. Infidelity is not a worthy characteristic of a virtuous knight."

"I will think on it, Captain."

"Just do it." Captain Purin's voice turned acidic, "Oh and Drystan, knight or no, next time you draw your sword on me, I'll stick your head on the end of it."

Drystan watched him go without saying another word. It wasn't the threat of having his head stuck on the end of a sword that troubled him, it was the choice the man had put to him. If it could be called a choice. Of one thing Drystan was certain: he would not give up Eselt. Not for anyone or for any reason. The realization that he would kill Captain Purin, if it came to that, was striking. But that, too, was a certainty, and he would do so without remorse. It didn't have to come to that. He would speak with Eselt about it later, and they would work out a plan. Besides, with the duke returning on the morrow, they would be back to their usual routine of seeing each other principally in the night again with no one the wiser.

Drystan pulled the chain from his pocket and looked at it closely. It felt too impure after Purin's touch to place against Eselt's clean skin. He walked to the privy in his room and tossed it down the dark hole. Immediately he felt satisfied that it was where it belonged. His lover deserved better. When he threw it away, a mad thought crossed his mind briefly. If only Captain Purin were so easy to dispose of . . .

CHAPTER 12

Confessions

"He knows about us, Eselt. I don't know how, but he does."

Eselt's eyes welled up with tears, and he moved to comfort her. He held her tight around her shoulders, and she pressed her face into his chest.

"What do we do now?" she asked, her voice was thick with emotion.

"We have to be especially careful. I don't know exactly what Purin knows, but he is not one to come to a conclusion unless he is absolutely certain. He said we were acting too familiar in public and that there were rumors. There must be more to it than that."

Eselt looked up at him. "Rumors? From whom and about what?"

"I don't know. Have any of your attendants ever tried to enter while your door was locked?"

She shook her head. "Never the attendants, only Lady Fedelmid on two or three occasions when she came to my room earlier than expected. I told her I was still frightened living in an unfamiliar place. I really don't think she would think to tell anyone about it, and she has never been the type to gossip."

Drystan pulled her over to sit with him at her bedside. "The rumors came from somewhere, and she's our best guess at the moment. I'll try and find out more about who she talks to."

Drystan knew he would have to act fast. Purin would probably only give him a few days to stop seeing Eselt before he felt the necessity of duty to go to the duke. He couldn't really blame the captain. If it were later found out that he knew about their affair and kept it to himself, he would be subject to the same punishment as he and Eselt, and that was likely death. Drystan had to find out where Purin was getting his information on them. It must be very reliable for him to be so confident. Lady Fedelmid might be the connection, although it seemed unlikely.

The next morning, Drystan was back in his own bedchamber thinking about the day. It was just after dawn, and he was lying in bed staring up at the new light of the morning slowly illuminating the whitewashed stone along the ceiling of his room. And it was cold. Reluctantly, he slid out of bed and set to work bringing a bit of warmth back into the chamber. In his haste to see Eselt the night before, he forgot to replenish the hearth, and now it would take a while to heat the large space he was given. Drystan wasn't in a hurry to get out of bed anyway—there was nothing he needed to do—so he stayed warm under his blankets and waited for the light and the warmth to pervade the entirety of the room.

The duke would be returning from his hunt that day and no doubt would want to tell everyone about it at the banquet that evening in the feast hall. Once, Drystan would have been enthralled with the stories that would be retold a hundred times. Now they were just part of his overall unhappiness that the duke returned and his freedom with Eselt was at an end. He briefly entertained a fantasy that the duke met with a riding accident and was forced to stay at his hunting lodge for months of recovery, but he quickly discarded the thought. He loved his uncle and would never wish misfortune on him. Duke Maruk just happened to be the source of his unending misery, and the duke didn't even know it.

It was midafternoon when Drystan heard the clanging of bells from the bell tower in the city followed by the blare of trumpets. Bells for the king, trumpets for the duke, the hunting party had returned. He walked to the landing on the fore tower and joined the throng of onlookers who watched the line of royals with their men-at-arms carrying long-haired deer on poles and steering wagons stacked with the carcasses of boar. Most remarkable were two wagons bearing the butchered remains of a woolly mammoth, the lead wagon displayed the head of the animal mounted on a frame for all to see. There would be meat to fill the cold larders for weeks.

Drystan went on hunts with his uncle and brothers many times in the past – at least once or twice each year. It was unusual to hunt a mammoth, since they were dangerous and traveled in herds across the open leagues of grassland and shrubland between the eastern shores of Loch Angu, the western coastline of Lake Virtue, and the forests to the north. They killed only two in his lifetime, and on one occasion lost three men trying to bring it down when its mate charged into them. From what he could tell, it looked like there were no casualties on this trip. Otherwise, a black pennant would fly in honor of the fallen.

There was a wealth of skill and decades of hunting experience between Duke Maruk, King Praeter, and High King Cadeyrn, not to mention their impressive level of competitive egos. So, it didn't surprise Drystan that the old bears had decided to hunt the biggest and most dangerous game in Lyonesse. He was just glad they managed not to get any of their men killed in the process.

Drystan returned to his room to change into more formal attire. He would be expected at the reception when they arrived. Eselt would be there as well. He didn't look forward to stepping back into the routine they were forced to follow—avoiding each other's gaze, speaking contrived words when they were forced to talk to each other in public, waiting through long days of agony for the few short hours at night to hold each other close. And then doing it all over again day after day, all under the real threat of their deception being revealed. The pressure was enormous, Drystan had to admit, but he would endure more, much more, if he must, if it meant he could spend those few hours alone at night with Eselt.

When he was a boy, Drystan had often read the poetry and prose of Gergain, Toghda, Vyvyan, and Wodanaz. Each of the masters wrote narratives about heroic characters with tortured souls. Drystan was sure that his soul was tortured. All he needed now was the heroic status, and perhaps he would be the subject of an epic story one day. If he ever was, he prayed it contained a happy ending.

~~~

There was a slight knock at the door, and then it opened. In walked Lady Fedelmid with another bucket of hot water, which she carefully poured into the perfumed bath where Eselt lay, enjoying the warm steam that rose from it. After a while, Lady Fedelmid prompted her to sit up so she could scrub Eselt's back and arms with a wool cloth. Lady Fedelmid had been in her service since she was a little girl, and there had always been a comfortable, maternal relationship. Eselt couldn't deny that she loved Lady Fedelmid, but after she spoke to Drystan, she was quietly furious at her lady-in-waiting.

"The bells and trumpets have sounded. The duke, your father, and the king have returned and should arrive at Valiant Keep soon. We must hurry to have you ready for him, Your Grace."

"And what of you, Lady Fedelmid?" Eselt turned her head to look over her shoulder. "What have you planned for the evening?"

"As usual, Your Grace, I will attend to you during the reception and again at supper, and once that is done, I will prepare your room for the night."

"And then what? Will you go and gossip with the other attendants, or is there someone special you spend your nights with?"

"Your Grace!" Eselt could hear the shock in her voice. "This is not appropriate conversation. Are you feeling well?"

Eselt rose from the bath and stepped into the thick cotton robe Lady Fedelmid held open for her.

"My understanding is that you are quite chatty after you have put me to bed each night. Otherwise, why would I hear speculations about why I lock my door at night?"

"I, I don't know, Your Grace," Lady Fedelmid stammered. Her face went almost immediately pale.

"You know that sometimes I wake up afraid at night because I am still not used to my new home, so I lock the door to feel safe. Only you have come to my door when it was locked. Why would anyone else know about that?" Eselt was not shouting, yet her voice quivered with anger.

Lady Fedelmid's gaze fell to the floor in shame. "I might have mentioned it to a friend once." Then she quickly added, "Out of concern, Your Grace, not to mock you!"

"And who is this friend, Lady Fedelmid?" Eselt asked sharply.

"He is in the guard. I thought he could help, maybe assuage your fears. I promise that I was only trying to help!"

Lady Fedelmid fell to her knees in tears, clutching to Eselt's robe. This was not how Eselt ever expected to treat her lady-in-waiting, but she had to know the rest.

"Tell me his name, and all will be forgiven," she told her in a soothing voice while stroking her hair.

"It is Captain Purin. We have been intimate for over a week now."

"There, that wasn't so hard now was it? In the future, please keep my personal affairs to yourself, no matter how innocent it might seem. I am the Duchess of Tintagel now, and I must not have any scandal attached to my name."

Lady Fedelmid stood again, wiping away her tears. "Yes, Your Grace, you can be certain of my discretion."

"Thank you, Lady Fedelmid." Eselt kissed her on the cheek. "I only have you that I can trust. Now make me beautiful. I have to remind my husband what he has been missing while he was away!"

Eselt felt sick inside from what she had done to Lady Fedelmid and what she had left to do that night, but everything was a matter of survival now. She prayed to Eriu that Drystan would be about his business quickly so that they could make their escape. Their luck was bound to desert them eventually no matter how much care they took. She thought, *Drystan be strong and remember I await you. Never doubt my love, and I pray you find forgiveness for the things we must do until we can be in each other's arms for eternity.*

~~~

Eselt was awaked the next morning by Lady Fedelmid. The sun was already high above the horizon and nearly to noon. She was up late the previous night, first attending the duke's reception and listening to the hunters' endless stories, then later when her husband came to her, drunk and groping. She did what she had to do to please him, and it ended quickly, leaving her weeping in her bed until near dawn.

Drystan was also at the reception, and he looked like he was doing his best to keep up a cheerful façade, except that she could see the suffering behind his deep brown eyes. All she could think about was how badly she wanted to tell him about Lady Fedelmid and Captain Purin, but there would never be a chance that night. It didn't make things any easier that Captain Purin had his eyes on one of them the entire evening.

What little sleep she had was fitful. The guilt and sorrow that kept her awake for most of the night transferred to her dreams. Fortunately, she could not remember them, but they left such a terrible impression of loss and sadness on her the next morning that she didn't need to recall to know what they were about. She lamented that only Drystan's enchanted kisses could wash the horrid feelings away.

Eselt hoped that she could see her lover that night. Maybe she would feign ill if Maruk came to her again. In truth, the idea of intimacy with him gave her a sick feeling. Not because he wasn't kind or attractive, both of which he was in abundance, but simply because she wasn't in love with him, and he wasn't Drystan. With luck, the duke would stay up all night entertaining her father and the king before they departed Tintagel the next day. Then life would return to normal, whatever that was.

She felt bitter at the prospect of waiting endlessly day after day, counting the minutes until she could see Drystan. She felt herself falling into a melancholy as she sat looking at nothing outside the window. She always mocked the idea of people losing the will to live and dying of depression, and now that she was experiencing it she understood why they would feel that way.

Lady Fedelmid had already dressed Eselt and brushed her hair, retrieved a tray of fruit for breakfast, and was moving around the room cleaning and tidying up. She hummed a tune Eselt remembered from her childhood, and hearing it brought up her spirits just a little again. Good Fedelmid, she thought, you know I am sad, and even after the way I treated you, there is still kindness in your heart to find a way to give me joy.

There was a knock at the door.

Lady Fedelmid answered, and it was Duke Maruk himself. She let him in, curtsied and exited the room.

Eselt put on her best face and curtsied. "Your Grace."

"Good morning, dearest. I trust you slept well?" Maruk asked before he kissed her cheek and sat down at the small dining table where he fumbled for some fresh grapes in a bowl.

"I did, thank you. I'm surprised my father and the king do not have all of your attention this morning."

"Oh, I'll be meeting them for the midday meal in a little while, but I wanted to see you a moment first."

"Is something wrong? Have I displeased you in some way?"

He seemed happy, perhaps concerned, but not angry. If he knew the truth, surely he would be in a rage. Fear began to rise in her while she waited for his reply.

"Of course not, dear. You are lovely and perfect. I am concerned with Drystan. Has he been well?"

"He has been fine as far as I can tell, what is your concern?"

"I don't think he's happy. I'm not sure. I don't recall ever seeing him this way. It's as if he's hiding something profoundly sad behind a mask of spurious smiles."

Eselt was taken aback. She had no idea the duke's perception was so astute. She hoped it was because he knew his adopted son so well and not some talent he possessed. Otherwise, she wondered what he saw behind her mask.

"Whatever it is, I'm sure it will pass." She put her hand on his.

"My darling," he began hesitantly, "maybe it is time to release Drystan from his obligation to you. He is a young knight who should be making his mark in the world and perhaps raising a family of his own. I'm sure he agreed to be your personal protector to please me, but you are here now and safe. He will soon find the life of a champion dull and unrewarding."

Eselt's heart plummeted at his words. Surely he did not know about them. Otherwise, the conversation would be much different.

Controlling her shaky voice, she tried to dissuade her husband. "He seems to enjoy his duties well enough and to be relieved for the change from his usual lifestyle. He even has an eye toward one of my attendants. Melandri, I think."

Duke Maruk appeared skeptical. "You don't know Drystan. He's a good man and virtuous knight, but wild as a stallion. I will speak with him and determine the truth of his mind."

Eselt almost stuttered, "I'm sure he will do what he feels best. I will not pressure him either way."

Duke Maruk rose and kissed her hand. "Very well, then, we'll leave it up to him to decide. Also, I don't expect to come by tonight, dear." He smiled sweetly. "You know us old men and our stories. I imagine I will be up most of the night with your father and the king and wake up stuffed in my chair in the morning!"

Eselt stood and kissed his cheek. "Enjoy your time together. It's so rare to have a gathering of friendly souls such as we have enjoyed for our wedding. I will see you in the morning."

She watched as the duke walked out the door. He wasn't a bad man. In fact, she would have probably grown to love him under different circumstances. As it stood, she felt nothing for him and instead felt excitement at the prospect of being with Drystan again that night.

~~~

The garden courtyard of the upper ward was beautiful in the summertime. This was where Drystan played as a boy. The great pine that he climbed, the wide fountain he swam in and almost drowned in on more than one occasion, the field of soft grass that he would tumble and run upon. Everything was so different then, a happy time that he wished he could remember better. Coming here allowed him to be away from people and their dramas. He could think and be calm. There were so many good memories in this space that it had a miraculous effect on his disposition, and he could feel content for a little while.

He sat on one of the secluded benches surrounded by taller shrubs near the entrance of a maze lined by high hedges, and he thought about the predicament he and Eselt found themselves in. Their world was like a treacherous maze; they never knew which turn might doom them or which could lead to salvation. At present, their way was fraught with danger, now that someone finally discovered their affair, and they were faced with dealing with the inevitability of the consequences. In a way, it was a small relief knowing that they were finally forced into a real decision about their future. Now they had to make a choice to either stop seeing each other or run away together. There really was no choice in the matter. They would have to leave, and soon.

Drystan stood and paced one of the parallel channels that framed the small grassy field and fed the fountain with water. They were only a few feet deep, but he had almost drowned in one of these as well, he laughed to himself. Water was not his thing as a child. So innocent then, uncorrupted by desire. He passed a bench where his adoptive mother, the duchess, would tell him stories about knights and trolls and giants. No one ever died in those simple stories. In the end, the knight would always chase them back into the wilderness of Fomoire. Back then he had a little wooden shield and a little wooden sword, and to the gardeners' eternal aggravation, he would give the hedgerows a proper thrashing two or three times a week. He could still hear the laughter from his mother urging him onward. *That hedge is a troll, this one is a giant! Save me Drystan!* His mind wandered while he pinched the small lavender flowers blooming on the hedgerow. He was so engrossed in his thoughts that he did not notice the approach of his uncle until he was standing in front of him.

"Good afternoon, Uncle." Drystan smiled.

"Good afternoon. Could you spare a moment to talk?"

There was no anger or malice in the face of his uncle, which was a relief. Purin had not played his card . . . yet.

"Absolutely, uncle, will you walk the garden with me?"

"I would like that. Do you remember when you fell from that pine there? Nearly broke your neck and your brother's." His uncle laughed. "He said he was trying to catch you. Both of you were lucky to walk away with only bruises and scrapes."

Drystan laughed with him. "My brothers and I had many good times here and our share of lumps trying to outdo one another."

"You all grew up to be fine men of honor and virtue. I couldn't be prouder, especially of you."

"Especially?"

"You had a much harder time in the beginning, with your parents absent at so young an age. We worried about you for a long time."

Drystan frowned. "If it had to happen, I suppose earlier in life the better. I never remember my birth parents. You and the duchess were always my parents as far as I was concerned, and I couldn't have asked for better."

His uncle put his arm around Drystan's shoulder and squeezed. "We've had a good life together, and now your brothers are married with children of their own. What about you Drystan? Don't you want the same thing, or do you wish to graze the pastures a bit longer?"

"There is one I love above all others, but it is complicated." Drystan felt the gloom coming on, even here in the garden, and there was a slight quiver in his voice. "I don't know how it will all work out yet."

"I have noted that your days of happiness have been fewer since you returned from Eriu, and it troubles me to see you this way. You know I appreciate your enthusiasm to please me by taking on the obligation as Duchess Eselt's protector and champion. The courage you displayed defending our family honor, as well as Eselt's against the Eriu knight Murhalt, was one of the noblest deeds I have ever known." The duke stopped and turned to face him. He placed his hands on Drystan shoulders. "But you do not need to prove yourself to me, Drystan. I know your heart, and it is traveling the kingdoms, the world for that matter, seeking your destiny. Not playing guardian to a lady with no need for more protection than I can provide."

Drystan was not expecting this conversation and had no time to prepare a logical argument for his continued service to the duchess. "Uncle, it is a duty I enjoy for the present, a little escape from the life of adventure I know will pull me back soon enough." He spoke as well as he could off the cuff. "Just for now, allow me this reprise until I am certain of my next endeavor."

"Fair enough, gallant knight, although I suspect there is more to your motivations than you divulge." Duke Maruk whispered in a very serious tone.

For just a moment Drystan was shocked and felt his heart lodge in his throat. He didn't know what to say.

Duke Maruk finished the thought with a laugh. "Don't break too many of Eselt's attendants' hearts. I would hate to have to replace them because they were too despondent to serve the duchess!"

Drystan laughed along with him, a relieved, nervous laugh that made the duke laugh even harder.

CHAPTER 13

Plans and Pines

So it was your own Lady Fedelmid, who is the lover of Captain Purin?" Drystan was almost amused. "How unexpected. Do you really believe she will stop telling him details about us?"

"Maybe for a time. How long could we keep secrets from each other, no matter what the disadvantage?"

He stood close to Eselt and whispered, "Not for a moment."

"Nor I, love, and I am afraid for it." Standing on tiptoes, she brushed her lips against his, then kissed him lightly.

He held her tight and close, feeling the perfect line of her back under the silky gown she wore. "For a time, we should meet in the garden, through the passages behind the walls. I will show you the way tonight. No one goes there after dark, and it is not patrolled regularly. I will leave the pine twig at the door, and you will know I am waiting for you."

Eselt gripped him tightly and placed her head on his chest, "When will we be gone from this place?"

"The very day I sell my lands, we shall leave this prison forever, and quickly, as we won't have a choice about it. Once my uncle finds out what I have done, he will have questions that I will have no good answers for. Be ready for that day, my love."

"I am as ready now as I will always be. With these frail clothes, a beating heart, and the breath in my body, I will follow you anywhere, my love."

Drystan took her hand and kissed her soft palm, the short blond stubble above his lips bending from the slight pressure. He breathed in her spicy-sweet fragrance from the scented oils on her skin; the scent teased his senses and filled him with desire. She looked up at him, her blue eyes trusting, confident of his love and devotion to her, and he knew that she saw the same in his. He felt joy in those eyes and pain at their suffering. Then her delicate lips were pressing his, and the taste of strawberry wine was on them, intoxicating his coherence, making him barely able to breathe. The time for proper conversation at an end, he lifted her gently and took her to the bed, Eselt kissing him all the more passionately for it.

They spent the night together not knowing when or if there would be another. Every night was like that now. Drystan was grateful for those moments, even with the fear and shame, the flame of passion burned brighter. Next to her, he slept fitfully, and when he awoke the next morning, he felt content. Looking toward the window, he saw it was still dark, with just a hint of the blue glow that indicated the sun would soon be breaking the horizon.

Eselt lay quietly next to him, one of her hands on his thigh as if to assure herself he was still there. *Why were they both so insecure?* He thought. *Never in my life have I felt so much uncertainty. Has it changed me?* Drystan stared up at the colorful ceiling and for the first time noticed that it was covered in painted images of nature and fantasy. He wished they could step through and into that place, which reflected a state of pure perfection and happiness. *I will find a place such as that for us to live in peace and to love each another as we please, Eselt. One day soon, I swear it.*

He planned to meet today the man who was quietly selling small parcels of his lands well south of the city. It would have been easier to find a single buyer for all of it, but doing that would have brought word to the duke right away. Everyone knew who those lands belonged to, and selling the whole at one time, especially since they were tenant farmed and making a profit, would have brought a great deal of uneasy speculation. Selling off small parts to unrelated buyers would take longer, but with luck, no one would realize what he had done until he and Eselt were far away. *Maybe we can go to the Emerald Isle, my love.*

He had heard that the Emerald Isle, home of the Enlightened Ones was a Paradise where the game was prosperous and the ancient volcanic-enriched soil was fertile. But would they accept them? Foreigners were allowed to travel to their amazing city, Atlantis, for trade, but could they also live there? He knew the duke journeyed to the isle once when Drystan was a child and had required an invitation from one of their nobles so that he could travel freely about their land. Perhaps Drystan could see their ambassador and inquire if their delegation had not already returned to Lyonesse City.

"I must leave you now, my love." Dawn was breaking, and Drystan needed to be away before Lady Fedelmid found Eselt's door locked again.

Eselt stirred and kissed his face leaning over her. Then he quickly dressed and drew back the bolt on the door, careful not to make any noise. He didn't want to leave her now—or ever, for that matter—but he knew he must.

"We must do our best to give the appearance that we have moved on from each other and accepted Captain Purin's bargain. It will be difficult for the both of us, but our anguish will buy us more time." He kissed her once more. "Remember the pine."

~~~

The fat little dwarf was the ugliest creature Captain Purin had ever seen. He was genuinely surprised at how surprised he was at the dwarf's appearance every time they met. It was as if his mind could not comprehend the excessive ugliness of it and chose to forget what should have been unforgettable, only to be astonished by it the next time. It wasn't just Purin; he saw the reaction from others the rare times the dwarf was out among the public. To most, he was more of a . . . thing than a person. Even from his distant vantage, Purin could see the details of his features—a large, bulbous nose studded with several large warts, each sprouting thick strands of black hair tilted off center to one side; a heavy brow with bushy black eyebrows; long, greasy black hair; and eyes as black as any night.

Purin stood across the dark street and watched the dwarf through the illuminated windows of his small two-story house and thought about how many times he had been there asking for assistance. Sometimes it was for help locating criminals, missing people, or stolen property, but tonight was for something entirely different. The dwarf had a talent for finding things, a kind of seeing, the captain thought, although he was not familiar with the ways and means of the magic, only with the knowledge that it was useful.

He walked across the street, advancing upon the long row of attached wood-and-stone residences that lined both sides of the boulevard, and knocked on the front door. He could hear the heavy footfalls of the dwarf's approach, the sliding of the locked bolt, and the creak of rusty latches as the door opened to reveal the chest-high silhouette of the short man holding a loaded crossbow. With a heavy grunt, the dwarf turned and walked back into the interior, leaving the door open for Purin to follow.

The dwarf, Firolin, led Purin down a short hallway, past another door and into a large room furnished with a single long table and a few scatted chairs. The illumination from several light globes floating in the air near the ceiling left the room dark around the edges. On the table were small piles of herbs and roots and other things Purin didn't recognize. There must have been over a hundred little accumulations scattered about. A pot hung over the hearth and looked as if it were about to boil over; the dwarf gave it a quick stir when he passed, calming the strange noxious liquid before he sat in a nearby chair. Purin found a chair on the other side of the hearth and adjusted its position away from the slightly putrid smell steaming from the pot. At least the stench was less unpleasant than it was the last time he was here.

"What'r ya here fer?" the dwarf asked in the rough grumble so well-known to his kind.

Purin pulled a gold coin from his purse and handed it to the dwarf. "I need information, Firolin, the usual sort."

"A'ight, watcha got?"

Purin pulled a tangle of golden hair pilfered from Eselt's hairbrush and a man's sweat-stained riding scarf from another pouch and held them up. "Will these do? I need to know what you can tell me about the relationship between these two people, a man and a woman."

Firolin took the items and held them close to his nose to sniff, inhaling deeply with each one. He stood then, grabbed a large bowl from a shelf, and placed it on the table, then cast the lock of hair and the scarf into it. He walked back to the hearth and lifted the pot off its hanger and poured its frothy liquid into the bowl until it was a little over halfway full. Replacing the vessel, the dwarf gazed about the table, taking a pinch of this and a stick of that and tossing them into the unorthodox stew. Finally, he took a thin branch and ignited the end of it with a snap of his fingers, then slowly placed the unlit end within the bowl and stepped back quickly.

Whoosh! The liquid flamed high into the air, barely missing the dwarf's long beard, and then settled into a steady blue flame that extended to the edge of the bowl. The dwarf Firolin peered deep into the flame and began to speak strange archaic words that conjured images that Purin could see. There was the face of an old lady, a man and a woman naked in the throes of passion, the black-and-white banner of the boar torn asunder, and a short twig of pine.

"Da pine will take-ya to what-ya seek," the dwarf rumbled, and then he took a thick piece of leather and placed it over the bowl, extinguishing the flame.

"A pine?" Purin was confused. "How will a pine help me? Do it again. I need more than a pine."

"Der ain't noth'n else-ta see." The dwarf put his thumbs inside the thick leather belt that cinched his long brown robe. "If der be more, it-ta show'd me."

Purin was annoyed. "You've shown me more in the past, dwarf. Is it a symbol for a tree, a painting, sculpture, or relief? Give me something helpful!"

"'Tis what it be!" Firolin fired back angrily. "Der be no more! It up-ta you-ta find what meanin' der is. Now go about yer bus'ness, ain' got noth'n left fer-ya."

"Very well, dwarf, I'll be seeing you again soon," Purin said and made his way out. He knew when the dwarf could not be pushed any further.

The only response from Firolin was an incomprehensible grumble.

Purin was frustrated. Usually, he got more from Firolin. These visions showed much he did not understand. Who was the old woman, and was the pine supposed to be abstract? He considered the possibility that the dwarf was holding back on him, but for what purpose?

He had only known Firolin for a few months and although he never appeared happy he was always willing to take his coin. Their relationship never changed from the first day Purin found him casting fortunes for a half silver under a small tent outside the city. He was new to Tintagel in those days, a rare dwarf outside of Tirnan Yog with magical abilities. Purin had, on a lark, asked the dwarf to tell him something about a jewel thief he was trying to track down. To his absolute surprise, Firolin provided him enough information to successfully find the nave and put an end to his thieving ways. From then on, Purin used him on a number of occasions that, more often than not, turned out well for him.

Crossing the street to retrieve his mount, he rode at a slow jog along the well-lit streets back to Valiant Keep. Purin wondered how often the dwarf sold his services to the thieves' guilds in the lower city. He was sure his coin alone did not elevate Firolin's living to afford a two-level home in a neighborhood situated in the heart of the upper city. He was sure the guilds could afford to pay much better than he could as well.

Arriving at the stable within the upper ward, he tossed the reins of his horse to a stable hand and decided to take a walk through Valiant Keep and look around. It was late enough that nearly everyone would be asleep, and he could search without being hindered. Exploring his memories, there was nothing that he remembered that resembled a pine in Valiant Keep or outside of it, except for the tall pine tree in the garden. *Could that be it?* It didn't make much sense, and the image was a twig, not a tree. He would simply have to look closely at the shields, heralds, tabards, sculptures, paintings, and reliefs that were everywhere along the halls and corridors. *This could be a daunting task,* he thought, but what better choice did he have?

Purin decided to start in the great hall and then move to the Gallery of Legends where portraits and accouterments of Tintagel's greatest lords and Temple Knights were exhibited. For several hours he alternately walked and sat staring at every detail on the walls and displays. Many heraldic symbols included pine trees and cones, yet never explicitly a branch or twig of pine.

Well past midnight, Purin was growing tired of staring at symbols on shields and decided to get some fresh air in the garden. While he was there, he would inspect the lone pine tree that grew there in case it held a clue. The corridors that he walked were well lit with light globes spaced evenly along the walls, and the only sounds besides his own footfalls were the low murmurings of his guards, who snapped to attention when he passed.

It didn't take him long to reach the garden in the dead of night. During the daytime, he couldn't walk twenty paces without becoming engaged by a noble for polite conversation or a soldier making a report. The night was a peaceful time in Valiant Keep; perhaps he would do more patrols after dark to clear his head and enjoy the quiet.

He sat on a stone bench within sight of the tall pine and wondered for the first time why it was even here. There were no other pines in the gardens. Other trees like leafy poplar and beech, but no pine. Where he sat there were no light globes or torches, since rarely did anyone stroll the gardens after dark. Still, Purin could see well enough with the moon far along its nightly path and nearly full. The gentle sound of water falling in the fountain and running across the stones that formed the canals feeding it began to lull him into a sleepy haze.

Images played across his imagination, a time decades past when he first came into service of the duke at Valiant Keep. A young boy was here then, a boy who liked to explore and climb the pine tree in the garden. Purin saw him often scurrying about Valiant Keep in those days, his tutors and nursemaids desperately trying to keep him out of trouble. He wasn't born to the duke and duchess, but they considered him their child and the youngest sibling of their natural children. Purin would come to find out that the boy was adopted by his uncle, the duke, after his parents tragically died.

The boy grew and was sent to squire a knight in another city. The knight would release him twice a year to spend the solstice with his family, and Purin would train with him. Despite the boy's high energy and desire to learn everything too quickly, he was a good student, and by the time the boy became a man and returned with his silver-trimmed cloak, he was among the best Purin had ever seen with nearly any weapon he chose to put in his hand.

To Purin's envy, the boy was good at other things as well. Whether it was riding, running, climbing, swimming, or winning the girls, he excelled. Especially with the girls. So often Purin would walk through Valiant Keep and hear the sound of the boy's name called by some girl or another in love with his fair locks and bright smile. "Drystan, Drystan," they would call.

Those sirens' calls echoed in Purin's mind: "Drystan!"

"Drystan, Drystan? Are you there?" a woman's whisper came out of the darkness, shocking Purin into full awareness.

"Here, love, under the pine," a man called back quietly.

There were fast footfalls from the other side of the hedge Purin's back was against, a flash of white fabric through the shrubbery, and then the dull impact of two bodies coming together. Purin dared not move. One clink of a buckle or creak of his leather armor would give him away. The hedges surrounded the pine, and he could hear the couple talking. Although he could not see who spoke, he knew their voices—

It was Drystan and Eselt.

Purin listened to them talk. There was nothing else he could do, and there was no point in confronting them. Besides, maybe he would learn something.

"I am so glad that you sent for me, Drystan. I thought I might go mad," Eselt whispered.

There were sounds of kissing before Drystan whispered back, "I as well, my love."

More kissing and Drystan spoke again, "I made sure the guards saw me stroll into the gardens, and they will see me leave them later as well. When they give their activity report to Captain Purin in the morning, he will not suspect that we were anywhere near each other."

"You're so very clever, my love, and handsome," she giggled.

The kissing went on for some time then, and Purin couldn't help but roll his eyes. This was not at all like his dalliance with Lady Fedelmid. He supposed that was the way of youth, and he prayed silently to Sunna that he would not have to endure much more of it.

Finally, Drystan said, "I have good news. I have found buyers for the majority of my lands to the south, and my man will formalize the arrangements by next week. On the day he hands me the payment vouchers, we shall run far away. Be ready."

"I'm so happy, Drystan! I will count the seconds until that day. Now let's go to my chamber and lock the door. After my talk with Fedelmid, she won't dare come to my room before dawn."

Purin stiffened for two reasons: first, they would have to walk right past him to leave the garden, and second, what was that about Lady Fedelmid? If he stayed perfectly still, they might not notice him in the darkness. There was movement behind him in the hedge again, a quiet grating sound of stone sliding on stone, and then silence.

Purin was confused. Where did they go?

He waited for a time, not moving, just listening. Nothing.

Then it hit him. There was an entrance to a hidden passage concealed in the wall that led to these gardens. He hadn't thought about those corridors in a decade. No one used them or had cause to. Drystan obviously remembered and was using them to his advantage. Purin walked around the hedges and shrubbery to a place on the wall of Valiant Keep where he thought was the source of the grating sound. Without a light globe, it took a little time, but he found the small hole in the wall, where he inserted a narrow stick from a nearby branch to lift the latch.

There was no light inside nor any sound. From what he remembered, the passages ran behind the chambers where the duke and duchess resided and could serve as an escape route in times of need. The narrow corridors went other places in Valiant Keep as well and offered another way out through the inner wall above the city.

Feeling around with his hands, Purin located a torch set into a sconce on the wall just inside the opening. Fortunately, he always carried his spark stones and had the torch blazing within minutes. Now with the aid of light, he entered the passage and closed the door behind him. The dust on the floor ahead of him was disturbed in such a way that it appeared as though Drystan had come this way several times already.

He traveled upward through the tight passage until he came to the vague outline of a door that he knew was the chamber of the duchess. Purin stopped at the duchess's door and stepped on something that felt like a narrow cylinder breaking with a slight crunch. A note left in a scroll case outside the concealed doorway? No, just a small branch of dried-out pine needles. *Pine needles.* Could this be the sign he had been looking for? Perhaps, but where would this pine branch come from and how would it get here? Maybe this was a sign to the duchess that he was in the garden waiting for her. Drystan must have forgotten to pick it up when they came back this way.

Purin listened at the concealed door and felt a flash of shame for doing so. He couldn't hear anything anyway and really did not expect to—these doors were made of solid stone. He was sure they were in there together. The duchess said as much in the garden. Drystan clearly defied Purin's warning to stay away from the duchess. He liked the boy once, but now he would have to do something.

CHAPTER 14

Traps

Purin did not sleep well that night—or what was left of it. He was tortured over what to do about Drystan and Eselt. On the one hand, he could do nothing and let the lovers run away, leaving the duke devastated and confused about what had happened to his new wife and adopted son. On the other hand, he could reveal their treachery to the duke, causing him to take punitive action against the treacherous lovers. Still the duke would be devastated. Either way, it would not end well for the duke.

What kept him starkly awake more than anything else was his own personal jeopardy in these scenarios. Going to the duke would be a hard thing to do and would require irrefutable proof. If he allowed them to escape and they were later caught, he could be implicated as an accomplice and bear the same punishment as them. He was not a conspirator, but if it were found out that he knew about their treason and did nothing about it, how could he prove himself innocent? That was the crux of it, and given this perspective, his best choice would be to go to the duke. First, however, he would have to come up with a plan to catch them in the act that would leave no uncertainty in the mind of the duke or rely solely on Purin's word against theirs.

He spent the remainder of the night tossing in his sheets putting it all together, and by the time dawn broke the horizon, he formulated an idea that would be as good as getting a confession from the lovers. First, he would have to see the dwarf again. Hopefully, he would have something that would help him succeed in his design. Then the duke would have to witness Drystan and Eselt's betrayal firsthand. It was the only way to keep Purin's own life out of jeopardy.

Purin washed and got dressed. With any luck, Firolin would be home at this hour, and he wouldn't have to go back again later. He walked through the hall that led to the stables, nodding to the servants and guards who were going about their morning duties. It was still too early for any of the gentry to be up and about, which he was secretly thankful for.

Taking a quick detour, he turned down the broad hallway that led toward the duchess's chambers and then turned once again down a narrower corridor. There, he stopped at the first door and knocked lightly.

"Lady Fedelmid? It's Captain Purin," he spoke quietly into the door.

A moment later the door opened and Lady Fedelmid, fully dressed in her blue corset and long skirt, beckoned for him to enter. He closed the door quietly behind him, took her hand in his, and kissed it.

She smiled broadly at his unexpected appearance. "I am pleasantly surprised to see you this morning. When you did not come by last night, I worried that you had tired of me."

"Never, dear one," he replied. "I was caught up in an unexpected adventure involving our young lovers."

Lady Fedelmid cast her eyes down in shame. "Her Grace forced me to reveal that we are involved with each other. I am sorry, Purin, I do not possess the strength for this that you have."

He smiled and wrapped his arms around her. "Don't worry, my sweet, I have found them out entirely." His left arm tightened around her waist, and he kissed her lips. "I'm certain you will not speak a word about us to the duchess in the future."

Her eyes widened when the point of his long dagger entered under the base of her skull, killing Lady Fedelmid instantly. Suddenly limp, her body slumped against his, and he gently laid her on the floor, cleaning his dagger on her blue skirts while blood pooled around her head. Light reflected from her glassy eyes staring into eternity, and her features still displayed her utter surprise. He wondered briefly what she saw now. Gently, he reached down and closed her eyes. Purin felt no remorse. He just didn't want her staring at his back when he departed. Who knew what the eyes of the dead saw? Then he calmly exited her room, unhurried on his way again to see the dwarf wizard, Firolin. One less end to tidy up.

~~~

Drystan and his brothers sat in the council room with Sir Wilhem and Captain Purin. The duke was in a rage. The body of Lady Fedelmid was found that morning, murdered in her room not far from the chambers of the duke and duchess themselves, and no one had any ideas about who could have accomplished such a brazen crime.

"If the assassin was able to get to the Lady Fedelmid, he could have just as easily found his way to the duchess or myself! Where were your guards, Captain Purin? Why didn't they see anyone? Is one of the guilds trying to send me a message? I will root each one out and butcher every one of them!"

The whole thing was a shock to Drystan as well. Was Eselt's life in danger? The sooner he could take her away from this place the better. And why was Purin's gaze so intent on him?

"It had to be someone very familiar with Valiant Keep," Captain Purin speculated. "Someone so typical that the guards would not notice them or give them another thought. A servant, perhaps someone from the kitchens or a housemaid with easy access to the servant's hall."

"Whatever the case"—the duke's voice boomed, causing Drystan to flinch—"find them, Captain. I want no excuses and a doubled guard. I don't want a mouse to creep through these halls unaccounted!"

Captain Purin stood at attention and left the room, his eyes hard upon Drystan as he departed. What was the man thinking? Could Purin believe that he had something to do with the murder of Lady Fedelmid? Unless she told him about her confession to Eselt. Still, what would his motive be? To keep her quiet? Perhaps.

Drystan's brothers were on their way out, almost on Purin's heels, assuring their father that the murderer would be caught soon, and Drystan decided it was a good time to exit as well. None of them wanted to be around the duke when he was in such an explosive mood. If only Drystan could chance seeing Eselt. No doubt she would be surrounded by attendants consoling her and would have no opportunity to see him alone. He would have to wait for the night and hope she could find him in the garden.

He left the council room troubled. Captain Purin knew about him and Eselt; he also knew that his lover, Lady Fedelmid, betrayed their relationship to the duchess and admitted to telling him things that should have never been said. Purin was either behind the murder or done murder himself, Drystan was sure. Purin was no Temple Knight bound by the Oath, and he could imagine the captain justifying in his own mind his actions for the benefit of the duke. It also served as a dire implication on him and Eselt when they fled the city, but how could Purin anticipate that?

Was it part of his plan?

Yes, Captain Purin was no Temple Knight. A knight of Sunna would never debase himself by murdering another, not if he valued his soul. Drystan considered the Oath. He had taken it three times. First, when he graduated to the silver-fringed cloak, again when he earned the gold-fringed cloak through his act of heroism, and the third time when he endured the Testing.

The Testing, he recalled with an uneasy shudder.

He was required to take the Testing. Only those who could not achieve an act of heroism within two years of receiving the silver-fringed cloak were compelled to do so if they wanted to be awarded the gold-fringed cloak. Drystan volunteered to undergo the Testing to bring honor to his family, in particular to the duke himself, as a kind of gratitude for everything his family had done for him. It was not unheard of for a knight to elect to endure the Testing voluntarily. However, it was very rare and highly regarded by other Temple Knights. The danger of the Testing was that if one failed, he would be stripped of his gold-fringed cloak and never allowed to repeat it. And it was no easy challenge. The Testing was a torturous event on mind and body.

For Drystan, it began when men in masks abducted him before dawn one morning. He was terrified, never having the opportunity to fight back before they had him tied and blindfolded. The men that handled him were rough but not severe when they loaded him into a cart and then down into the cavernous depths under a nearby building. The smell of wet, mineralized earth and the uneven descent were easy enough to discern, and he worried that he had been taken by some dark cult to be sacrificed to an obscure god.

Then he heard the chanting. He vividly remembered it and how relieved he was. For it was the Song of Sunna that they hummed, and he knew that he had been brought for the Testing. He had not been taken to be sacrificed or murdered.

The Song began low and steady at first then slowly risen in pace and volume until he reached their destination where his blindfold was removed. He was brought to the inner sanctum within the lowest subterranean level in the Temple of Sunna. There had to be at least two scores of the Temple Knights who gathered around him, and each one wore a solemn, hard expression. Drystan remembered how much like a tomb the place felt and quiet. He remained silent as well, waiting for it to begin.

The room around him was a massive underground dome crowded with columns throughout except for the center space where two heavy stones were pulled from the floor, revealing a small cavern below. It was into that cold, black void that he was lowered, and then the stone slabs were replaced, leaving him bereft of any light. The last thing he saw before he could see only the black ink of darkness was a small barrel of fresh water, a loaf of bread, and an empty bucket. A voice from above informed him that if at any time he called out to be released, the Testing would be over and he would have failed. Drystan laughed to himself at the absurdity of the whole thing in retrospect. Who couldn't endure a few days relaxing in a cold dark room with the option to leave at any time one desired? It was different when he was there, and his mind conjured all manner of terrors in the eternal darkness with no method to measure the passage of time.

Somehow Drystan managed to hold firm and keep his sanity until he was removed three days later. For some, the Testing was intolerable, and there were instances where initiates went mad and sometimes even died while in the cavern rather than suffer the humiliation of ending the Testing early. For those who survived intact, the most spiritual experience of their lives took place, as it did for him.

Tears ran down the sides of Drystan's face as the memories flooded back to him. When the stones were removed, he was illuminated by a bright light emanating from the pinnacle of the domed ceiling above, so bright it was blinding, and he had to feel for the rope sent down to hoist him up. Pulled out of the cavern, he knew he was surrounded by others because of the Song of Sunna that they sang, although he could not see them from the light blindness. Then one began to speak in arcane words he had only heard a druid or wizard speak before. It was the ritual of his solemn rebirth.

The words echoed in his head as if spoken forcefully from inside of him, in a woman's voice, and he knew he was receiving the Enlightenment. It was the Wisdom of Sunna, and through her spirit, he understood their meaning. He could still remember every word clearly.

"I hear the call from darkness and come into the light

Born once again unto Sunna, to bask in her radiant wisdom.

Pledged to defend her teaching and follow her faith

Hold close the secrets of the Order to which body and soul I am endowed

Ne'er to commit murder, deceit or lie

To honor and serve Country and King,

Upon pain of death and ruin upon my soul if ever I should fail.

In her Grace I shall serve with bone and blood and spirit

With every breath within me unto the end of days."

No Temple Knight could ever forget those words. They were the foundation of the Order, the Oath of Enlightenment, a dedication to a way of life until their death. Of course, all Temple Knights learned the words from the day they started training, but to receive them from the Goddess herself in the final ritual of the Testing brought a kind of sanctity that could not be endowed in any other way.

The Testing concluded with the presentation of the gold sun pendant that would be the clasp of his gold-fringed cloak. Only those who successfully completed the Testing received the pendant, to be worn as a badge of honor for what they endured and survived. It instantly became Drystan's most valued possession in the world. Some knights whispered that the pendant was imbued with sacred magic to ward off evil. He didn't know anything about that, but it didn't matter to Drystan. There was magic enough in the accomplishment.

Those who failed the Testing were returned to society to pursue whatever trade they wished, but they would never be allowed to attempt the Testing again. Even a king or heir in the agnatic succession of Lyonesse could lose their status and become a common citizen in this way; the line of succession simply passed to the next in line. Drystan knew of many royals in the histories of the kingdom to whom this occurred. The general opinion was that it filtered out the weak-minded and kept only the fittest in power to rule. He tended to agree.

Captain Purin was no knight and could take a life by murder without conscience if he was so inclined. It pained Drystan to think that Purin would be capable of murder, yet the captain's fanatical protection of the duke had driven him to cross many lines over the years. Only recently, Drystan's brother confided that the captain flew into a rage when he found out that Drystan accepted Sir Murhalt's challenge in defense of the duke's honor. It seemed that Purin believed that he should have been the one to retrieve Eselt and take up the threat.

Drystan would have to keep a close eye on the captain. Purin was becoming more unpredictable and daring, which worried Drystan, especially with Eselt so vulnerable and alone. He prayed that she kept her door locked at night, considering the recent events, and he would tell her as much if he could only see her. They didn't have much time now before Purin either gave them away to the duke or attempted something even more drastic. Drystan doubted that it made a difference to Purin how he resolved the problem with him and Eselt, as long as he resolved it. If there was any solace at all, then it was only the assurance that Purin would come for him first. He was sure of that. If Drystan were dead, then Eselt would have to find comfort in the duke's arms, and all would be right in Valiant Keep again, at least in Purin's mind.

~~~

"What sort of encounter are you expecting, Captain?"

Purin was not a nervous man. Not by any stretch of the imagination. Except when it came to the duke. He never liked lying to the duke, and it seemed to be happening so often of late. Tonight, his capacity for persuasion and control had to be on the mark, for any stumble could send the duke in a direction that might leave Purin's own head on the chopping block.

"I'm not exactly sure, Your Grace. The wizard Firolin could not see more, although he did advise caution regarding the delicacy of the situation."

The duke paced back and forth in his private office, clearly annoyed. "Delicate? How so? I can put a hundred guards in the garden and capture anyone who arrives. Whoever it is will break quickly under questioning."

Purin had to get control of this conversation quickly or everything could be compromised. "This meeting has a complexity that makes me believe it would be in our best interest to involve as few others as possible. The way Firolin described it, we will learn more with observation rather than apprehension."

Duke Maruk threw his hands in the air. "Spies? You want us to be spies in my own home?" He was getting angry and nearly beyond the point of reason. "And what is this 'complexity' you speak off?"

Purin's mouth went dry. He was hoping to avoid what he was about to say. "The Duchess, Your Grace. It has something to do with Duchess Eselt."

The duke stopped mid-step and turned slowly on Purin, speaking in a dangerous, low growl, "What does any of this have to do with Duchess Eselt?"

Calming himself, he knew that the next words out of his mouth would have to be carefully considered, otherwise he might find himself in a very perilous position he could not back away from. Firolin dissuaded him from going with his original plan to just tell the duke his suspicions about Drystan and Eselt, which would have required a considerable leap of faith to expect the duke to believe. Especially after Lady Fedelmid's body was found. That at least had given him what he hoped would be a better plan that would expose the duke to the lovers incidentally.

Clearing his throat, Purin soothed his words, "Firolin assured me there was no danger, and I'm not saying the duchess would be an accomplice to the meeting, only that there are connections to her, in some way, that would be better if they remained a private matter. I nearly rattled the dwarf to get more information myself, but he had none left to give."

Visibly calming, the duke sat in a nearby chair. "Very well, Captain. I will follow your lead on this one, but I will come armed."

"Of course, Your Grace." Purin tried not to show his relief. "Firolin has also been good enough to provide us some assurance against detection."

"Magic foolery. I don't trust it. When will this meeting take place, Captain?"

"Late in the evening, perhaps tonight or the next; I will watch for the signs."

"Signs?" The duke shook his head in disgust.

"Yes, Your Grace. Firolin advised me of certain signs to watch for. Then I will find you immediately so that we may make ourselves ready."

"And then we'll have a neck to stretch." The way the duke said it, it wasn't exactly a question.

"Yes, Your Grace," Purin hoped it wouldn't be his.

CHAPTER 15

The Garden
SY5490

The bright moon cast its illumination through the branches of the pine, forming strange shadows on the grass beneath. Drystan sat on the bench underneath the tree, watching the movements of the shadows and imagined familiar forms in them. He had been here an hour already and wondered if his lover would be free to meet him that night. If not . . . he didn't want to think about that, but unbidden images came into his mind anyway of his uncle, the duke, happily fulfilling his husbandly obligation to the duchess. To his relief, they never spoke about that anymore. He didn't want Eselt to feel guilty about it, although he was sure that she did. He knew that to her it was like submitting to rape, except that it was not violent in any way—thank Sunna—and it affected her in a very emotional way. It was similarly painful to Drystan, causing him to fall into a deep despondency that would not let up until he was with her again. It was better that they each dealt with it privately. Otherwise, it would be too easy for it to corrupt and destroy the love that they shared.

Drystan turned his thoughts away from the subject. She was later than usual, but she still might come. There was no reason to continue down the path of those dark thoughts. Not yet.

He always enjoyed the garden, despite his excitement and anxiety. The fresh fragrance of spring blossoms was on the night air. Eselt would surely find it delightful, and perhaps she would relish the idea of spending part of the night under a blanket right here on the soft grass between the hedges. Either way, he was almost bursting with the anticipation of seeing her this evening, a feeling tempered only by his concern for her emotional state, considering they had not spoken with each other since Lady Fedelmid's murder.

Glancing around the small glen where the pine grew, he found the space strangely silent. Usually, the warbles of night birds and buzzing of frogs created a symphonic background that complemented the hypnotic circulation of water in the nearby fountain. Not tonight. The sounds of life were absent, leaving the fountain as the solo player to prevail undaunted. It was troubling, and he felt down to his spine as if something unnatural was happening. Then he spied a brief wink of light off something reflective through the hedges several paces away. He didn't look directly at it, but he watched from the corner of his eye until it happened again, a flash of shiny metal where no metal should have been. Had the moon not been full and at the perfect angle to cast its light upon those hedges at this precise hour, he would have never known there was a witness to his duplicity and would have fallen naively into the trap.

His heart fell to his stomach knowing that his night was ruined. Someone, perhaps Captain Purin himself or one of his spies, discovered their meeting place and waited to catch him and Eselt in the act. It made him angry to be interrupted, especially knowing how afraid and lonely Eselt would be in the darkness of her chambers worried that the killer was lurking outside her door. He almost walked over and stuck down the cowardly watcher, no matter who it might be.

Before he could decide anything, a light cut through the darkness from the direction of the secret door that led into Valiant Keep. Drystan's heart leaped. It had to be Eselt.

"Drystan?" she called quietly while stepping into the glen holding a small light globe in her hand.

"I am here, my lady," he whispered in reply.

They prepared for this very circumstance, and his formal reply would alert her that they were under observation.

"Thank you for meeting me again, my lady," he said.

"So why have you summoned me again this night?" Her voice held a hint of agitation, but her eyes were the picture of longing, and Drystan was glad whoever watched them would not be able to see their faces well in the darkness.

For several long minutes, they conversed about the duke's birthday coming up in the next month and plans for a surprise celebration. Eselt even elaborated on the forms of entertainment and who not to forget on the guest list they would put together. Of course, there were no real plans for a party; they expected to be long away from Tintagel by that day.

Drystan felt the turmoil inside of a man dying of thirst staring into an ocean of water he could not drink. It took enormous self-control not to reach out and touch her. She was so beautiful in the luminescence of the moonlight, and he was sympathetic knowing that it was just as arduous for her. He didn't doubt that they both could have stood there all night conversing endlessly about matters of no consequence, but he knew he had to end it before one of them made a mistake.

Concluding the discussion, Drystan said, "It will be a grand celebration! Please allow me to escort you out of the darkness, Your Grace."

They left the garden through the hidden passage and into Valiant Keep. Drystan was annoyed that the watcher now knew how they traveled unseen around Valiant Keep. Hopefully, that person did not also have the knowledge of how to access them. Safely inside and away from prying eyes, Eselt fell into his arms. She was trembling and breathing fast. "Who was it, Drystan? Do you know?"

"It had to be Captain Purin or one of his spies. Who else would know as much to find us in the gardens?"

"Drystan, I . . ." Eselt began, but he interrupted.

"Say nothing right now, love. I want to go out at the kitchens, circle back, and try to glimpse who was watching us. I will come to your chamber in an hour if it is safe. There is much to discuss."

He quickly kissed her on the forehead and headed toward the kitchen exit.

～～～

Purin was incensed as he watched Drystan and Eselt leave the clearing under the pine tree. *How could Drystan have known they were there?* He had activated the bubble of silence that Firolin's trinket had created to keep them from being detected. He removed the spell so that he could speak once he was sure the lovers were no longer in the gardens.

"Your Grace, I am sorry . . ."

Duke Maruk was furious. "Is that what you wanted me to see? My wife and son planning my birthday party? I don't have time for this foolishness, Captain!"

Purin indeed felt like a fool, which only heightened his determination to expose them, but right now he had to try and salvage a scrap of the duke's confidence. "Please, Your Grace, this was clearly not the convention I expected. I beg your opinion not be altered too severely by this error."

"Don't involve me in your witch hunts, Captain. When you have something certain, then inform me, and I will take appropriate action."

Purin bowed to the back of the departing duke. "Yes, Your Grace."

He watched the duke disappear into the black night of the garden and fumed at the utter humiliation he had suffered. Even a stupid man could see that, if Purin hadn't already lost His Grace's confidence, he was on the verge of falling out of favor with the duke. From the duke's point of view, Purin was responsible for a string of negligence since he had returned from Teamhrach. It had started when Purin asserted that the two brutes killed by Reskalin at the inn were the thieves responsible for the burglaries in Valiant Keep. It was a stupid mistake on his part, how could he expect that the duke would believe those louts had managed to get in and out of Valiant Keep unnoticed? It just made Purin look incompetent. Then there was the murder of Lady Fedelmid, another one of his miscalculations. His pride had gotten the best of him on that one. Had he just let her be and stopped seeing her, or at the very least had the wisdom to murder her outside of Valiant Keep, then everything would have been just fine. It was the idea that a mere woman defied his wishes that set him off.

There could be no more mistakes. Purin would come up with a new plan that held little danger of failure. The stakes were higher than ever because if it did fail, Purin knew that he would be finished at Valiant Keep. And if that happened, he would not rest until he watched the last light of life flicker away in Drystan's dying eyes.

~~~

Drystan's gaze identified the silhouette of the man he knew as Captain Purin standing alone in the darkness of the garden. Purin had his back to him, looking toward the place where he and Eselt were conversing earlier. Drystan was surprised the captain was still there, as it had taken him longer than expected to get back through Valiant Keep while avoiding the additional patrols the duke ordered.

He glided closer to Purin, moving silently on the stone pavers and doing his best to avoid the twigs and leaves scattered on the ground that might give his presence away. Drystan was no stealthy footpad, and he knew that Purin must have been deep in his thoughts not to hear his approach even as quiet as he was trying to be.

Close enough, Drystan broke the silence. "What a charming reunion we had here tonight."

Startled by the unexpected voice out of the darkness behind him, Purin drew his sword and in one quick motion spun on his heels and lunged blindly. Drystan barely had time to pull his long dagger, and instead of Purin's blade finding its mark, his strike met with the clang of opposing steel. The captain stepped back from the smooth counter-attack and stood ready to meet his adversary.

Drystan drew his sword and stepped into the moonlit clearing, but the lack of surprise on Purin's face told him that he already knew who it was, and he surged forward, striking with the quickness of an adder straight toward his heart. Again, Drystan batted away the attack with little effort. Purin spun away, feigned low, and then pressed a blistering attack of precisely timed strikes that Drystan beat back with his blades with hardly any exertion. There was a heightened strength and agility in Drystan that never left him after his experience with the High King and the Liafal Stone. Purin's attacks seemed slower than he remembered from the days they would spar together, years ago, when he was the apprenticed to Sir Clavemore of Bours.

"Not like training a child, is it, Captain Purin?" Drystan taunted.

Purin stood panting while Drystan casually waited for his next attack, not breathing heavily at all. The captain was considered one of the best Master Swordsmen in the Western Kingdoms, yet Drystan was confident that he could kill him at any moment if he pleased.

"I loved you when you were a child," Purin spat back, "and protected you from the nasty words the other little nobles had for you. They were jealous and cruel, the little terrors, but they were innocent in their cruelty. That's how children are. Your heart was pure then. What has corrupted you Drystan? The stink of a woman?"

Drystan was stunned by his words. *What could he mean?* Drystan was a Temple Knight of Sunna: he was incorruptible. "Corrupted? How can one such as you speak of corruption? Because I love a woman? You should be wary about casting stones of accusation Purin. I too have a stone for you, and it bears the sin of murder!"

Purin's features registered shock, as if he couldn't believe Drystan might guess that he had killed Lady Fedelmid. "How could you know that?" Purin's face grew red with fierce rage. "Is there no limit to your witchcraft?" He drove at Drystan again with a flurry of strikes intended to force him back and off-balance. But Drystan did not retreat and countered each attack impossibly until, with a clash of steel, they stood nose to nose with each other.

"What kind of knight are you? Where is your honor?" Purin growled.

Drystan sent him tumbling backward to land five paces away on all fours. It felt like tossing a children's doll. Drystan made no move toward him. He just stood there and smiled . . . and waited.

"I am a Temple Knight of Sunna, as you know, and my honor is intact. You, sir, have no honor. No murderer may have honor in that deed."

Purin began to laugh. Drystan was appalled that he would laugh at such an accusation and he wondered if Purin might be delusional.

"How can you say you have honor, knight? What about this love for a woman you speak of? Can you love her in the light of Sunna?"

Drystan was confused. What was he talking about? Certainly, Sunna must know and approve of the pure and innocent love he shared with Eselt.

"Speak your oath now, good knight! Can you remember it?" Purin slowly stood and lowered his sword. "I remember one very important part: 'Ne'er to commit murder, deceit, or lie.' Did I get that part right, Drystan? We are in good company, aren't we? Brothers in sin are what we are, and you are no better than I!"

Drystan took a step backward, feeling the force of the words as if he had been dealt a blow. Why had he never contemplated the hypocrisy of his unholy adultery with Eselt? Purin was right. He was no better than a murderer. He never once considered—not even once!—that what he was doing had put himself at odds with his sacred oath. He was a fallen knight, dishonored and subject to summary execution by any Temple Knight in any place once he was found out.

Without a word, Drystan retreated into the darkness overcome by shame, leaving Purin standing alone in the glen under the pine. He ran through the gardens and into the upper ward, startling the guards who demanded that he halt until they realized who he was. Drystan wouldn't have stopped anyway. He ran through the lower ward and out the eastern gates, which never closed unless the city was under threat. Drystan shrugged off the cold rain that began to fall, a chill drenching deluge that soaked him in an instant, but it did nothing to slow him, and he continued his flight into the forest. Even when the branches swatted at his face and he nearly fell running over the uneven ground, he barely noticed any of it. He was deep in his thoughts, weighing what he came to know. One terrible realization stood out more than all others: he had no idea who he was anymore.

~~~

It was late, far past the time when Eselt would still be expecting him, when Drystan returned to Valiant Keep through the hidden passage that connected to the outside wall. He didn't care; he had to see her. The way was dark and oppressive, even with the thin illumination of the light globe he carried. He wanted to run, hasten as quickly as possible to Eselt, but the noise might draw attention through even Valiant Keep's thick stone walls. He wasn't far away, and as much as he wanted to be with her, he didn't know quite what to say. His life was now a paradox of his own making with no clear resolution. How could he have been so blind? Purin was right. In the eyes of Sunna, he was no better than a murderer for his deceit. And it was the worst kind of deceit, against a man who was like his father, who he loved and honored and then stole his wife away from. Something was breaking inside of him, changing him, for as much as he knew how wrong it was, he also knew that he could never leave Eselt, no matter what the cost, and that made the rest of it almost irrelevant. He could not serve Sunna and love Eselt the way he had up until this night. His Oath was shattered the second he fell in love with her and allowed himself to act upon that love.

Drystan stood at the concealed door to her room. The pine was there, so he quietly triggered the latch and slowly pulled open the door. He didn't need to open it beyond a crack or pull aside the tapestry to know that the candle was not lit in the dressing room. The sounds of passion filled his ears, and he knew she was not alone. Numbly, he closed the door and sat in the forgiving silence of the corridor with his back against the cold granite wall. All thoughts of Sunna and oaths and Purin were gone. Now he fought his rage and jealousy. He wanted to rush into that room and put his sword through the duke and run away with Eselt, but that would have spelled their doom. Even if they managed to escape Valiant Keep, they would be hunted relentlessly by the entire kingdom until their heads were on spikes at the gates of Tintagel. At least if they ran away without causing harm to anyone, it would be considered a family matter and the only pursuit, if any, would be that sent by the duke.

He felt wholly devastated by this night. He could never have anticipated the sorry turn of events that it had taken. Rising to his feet, he walked the hidden passages back to the secret exit overlooking the city. It was raining hard, but he didn't care. He was already drenched to the bone. He sat in the downpour and looked at the lights that flickered in the homes below and wondered if they were happy families who lived there. Would he and Eselt ever be among them, in another city, far from here? He wept bitter tears, unable to contain his emotions any longer. He was glad for the rain, for he could not feel the tears of shame that ran over his cheeks and fell to the ground to be washed away with the rest of his immodesty.

CHAPTER 16

Firolin's Ploy

There is something about an absurdly ugly people who are nearly as wide as they are tall that gives me pause, but that would be an unfair judgment of who they really are. I have sung the greatest ballads in their homes under the mountain in Tirnan Yog and watched them weep, I have moved them with rousing melodies that made them dance, and I have whispered the sweetest love song, and, well, their ladies don't hold back their passion. For me, their greatest asset is their word as bond. I admire that above all else and only the worst of them dare to ever break it.

Wodanaz the Wanderer

Another early morning, and Purin was once again on his way to see the dwarf Firolin. Only the morning before when he walked this way, he made a turn that ended the Lady Fedelmid's life. Today he walked straight to the stables with no detours. He had plans to make, plans that were vital to putting an end to Drystan and Eselt and placing him back in the good graces of the duke.

An hour later, dawn was breaking while he sat in the large, dimly lit room where the dwarf did his work. Firolin was grumbling over being awakened so early after staying up most of the night with his experiments, the results of which lay in piles of scorched, mangled pieces on top of his sturdy work table. Purin could not make heads or tails of the contraption, but it had apparently not produced the results the dwarf was anticipating.

Purin decided to lay out the whole story for the dwarf. He needed Firolin's crafty mind to help him come up with a way to entrap the lovers. It had to be foolproof in its design. The duke might decide to relieve him of service, at best, or hang him, at the worst, if they had a repeat of the previous night's debacle in the garden. He waited quietly while Firolin pondered the task, his face moving in curious contortions with frequent mumbles and grumbles. It was one of the oddest displays Purin had ever seen.

Finally, the ugly dwarf smiled, his large yellow teeth making it appear grotesque. "I 'ave de plan. All'ya need-ta do is get-ta duke to-ta duch'ess room when I tell ye."

Purin hated the idea of leaving so much in the hands of the dwarf, but his options were diminishing. "This better work, dwarf, or my time as your benefactor will come to an end."

By the time Purin left Firolin's home, he felt confident again. For all of his uncouth mannerisms, the dwarf had come up with a cunning plan that had a good chance of working. Of course, much of it would be dependent upon the dwarf himself. One thing Purin was sure of if this turned out badly for him: Firolin would not survive the outcome.

His challenge would be to get the duke into Eselt's bedchamber at the right time. His intuition told him that the lovers could barely stand to be apart, which meant that Drystan would likely be with Eselt again that very night. And given the heightened alarm because of Lady Fedelmid's demise, he believed convincing the duke to go to his wife's room wouldn't be too difficult under the right circumstance.

He thought more about the dwarf's scheme. The dust that he would spread in front of the concealed door leading to Eselt's chamber was invisible except when viewed with a particular light globe that cast a blackish-blue illumination that caused the dust to glow. The demonstration was fascinating. Most remarkable, however, was a spell the dwarf cast upon himself that allowed him to meld into a solid stone wall. Watching Firolin step into the wall of his workroom and then stare back out with only his eyes visible, blinking, was a shock Purin would not soon forget.

The dwarf would use this same method to hide in the stone wall of the concealed passage and wait for Drystan to arrive, observe him entering Eselt's room, and then perform one final spell before signaling Purin. From there it was all up to him and the duke seeing firsthand what needed to be seen. Purin was not a man who went to pieces with nerves, but in this endeavor, he felt the pressure of what they were scheming. So much was beyond his control with only the word of a corrupt, mangy dwarf to rely upon.

~~~

The sun had finally set on what Drystan was sure had been the longest day of his life. After a sleepless night soul-searching at the edge of the forest facing Tintagel, he greeted the dawn of the new morning with a certainty of who he was now—just a man in love with a woman. He prayed that Sunna would take pity on him and accept him for who he had become, but he would be serving her in a very different way from now on. The gold-fringed cloak that meant so much to him once now lay on the ground, the edges flapping in the breeze, with his sword driven through its center. No longer could he be called a Temple Knight. He would be cast out and scorned by his family and peers, and they would all know it soon enough. He considered leaving a note when he departed with Eselt, a letter explaining everything. Did it matter if he did? Their actions would convey explanation enough, and not even his family would care what he had to say about it. The Temple Knights wouldn't care about the why of it either.

In a way, it was a huge relief. He no longer struggled with himself or worried about what he would do or say. All he cared about now was his life with Eselt and keeping her safe and happy as far away from this place as he could take her. At least that would be the simple truth of it when they were gone from Tintagel.

As fortune would have it, tonight would be the beginning of their new life together, and he couldn't wait to tell Eselt. A short while after returning to his room, a runner arrived bearing the vouchers for the lands he sold, which he could exchange for gold at any Temple of Sunna. He was glad for it, considering he was not sure how much longer he could endure the hiding and running, especially with Purin on his heels now. That man would hang himself before he gave up.

The day dragged on, and twice he saw Eselt, each time from afar, and he had to compel himself to go in a different direction from her each time. He didn't trust himself not to make a mistake when they were so close to the end of their odyssey. So, he waited in anxious anticipation, finding himself amazed at how slowly the sun seemed to move across the sky until finally it had the mercy to take refuge below the horizon.

Still, he waited. He would wait until most of the servants retired and Eselt left the pine sprig outside her door. If he found the duke there again, he didn't know what he would do. Drystan didn't think he could wait another day to be away with her. Everything was ready for their quick departure, including the travel satchels he and Eselt prepared days ago. He planned to carry those with him when he went to her chamber since they would leave by way of the hidden passages into the city when they made their escape

One hour passed and then two. Drystan tried to eat, but he didn't have the appetite, and he couldn't sleep given his excitement and anxiety. He paced his room for another hour and then one more before it was finally time. Taking the satchels, he quietly made his way to the kitchens, avoiding any lingering servants and a patrol of Purin's guardsmen along the way.

He felt the tension leave his body once he stepped through the concealed door from the kitchens and into the safety of the passage beyond. There was no one left to avoid or be seen by, and all that was left was to find Eselt and make their way unseen to freedom. Fear was replaced by enthusiasm as he walked toward the secret door to her room. He felt almost giddy when he arrived and was elated that a fresh pine sprig was there waiting for him. He smiled. All was going as planned.

He took a deep breath and made a prayer to Sunna. Please let the candle have flame! He held his breath and cautiously opened the door to peer inside. He could see the light from the taper in the dressing room at the corners of the tapestry that hid the door from the other side, and his heart leaped with joy. She was there and alone. Leaving the satchels and his sword belt outside, he quietly moved into the room and stood at the entrance to Eselt's bedchamber. There she was, sitting at the side of her bed with her back to him, humming a soft tune as she toiled nervously at her needlework. She had not heard his entry, and for a moment he watched and savored the life-changing news he was about to bring her.

"My love . . ." he whispered, trying not to startle her.

She turned with a smile that was genuine and lovely on her face. "I knew you would come." She ran to embrace him.

They kissed long and passionately before he pulled back just a little. "We leave tonight," he said. "Right now."

The look of relief on her face was beautiful, and her eyes began to tear. "Finally, it will be just you and I forever!"

Then her ocean-blue eyes went wide with fear at a violent pounding on her chamber door.

~~~

The night was clear, with no rain clouds in sight. A light breeze blew in the chilly air that sailed over Lake Virtue before rising up the steep cliffs and over the city from the west. Standing at his perch on a tower balcony not far from the duke's apartments, Purin watched and waited. He had been standing outside for some time, and the humid air started to saturate his leather armor and invade his clothing, giving him the shivers. Absently he scolded himself for not thinking to bring his heavy cloak. Heedless of his discomfort, he was determined not to leave until the moon was closer to the horizon or the signal came.

It was only the first night of his watch, and if this was anything like fishing, it could be the first of many. Except that fish were devoid of emotion, as far as he knew, and he anticipated lust, human nature, or actual love would end his vigil sooner rather than later. For now, he would wait and try not to think about it.

Purin sat on a stone bench and tugged the short coat of his uniform tight around him. He felt tired. The irritation of the cold air kept him alert for a while before the long minutes waiting turned to hours and he began to doze. He did not sleep, nor was he fully awake, but somewhere in between, and in that haze, half-conscious thoughts of his mother rippled through his mind unbidden.

"Purin? Purin?" a regal, feminine voice called from upstairs. It was his mother.

"Yes, Mother?" he replied loudly.

"I am going out again tonight dear. I will be home late. There is bread and cheese in the larder and a sweet for later."

He was only eight, and already he found it odd that she would always go out late when his father was away on the king's business. "Thank you, Mother!" he called back distractedly.

They lived a comfortable life in a well-appointed house in the upper city, and as far as he could tell they were happy. He was the only child of a minor noble family, and his father was the magistrate of the livestock trade. Often his father was away from home for days at a time, traveling the duchy, keeping tallies and inventories of all livestock bought and sold as well as assigning grades to the quality of their breeding.

Tonight, Purin was lying on a thick green scatter rug below the finely upholstered beige settee in the family room reading stories from a new book his father had given him before he departed. It was by the famous poet Boeger Penhallow, and in it were short stories about knights, ferocious beasts, fair maidens, and perilous adventure. He loved the stories and poems by Penhallow and greedily churned through each page hungry for the next exploit. He imagined that his life would be much like the stories he read one day when he was a knight.

In less than a month he was to be squired to Sir Gramercy of Oswalt, and in a few short years he would be wearing the silver-fringed cloak and looking for an adventure that would earn him the gold fringe. He could hardly contain his excitement and already begun to practice some of the skills required of a good squire.

"Don't go to bed too late, sweet pea." His mother stood above him, dressed in a fine black gown trimmed with blue silk and a suggestively open bodice. The surcoat she wore over it barely concealed more than the bodice, and Purin hoped she would close it for the sake of decency before she left their home.

"Won't you be cold?" he asked.

"I will be just fine, dearest. Good night!" She blew him a kiss before disappearing through the front door and into the dark night.

He didn't mind being alone in the house and left to his own devices. He had a good book and plenty to eat and no one to interrupt his fun. His life was simple then and innocent. He had not yet been exposed to the corrupting influence of the outside world, especially the women.

The rush of sizzling flame jolted him back into full awareness. An orange bolt of liquid fire arced through the air, followed closely by another, and he knew that was the sign he was waiting for. Time was of the essence now that the trap had been sprung, and adrenaline tinged with fear drove him forward. He sprinted down the stairs calling to the startled guards that were stationed outside the anteroom where two hallways split separately to the duke's and duchess's chambers. Arriving at the duke's door with four guards in tow, he hesitated. Once he knocked his fate would be sealed, for good or bad, there was no turning back after.

"Captain?" One of the guards asked uncertainly.

Purin didn't bother to answer, his decision was made. He banged urgently on the duke's door and waited. Seconds passed, nothing, and he knocked again.

Finally, the door opened, and the duke stood in the doorway wearing nothing but a long shirt and stockings. His expression upon seeing Purin might have been worrisome any other time, but not now. Purin was about to put on the most crucial drama of his life.

"Your Grace! Something is amiss in the duchess's chamber! A servant reported hearing a scream, and the door was locked!"

The duke's expression immediately changed to one of horror and fear. "Let's go, then!" he cried, pausing only a second to grab a sword standing next to the door.

They all rushed through the antechamber and down the hallway to the duchess's rooms. The guards had their swords in hand, unsure of what they would encounter, and all except Purin had the recent murder on their mind. After finding the entry locked, the duke began pounding on the heavy wooden door.

"Eselt! Open the door! It is your husband! Open up immediately!"

A moment passed. He shouted again and again, his calls clearly growing more panicked by the second. Finally, there was the metallic grating of the bolt pulled back, the turn of the latch, and the door opened. Eselt stood on the other side in her night clothes. She appeared as if abruptly awakened.

"Is everything well, my dear? Are you hurt?" the duke asked.

She seemed confused for a moment before she answered. "I am fine, dear. What's the matter?"

"Your door was locked, and a servant heard a scream."

"It was a bad dream, and I was afraid," she replied. "Everything is fine now, husband."

Purin knew she was lying. He needed to get inside. He had to get inside.

"May we come in, Duchess, and confirm you are safe and not held against your will by some hidden danger?" Purin asked quickly.

Eselt opened her mouth to answer, probably a reasonable denial that all was well, but the duke spoke for her. "Go ahead Captain, clear out the boogeymen so my wife may sleep unworried."

The bed linens appeared disrupted, with half of them flung on the floor. The windows were closed, and there were no other exits . . . except one. Purin tried to approximate the position of the concealed door from the inside and soon decided it had to be behind a tapestry that hung from the ceiling to floor in the dressing room.

Eselt was speaking urgently to the duke, "Send them away, dearest, and come to my bed." Desperate. "Please, husband, send them away."

Purin approached the tapestry and took a deep breath. This was it. His life was riding on the next few seconds. He tore the tapestry from the wall and exhaled. Everyone else in the room inhaled in astonishment. There was Drystan, crouched on the floor with both of his hands sunken inside the concealed stone door. Eselt screamed in a voice thick with mournful emotion. She knew what this meant, and even to Purin, it seemed that a beautiful dream had just died. Then she collapsed on the floor, unconscious.

Drystan just glared at them all, and Purin was sure if he was not trapped in the stone there would have been a battle to the death right then. The duke, on the other hand, was a study in disbelief and confusion. He stared at Drystan, mouth working, but no words came forth.

Drystan spoke first. "It is true, Uncle. Everything you see here is true. Your eyes do not deceive you."

The duke finally found his voice, but it came out as a hoarse whisper. "Why, Drystan? Why have you done this? Have I not been a good father to you and given you everything the same as my own children? Do you feel slighted in some way I could not know?"

"You have been a better father than I deserve. My actions have not been caused by you. My sins are my own, mine alone. Even poor Eselt is innocent in this. Tempted by my guile, she succumbed unwillingly. Do not treat her ill, Uncle."

The duke looked around the room. "Is there witchcraft at play here? Some chicanery I do not comprehend?"

Purin spoke up, "No, Your Grace. I have long suspected their deceit, but I had no proof to show you. They are simply two people in love, and they have met many times to share it with each other."

"Not true!" Drystan's hands were stuck fast to the stone no matter how hard he tried to free them. "The deception has been mine! She was innocent and without defenses to repel my advances! Believe me, Uncle!"

"He speaks like a man desperate to protect his lover, Your Grace." Purin sheathed his sword. The battle was over, and he had won.

Duke Maruk sighed depths of sadness. "Take Drystan to the cells below and put Eselt under guard in a maid's chamber away from the servants. I will get the truth soon enough."

The duke turned and left Eselt's chamber, not sparing a glance for the still-unconscious duchess, who had been placed on her bed by the guards.

Drystan glared at Purin. "If any harm befalls her, you will pay with your life."

Purin smiled, but he felt no mirth in it. "I did my duty. I defended the honor of the duke, and I exposed adultery and treachery to the Light of Sunna. You placed yourself in this quicksand and pulled the duchess down with you. No one will place the fault of her peril on anyone's head but your own."

Drystan did not respond. Instead, he bowed his head and wept violently. For what, exactly, Purin did not know.

"Release him!" Purin shouted loud enough for Firolin, standing on the other side of the concealed door, to hear.

The stone softened enough for Drystan's hands to fall to the floor next to where he sat. Purin ordered the guards to seize the fallen knight. He did not resist, and they dragged him as if from a womb out of Eselt's chambers to a cell below Valiant Keep. Two more guards were summoned to take Eselt, and soon Purin stood alone in the duchess's chamber. It was over—well, almost. There would be interrogations, judgment, and finally sentencing. It could take weeks if they put up a strong defense.

He worried that Drystan would accuse him of murdering Lady Fedelmid, but it would be each one's word against the other, and there were no witnesses. He should be able to brush that off as a distraction and come under no judgment himself. In the end, Drystan and Eselt would both likely be exiled from the kingdom with the blessing of the king. He sighed. That's what they wanted anyhow. Now they would be forced to do it in the daylight with the full weight of shame on their shoulders. Purin didn't care. He would be back in the duke's fair graces and might even receive a reward for his diligence.

Purin was still filled with adrenaline and wondered if it were too late to take a ride down to the lower city and spend a couple hours in his recreation room. He wouldn't even be too particular about who Lewys could find at the last minute to satisfy his needs. He wanted to celebrate, and he had the energy to burn.

CHAPTER 17

The Hunt

"You old fool, quit stepping on my robe."

"Who are you calling an old fool, Myrllin? You're older than I am!"

"By less than a minute, Wodanaz! And that's only because you were probably so drunk you couldn't find your way out!"

"How old are we now, by the way? A thousand? More?"

"Poor Wodanaz. You never learned to count well. We are nearly twelve hundred years old, and you are already showing your age. You need to go home more often and sleep for a century or two."

"What's the point, Myrllin? Didn't you tell the Assembly of Nine that the world was going to end in a millennium or so anyway?"

"No, no," Myrllin scolded. "You need to temper your tongue. Rumors get started otherwise. I told them their world will end, humanity will go on, and you well know your part after. We have much work to do in the centuries that follow."

"Bah," Wodanaz scoffed. "Are these humans worth it?"

"I think so, and so do you. Look how they light up and croon your songs and ballads. How many love stories have you inspired, how many poets? I may be able to glimpse the future, but you are the one these people love, and that will never change."

"I suppose, brother. At least the Vikja don't bore me like the Dwarfs and Sylvan people. Although the Dwarfs are a great bunch to drink with. Too bad their women are so trollish."

"Careful, Wodanaz, I've heard about you and the human women, especially the Vikja. How many demigods do you think to create?"

"Only a couple here and there. Don't worry. I strike my lovers barren before I grant them the privilege of my seed."

"You're so considerate," Myrllin chided.

"Except for a few of the Vikja women. I wouldn't mind a few progenies with them.

"What is your obsession with those people, anyway? It's so damn cold where they live, and they rarely wash."

"They are a strong, vibrant people who enjoy my ballads and arias which are always accompanied by copious volumes of strong mead and wine. Not to mention they have been quite grateful that I introduced writing symbols to them five centuries ago."

"Yes, they practically worship you. And it was six centuries, not five."

"So, what are we doing in the middle of the Wilds anyway? You think the witch Aja is nearby?"

"You know she's not a witch, Wodanaz. She is far more dangerous than that. I'm just not sure how much more dangerous she is yet."

"I knew her as the Wandering Healer, a sweet old lady who didn't care for riches or fame, just the well-being of those she would visit in the out-country." Wodanaz scratched his short black beard. "We traveled together a few leagues a couple decades ago. She had quite the humor, and I enjoyed the conversation to pass the time while we walked between villages. Too bad we have to kill her."

"She is not who she was," Myrllin's voice was low and sorrowful, "and we kill what has taken her body and soul. Just like the troll a few months back."

They walked in silence for a bit while Myrllin contemplated what it was they were set to do. So many leagues they had followed Aja, each time arriving just after she departed a village, yet still in time to reverse the terrible effects of her intrusions. Without their interventions, dozens would have perished due to her poisons and dark magic. These were the only clues they had as to her power, and unless she was hiding something more significant, Myrllin believed he knew what she was and the genuine threat they thought she might be.

Myrllin broke the silence. "It will be a simple matter if she is just a Chaos Demon."

"And if she is something more?" replied Wodanaz.

Myrllin was noncommittal. "We will find out together." He smiled.

"Do you really think even a Named Demon can overcome the two of us?"

"Not a chance." Wodanaz's simple reply was riddled with sarcasm.

"If I were to guess, I would say it was the same damn demon that escaped the Troll. Wish that I had known it then." Myrllin stamped his staff on the ground mid-step in anger. "I won't make the same mistake this time."

"There was no way we could have known then," Wodanaz tried to comfort him. "Now we do, so let's find this bitch and get it done."

Myrllin appreciated his brother's words, but he also knew that the Chaos Demon had taken many innocent lives through Aja that could have been saved if they captured the demon when it escaped the Troll. "Summon your steed, brother, and let's ride. I believe my backside can handle a few leagues on a mount."

Wodanaz stopped and waved his arms in the air along with a brief incantation, then from a burst of smoke, a mighty steed appeared, eight legs in all, standing before them with steam exploding from its nostrils with each breath.

"Sleipnir, good boy," Wodanaz's voice was calm and soothing. "We need to travel swiftly."

Wodanaz hopped up quickly, and Myrllin followed with a little more hesitancy. He didn't trust this strange mount, but he respected its haste in arriving at its destination.

Looking back over his shoulder, Wodanaz laughed. "Are you ready, you crone?"

Myrllin checked his staff was secure on his back and clasped his arms tightly around his brother's midsection. "I suppose . . ." The eight-legged steed took off like a bird startled out of the fens, and if he weren't sure he might lose his grip, Myrllin would have thumped Wodanaz on the head.

The next village they planned to visit in search of Aja was over six hours away on the best-conditioned horse, but Wodanaz's steed, Sleipnir, could travel the distance in less than a third of the time. Myrllin secretly envied his brother's conveyance, since he had nothing like it himself and generally walked or rode a regular horse wherever he went. Of course, he could always use his craft to stimulate a mount to greater speeds and longer endurance, although most of the time he ended up killing the animal in doing so. Instead, Myrllin preferred to take his own time getting to where he wanted to go and planned carefully unless urgency dictated otherwise.

Almost a quarter league outside the village, Wodanaz dismissed Sleipnir back to wherever he went, and they walked the rest of the way in.

Two middle-aged men dressed in traveling clothes, carrying staves, and walking into a village inspired far less discussion than two middle-aged men riding in on a fantastic eight-legged horse. Considering who they hunted, they preferred she not find out through rumor that they were asking after her. Instead, it would be best to come upon her with surprise. Aja likely did not know who he was, but she had spent a little time around Wodanaz, and no doubt sensed that he was more than what he seemed. The demon that they supposed controlled her would know that as well.

They were on the edge of the Wilds near the southern face of the Kenno-windo Mountain Range on the Eriu side of the border with Lyonesse. This village was the last vestige of civilization between Kenno and Stoddenferry Castle. No one ventured any farther west unless they were foolhardy or deliberately searching for the legendary Valley of the Leprechauns. Myrllin caught wind of rumors about hunting parties that found sport in trying to capture one of the elusive creatures. He also heard that few of those ever returned from their exploits, and those who did were changed forever, and not in the fortunate way they always expected.

There was no challenge from the four guards who stood watch at the entrance of the high wooden palisade that surrounded the village. Myrllin knew two men in robes didn't present a threat in their eyes. This far into the Wilds, the guards were far more concerned with bandits, brigands, and beasts. Beyond the walls, the village appeared normal enough, with children running freely at play and merchants hawking their wares in the streets. Wooden structures with moss on their roofs and ivy crawling up their walls formed rough, unpaved avenues. Some had pens for livestock and shacks for cover attached to them. The only stonework was a fountain on a broad mound of grass in the village center and the odd statue or carving here and there.

Myrllin patted Wodanaz's shoulder. "Well, brother, why don't we do what we do best? You see what you can unearth at the tavern, and I'll go find a druid if one is around. If you find Aja is still here, send a raven; I'll do the same."

"A plan as good as any," replied Wodanaz. He mumbled to himself as he walked away in search of a tavern, "Let's see what passes for a drink in this backwater."

Myrllin smiled. He missed his brother. Perhaps he had let himself hibernate too long this time. Five hundred years was a long time in this world. He could have spent those years alongside Wodanaz living on the road, seeing the world and carousing with the locals. Bah, what was he thinking? Myrllin didn't like to drink, he didn't find most people very interesting, and he enjoyed a far more comfortable way of life. Besides, the two of them would be hurling orbs of fire and lightning at each other before long if they didn't have a common objective to keep them focused.

It was not always easy to find a Druid in a village, and even less so in a city. They preferred the seclusion of the wilderness and the company of trees. Myrllin secretly believed they enjoyed the company of the Dryads more than anything else, and from the few he had seen, he couldn't blame them for desiring the extraordinarily beautiful creatures. Of course, there were no male Dryads, so the females were dependent upon human men to propagate their species. He wondered absently if a male child was ever born to one and, if so, whatever happened to them. Perhaps he would study their ecology more intimately one day. He chuckled quietly to himself. Now he sounded like his brother!

Myrllin's best choice would be to seek out a soldier of the guard. They usually had an idea of who came and went, and in a village this size, there weren't so many to keep track of. It didn't take him long to find one.

Equipped with his best smile, Myrllin walked up to a soldier standing next to a short circular stone wall that surrounded a pit dug for a well. He stood casually, shifting his eyes constantly as if searching for something, paying no attention whatsoever to Myrllin's approach.

"Hello, lad, might I have a word?"

The young soldier appeared surprised that Myrllin spoke to him.

"Of course, sir. How may I be of service?"

"Would you know if there are any druids in the village today?"

The man scratched at his head were brown hair met the edge of his helmet. "I haven't seen one today, sir. Are you feeling unwell?"

"Just looking for a bit of salik for a headache."

"Surely you can find that in the market." He gestured down the street. "We had a healer here just yesterday, the Wandering Healer. Maybe you've heard of her? Anyway, she's already left. I was at the west gate and saw her leave."

"The west gate?" Myrllin was surprised.

"Yes sir, I thought that odd as well. Not many travel west from here."

"Do you know if she treated anyone while she was here?"

"Just a woman at the bakery. She cut her hand bad while slicing bread. Got her blood all over twenty loaves of it when she carried on screaming and flapping about like the King of the Fir-Bholg was committing murder upon her. She calmed right away when the Wandering Healer got to her, bandaged her up, and gave her some salik tea." The soldier began to laugh. "The baker, old Eignach, is still trying to sell the bloody loaves half off!"

Myrllin laughed politely. "Where is this baker? I wish to see these loaves."

"Just up that road and on the right. You can't miss it."

Myrllin turned to leave and then stopped. "Why are you guarding the well, lad? Do you have a need to ration the water?"

The soldier's eyes narrowed, and he forced his voice near a whisper. "It's those leprechauns, sir. They think it's a load of fun to sneak into the village and throw a dead animal in the well or one of their vile potions. The last time half the village shit themselves for a week because of something the little devils managed to get into the water. Now we guard it day and night."

"Keep at it, then." Myrllin smiled and walked in the direction of the bakery.

He could smell the aroma of baking bread before he saw the sign on the door. The bakery was just where the guard said it would be. Outside the entrance to the sturdy wood-built shop was a basket filled with several loaves of bread. Red speckles were visible on the crusts in random places. They were marked half off. Myrllin shook his head and chuckled to himself as he walked through the door.

An obese, balding man wearing a brown robe with rolled-up sleeves and covered with powder marks from flour looked up when he entered. "What can I get you, sir?"

"I came to inquire about the girl who cut her hand yesterday."

"Moina? She's home resting. Caught herself a fever now, and I'm stuck doing all her work. What do you want with her?"

"The Wandering Healer, Aja, left me with medicine to give Moina after she left, but I forgot to ask where she lived."

"I can give you that, and when you see her, tell her to hurry up and get well enough to come back to work. Not well, mind, just well enough!"

Myrllin took the directions to Moina's house and then bought two fresh bargina loaves before he left.

As fortune would have it, Moina's home was not far away. It was a small wooden house, barely a cabin of maybe two rooms, yet it had a very well-tended garden in the front, and the exterior walls were clean and intact. A short trail of flat stones led to the front door, on which he knocked. Moments later the door was opened by an older woman. She had a sad expression that turned to surprise to see him standing there.

"Can I help you, sir?" Her voice was thick with emotion, and her face still showed the trails from tears she had been crying.

Myrllin felt sympathy for the woman. He knew she must be Moina's mother, by age and emotion. He reached out and gently took her hand. He needed to calm her if she were going to trust him.

"Moina needs my help," he told her quietly, tenderly.

He kept his eyes on hers, willing her to be calm, and she immediately ceased to wring her hands and shift her gaze. He had her.

"Yes," she replied in a placid tone. "Moina needs your help. Please come in."

Stepping into the small house, he was immediately struck by how clean and organized it was. A small hearth in one corner kept the room a little too warm, but not unbearable. There was also a small table with two chairs and a bowl of fresh fruit.

The woman turned and led him through another door to a sleeping chamber where a young woman lay motionless on a bed covered by tangled white sheets. A man wearing a brown robe stood over her chanting in a deep, rhythmic diction that was tiring on the ear.

Moina's mother spoke quietly to the man when they entered, "Lochlann, this man is here to help Moina."

He looked Myrllin up and down blandly. "Who is this?" he demanded.

Lochlann was short and a little overweight in his fine, long earthy robe trimmed with fur and decorated with colorful feathers that hung from leather thongs here and there. His face was covered with blue tattoos typical of the druids, and there were more on the skin of his hands and arms that Myrllin could see. He was not old, probably in his early thirties, and exhibited the defensive characteristics of inexperience that Myrllin had seen in so many of the younger druids. There was a druid's stone around his neck, which meant that he was sanctified as a full druid, but Myrllin suspected he had risen in rank only very recently. All of this he took in with a brief glance.

Myrllin stepped up beside him to get a better look at Moina. "I am Myrllin, brother of Wodanaz, and I am here to help."

"Brother of Wodanaz? The minstrel?" The druid had the most incredulous look on his face. "How can you help this sick girl? Your interruption is costing me time that I need to save her."

Waving one hand dismissively, Myrllin placed his other on Moina's forehead. "I can see what you are doing, and it is not helpful."

"What do know about healing?" Lochlann put his hand roughly on Myrllin's arm. "You need to leave here at once!"

Myrllin swung his head around and fixed the druid with a gaze so fierce that the man stepped backward startled. "Listen to me!" Myrllin growled. "You are trying to treat a disease, and she is dying of poison. Now be quiet, or I will freeze you forever where you stand!"

The druid's face was livid with rage, but fear stayed his tongue. Myrllin almost laughed in the poor man's face. Why did the young ones always have to be so arrogant?

Turning back to the girl, Myrllin placed his hands gently on Moina's chest and began to whisper the healing charm that he needed to counter the poison. If it already advanced too far, then there would be nothing he or anyone else could do, and she would die. Myrllin was no great healer by any stretch, but he was reasonably capable with certain ailments, and poison happened to be one of them. Moina's body began to convulse, and a blue glow appeared around the area were Myrllin's hands lay. Her breathing came in rapid gasps, then her eyes shot open, staring into nothing while he continued to speak the arcane words only one of the Tuatha De Blood would understand. Then everything stopped at once, her body lay calm, and her breathing slowed to normal. The pallid hue of her skin began to regain color, and she shivered a little from the cold wetness of her sweat-drenched gown.

Myrllin stopped speaking the ancient tongue and gently pulled the discarded sheets and blankets up to Moina's neck to warm her. His hands no longer glowed with the powerful magic he called upon to heal her, and he sat heavily in a chair next to the bed, feeling exhausted. Quickly, Moina's mother rushed over and kissed her daughter on the forehead, wiping the sweaty hair from her face while thanking him profusely over and over.

"What did you do?" asked the druid, a hint of respect in his voice now.

Not taking his gaze from Moina, Myrllin replied, "I took her poison away. She was nearly to the point where she would have been beyond my power."

"How did you do it? Are you a healer yourself?"

"Some." He did look up from his chair at the druid then. "I took her poison into me."

Lochlann gasped. "Won't it kill you just the same?"

Recovered from his initial exhaustion, Myrllin got up from the chair and headed for the door. "Nope," was his only reply before leaving the house to go in search of Wodanaz. He needed some strong drink.

CHAPTER 18

Judgment

Drystan was sure that the sun had finally risen based on the thin sliver of light that cast its faint illumination from somewhere down the dark corridor. If it weren't for that faint light, he would have no way of marking the passage of time in his dark cell under Valiant Keep. He was alone here. There were no other prisoners to keep him company nor even a guard to stand watch. He assumed the guards, if there were any, preferred to stay upstairs in the daylight where the air was fresh. There was not much to the cell—a wooden bench, a matt on the floor to lie upon, and a pot to defecate in. He supposed he was fortunate that the duke had not thrown him in the common dungeon with thieves and murderers. Perhaps they worried that his allies might find a way to free him there. Regardless of where they decided to confine him, he was determined to escape. Not for himself, but for Eselt. He had to find her and free her from the punishment they planned for his love.

He could not believe that his uncle would execute them both. Drystan was fairly confident that he and Eselt would be exiled from the kingdom, but he couldn't take that chance. If he could escape and rescue her, then everything else didn't matter. The problem was, he would have to get out of this cell first.

It was heartbreaking the manner in which their dreams were shattered just when they were on the cusp of leaving forever. That damned dwarf with his magic and Purin's luck to come when he did. Was it luck? No, it was a well-thought-out plan to trap them. Maybe the schemers had planned precisely for their capture that night, and it just happened to be the night they were running away. He wanted to hit the wall of his cell again, but his hand was still throbbing from the first time, and he may yet need his hand healthy if he was to have a chance at freedom.

He worried for Eselt, and he was thankful that she was unconscious when they took him away. Her pleas and screams would probably have caused him to get himself killed or, worse, beaten so severely he would be unable to attempt escape. Drystan put a lot of thought into his plans—there was nothing else to do anyway—and he had some idea of what he was going to do. If he were honest with himself, he would have to admit that it was the only chance he'd have once they brought him into the daylight from below. The plan would be considered daring and possibly heroic by those who still admired him if any of his supporters remained. His reputation and popularity were second only to the duke himself. Now he was at odds with his uncle, and adultery was generally considered a heinous crime. No matter, he thought. There was no one coming to free him, and he was on his own.

From somewhere far away he heard the clang of a metal door opening, then men walking and the jangle of another door nearby. The heavy stride of boots came closer, preceded by illumination from the light globes the walkers carried. Within moments there was Purin, the perfect portrait of puffed-up arrogance, with three guards standing outside of Drystan's cell.

"Look at the great Temple Knight Drystan. What a sight of magnificence you are now," Purin taunted. "Do you like your new accommodations? The comfy mat, plush bench and fabulous views—oh, and the fresh aroma of a chamber pot. You must be pleased with yourself."

Drystan didn't care about himself. "Tell me how Eselt is doing."

"Still you think only of the duchess? She is fine, of course, and would be better if she would stop crying and eat. The duke even allows her to have attendants and a bath when she wants it. I think he might forgive her if she begged his forgiveness."

"What is to become of us?"

Purin tapped the bars in mock consideration. "There will be a public trial. The duke has already made his formal accusations, which have been substantiated by witnesses. Tomorrow you and the duchess will be brought before the high magistrate to plead your case."

Drystan looked at him with contempt. "Is that what you came to tell me?"

"In part," Purin admitted. "I could have sent a guard to pass along the news, but I preferred to see the great knight myself."

"I am no longer a Temple Knight. You know that."

Purin laughed. "Finally, just to hear you say it! And now we are the same." He turned away followed by his men and the light, and his laughter receded into darkness once again.

~~~

"You are here before the high magistrate, the duke, and a panel of judges because you have been accused of adultery against His Grace, Duke Maruk himself, which carries the penalty of death," the herald announced to the assembled crowds as much as the accused. "You will now be allowed to address the esteemed high magistrate to state your position. As the duke's adopted son by law, Sir Drystan, you will speak first."

Drystan's hands and feet were in shackles chained to a ring that was driven into the ground between his feet. To his relief, Eselt stood without restraints of any kind between two members of the duke's Guard. Behind them, the upper ward was crowded with hundreds of onlookers, noble and commoner alike, listening intently to the events that transpired before them. Ahead, sitting in high-backed wooden chairs bearing ornately carved trees, boars, and spears representing the house of the duke, convened the panel of the judges and the high magistrate. The duke was seated in a similar chair constructed wider, like a throne, off to the side near Eselt, and behind him sat the witnesses, Captain Purin and the guards who found him in Eselt's chambers.

Drystan was vaguely aware of it all, but his full attention was on Eselt, and hers on him. Her eyes were red from weeping, and her legs trembled where she stood. The look on her face was sorrow, but he knew her well enough to recognize that there was something more. Anger? Could she be angry at him? He prayed to Sunna that it wasn't so, although she had every right to be displeased with him. She wanted to leave days earlier, but he insisted they wait until he sold his lands and had money. Now they were here, and even if they managed to escape, they would have nothing.

"Sir Drystan!" the herald shouted. "If you wish to say something, do not keep the high magistrate waiting, or your chance will pass."

Drystan glanced over at his uncle—Duke Maruk wouldn't even make eye contact with him—before staring defiantly at the high magistrate. The way the herald addressed him as *Sir* sounded more like a slur than an honorific. He knew this man, the high magistrate, as an old dotard with a few wisps of white hair that clung desperately to the top of his head and a long shaggy beard that was always unkempt. He would rule however the duke required, and the judges sitting behind him were merely dressing for the tapestry. On their own, they were fair and just, but when it came to a trial of this sort, with the duke squarely at the center of it and so many witnesses, it would be a matter of sentencing.

Speaking loud and clear for all to hear, Drystan declared, "I have no defense!" There were gasps and screams of astonishment that rippled through the crowd. No one expected this. "I do not deny the accusation! I have abandoned my rights as a Knight of the Temple, I have betrayed my Oath, I have deceived the uncle who was a father to me, and I have forsaken Sunna! And there is one more thing! I have seduced the duchess with chicanery and trickery so much so that she was bemused and knew not what she was doing. I do not ask mercy for myself, I ask it for the duchess who is innocent and a victim of deceit!"

The upper ward was silent. The crowd must have been stunned by the things Drystan said since his reputation should have claimed the opposite. Even the high magistrate was speechless and at a loss for an appropriate response. The silence was deafening for all the people within his proximity. *Quite amazing*, he thought.

And then a word pierced the silence, shocking in itself that it was spoken and more so from the person from whom it was said: "No!" Eselt screamed the word with heated anger so vehement that it took Drystan a second to register that it had come from her.

"I am not innocent!" she wailed loudly.

The previous spell broken, the crowd responded with a confused murmur.

Drystan felt panicked. "No, Eselt, you are! Say it, please!"

She looked at him fiercely, and he knew his cause to spare her life was lost. He hoped that in the event he failed to escape, she would be afforded leniency and avoid the sentence of death or banishment, or worse.

"I . . . am . . . not . . . innocent!" Eselt proclaimed again to the high magistrate. "I am in love with Drystan, and everything he said was untrue is true! He has not betrayed his goddess, the temple, the Oath, or even the duke if love means anything! Love means everything! If you expect an explanation from me, you will be sorely disappointed. Love has no reason!"

Again, the high magistrate sat speechless, but not the duke.

He stood from his chair, face livid and his voice tight with rage. "What of your husband?" he shouted. "Where is the love you owe for the vows you took in the presence of goddesses and kings?"

The expression on her face turned genuinely sorrowful, and she took a step toward him before the guards held her back. "I am truly regretful for misleading you, Your Grace. I never should have allowed the wedding to proceed when my heart was not in it. We should have run away before that day."

"You loved him even then?" he said, astounded. "How long before then?"

Her voice lowered so that only those closest could hear. "Almost from the moment our eyes met."

Duke Maruk roared with outrage, "You have brought shame upon me, my house, the duchy, and this fair city! As the duke of this land and the highest authority under the king, I find you each accountable for your actions and pass the sentence of death to you both!" The upper ward exploded with a mix of emotion, some supporting and others condemning the lovers. Fights broke out in the throng of onlookers, and guards rushed to quell the violence.

Drystan hardly noticed. He was horrified that his uncle just ordered their execution. He aspired to a much different outcome, and now the absolute worst had happened. There was only one option left to him now, and the odds weren't looking good for his success.

The duke continued when the high magistrate nearly shrieked for the crowd to calm. "On the morrow at noon, Drystan shall be taken to the lower ward, in sight of Sunna and the general populace of Tintagel and hung from the neck until he is dead!"

Eselt screamed at the pronouncement, and gasps rippled through the crowd, but they remained subdued in anticipation of the next sentence. Then she began to sob loudly with her hands on her face. Drystan held his breath. It made no difference what happened to him. Only Eselt mattered now.

Duke Maruk turned to look at Eselt. She lowered her hands and returned his gaze with sadness and regret in her eyes, but it did not soften the duke's words. "Immediately afterward and in the same place, Duchess Eselt will be brought before Sunna and the general populace of Tintagel and be put to death by burning!"

The crowd erupted in shouts and shrieks. Burning was a cruel punishment customarily reserved for the most vicious of crimes, like murder, mutilation, and assassination. Even then, no one had been burned for any offense in the last century or more.

Drystan lost all sense of sound and time after the duke pronounced his sentence on Eselt. He found himself on his knees, straining at the chains that held him to one awful spot, unable to rush to Eselt's side. She had collapsed as well after running toward him, only to be restrained by the guards next to her. She was screaming and crying. The sounds she made were heart-wrenching, and the sight of her was no better. They clawed toward each other in desperation but made no advance until somehow, he felt the release of tension and he surged forward. He felt a wave of euphoria as he realized the chains had broken, and his mind raced to calculate how he would defeat the guards who held her and escape from the upper ward. Then something hard smashed into the back of his skull.

Blessed darkness . . .

~~~

It was almost time.

Drystan regained consciousness in his cell several hours after he and Eselt had been sentenced. His head hurt where he was hit with a pommel or club, and he was sore all over from rough handling by the guards. Unable to sleep, he prayed most of the night, seeking whatever redemption Sunna would offer, and spent the remainder of the time going over the details of his final plot. There would be no second chance, there would be no pardon of his offense, and there would not be another sunrise for him or Eselt if he failed. No matter what happened to him, if he failed, Eselt would burn, and it tore at his heart so severely that he almost couldn't function. Drystan put those thoughts out of his mind. He had no choice. If he dwelled too much on them, he would fulfill his own fears. No, he would trust in his training, resourcefulness, and abilities to see this through, and maybe a little help from Sunna. His hopeless situation gave him the courage to face whatever came. He knew his back was against the wall, with a very tough road forward, and he was determined to prevail. Somehow.

For Eselt.

Drystan allowed himself to wonder what they would do if they did escape together. Would her father shelter them or be as likely as the duke to condemn their actions? Eselt would have to decide that. Otherwise, where would they run? Far away to the Eastern Kingdoms? South to Ys or Courth? Maybe even to the Emerald Isle. He never had the chance to speak with the Atlantean ambassador. They were probably unlikely to harbor fugitives, he reasoned. Wherever they went, they would no longer be Drystan and Eselt. They would change their names and their appearances as best they could and lead ordinary lives if they were lucky. He hated the idea that he had no money and that Eselt would want for everything she was used to. Except that they would have their lives and each other. He hoped that would be enough. It would be enough for him.

If he did escape from the upper ward, where they held him now, maybe he could get back into Valiant Keep through the hidden passages and collect a few valuables that would ease their burden for a while. It would be risky, but every moment from here on out would entail significant risk until they were far away. Putting those thoughts away for now, he focused on the first crucial stage of his plan—escaping from his captors.

Four guards came for him just before noon. He was glad Purin was not among them. That was one of his biggest worries. If Purin came, then everything he was planning would be that much more difficult. Purin was a talented soldier who could think on his feet, and that could have been the tipping point in Drystan's success or failure.

"It's time to go, Drystan," one of the guards said as he opened the door to his cell.

Drystan just nodded. He didn't know these men, and he didn't want to know them. He might have to kill one or all of them soon.

"Leave the leg irons off," one guard said to the other. "Otherwise we will have to carry him up the stairs."

A point in his favor he had not expected, Drystan noted. He rose from the wooden bench with only the shackles on his wrists and a length of chain between them. Then the guards led him down the dark hallway to the stairway assent out of the cell block. They passed under a small column of light from a shaft in the ceiling that served as ventilation. It was bright and unobscured, indicating that it was a clear, sunny day. He hoped it would be gloomy and overcast to better conceal his flight if he managed to get away from the guards. He would just have to move faster.

There were only half a dozen cells under Valiant Keep, and not a single one was occupied by more than rats. They probably had not been used for a century or more. The histories he studied as a child recounted that they generally held political prisoners or high-ranking prisoners of war. Those were dark times in this land.

The first flight of stairs took them through a hall with a series of rooms designed for interrogation. He was glad that he had not been a subject in any of them. Drystan kept pace with the guards and, in an effort to adjust his eyes to the light, did his best to keep his gaze on the soft glowing light-globe the guard beside him carried. When they arrived at the end of the corridor, there was another flight of stairs that brought them into a spacious hallway that led outside and into a secluded area of the upper ward. From there he would be taken on the back route down to the lower ward where the gallows waited to embrace him.

It was almost time.

Drystan felt himself growing tense as they approached the outer doors, and he forced himself to relax. Almost there. He prayed his memory of the coast was accurate. They stopped in front of the entry, and the two guards ahead moved to hold open each of the very tall and heavy wooden doors, leaving one guard on each side of him. Perfect.

The doors opened, and bright light flooded into the darkness. The four guards immediately thrust their hands in front of their faces to shield their eyes, and that's when Drystan bolted forward and through the door untouched, taking the guards completely by surprise. It was the chance he had been waiting for, and his legs did not fail him.

He ran for the low wall of the upper ward trailed by the guards tripping over themselves in pursuit. With his hands shackled in front of him, he thought it would impossible to make the leap to the top of the wall, but the shackles' metal edges dug into its surface, finding traction enough to pull himself up rapidly, if painfully. Sunna must have been with him because the guards were still several paces away, giving him the precious seconds he needed to choose a spot. Then he jumped, leaving the frantic guards behind.

Far below and into the waters of Lake Virtue he fell, barely missing the jagged rocks and shallows. Then he swam as best he could, with the shackles weighing him down, under the water toward a sandy part of the shore and out of sight of the guards on the wall above. He was a good swimmer, and with any luck, the guards would not see him resurface and assume him dead before they ran to get help. Certainly, none would follow his route down.

Making his way to the shore, quickly he found a sharp rock and pounded at the chains between the shackles until they broke. Those he threw into the sea. Then he ran as fast as his feet would carry him to where the fishing shanties lined the shore north of Tintagel Castle's walls. The shore was deserted, with the fishermen either out in the lake fishing or, more likely, in the crowds gathered to watch his execution in the lower ward. It didn't take long to find a shanty with tools to remove the shackles from his wrists. He hurriedly got to the task and considered the next part of his plan—freeing Eselt. Drystan shuddered to think that what he had already done was the easy part.

CHAPTER 19

Despair

Eselt paced the maid's chamber where she was confined, alternately crying hysterically and raging over the inhumanity of the duke to have them executed out of jealousy. Her emotions were swinging wildly from one extreme to another, and there was little she could do to control them. She was on the verge of a nervous breakdown that threatened to leave her a quivering mass on the floor if she didn't get a hold of herself. Eselt tried to respond to her attendants' efforts to calm her, but they were nearly as hysterical as she was. She had never known this level of despair, and she wished she could just die right then rather than wait for the flames to consume her.

When the hour of Drystan's execution grew close, Eselt began to shake involuntarily with fear that filled her entirety, both for what would become of Drystan at the end of a hangman's noose and the terror of facing death by burning. She was beginning to succumb to despondency when a visitor arrived. It was the Captain of the Guard, Purin, and she hated him for what he had caused. His presence alone was enough to focus all of her rage and anger, allowing the chaos in her mind to calm. She refused to face him or even acknowledge he was there when he entered the room.

"Your Grace"—he spoke to her back—"I have a message from the duke."

She did not care what the duke had to say. He might as well cast his words to the wind for all it mattered to her. What worse could he do now?

Purin hesitated for a response, but when she did not give him one, he continued. "Duke Maruk has had a change of heart and can't bear to see his wife die of burning, regardless of her crime. Besides, King Praetor is concerned that a sentence of this brutality, no matter how much deserved, could start another war with Eriu."

Eselt spoke without turning. "So how am I to die now, Captain? What less brutal method has the duke imagined?"

She could hear him shift uncomfortably before he said, "Your title will be stripped from you, the marriage will be annulled, and you will be banished from the kingdom by the declaration of the king."

"So I will be sent home to Teamhrach?"

"Not exactly." His response was unemotional. "You will be escorted to the Valley of Leprechauns to live the remainder of your life as a slave among the vile creatures and their Halfling spawn."

"Don't you think my father is just as likely to go to war if you send me to the Leprechauns?"

"Perhaps you are right, and he will bring war upon the Leprechauns to get you back. However, that is none of our affair."

Just as he turned to leave, Eselt spun around angrily. "What about Drystan? Will he receive the same mercy?" The last part was spoken as mockery.

"He's already dead," was his simple reply before he resumed his turn and walked out the door.

For a long time, Eselt stared in shock at the door Captain Purin had just exited, and by the time her attendants hesitantly arrived at her side, she fell to the floor, screaming with uncontrolled rage and sorrow. "Drystan! Drystan!"

If there had been a window of height to leap from, she would have jumped; if there were a blade, she would have cut her own throat; and if her attendants would have allowed it, she would have taken the sheets and hung herself. Such was her complete hopelessness. Eselt couldn't accept that Drystan was dead. She couldn't feel his absence inside of her. Surely she would know the moment of his departure from this cruel world if it were true?

Desperately she ran to the narrow window and looked up at the sun. It was near to the noon hour. Would the captain be so cruel to lie to her, or did they take Drystan to the gallows a little early? Maybe he assumed Drystan was dead because of the time. Eselt prayed and prayed to Eriu that it was not true and that the duke had banished Drystan as well.

She had to know. Selecting one of her attendants with a violently shaking hand, Eselt bid her go to the lower ward and return with news, no matter what it was. She would know the truth, and if Drystan were truly dead, then she wouldn't care if they sent her to the Leprechauns or the shores of Fomoire.

~~~

Drystan quickly ransacked a few more of the fishing shanties, finding food, two long smelly cloaks, and a rusty but sturdy old sword. In a wheelbarrow he piled fish that had been hung to dry, then he took the wheelbarrow up and walked quickly along the trail that led from the shanties to the main road and then onto the city. He wanted to hurry, but he had to be careful now as well. Disguised in the cloak, no one would expect him to be going into the city, but if he were stopped and questioned, then he would almost certainly be recognized. He had to take the chance.

Nearly to the main road, he could see a group of soldiers riding along the base of the curtain wall surrounding the city. They were rushing to the area where he had jumped into the water, most likely expecting to collect a battered body. Drystan needed to be well into the city before they sent word that there was no corpse to be found and expanded their search. Looking up at the sun, he realized that it was past noon and he had to get to the place where they would bring Eselt from Valiant Keep. If he could ambush the guards just inside the narrow corridor, before they were out in the open, and dispatch them quickly, then he had a chance to get her into the hidden passageways by way of the kitchens before pursuit could be organized. From there he would cover Eselt with the long cloak he found in one of the shanties, exit into the city, and be out the gates before a general alarm was sounded.

Fortune was with him, as the guards at the gate quickly waved him through. No one wanted to search a foul-smelling man with a barrow of rancid fish. Once inside, he abandoned the wheelbarrow in an alley and hastily made his way through the crowds to the hidden entrance below the lower ward. Before he entered, he became aware of a stir in the gathering above him. Had Eselt already been brought out? He felt panic rising as he ran up the ramp to the lower ward. Many others were running with him to find out what was happening, so he was confident he didn't attract any undue attention.

He arrived just in time to hear a herald making an announcement to the pressing crowd. "Be still! Be still!" he shouted. "By decree of the duke, he has mercifully suspended the execution of the duchess for the high crime of adultery! Instead, she will be banished to a place of seclusion never to return, nor to be granted clemency in her lifetime. So says the duke!"

Drystan was relieved, although he knew that Eselt would be well guarded when she was brought to wherever they would take her. No matter the destination, it would be several days travel, which would allow him more time and opportunity to recover her. It would also give him time to collect supplies and find out when she would be removed from the city. With more confidence, he made his way to where the entrance to the secret passage was concealed. He wanted to go to Eselt's chambers and collect a few things for her while he waited for nightfall, when he could move around the city with less chance of being recognized.

The passage was dark, and Drystan realized to his dismay that he didn't have a light globe. With no other good choice, he felt his way along the walls in complete darkness. Fortunately, he remembered them well and had a pretty good idea of how to navigate his way to where he wanted to go. After what seemed like hours, he found the door that he was sure was Eselt's chamber and gently pulled it open.

Inside it was dark, no light at all, and he had to feel his way through the darkness to Eselt's bedside, where he expected to find her light globe. Before he covered two paces, his foot nudged something on the floor that rolled a short distance. Feeling around in the darkness, he recovered the object and removed it from the leather bag where it was stored, immediately illuminating the room in soft white light.

Surveying the room, he noted much of the furniture remained toppled where the guards overturned it days before. Otherwise, everything was just as he remembered. Then, to his amazement, he discovered the packs that he brought with him for their escape. Someone brought them into the room and placed them out of the way behind an overturned divan, and there they lay forgotten. Everything he needed for him and Eselt was right there in those packs. Even the vouchers from the land purchases and his sword! If Sunna wasn't guiding his purpose, he surely didn't know who was.

Taking clean clothes and a long cloak from his pack, Drystan changed, strapped on his sword belt, and discarded the smelly fisherman's cloak in a pile of clothes in the closet. At last, he was ready to leave the city. After some consideration, he decided to watch Tintagel's north gate from the safety of the nearby hills for the guarded procession that carried Eselt. They would likely depart by the next morning or the morning after.

Pulling back the tapestry on his way out, he was stunned to see deep hand impressions on the inside of the stone door. His hand impressions. If only he had the time to bring an end to that damned dwarf, he thought. Begrudgingly he had to respect the thing for its creativity, and he pushed through and out into the secret passage beyond.

Through the dark corridors, he walked back the way he had come much more quickly than when he came in, thanks to the illumination of the light globe. For the first time in days, he felt hopeful and as though somehow everything would work out no matter what the odds, which seemed to be in his favor today. He turned the last corner, arriving at the concealed door that exited into the city, and was stopped short by a man standing, sword drawn, five paces in front of him: Captain Purin.

"I had a feeling you would be here," the captain said grimly.

Drystan slowly dropped the bags from his shoulders and drew his sword. Thank Sunna he had his own sword rather than the rusty one he had earlier, he realized.

"Let me pass, Captain. You are in the clear. Eselt will be sent away, and I am assumed dead in Lake Virtue."

"I want to," the captain's voice was strong with mock emotion, "I really do, Drystan, but you are a fallen knight now, and my duty to the duke demands that I take you . . . alive or not."

"Have you ever been in love, Captain?" Drystan asked as he moved casually closer, sword down at his side.

"What? In love? Yes, maybe once," Purin replied uncertainly.

"Do you remember how you felt at the time? Like you would do anything to keep that love protected and alive?" Drystan kept his sword low and moved closer.

"I do, but I was young and was not thinking as I do now."

"But you remember well enough, don't you? What became of your love?"

"Her father forced her to marry a noble," he said flippantly. "I wasn't crushed by the cruel emotion, if that's what you're after. She came from a good family that would have restored my family name and produced children for me."

"Did you continue to see her? Try to stop her from marrying another?"

"For what? Love?" He shook his head in disgust. "That is your weakness, Drystan. Imagine who you could have been, the honors attached to your name, the fame and fortune you would have acquired in your lifetime. Now what do you have? Nothing! You tossed it all away for a whore. You could have gotten better than her on the street."

Purin's words angered Drystan, but he stayed calm. "Is that what you would have for me, Purin? Someone you have cared for and trained from the time I could carry a sword? To mingle with whores as you do and never follow real love that is in my heart?"

Captain Purin looked at him sharply. "What do you know of what I do?"

"Rumors, talk among the soldiers." Drystan shrugged. "Enough to know that you are corrupted beyond pardon if the duke were to ever find out."

"No worse than the whore your Eselt will be soon enough!"

Drystan ignored that. "Where are they taking her?" he demanded.

In almost a whisper, Purin replied, "The Valley of the Leprechauns. Even I was surprised at the duke's cruelty."

"By the Gods, Maruk has sent her into the slavery of little beasts. They would torment her and force her to breed their Halflings." Drystan could feel rage building in him, the same as when he faced Sir Murhalt.

Purin was smiling openly. "She will be concealed in a carriage and escorted under guard tomorrow night. And these guards are special," he sneered. "I handpicked them myself. They are among the most depraved and brutal men you will find anywhere, and they will no doubt abuse your Eselt when they are out of sight of the city. It gives me pleasure to know that you know that before you die."

Purin began to advance with sword level.

"Just one more thing, Purin. Why did you have to kill Lady Fedelmid? She was innocent in all of this."

The blackest look of pure evil crept into his eyes, a look Drystan would never forget. "The stupid bitch betrayed my trust, but more than that, it was fun."

Purin's sword thrust at Drystan expertly just missing his ribcage. Nonetheless, there was a sharp pain on his right side accompanied by a quick flash and the crackle of electricity that left his ribs numb afterward. Drystan fell back a pace and looked closely at Purin's blade. It looked like a finely crafted weapon, but nothing unusual otherwise.

Purin moved in fast a second time, thrusting and feigning as best he could in the narrow corridor. Drystan made sure to keep his sword farther out from his body in a purely defensive stance, and each time their blades connected, Purin's sparked an electrical wave up and down its length. The captain smiled broadly, clearly enjoying his advantage, no doubt an enchantment by the devious dwarf.

Purin pressed harder, and Drystan, falling back with each assault, knew he was in serious trouble. Even the slightest contact from the bewitched sword might well cause enough injury to overcome him. There was no doubt that Drystan was the better swordsman, but with his lightning-charged blade, the odds were now more evenly matched. Still, Drystan had the additional advantage of strength and endurance thanks to the Liafal Stone, and soon he could see Purin begin to tire.

"Come on, Purin," Drystan taunted. "Can't you hit me once with that pretty toy you call a sword? Or is it just for decoration?"

Purin came on again with a flurry of strikes that sent electrical sparks flying in every direction. Drystan calmly parried and deflected each blow, leaving Purin breathing heavily and slowing the onslaught. This was his moment.

Deliberately leaving his center open, he knew Purin couldn't resist a thrust for his heart. The tip of his blade cut through the fabric of Drystan's tunic and scarcely broke his skin. Worse than the scant cut, he felt the expected charge of electricity course through his torso. Barely able to keep his footing, he slapped the pommel of Purin's sword with the flat of his blade, causing the captain to lose his grip and drop it to the floor. Then Purin's eyes went wide as Drystan's long blade slipped under his leather breast guard and deep into his chest cavity.

"Scream if you like," Drystan whispered. "Anyone who hears will not care that it is you."

Purin never got the chance. With a second thrust, the blade penetrated deeper into his sagging frame. Drystan held the captain's body suspended for just a moment before allowing him to collapse on the floor, twitching from the violence done to him. Drystan bent over and cleaned his bloody sword on Purin's ermine-trimmed cloak, his knees still shaking from the electricity he had absorbed. The front of his tunic showed blackened trails where it touched him, but there was no blood, with the wound instantly cauterized.

Carefully, he picked up the enchanted sword by the pommel, sheathed it in Purin's scabbard, and strapped it around his own waist. "This might come in handy," he said to himself, while at the same time hoping he didn't manage to kill himself with it.

It was time for him to go find Eselt. He stepped over Purin's body to retrieve his bags, then put up the hood of his cloak and made his way toward the southern gate. The southern gate! Had he not run into Purin, he would have been watching the northern gate, never expecting that they would take the southern route into Eriu.

~~~

The next night Drystan was lying atop a hill with a view of the southern gate of Tintagel illuminated by a dozen torches. He wasn't close enough that he could recognize the people passing through the entry but the unusual occurrence of a guarded carriage, especially after dark, would be easy to spot.

An hour passed, then another. Drystan was growing tired and feared he might doze off until, an hour after midnight, a small black carriage rolled through the gate pulled by four horses. There were two men driving the carriage and four riding on horses close by—two in the front and two bringing up the rear. They were all wearing the uniforms of the regular guard and carried no pennants with house colors. Most importantly, Eselt was in that carriage. He could sense it.

Drystan was familiar with the route they would take on the coastal road around the south end of Lake Virtue before turning north along the eastern edge of Loch Angu. Just before the forest on the border with Eriu, the north road and the south road from Tintagel would merge into one all the way to Teamhrach. They wouldn't leave this road until they reached the Kenno-windo Mountain Range. That was where the Leprechauns would be expecting them, and that was where Eselt would be handed over, since the carriage was not built to travel off the road. He calculated the distance around the lake and to the mountains at about ninety leagues. At the pace the carriage would be moving, that would give him about ten days to free her. Once the Leprechauns had her, it would be too late.

He mounted and followed the guarded carriage at a safe distance from beyond the hills on their right flank, checking on their movement from time to time so as not to overtake them too quickly. Purin's words about the men escorting his lover weighed on his mind. If what he said about them were true, then Drystan would be facing them sooner rather than later. That was just fine with him.

They traveled all of that night and the next day, only resting the horses when needed, before setting camp the second evening. They moved off the road far enough not to be noticed by anyone that passed by, built a fire, and erected small tents. Drystan watched them closely from just over the rise of a nearby hill. Then, he caught his breath as Eselt was allowed to exit the carriage for the first time since they had departed Tintagel. She was lovely as ever, even as she looked tired and sad. She was alone, with none of her attendants to keep her hair brushed or her blue dress pressed, but none of that mattered to Drystan. He thought she would be beautiful wearing a sack and with nettles in her hair.

A guard grabbed her roughly and pushed her onto the loose dirt near the fire, slamming a wooden stake into the ground next to her. He tied one end of a short rope to the stake and the other end around Eselt's neck. The other guards just laughed at the spectacle while they unpacked the bags containing pots and provisions from the back of the carriage. It was all Drystan could do to keep himself from rushing into their camp right then and cutting them all down. He reminded himself to stay calm, observe, and take the measure of his adversary.

When they were done, one of the guards placed the packaged

supplies near Eselt and demanded that she prepare food for them. She looked around uncertainly, then slowly started to boil water and cook a light stew. In the meantime, the men brought down a keg of ale and started to drink heavily. Before long their true natures began to reveal themselves, and Drystan could make out portions of their relentless stream of unseemly jokes and remarks directed at Eselt.

The situation was becoming dangerous, and Drystan was by the moment becoming more and more alarmed watching the men continue to drink and leer inappropriately at his beautiful Eselt. Leaving his horse tied up and out of sight, he quietly moved closer to the camp—close enough that he could hear their words clearly, and to his ears, their intent was becoming obvious. No matter the danger to himself, he would let no harm come to her.

Knowing where this was going, Drystan retreated back to his horse and donned his leather cuirass, greaves, and gauntlets. Then he crawled back up the hill where he could continue to watch the camp without being seen. He hoped she would be safe until the guards were drunk and went to sleep so he could come upon them unaware and steal her away in the darkness. This wouldn't end without bloodshed, he silently predicted.

Eselt finally completed the stew and put ladles of it in bowls that she served to each man. After the stew cooled enough to eat, one of the guards took a drink from the bowl with a loud slurp and then immediately spit it on the ground.

In a rage, he stood and screamed at Eselt, "Are you trying to poison us? What woman can't make a decent stew?" He grabbed Eselt and pulled her close. "Well maybe you're better at being a whore!" He jerked her head back by her hair and attempted to force a kiss on her. Breaking from his grasp, she screamed and tried to run, only to be brought to the ground by the length of rope around her neck. The men laughed while several began to remove their boots and armor.

Drystan was filled with rage like he had never felt before in his life. Why his uncle would ever have men like these in his service, he could not guess, unless Captain Purin recruited them specifically for this task. It was also likely that whoever escorted Eselt to the Leprechauns were as doomed as she was and never expected to return. Drystan could not contemplate the reasons why these men were the way they were, only that they would die tonight.

Trotting quickly down the hill to the edge of their camp, he arrived just as the guard grabbed Eselt a second time. He stood above her, laughing maliciously and holding her arm while she cried and struggled to get away from him.

"Release her now, or every soul here will die." Drystan's voice was hard with barely controlled rage.

"Look here, fellas," the one holding Eselt's arm snorted. "A fool has come to die for a whore. Do you think you're going to kill us all, boy? I don't see anyone else with you."

The other men laughed nervously, each in various stages of undress and fumbling for a sword or ax. The guard that held Eselt released her to the ground and walked confidently toward Drystan, his sword in hand. And Eselt, no longer paralyzed by her terror, looked for the first time in many days on her lover's face. "Drystan!" she screamed in disbelief.

"Drystan?" The guard stopped. "You're the Temple Knight Drystan? Word was you died going over the walls into the lake. No one could have survived that fall."

"Yet I am here, or is it my ghost who brings your death?"

He could sense the fear in the other guards hesitantly backing away. Drystan was a well-known figure in Tintagel, and everyone knew he was one of the finest swordsmen in the kingdom. Most recently, his triumph over the great Eriu knight Sir Murhalt only reinforced that reputation. Now he was considered a disgraced and fallen Temple Knight who died trying to escape the duke's justice.

Maybe it was the seduction of the fame that the guard who stood between him and Eselt would receive if he brought back the head of Drystan, or maybe it was just the ale that gave him courage—whatever the motivation, he charged Drystan, sword held high. Stepping into the charge, Drystan thrust his longsword straight into the man's neck, and the foolish guard impaled himself with the force of his own weight. Drystan held the man on his feet for a moment, staring into the dying man's eyes until there was no life, before casually dropping him to the ground.

The remaining five guards immediately ran toward the carriage or their mounts. Two of the guards never made it to their destination, cut down as they ran. Another Drystan disemboweled while he sat in his saddle, and the last two spurred their horses to flight. Pulling the dead man off his horse, Drystan gave chase. Quickly he caught up with the first one, severing his arm from his body. That one would bleed out, he thought, and he continued in pursuit of the last guard.

The fool stayed on the road leading back toward Tintagel, leagues away, instead of trying to lose Drystan in the rolling terrain. He would never make it. Pulling up close, Drystan cleaved the man's skull, dropping him from his saddle. On his way back, Drystan collected the guards' horses and passed the man with the severed arm, who stared up at the night sky and breathed rapidly.

"It won't be long now," Drystan told him without slowing. He had to get back to Eselt.

When he arrived back at the camp, Eselt apparently found a sword and cut herself free of the rope. Drystan was elated at the sight of her unharmed and free. He jumped off his horse and rushed to her, and they held each other tightly.

"I thought you were dead!" she sobbed, gasping between tears of joy.

"How could I die and leave you in the clutches of these barbarians?" he laughed.

"They were taking me to the Leprechauns, and I felt so helpless," she said with a shudder.

"There is nothing left to fear, my love. We will never be apart again. I promise."

She looked him in the eyes, serious and unwavering. "Give me your long-blade dagger, my love."

He was confused about what she was asking. "My long-blade? Is there something you need help with?"

"Just give it to me, please. I will never be helpless again."

He understood then. Even if it was symbolic, she would carry a weapon and feel a little more secure.

He handed over his dagger in its scabbard. "When you're ready, I'll teach you how to use it."

She stood on her tiptoes and kissed him on the cheek. "What makes you think I don't know already?"

He laughed at that, but not too much. The wicked smile on her face left him wondering.

Clearing the camp of the dead, they spent the night in each other's arms. After what seemed a lifetime of hiding and running, they were finally free to be together. With any luck, it would be concluded that Eselt was lost to bandits, or worse, and they would now both be presumed dead as far as the rest of the world knew. As of tonight, they could be anyone they chose to be.

CHAPTER 20

Illusions

I always wanted to get drunk with Leprechauns—at least that was a small dream of mine. I could imagine their feast hall teaming with the little buggers—dancing on the tables, jumping among the rafters, playing tricks like exploding mugs and sending fountains of mead bursting from barrels. But invariably I fear I would only wake up to find that it was all an illusion and I had been robbed of everything down to my smallclothes!

Wodanaz the Wanderer

She is heading straight into the valley," Wodanaz commented.

Myrllin shifted and dismounted from Sleipnir. "We better walk from here."

Wodanaz also dismounted, and with the flick of his wrist, Sleipnir disappeared in a pillar of smoke. They walked on toward the valley, and already the rarely traveled road turned into something resembling a trail. The trees formed a canopy that blacked out much of the sunlight, leaving them in a hazy twilight that almost felt otherworldly. Oddly, there were no sounds of nature in the valley, and even had there been, they would have seemed contrived. Rather, there was an eerie silence and a vague sense of being watched that pervaded the stillness of the wood.

Myrllin was sure of what it was—he recognized the weaves of magic around them—and he also knew that he could dispel the illusion at any time he chose to. For the present, he decided not to and preferred to let whatever was happening to continue without his interference. The creatures that lived here could be very dangerous if underestimated, and as a rule, Myrllin never underestimated anyone or anything.

He glanced over at Wodanaz. "They will test us soon. Are you prepared?" he quietly asked.

"I have been prepared since a league before I dismissed Sleipnir." He stamped his ordinary-looking staff on the ground, causing it to briefly flicker into the shape of a spear and then back. Only Myrllin, or one with his rare ability to see the forms of magic, could appreciate the staff for what it was, and he smiled knowingly.

Wodanaz and his wondrous toys, Myrllin thought with a small sigh of envy. His own staff was just a stick, although it could take the form of different magically conjured entities, like a venomous snake or a steel sword. It was a great tool, but still just a thing. Whatever the staff was that Wodanaz carried, Myrllin was sure it was far more than a simple spear hidden by an illusion.

As much as they were alike, he and Wodanaz were different in more than a few respects. Myrllin was much stronger in the arts of magic, and he possessed the power of Seeing the environment around him as it truly existed. Most profoundly, Myrllin often had visions during his hibernations that foretold of future events. Wodanaz, on the other hand, was more dependent upon the magical artifacts that he carried to wield the full potential of his power. It was not that Wodanaz's capability was any less than Myrllin's own; it was about the way he accessed his power and his ability to magnify it by channeling through these artifacts. Not only that, his brother was far stronger physically, with a powerful build and the unnatural strength of fifty men. More than all of that, the one thing he envied above everything was Wodanaz's incredible charisma. Whether he sang, recited poetry, or simply spoke, men and women alike hung on his every word. He often joked that he could travel the world without a copper in his pouch and still live in the lap of luxury the whole way.

A strange laugh echoed through the forest around them, from what direction, it was impossible to say. Myrllin didn't even bother looking around for the source of the sound. There was nothing to see except what the watchers wanted them to see. Myrllin knew their strategy—the little monsters were hiding behind their illusions and trying to strike fear into them, eventually expecting them to panic and run. That's when the Leprechauns really had their fun, tormenting their prey with fear and illusions for days on end until they died from exhaustion.

"Do you think this Aja controls the creatures that live here?" Wodanaz asked.

Myrllin shook his head, "I don't think she has that kind of power, although she has probably warned them that we are dangerous and a threat to them in some way."

"Why do you think they would allow her in their territory to begin with?"

"I would guess that even before the demon took her mind and body, she was well known here. I suppose that even Leprechauns get sick or injured once in a while too. She may be one of the few outsiders welcome in their valley. I doubt they know what she is now."

Wodanaz scoffed, "Until she kills one with her poisons or alters the life of another with her love potions."

"The Chaos Demon is limited to the talents of its host," Myrllin agreed.

Myrllin gazed nonchalantly at their surroundings. With his Inner Eye, he could see through the illusion presented to them. On the surface, the valley was still a hazy, canopied forest that felt dangerous and foreboding with dark shadows that were cast from no logical direction. In reality, it was a bright, thickly wooded landscape with green patches of lush grass and gentle forested slopes ascending to high hills on each side in the distance. The narrow entrance to the valley would have been considered beautiful scenery under normal conditions. And there was movement as more and more Leprechauns shadowed the brothers' course behind the illusion on each side of the path they followed.

"The creatures are becoming frustrated that we are not succumbing to their fear tactics. I believe they will be upon us soon. When they attack, I will lift the veil of their illusions and the Leprechauns will be visible to you. Try not to kill too many, brother. Once they realize they are outmatched and visible to us, they will flee."

Wodanaz chuckled. "If they weren't about to try and kill us, I'd feel sorry for the little bastards."

Myrllin spoke a few arcane words and made a quick swirling motion with his hand. Immediately the two of them were surrounded by a fast-moving current of air that made no sound and was invisible except for the occasional draft that lightly ruffled a robe or sleeve as it moved with them.

Keeping watch on the diminutive creatures from the corners of his eyes, Myrllin was struck by their appearance. Of course, he had read much about them and heard the stories traditionally told in taverns for entertainment. Even his brother had numerous songs and narratives that he would recount to attentive crowds, most of which involved large volumes of wine and mead. In the stories, the Leprechauns were generally depicted as mischievous tricksters that would steal your gold and convince you to trade your valuables for conjured illusions. The truth was that they were thieves and would scavenge what they could from the fringes of populations.

Livestock, food stores, textiles, and anything else of value they could get their hands on, often causing illusory chaos as a distraction. They even went as far as luring foreign ships to the western shores of Loch Angu with their illusions of beautiful Nymphs and Mermaids, only to wreck the doomed sailors on its rocky coastline and plunder the remains.

The darkest side of their nature was the abductions of female humans, mostly young women, who they would enslave and mate with. The offspring of these couplings were a kind of Halfling that lived to serve the Leprechauns in the valley where they lived. There was no account of how Leprechauns reproduced themselves, although the ancient Eriu poet Toghda speculated that they were grown from a magical root that produced a plant with a pod from which they were later hatched. Myrllin was sure they were another creation of the Tuatha De that ran amuck, but he had never come across a record of it.

There were about twenty of them who came together on either side of the trail they walked. Some carried spears, others bows, and they all had a long dagger they held like a sword. Other than the weapons they carried, they hardly appeared very threatening at all. Only about the height to a man's waist, they looked very human—dressed in fine trousers, tunics, and short overcoats—except that their ears were pointed on top and their noses were long and bulbous. Most wore long beards and mustaches of red or blond coloration and a hat that was tipped or with a brim. Their disposition was intense and greedy, and Myrllin knew any one of them would happily cut the brothers' throats just to find out what they carried in their pockets and never feel a bit of remorse over it.

The little men raised their bows, and Myrllin put a hand on Wodanaz to give warning just before they released. Arrows and spears sped in from point-blank range and would have killed them instantly if it wasn't for the column of air that surrounded the two of them. The projectiles bounced off harmlessly just as Myrllin shouted a word and clapped his hands. The illusion of the hazy forest disappeared, revealing the Leprechauns, staring and stunned. Wodanaz did not waste a second and threw his spear at one nearby. It went through the creature and then sped into another and another, achieving impossible turns at high speed before returning to his hand.

Myrllin worked the opposite side of the trail, felling three more with a blast of electricity from his hands, leaving them charred and twitching on the ground where they had stood. Within seconds, half their number was dead, and the rest were sent running away in a wild panic.

"Well, that was quick. You think they will come back?" Wodanaz was wiping the blade of his spear on one of the dead Leprechaun's coat.

"I think that depends how close we get to their village or lair. The

Leprechauns thought so little of us that they did not use their magic when they attacked other than the environmental illusions. I doubt they will make the same mistake twice."

Myrllin looked at the spear in his brother's hand, no longer hidden by the illusion of a staff. "Is that new?"

Wodanaz lifted the spear proudly. "I call it *Gungnir*, from the Vikja word meaning 'it turns.' The Dvergr Dwarfs crafted it for me a decade or so ago. It's come in handy a few times."

"It made a mess of those Leprechauns, I'll give you that."

"And a song." Wodanaz winked. "I'll have a song about this adventure before we're done!"

Myrllin laughed. "So you will, brother. Now let's find this Aja and get it over with so we can go home."

With the illusion of their surroundings dispelled, the sun illuminated the wooded area immediately around them and well along the trail they followed. Nothing stirred. Still, Myrllin could sense . . . something. It was a stirring of magic, more powerful than what he would expect from Leprechauns, and he suspected Aja must be nearby. Then there was movement. Something far down the trail rippled toward them, or bobbed, he wasn't sure from a distance, and it was moving fast.

"Something is coming, brother."

"I see them," replied Wodanaz.

"Them?"

"Dozens, maybe a hundred of them. They look like the Halflings you were describing earlier. Definitely not Leprechauns."

Myrllin could see them clearly now. "They are charging us?"

He couldn't believe the Leprechauns would send a small horde of Halflings to assault them. It must be a ruse or a distraction. Myrllin sent his senses out in every direction, expecting an ambush.

Wodanaz spoke again, "I don't think they are charging, I think they are running from something."

Looking back down the trail, Myrllin could see the trees moving behind the onrushing Halflings. They appeared odd, like something big was trying to break through behind them. Except it was the trees themselves that were moving forward.

The trees . . .

"Those are Tree Guardians, Wodanaz!" Myrllin shouted. "Aja must control them. Get off the trail and let the Halflings pass."

Moments later the Halflings were streaming by them in terror, and none of them paid any attention to Myrllin and Wodanaz standing off the trail as they passed.

Three Tree Guardians were close on their heels, stomping forward in long, slow strides that covered a great distance with each step. The towering oaks must have been ten times the height of an average man, with thick branches for arms and a massive split trunk for legs. Myrllin had seen them before in Avalon, guarding the forests of the Elves, but never moving aggressively as they were now.

"Take the one on the left," Wodanaz shouted, "until you can help me with these two!"

Myrllin moved to the left side of the trail to intercept the Tree Guardian on that side. The trio would be upon them in moments. Myrllin watched as, back where Wodanaz stood, he began to grow. Larger and larger he grew until he was easily the size of the Tree Guardians, immediately attracting their attention. All three angled toward their new target. None noticed Myrllin yet.

Taking advantage of the oversight, Myrllin cast a shield on himself and then slammed the base of his staff into the ground in front of him. A crack formed in the earth and ran away from him at an angle that would intercept the last Tree Guardian if he timed it right.

He had.

By the time the crack in the ground ran in front of the monster, it was wide enough to trap one of its knobby legs, causing it to fall forward flat on the ground. Myrllin ran toward the fallen Tree Guardian, jumping on its back and thrusting his shifting staff, now transformed into a sword, deep into the bark-like flesh between what he supposed was its shoulder blades.

Nothing.

The Tree Guardian continued to struggle to remove its leg from the fissure in the earth and stand up. It didn't seem to notice Myrllin on its back any more than it would have been bothered by a chipmunk. The enchanted blade had encountered no vitals, and there was no blood, refuting Myrllin's assumption that the terror had a humanoid anatomy under its thick bark skin.

Damn, thought Myrllin. He couldn't fight this like a living thing. He would have to fight it as an enchanted thing. Glancing back over his shoulder, he saw Wodanaz fighting off the other two Tree Guardians with his giant spear, spinning it like a staff, to counter the pummeling of their branches. Distracted for only a second, Myrllin was hit by an unknown force from behind, knocking him off the back of the Tree Guardian and toppling him to the leafy ground. Quickly regaining his feet, he was just able to avoid another bolt of energy coming from somewhere near the tree line.

It was Aja.

But this was not Aja, the old woman healer. It was something corrupted and altered . . . changed. Still in vaguely human form, her skin was completely black, with piercing green eyes that glowed from their sockets and giant antlers that protruded from her head. She was a corruption of druid magic, an abomination of nature twisted by the demon inside her. And right now, she was wholly determined to make an end of Myrllin with waves of dark energy that exploded around his magical shield.

Rolling to the side to avoid the crush from the Tree Guardian's huge brachy arm, Myrllin sent balls of fire into the leafy portions of the Tree Guardian's head, igniting it in a burst of flame. Despite the blaze, it continued struggling to free itself from the fissure, while Myrllin moved around it trying to keep its mass between him and the slow approach of Aja.

Out of her line of sight for the moment, Myrllin turned and sent balls of fire into the Tree Guardians Wodanaz was fending off. Very quickly, they too caught flame. Even so, they did not break off their mindlessly determined assault either. His brother stood steady against them releasing a stream of curses with every blow he struck. Split and broken branches hung uselessly from both Guardians, but they had many limbs yet, and Wodanaz's robes were ripped and torn in multiple areas showing the stain of blood that crept from beneath the fabric.

Myrllin first had to deal with Aja, or they would be lost. Running back around the burning Tree Guardian on the ground, he got clipped by its branchy arm, which sent him tumbling back onto the trail in front of Aja. Rising to stand, he felt his legs and arms suddenly seized by thick roots and vines that sprouted from the ground. He couldn't move, and the grappling vegetation rapidly climbed up his body, twisting around his torso and constricting his breathing almost until his chest could no longer rise. *Well done*, he thought, genuinely impressed by Aja's inventiveness.

"Mer-lin," the thing that was Aja rumbled. "You have found me once again."

While he struggled to take in air, Myrllin's voice sounded shriller to his ears than usual. "It seems fate grants me fortune once again."

"Maybe not so fortunate as last time, Mer-lin." It spoke from somewhere nearby, probably still near the tree line. Myrllin couldn't see with the thrashing of the Tree Guardian and the smoke billowing from its leafy head and torso. Soon it would be fully engulfed in flames.

"Has the High King sent you to punish Aja for giving his daughter what she truly desired?" It was closer now, but still out of his view.

Myrllin was confused by the question. "The medicine you gave her in the village of Sundy had no ill effect on her or the boy. If you were expecting to assassinate her, you failed."

The Aja creature barked a laugh, "If I wished her dead, she would have been dead. No, Mer-lin. I only opened her heart to the boy and his to her. An amusing paradox given the purpose of their journey."

Suddenly so much made sense—the obvious flirtations, the magical auras around the two of them, Drystan's behavior at the wedding. "You gave them a love potion," he stated flatly.

Aja laughed with high-pitched screeching laughter that assaulted Myrllin's ears mercilessly. "Did she still marry the one she was intended for?"

"Yes." Myrllin was busy calculating his best escape options and needed to keep her talking for a few more moments while he made mental preparations. "However, I doubt she will be married much longer from the way the boy looks at her."

"Too bad you will not live to see the results of my influence, Merlin. I'm sure it will be quite amusing." The roots quickly tightened, ceasing Myrllin's ability to take another breath entirely.

With the last bit of air in his lungs, he had one final breath, and with its expulsion, he shouted a word. His staff grew cold, and all the roots and vines binding him immediately froze where they touched his body. It happened in a second, and Myrllin burst forth from the fragile mass, sending shards of brittle foliage in every direction, freeing himself.

Aja roared, and more dark energy followed. Myrllin dove behind a stand of trees to avoid it. Aja was visible now and much closer than before. Close enough. Still enshrouded by the frosty air he created, he quickly conjured a breath of powerful wind and spoke a charm with its release that sent a fierce blast of frozen death upon the figure of Aja just as she rounded the shrubbery to face him.

Whatever she had planned for him, she only had time to throw her arms up protectively in front of her antlered head. It was the last motion she would ever make. The blast of freezing air that enveloped her froze her solid in less time than the flutter of a bee's wing.

"That's how it's done," Myrllin snickered, and then panic nearly took him when he remembered Wodanaz was still facing two of the Tree Guardians.

Frantically Myrllin found clear air away from the smoke to see Wodanaz with one of the burning Tree Guardians flailing uselessly, pinned to the earth under the brother's great spear, while he methodically tore the branches off the other with his bare hands. The third Tree Guardian never could free its leg from the crevasse Myrllin created, and it burned unmoving where it lay.

"You need any help, Wodanaz?" Myrllin called up to his brother.

"Nah, just stripping this log. Shouldn't be but a minute or two."

Turning back to Aja, Myrllin took his staff and with one mighty swipe smashed the frozen thing to pieces. Then he waited for the Chaos Demon to emerge from its dead host. At first, a few wispy strands of thick black smoke like tendrils rose from the loose pile of frozen pieces that was Aja's remains. Then they slowly coalesced into a dense ball of the blackest evil that hovered briefly above what was left of the body of its host. Myrllin knew this was when it was most vulnerable, and with quick action, he captured the demon in a magic bubble and took it in hand. This one wouldn't be getting away again, he thought.

Wodanaz, back to his normal size, walked up to him holding his spear. Lashes and scratches covered his face and exposed arms while torn ribbons of his blood-stained robe hung freely all around him. Behind him, a large bonfire roared with the forms of his two adversaries now no more than a pile of burning leaves and branches.

"Are you OK, brother?" Myrllin asked with some concern.

Wodanaz ran his hand through his disheveled hair. "Well enough, brother," he replied with a smile. "They messed up my hair a bit, though. Oh, and thanks for the fire. I don't know why I didn't think of that."

Myrllin held up the bubble containing the angry Chaos Demon writhing inside and smiled back. "Here's the demon, and down there is what's left of Aja. I guess we're done here."

"I suppose the Leprechauns won't trouble us any further." Wodanaz tapped one of the shards that were Aja with the butt of his spear. It clinked like glass.

Myrllin snorted. "I would be surprised if there were one within a league of us. By the way, do you remember Drystan, the duke's adopted son I told you about with the strange auras around him that strangely matched the auras around Duchess Eselt?"

Wodanaz nodded. "I always take your word for those things, brother. You know I can't see the auras."

"Apparently the 'medicine' Aja administered to Eselt in Sundy was actually an enchanted potion that put some kind of a love geas over the two of them."

"Interesting. Rather than simply poison Eselt, the Chaos Demon sowed chaos. Fitting, I suppose. Are you going to do something about it?"

Myrllin shook his head thoughtfully. "I don't know. Imagine the chaos this will cause in Tintagel if it hasn't already."

"So, what now for you?"

Myrllin shrugged and held up the orb with the entrapped Chaos Demon. "I'll make my way to the Emerald Isle and drop this thing into the Ourea first. Then I have to oversee a new bloodline in Lyonesse."

"The Ourea? The volcano in the Atlas Mountain Range?" Wodanez asked with some surprise. "Why do you have to take it there?"

Myrllin shrugged again. "In the purgatory of its hellish depths is supposed to be a one-way portal into the Infernal Planes, according to Dhroghan."

"Father would know, I suppose." Wodanaz tapped on the edge of the magic bubble, causing the black form inside to shift violently. "Is there no way to just kill it?"

"Not that I know of." Myrllin absently kicked at the frozen shards of Aja on the ground. "If Dhroghan knew, he never included it in the stories he told when we were little."

"Bah, I never paid attention to those stories of his. He and the rest of the Tuatha De Blood were never much of a family to us." Wodanaz spat on the ground in disgust. "Just because he showed up every couple of years with stories to tell didn't make him much of a father. The only thing he and the Blood ever gave us worth anything before he died was Hy Brasil, and they probably just wanted to move us far away so they wouldn't have to listen to your damn prophecies."

Myrllin nodded in agreement. "Even the Tuatha De didn't want to hear about their eventual demise. The island was better for Mother anyway. Nymphs like to be near water, and not the frozen kind in Falias."

"And what's this about this bloodline in Lyonesse? Are you playing kingmaker again?" Wodanaz chided.

"I don't know. He hasn't been born yet, but he will be soon enough."

Wodanaz shook his head. "So many mysteries with you, Myrllin. I think I will just go spend some time with the Vikja and teach them a few more songs to sing about me."

CHAPTER 21

Wizards

It was moments before dawn, and Drystan was up before the first rays of light crested the horizon. To his surprise, Eselt awoke with him and was eager to be away from the camp where they buried six soldiers of the Duke's Guard the night before. It was an exciting time as well, for it would be the first day that they would face a new life free from any constraints or limitations, expressing their love for each other openly and without fear. Of course, they would have to stay away from Lyonesse and Eriu for at least enough time that no one would recognize them if they returned, and that could be forever.

For long hours into the previous night, they discussed their newfound freedom. Eselt expressed her astonishment and fear at what he had gone through to find her, and Drystan told her how much he admired her strength to endure her captivity and the terror that awaited her among the Leprechauns. They agreed that their destinies had been guided by the benevolent hands of the Sister Goddesses, Eriu and Sunna, because of the pure love that they shared and dedication to each other that never wavered, even in their darkest hours.

They decided they would travel first to Ys and then somewhere beyond where they could live in peace and without fear of being recognized. With nine horses, a fine carriage, and enough supplies for several weeks, they were optimistic that they could overcome any challenge as long as they were together.

"What about Teamhrach, love?" Drystan asked. "Would your father protect us or turn us away?"

Eselt's eyes dimmed with sadness at his suggestion. "He would accept me back and likely send me to the druids to live out the rest of my days unseen and unheard. As for you, the light of my heart, he would likely remove your head."

"That sounds severe, don't you think? Surely, he would understand how much we love each other and allow his baby daughter happiness. He has nothing to gain from either of us politically." Drystan paced as he spoke. "And what of your mother? Wouldn't she want only the best for you?"

"You don't understand my father, Drystan." She stood from the water barrel where she was sitting. "He is a good man but also very political. Remember, he is the High King of Eriu, and only through strength and unity does he maintain that position and the safety of our family. To him, I am an embarrassment, especially after what happened with Sir Murhalt. The knight's mother, Queen Gwyr of DunDwai, is very likely looking for any reason to take revenge on our family now. As for you," she stopped in front of him and took his hands, "he would execute you on principle. From the High King's perspective, you have put him in a position of weakness within Eriu and caused an irrevocable rift with his closest trading partner and ally, Tintagel. And we can't forget that Duke Maruk was sending me into exile with the Leprechauns. Would anyone truly believe that would be a better fate than death? As a father, he would see you as the cause of all that as well and use you to take retribution on the duke for his decision. It will be better if everyone concerned thinks us dead."

She kissed him lightly on his cheek while Drystan stared into the dense morning fog that surrounded their encampment. He looked at her, then and put his arms around her waist. "You sound like your father." He smiled. "How impressive you would have been in the political circles of Eriu, or Lyonesse, for that matter."

"I am the youngest of my siblings. None of my older sisters wanted to play dolls, so I would sit and listen to their 'grown-up' conversations every day, and our father often considers my oldest sisters, Mairwen and Gwynn, among his closest advisors."

Eselt was shivering in the cool air of the morning, prompting Drystan to set about restarting the fire that burned out overnight. "Then it appears we need to decide which route would be the safest to take us to Ys."

They discussed their options while preparing a light porridge for breakfast and warmed themselves over the low flames of the small campfire. If they continued west, it would take them into the Valley of the Leprechauns. That was not a good option. They could go north and around the eastern slopes of the Kenno-windo Mountain Range to the port of Kenno and take a trade ship to Ys, but that route would force them to skirt Teamhrach, where Eselt was well-known and might be recognized. The most direct route would be south back the way they had come along the coastal road adjacent to Loch Angu and then on to Ys, but that was also a dangerous route considering that anyone on that road would surely recognize them given the recent events in Tintagel. That left the lane east to Oswalt, then a riverboat to Bours, and finally through the Wilds along the southern coast of the Lake of Mists before they reached Ys. Sunna only knew the horrors they might encounter that way. It would be a tremendous risk no matter what they decided.

For now, they focused on getting everything cleaned and packed on the carriage and horses. The thick fog in the hills that morning still obscured the view beyond the camp and distorted the sounds they made. Even though they were out of sight of the road, Drystan cautioned Eselt to avoid attracting any attention by not making too much noise. Not that they had heard a single cart or horse during the night anyway.

Everything was nearly packed and put away when Drystan noticed what looked like the outline of a small boulder at the edge of the camp in the fog. It was odd that he had not seen it before. Then to his surprise, it shifted left to right as if it might turn over. He turned to face it and took a step forward when it expanded upward into the form of a short, stocky man in gray robes and a travel cloak. He was a Dvergr dwarf, the same one who made his hands stick to the door in Eselt's chamber the night they were captured.

Heat rose inside Drystan as he strode forward. "What are you doing here, dwarf? Do you intend to avenge your master? You would have to face me on a fair field this time."

The dwarf chuckled, a sound like gravel rolling over rocks. "Ain't no masta I care 'bout, human. But yer head got-ta be worth-a coin 'r two."

He thrust his hands forward, and wind as forceful as any gale Drystan ever encountered hit him right in the chest, sending him tumbling backward several feet. Eselt noticed the commotion from near the carriage and came running over to him.

"What's happening?" she cried, as yet not noticing the dwarf slowly approaching.

Drystan gestured with his sword as he got back on his feet. "We have a visitor. Go back over by the carriage, love. I'll take care of this."

Eselt ran over to huddle behind a barrel attached to the rear of the carriage.

The dwarf continued toward Drystan yet called over to Eselt, "I be wit-ya shortly, gerl, ta bend-ya over-da barrel der!" He laughed harshly.

Drystan moved forward carefully, not sure what the overconfident dwarf planned for him next. He carried no weapon, although a wizard wouldn't need one. Drystan would have to get close enough to strike, and so he began to angle forward slowly. The dwarf's hand snaked out from his robes again, propelling several bright sparks that looked like tiny stars racing toward Drystan. He avoided a few, but the others slammed into him, burning his flesh with intense heat where they struck, leaving smoking holes in his clothing. The dwarf just laughed raucously. The evil wretch of a man was toying with him.

Moving with haste now, Drystan charged. Only a few steps into it there was an intense flash combined with a loud boom like thunder that hit him like a club on the head. He was still running, but he was forced to slow, so dizzy that he might lose his balance, and the horrifying realization that he could no longer see or hear. Drystan stopped abruptly and desperately tried to clear his eyes. Nothing. All he could see was the vague outlines of light and shadow, and there was a growing buzz that filled his ears.

Drystan took a blow to his gut, taking his breath away, and he fell to the ground gasping. Seconds later there was a force on top of him, and he could feel the rock-crushing grip of the dwarf's hands around his neck. Drystan was strong, very strong, especially since the experience at the Liafal in Teamhrach, and it was all he could do to keep the powerful dwarf's grip from collapsing his windpipe. *Sunna, I can't die like this! Not after one brief moment of freedom! What of Eselt?* Drystan prayed.

Abruptly the dwarf's grip relaxed, and the impressive strength behind those massive hands dissipated. Drystan hurriedly pushed them away from his neck, rolling the heavy weight of the dwarf off of him at the same time. Then he righted himself onto all fours and coughed violently. By the time he could stand, his vision and hearing had slowly returned, and the first thing that he saw was the face of the dwarf, dead eyes staring back at Drystan. The dwarf's head was lying in a pool of blood, and the pointed end of a blade was sticking out the front of his neck. Behind him, he heard Eselt's heavy breathing, and when he fearfully looked around, he found her on her knees, panting as if she had just run a league uphill.

They looked at each other, and she smiled weakly. "I told you I would no longer be helpless."

Drystan coughed a choking, sputtering laugh. "It's a good thing, my love. You have saved us both."

"Looks like we came a minute too late," a deep voice rumbled from the edge of their camp.

"Or at just the right time," another added.

Rolling onto his feet, Drystan stood sword in hand. Behind him,

Eselt nonchalantly pulled the dagger from the thick neck of the dwarf and then crouched beside him. Absently, he was impressed with her form.

Facing them across the camp was too tall figures shrouded in the fog.

"Now that is a heroic picture!" one of them said.

"Agreed," said the other with a laugh. "Quite different from the last time we saw the two of them."

The two men emerged from the fog, and recognition flooded over Drystan.

"You are Wodanaz," he pointed to one, "and you, you are his brother . . ."

The one he indicated rolled his eyes. "Myrllin, my name is Myrllin."

"Right, Myrllin," Drystan repeated. "Are you hunting us as well?"

"Hunting you? Why would we be hunting you?" asked Wodanaz.

"For the same reason this one was." Drystan kicked the dwarf on the ground.

Myrllin looked at his brother. "Looks like we have missed a lot since we departed Tintagel."

Wodanaz looked closer at Eselt. "Aren't you the newly betrothed duchess?"

Eselt shrank back from his gaze, hiding behind Drystan.

"That's none of your affair," Drystan growled threateningly.

"Relax, young boar," Myrllin said soothingly. "We are not chasing you, and you are correct, it is none of our affair. I knew the two of you were in love when I saw you at the wedding, I just didn't expect things to move along so swiftly. You didn't kill the duke, did you?"

Drystan was hesitant. "No. We didn't kill anybody except for the men who brought Eselt to this place and attempted to rape her. And the dwarf here that came for his own reasons. Oh, and Purin. I killed Captain Purin because he was an evil man who murdered for the pleasure of it."

The two men just looked at each other in what Drystan could only interpret as amusement. Then Wodanaz pointed at the body on the ground.

"That dwarf was Firolin? He was quite adept in the magical arts for his kind. You were fortunate he was overconfident and reckless."

"Will you report that you've seen us when you return to Tintagel?" Drystan asked.

Myrllin huffed, "Report you? Hardly. We have our own agenda, and it certainly does not include returning to Tintagel to report you."

"Thank you," Eselt spoke up meekly.

"Where will you go now that there are no barriers to your spurious love affair?" Myrllin asked.

"To Ys," Drystan replied, sheathing his sword. He was a little confused by Myrllin's choice of words. "But we are unsure of the best route since we could be recognized, and there is danger in every way from here."

"It looks like you two can handle yourselves pretty well, but perhaps I can help a little." Myrllin handed a small bubble filled with swirling smoke to Wodanaz and bent to pick up two small stones.

He held one in each hand, deftly shaping each into perfectly round, smooth gray spheres as if they were putty. Then he produced two leather thongs from his pocket and threaded one sphere on each. He handed both to Drystan.

"When you wear these, you will look like no one special or memorable to anyone else and like yourselves to each other. Now you may travel any way you choose," he told them.

Wodanaz mumbled to his brother, "Show-off."

"Thank you, Myrllin. I will not forget your name again if we meet in the future." Drystan bowed.

Myrllin had a strange expression on his face as he replied, "Perhaps we will. One day."

Drystan gestured to the transparent sphere filled with black smoke that Wodanaz was holding. "May I ask what that is? It looks familiar to me."

Myrllin took the sphere from Wodanaz and held it up in the dim light. "This was what was in Aja."

"It looks much like the black wisps that escaped the body of a knight I defeated not long ago. I thought I imagined it at first, but the stark feeling of the purest evil seemed to reach out to me from it, and I assumed it was his dark soul."

Myrllin and Wodanaz looked at each other again, and looks of worry flashed across their faces.

"What is that thing, Myrllin?" Eselt asked.

"It is the essence of a Chaos Demon," Myrllin replied. "There are a few in this world that travel from host to host, spreading chaos and death where they can until they are banished back to the Infernal Planes where they came from."

The more Drystan studied the demon's essence, the more he was sure that it was the same thing that departed from Sir Murhalt. "How did it get here? Is it so easy for demons to come into our world?"

Myrllin shook his head. "It should be impossible. There was a time, many millennia ago, when there was a tear in the fabric of space and time in the only portal that separated our world from theirs. A few were able to escape before that tear was mended. Most were like these"—he shook the angry sphere—"but there were a few that got through that were much more powerful. For a time, they reigned on this and every other land when humanity was in its infancy and barely evolved beyond the animals they lived among. Then, the Tuatha De, along with the people you know as the Enlightened Ones, gathered the demons up and sealed them together in a Pithos for all eternity. Now, many centuries later, through trickery and manipulation, the Pithos has been shattered, releasing the demons back into the world, and it is up to the sentient beings of this planet to find a way to banish them for good."

"How can they be destroyed, Myrllin? You say that you captured that one from Aja. Will they not die when their host dies?" Drystan asked.

"It's not nearly as simple as that, I'm afraid. If the knight you killed was truly possessed by one, then it is in search of a new host. What I have gleaned from the ancient texts of the Tuatha De is that the demons must be excised by the holy representative of a just deity, such as a priest or druid, or their essence can be captured and thrown into the Ourea on the Emerald Isle. Although that last one is of no certainty since I only heard it in a story. I plan to test the theory with this one."

"That is terrifying." Eselt's voice wavered when she spoke. "You mentioned that there were other Demons even more powerful that have escaped?"

"Yes," Myrllin nodded. "There are a few that are so-called Greater Demons. They are far more powerful and capable of possessing stronger-willed beings such as king or high priest, even those practiced in the most powerful arts of magic. They are dangerous, and with the right host could wage wars or cause the death and suffering of countless innocents in a variety of ways."

"And they can be banished in the same manner as the Chaos Demons?" Drystan reached over to hold Eselt. She was shivering again, but not from the cold.

"We believe so. As powerful as the Greater Demons are, they have a particular weakness the Chaos Demons do not." Myrllin glanced over at Wodanaz. "They have names."

"Names?" Drystan echoed.

Myrllin smiled, but the smile did not reach his eyes. "That's right. If the Greater Demon's 'True Name' can be found out, then it can be banished back to the Infernal Planes by anyone with knowledge of it."

"How do we find these names, Myrllin?" Drystan wanted to know. "Is there a source or a list that contains them?"

"That is a good question, Drystan, that even I do not have the answer to at the moment."

Drystan found himself holding Eselt tightly to his side. "If I thought we lived in a frightening world before, it seems even more so after speaking with you today. Will you pursue the demons, Myrllin? Or you, Wodanaz?"

"After a fashion," Wodanaz replied. "I am a wanderer, and wherever I go, my eyes are always open to the world around me. If I come across one, I will deal with it the best I can."

"Hopefully, you will call me first, brother," Myrllin commented.

Wodanaz laughed. "One minute older and you think you have to look after me! I can take care of myself, you know."

Myrllin had what Drystan would describe as an annoyed look on his face, one Drystan might have seen on one of his older brothers in the past. "You know what we had to go through just to get this one." He held up the smoky sphere, and then he glanced at Drystan and Eselt. "We'll talk about this later."

Wodanaz continued to chuckle.

"I and others are on the lookout for them, but the world is vast, and they could be anywhere. Humanity is not the infant it was the last time the demons were free, and there are many heroes among us now who will find a way to overcome them. At least, that is my hope." Myrllin turned again to Wodanaz. "Shall we continue on, brother?"

Wodanaz nodded, and Drystan and Eselt said their goodbyes. Drystan watched as they walked back into the fog and could hear the last of their words carry back to him from a distance.

"Why didn't you remove the geas?" Wodanaz asked.

Myrllin replied, "Do you think I should have? After all they have been through, that would have been cruel. Besides, what's left for a fallen knight and a fallen princess if they don't have each other?" And they were gone.

Drystan wondered briefly what he meant, then promptly turned to Eselt and hugged her close. "We are free again, love!" He handed her one of the necklaces Myrllin created.

"So which route shall we take?" she asked.

"The safest one—north to Teamhrach and then over to Kenno. With luck, my vouchers will be good at the Knights Temple there, and we shall have enough gold to go anywhere and live comfortably for the rest of our lives!"

Eselt laughed with joy he had not heard from her for far too long. "Well, let's depart from this place before any more wizards show up!"

CHAPTER 22

To Be Alive

Purin opened his eyes, straining to focus on the figures standing over him in the dimly lit room.

A voice he did not recognize spoke from one of the figures, though he could not tell which one. "He's coming around, Your Grace."

"Very well, Greallán. How soon will he be able to speak?" That voice he *did* recognize. It was his lord, Duke Maruk, and it filled him with joy that the duke was there to look after him.

But why was he here, lying in his bed with the duke standing over him? He couldn't remember what had happened to him. Was he dreaming? His vision was getting better, and he could almost see the face of the man the duke addressed as Greallán when the man leaned close to put a cup of water to his lips. He was a druid Purin guessed from the earthy smell of his clothing, the brown hooded cloak, and a string of stones and feathers that hung around his neck. They were all still a blur, but Purin knew what they were.

Purin's lips were dry, and it was difficult to swallow even though his head was propped up on pillows. He adjusted his arms underneath himself and tried to sit up for a better angle on the cup, but pain like Purin had never experienced in his life coursed through his body. He heard someone in the room screaming like a wild animal, except through human lips. *Was it he that made that sound?* Then the druid was chanting words Purin could not understand and waving his arms over Purin's chest, and the pain began to subside to a tolerable level. Still, it was there, and he realized it must have been there all along, except that he had not noticed it.

"Be still," Greallán told him, "and try not to move. I can take only so much of your pain away. The rest is there to remind you that you are healing and not to do what you just did."

Purin tried to speak, "Healing . . ." It came out in a croaking whisper that he barely recognized as his own voice.

"Yes," the druid replied. "You have been gravely injured, but don't worry about that now."

The druid moved away from him and spoke to the duke. "He will need to drink more water and maybe a little warm broth before he will have the strength to speak more. I will send word as soon as he is ready."

"Don't coddle him like you do with most under your care, Greallán." The duke sounded very serious, and Purin worried that he displeased his lord in some way. "I need to know who did this to the captain of my guard soon rather than late." Then the duke leaned in close and placed his hand on Purin's own. "Get well quickly, noble Purin. I will return when we can speak."

Purin felt relief flood through him. His lord was not displeased. Then he watched as the duke's blurry figure retreated from the edges of his vision.

"Let's try this again." Greallán was over him again. "But this time, let me do the work. Just drink what you can slowly." Purin sipped a little of the water. "That's it," the druid coaxed him, "a little more."

Purin carefully sipped more of the cool liquid, and it felt good in his throat. "More," he tried to say, but he coughed when he said it, causing his chest to burn with intense pain again.

"Don't try to speak," chided the druid. "Just let the liquid do its work. In a few days or so, you will be singing like a songbird."

Purin wanted to laugh at that. He doubted that he had sung anything in his life, but he knew that the laughter would cause him more agony. *Why couldn't he remember what happened to him?* The druid finally pulled the cup away. He could have drunk more, much more, and thought to protest, but all the activity had caused him to become so tired. Even with the pain, he could barely keep his eyes open, and then he was drifting off, and dreaming of singing a happy melody he heard somewhere once when he was young . . .

Purin awoke with a start. He had no idea how long he was asleep. The room looked exactly as it had before. Greallán came into view and hovered over him again with a cup. He drank the liquid more easily this time, and he drank much more of it. Then he was falling asleep again, unable to force himself to stay awake.

The next time he woke, the druid was there again with more water and a little warm broth. It tasted wonderful. He doubted that he enjoyed anything in his life as much as he did that broth. He was feeling stronger, yet he resisted the urge to speak. He really didn't feel like it anyway. By the time he had drunk some water and swallowed a little bit of broth, he was so exhausted all he wanted to do was sleep. He didn't fight it anymore and let himself drift away again.

So it went, repeated over and over countless times. He never knew what time it was or for how many days he lay there sipping water and soup and sleeping. Once or twice he thought maybe the duke was there, but he wasn't sure. Always Greallán was there. Purin could see his tattooed face clearly now, heavily whiskered with gray and smiling. The Druid Stone hanging from his neck was almost mesmerizing with its swirling patterns that seemed to slowly shift and move on their own . . .

Purin began to dream while he slept. First vague images that didn't make sense, nor much that he could remember, and then they coalesced into vivid scenes that he recognized. He recognized not so much the people or what was happening in the dream, but that they were people and that things were happening, and those images tugged on his memories. He dreamed these dreams over and over as if they meant something: a young knight, a beautiful yellow-haired woman, and once in a while, the duke made an appearance. The young couple seemed to go together. They were always happy and in love until the duke was present, and then there was fear and darkness. It was all very confusing, but he knew that they hinted at real memories, and he awoke feeling concern for the beautiful young couple and sorrow for the duke. He could not explain it.

He awoke once, and the light was not as dim as it usually was. Glancing toward the source of the illumination, he observed Greallán peeking through a shutter out into the daylight beyond.

"Does it hurt your eyes?" the druid asked. He had not even turned to notice that Purin was awake. *How did he know?*

"No . . . it's . . . fine." His voice! It sounded rough and hesitant, but he knew it was his own.

The druid left the shutter open a little and walked over with a cup of water and a bowl of warm broth. "The duke wanted me to call him as soon as you spoke, but I think I will let you rest a little more just to be sure."

Purin nodded. His chest felt very sore, and he found it difficult to breathe after the few words he had spoken. He barely got through the broth before he was dosing off again.

The dreams came in a rush this time. The duke was there, and so was the pretty girl. He almost remembered her name. For some reason, it felt disrespectful to think of her as a girl. The name *Eselt* came to him, but there was more to it than that, he knew. She was a princess, still more, a duchess.

A duchess! That was it. But there had to be something else. A grim realization came over him—she was the duchess to Duke Maruk.

His wife.

A chill spark of understanding infused his body for just a second, but he was vague and unsure. What he was sure of was that something was wrong and he desperately wanted to break through the fog of comprehension and see clearly what eluded him. His dreams went on.

Purin watched images and short scenes flash by. The knight and the duchess picnicking on a grassy slope during a sunny day. The duke searching for something in a dark corridor. The knight and the duchess riding their horses and laughing in a colorful meadow of wildflowers. The duke brooding over his mead alone in his dimly lit office. The knight with the duchess, dancing in a brightly lit ballroom among others dressed in fanciful clothing. The duke standing on a watchtower looking over dark lands shadowed by storm clouds. The images were coming faster and faster, and his memories were returning with them. He felt pain through the dreams, in his chest, he knew his breathing was rapid, and the cold beads of sweat that ran down every nook and crease of his body were so real he could even trace them. Yet more of the images came until they finally stopped altogether, and he saw himself in a dark corridor facing the knight holding his sword. The knight was saying something, but he couldn't hear the words. His face looked so familiar now, and then like the rush and crashing of the violent waves off the cliffs of Tintagel, he knew.

"Drystan!"

Purin's scream echoed through the chamber, where he was nearly sitting up in his bed. He was drenched with sweat, and his chest was in agony. He breathed rapidly, and each inhale brought to his lungs the sting of a thousand needles and not enough air.

He barely noticed any of it.

He had only one thing on his mind, and that was the man that nearly killed him: Drystan. Hot rage pulsed through him, drowning out every other sensation, including the efforts of the druid to calm him. It was rage unmatched by anything he experienced before, compelling him to get out of bed and find Drystan right then and there in his delirium. He was vaguely aware of a force against him trying to keep him where he was, but he pushed past it and felt his feet land on the floor. He was seething, uncontrolled, unhindered in his purpose, and triumphant with all his weight supported by his powerful frame.

And then everything went black.

Purin opened his eyes, straining to focus on the figures standing over him in the soft light of the room.

He was in his bed again, but nothing was as it was before. Except that he remembered! He felt the rage returning, but this time he was in control. And there was something new: his head hurt.

"How are you feeling?" the druid asked. He was still smiling, and Purin wished he could punch him in the face.

"Alive."

"You gave Greallán quite a scare, Captain, and nearly killed yourself last night." It was Duke Maruk.

"I am feeling much better now, Your Grace."

The duke smiled. It was a hard smile that the duke always wore when he was ready to get down to business. "Good. Do you remember how you came to be in this condition?"

"I do."

"Tell me who did this to you."

"First, you should send a company of soldiers on the south road to discover what happened to the men escorting Eselt to the Valley of Leprechauns. I doubt they ever made it."

The duke's dark eyebrows furrowed. "You may be right. They have not returned, and it has been weeks."

"Weeks?" Purin was astonished. He would never have guessed he had been out that long.

"Yes, several weeks, as a matter of fact," the duke confirmed. "You were lucky that your dwarf friend found you when he did. Otherwise, you wouldn't be here now. Why were you in the secret passages anyway? And how did he know to find you there?"

Purin ignored that. "Where is Firolin? The dwarf?"

The duke shrugged. "We haven't been able to find him since the day he brought your nearly dead body to Greallán here." He leaned closer over Purin, his eyes gleaming and determined. "Now, tell me. Who did this to you?"

Purin felt his rage rising at the thought of the name, but he held it in check and nearly spat when he said it. "Drystan."

"Drystan!" exclaimed the duke. "How is that possible? I was told he died when he jumped from the upper ward. No one could have survived that!"

"He did, Your Grace." Purin had to adjust his position. "He survived it so well that he nearly murdered me on his way out of Tintagel. It's also likely he survived well enough to kill every one of the soldiers we sent to escort Eselt to the Leprechauns. Maybe even Firolin if he is still missing."

Duke Maruk just shook his head. "None of what you are saying seems possible."

"Yet it is, Your Grace." He glanced up at Greallán. "Now I need your druid here to work his magic and get me healed enough to ride a horse. I'm going to track down Drystan if it takes me the rest of my life."

"I appreciate your ambition to please me," the duke sounded less enthusiastic than Purin would have expected, "but I'm going to need you here for a while."

"Why is that?" Purin almost demanded.

"Teamhrach and the greater part of Eriu are mobilizing for war."

~~~

Eselt arrived with Drystan at a village outside of Teamhrach nearly three weeks ago. They found a small inn that was comfortable and frequented mostly by locals for the mead and the large portions their kitchen served. Eselt was not familiar with the inn before they arrived, nor had she ever set foot in the village, as far as she knew. Although she was the youngest princess of High King Cadeyrn and lived in the Tower House less than a league away, she had rarely gone among the common people. It wasn't that she felt herself above them in any way, not exactly. She simply never had a desire to do so. Everything she and her sisters needed was provided for them right there on the grounds of the Tower House, including a full market with fruits, sweets, textiles and much more. It was open every day, was shopped by all the nobles and royals, and was conveniently located in the upper ward.

Having been immersed as a commoner for several weeks now, she found them a most kind and good-natured people that loved to sing and dance and tell fanciful stories. She liked her people, even if she shouldn't think of them as her people any longer. Drystan fit in with them more quickly than she did, laughing and joking with them, at ease as if he had always been one of them, and it made it easier for her to adjust to their new life. She loved that about him.

They had not intended to stay so long so near to Teamhrach, but it took a while to sell their carriage and seven of the nine horses they brought with them without attracting unwanted attention. Then they began to hear rumors. Rumors that revealed themselves as true when camps of armed men started to sprout up all around Teamhrach under the banners of different noble families from around Eriu.

Her people were going to war.

That in itself was very distressing. Wars brought death to hundreds or thousands of people and suffering years after for the families of the fallen. Even more disturbing than that was they were going to war with Tintagel, which would undoubtedly bring the rest of Lyonesse into the fray. But most worrisome of all was the reason Eriu was going to war: to avenge the murder of the former Duchess of Tintagel, Princess Eselt, youngest daughter of the High King of Eriu. They were going to war for her.

A few weeks previous, word arrived in Eriu that Duke Maruk decided not to have Eselt executed and instead sent her into exile in the Valley of the Leprechauns. However, it was later reported that she never made it to the valley, and speculation turned to the conviction that the jealous Duke ordered her murder along the way, then buried her in the remote forest where her body would never be found. She heard rumors that her father was enraged by the transgression and declared war upon Tintagel, but Eselt knew her father well, and this was about far more than just the loss of his fourth daughter. He had been embarrassed by her adulterous affair with Drystan, and this was a political move to strengthen his position by uniting Eriu in a common cause that would quickly shift attention away from the ugly truth.

The problem for Eselt was that she wasn't sure if she could live with it. "They are going to war because of me, Drystan." She lay snuggled tightly at his side in the room they rented at the inn. It was late in the evening, and the single lit candle cast flickering shadows on the wall that were almost hypnotic.

"Don't worry, love, surely the druids will put a stop to it before the battle lines are drawn. Nobody wants another War of the Oak."

"I don't know." Eselt felt unconvinced. "This war isn't about the Druids, and they may choose not to get involved on either side. Especially if they believe the conflict will be brief."

Drystan hugged her and kissed her on the forehead. "I'm sure that King Praeter is working hard behind the scenes as well. Often there is a certain amount of chest thumping before any real hostilities break out. If you're right about your father's motives, then this is exactly what he wants. It would work to his advantage to gain a favorable peace agreement from Lyonesse that would make him look like a hero to your people without any hostilities ever occurring."

"I hope you're right, love. My father can be stubborn and push things too far sometimes." She worried that this might be one of those times. "I could never forgive myself if any innocent soul lost their life because of our deceit, let alone thousands."

"Let's wait awhile and watch the course the matter takes. If armies begin to march, we will think of something."

Eselt was sure she had never heard so much uncertainty in her lover's voice before, and it made her worry even more.

CHAPTER 23

Drums of War

We'll be marching out in a week'r so, I'll wager." Nearly drunk, the captain from the coastal city of Dunon sat with Drystan and blithely gave him the information he was seeking.

"Are you sure the army is ready and the supplies are in place to get you through?" He found it hard to believe that Eriu would be set to march after only six weeks of preparations.

A serving maid stopped by to fill their cups. Drystan's was almost full, but the captain's was nearly empty. That was the thing about warfare. It encouraged men to drink and numb their worries, often loosening their tongues in the process.

"Ah, that's what the commanders say. I concern myself with the banner of House Kunagno and keeping my head firmly planted on my shoulders."

Drystan was concerned over the rapid acceleration of hostilities between Teamhrach and Tintagel. He was sure that King Praeter of Lyonesse might have intervened to de-escalate the tensions and call for a truce. Rumors abounded that he tried, but that emotion ran too high, and not even he could bring about sensible negotiations.

The best that could be hoped for was that the conflict would be limited to the two great cities involved. Unfortunately, even that seemed improbable considering that the captain of a house from Dunon was sitting with him now.

"What is the company that you lead, Captain?" Drystan asked. He didn't really care, but he wanted to keep the man talking a little longer. After a few more drinks, he might learn the route they planned to march. He reasoned that if they traipsed across the headland at the northern end of Loch

Angu, they would be vulnerable to attack from Lyonesse City—that is, if King Praeter decided to enter the war. The other routes would require ships to either land them somewhere along the southern shores of Lake Virtue or ferry them across the loch from the mainland. Drystan wasn't a spy, and he certainly did not intend to warn his uncle no matter which way they went, but it would tell him how much time he had to do what needed doing before violence erupted.

"Why, don't you know, lad? The men-at-arms of House Kunagno are the greatest spearmen in the Western Kingdoms!" the captain boasted and raised his mug. He spoke loudly enough that his comment brought cheers from a few others sitting nearby, and Drystan raised his mug too.

When they settled back again, Drystan slapped the captain on the shoulder. "I knew I sat with a man of fame!" Then he hushed his voice and leaned close, "But, Captain, won't your spears be at a disadvantage against the bowmen of Lyonesse?"

The captain leaned back and snorted loudly. "Not at all, lad! I would put any one of my spearmen against a bowman from anywhere, anytime! My men are powerfully built, with arms that could throw a spear through a bowman at two hundred paces!" Then he stood and spoke loudly enough for everyone in the inn to hear, "And what happens when you rush a company of bowmen?"

The crowd responded almost in unison: "They run!" The room filled with raucous laughter.

Drystan had not expected such an entertaining show from the captain and was glad he chose his mark well as he laughed with them. When the din died down, Drystan leaned back in his chair and casually asked the question he needed the answer to. "I'm impressed, Captain. Will your men do just as well on a ship if they are attacked at sea?"

The captain's jovial expression changed into a look of angry suspicion. "What are you, boy? Why don't you wear a uniform like most men your age?"

Drystan feigned innocence. "I wanted to, Captain. Believe me, I did! But my clan chief chose me and a few others to stay back and tend to the supplies that will provision hardy souls like yourself that go into the fray."

The captain snorted another laugh. "I knew it! You don't have much of a head for military matters, that's clear! Bah, my men won't be on ships. The High King is gonna take the whole army across the headland and set siege to Stoddenferry Castle on his way to Tintagel. And since we don't need cavalry for sieges, he'll keep them to protect our rear in case old King Praeter decides to wade in with us!"

"Brilliant!" Drystan applauded him. "I'll bet you'll be right at the High King's side, Captain!" Together they laughed and drank for a while longer until Drystan left the poor man passed out on the table they had shared.

A little bleary-eyed himself, he made his way through the darkened village back to the inn where he and Eselt lived for the time being. Since they had been here, he quietly sold the carriage and seven of the nine mounts they had arrived with. They kept the best two horses for themselves in the care of a stable boy at the inn who had taken a shine to Eselt. It was probably the young man's first infatuation. All Drystan cared was that he gave their horses extra care and rations with so little available that had not been seized for the war effort.

Drystan was in a good mood. He had gotten what he was after from the captain, which would enable him to make a proper plan. It was simple, really. Now that he knew the army was going east over the headland, he and Eselt could go west down the river to Kenno and board a ship from there to anywhere away from Eriu and Lyonesse. The toughest part might be convincing Eselt to leave.

He was worrying about her more and more every day since the war began to appear inevitable. Drystan assured her that it would never come to that and in the end, cooler minds would prevail, although it didn't look like that was going to be the case. She was still holding out hope and accepting his assurances, but he found her more often staring out a window or lost in the swirls of a pot she stirred. He knew Eselt was conflicted between her guilt for being the cause of hostilities between her father and the duke and her love for Drystan.

He walked into their one-room home at the inn and found Eselt already asleep with the single candle still lit to keep her company while he was away. He removed his cloak and boots and lay next to her, his chest against her back.

"I'm happy you are back, love," she whispered.

Drystan did not expected to wake her, but he was glad she'd woken anyway. "I am happy too," he said. "I never wish to close my eyes at the end of the day without your kiss on my lips."

He snuggled up closer when she turned to face him. "The way is clear to Kenno," he told her. "I think we should take it."

She stared into his eyes a long time without saying anything before a tear slowly ran down her cheek.

Drystan was alarmed. "What is it, love? Have I upset you in some way? Please tell me."

She began to sob. "I can't leave here, Drystan. And I can't leave you. My love for you is so deep that it hurts, and at the same time my guilt for what we have done and what will be done is tearing me apart inside. I don't know what to do, and I've been having terrible thoughts about ending my own life. How could I live with the deaths of so many on my hands?"

"Eselt!" he said and held her tight. He didn't know what to say. What could he say? Would he feel any different after men died in a conflict of their making? Would he be able to live with himself?

They lay together in silence and tears until the light of the candle finally burned out and they fell asleep, clutching to each other, unable to speak words of comfort to each other because there were none.

~~~

Eselt awoke late the next morning. She didn't know when they fell asleep, but it had to have been only hours before dawn, and she still felt tired. If she could have gone back to sleep, she gladly would have, except that her mind was already churning over her predicament. She would be lucky if she could ever sleep again.

Looking around the room, she realized that Drystan was not there, and she began to worry. *Had he run away?* Maybe he had enough of the hiding and running and agonizing over every moment of their lives. It was exhausting. She wouldn't blame him if he did, but she also knew that she would follow him if he did. To live without him would be worse than depriving her lungs of air. Even if it meant that she ran away to find him and thousands died, millions for that matter. She would become a thing of misery, perhaps eventually take her own life, but she would follow.

Eselt went about the room hurriedly collecting her things and noticed that Drystan left in such a rush that he had not taken any of his belongings. She would have to hurry if she was going to catch him. Hopefully, the stable boy would know the direction he traveled.

The door opened, and Drystan walked in with a bowl of water for washing. Relief flooded through her, and she ran to him, hugging him tightly. The bowl of water spilled from his hands when she did, but she didn't care. He was there.

"Are you OK?" he asked quietly.

She kissed his face all over before she sheepishly replied, "I thought you ran away."

He took her face in his hands and kissed her lips softly. "Never think that, love, never. You could plant a knife in my chest, and I couldn't make myself retreat from you."

She stood back a little and looked down at their wet clothes. "I guess we have bathed for the day," she giggled.

They shared a long laugh in each other's arms. It felt good and normal. Eselt missed laughing with him. They had done little of it since that night in the camp, when Drystan rescued her. She sat down on the edge of the bed, and Drystan sat with her. The mood was turning again, the reality was setting in, and they had to decide together what they were going to do next.

Drystan was the first to speak. "I have thought of almost nothing else since last night, and I still don't know what to do. Tell me, Eselt. Tell me what we should do now to rid ourselves of these demons and live a normal life. Together."

Eselt too thought much about what they could do, and no matter how much she tried to convince herself that there were other options, she always came back to one. "I have to go see my father and put an end to this."

Drystan just nodded his head. What did that mean? She expected him to try and convince her not to go, that there were other ways, anything.

"I will go this afternoon," she said reaching for his hand. He took it and held it firmly.

"We will go this afternoon," he replied.

Her heart leaped with joy that he would not leave her to go alone. Then fear crept upon her. What if her father seized him and threw him in the dungeon? Or worse, had him immediately executed? Would even she be able to save him from her father's anger?

"Maybe I should go alone," she cautioned. "My father has a terrible temper where his daughters are concerned, and you may be in mortal danger if you come with me."

"I will face it boldly, then, next to you." He smiled.

Eselt knew there was nothing she could say that would dissuade him. She wondered if their positions were reversed, would he be able to dissuade her? No, he couldn't. They would face the future hand in hand no matter what came against them. They made it through so many impossible situations already that, inevitably, Eriu and Sunna would not forsake them now. Would they?

Standing, she continued to pack her belongings, and Drystan followed suit. No matter what happened at the Tower House today, they knew they would not be returning to the inn. Even under the most optimistic scenario, they would be lucky if they were allowed to leave the Tower House unsupervised for months.

It didn't take them long; there wasn't much that needed packing other than a bit of clothing and a few personal items. Drystan grumbled about the gold and silver he carried. She knew he accumulated a substantial sum from the sale of the carriage and horses with nowhere to keep it stored since the Knights Temple was closed to the populace due to the hostilities with Lyonesse. He worried that it would be confiscated and never returned if he brought it with them to the Tower House. Ultimately, he decided to bury it outside the village near a clearing in the forest where they often picnicked.

After he left, Eselt took the opportunity to comb her hair and apply some color to her face. It seemed like ages since she dressed up. She still carried the fine gown they were going to burn her in, and pushing that thought aside, she put the dress on. When she presented herself to her father, it would go better if she at least looked like the princess he remembered. Eselt had changed so much since the time she lived there just a few months earlier. She was more mature and understood the nature of people better. Despite the hardships she endured, she was still generally a happy person, even if the innocence she once enjoyed had been dragged out of her.

Drystan returned shortly after noon and stopped dead in his tracks when he walked through the door. "You look beautiful," he said and walked over to kiss her.

He was calmer than before he left, having secured their wealth for future use, and it made her feel good to see his eyes light up at her appearance. She knew it wasn't as if he loved her more when she was preened and pretty—it was pride to be hers and to have her be his. In that second, she almost told him they should run away again, but it passed quickly. Why did there always have to be a cloud of depression over them?

Quickly he washed and changed into his finer clothes before they collected their packs and made their way toward the stables. They didn't bother to inform the innkeeper of their departure. The room was rented for another two weeks, and on the off chance they were able to return, it would be waiting for them. At first, they feared that their dress would make them stand out, but Myrllin's charms were true to their design, and they attracted no more attention than a scullery maid on her way to the market.

Until they arrived at the stables.

The stable boy nearly tripped over himself greeting Eselt. "You look like a lady in that dress, miss." She knew it was meant as a compliment.

"Thank you, Isaro." She curtsied, bringing a blush to his cheeks. Then she assumed the air of a lady taking command. "My lord and I will be taking a ride in the country," she said in the most dramatic voice she could summon. "Prepare our mounts for departure!"

Isaro giggled and feigned a proper air while he prepared their mounts for riding. Then he brought them forward and bent with a flourishing bow. "Your mount is ready, my lady."

Before she mounted her horse, she leaned forward to kiss the young boy on the cheek, producing another blush. "I will miss you, Isaro," she whispered. He appeared confused by her words but said nothing, most likely assuming it was part of the characters they played.

With a pair of regal waves, they rode from the stables into the bright afternoon sun and through the busy village. Teamhrach was a little over a league to the west, and the road into the city was packed with merchants and soldiers headed in the same direction they were from the dozens of military camps that they passed. Eselt wasn't sure if it was the charm or Drystan's long blond hair that gave him the appearance of a native of Eriu. Whichever it was, she was glad for it after hearing some of the ribald songs sung in the camps concerning the brutal treatment the soldiers intended for their adversaries' most delicate parts.

Almost two hours passed before they came to the gates of the lower ward. Eselt was unsure with mixed feelings. The last time she was here, her heart was filled with joy and wonder at what her life had in store for her. Now she stood with another man in a less-than-triumphant return to her home with no idea what the next hour of her life would hold.

Gaining entry into the lower ward was not difficult. Drystan told the guards they were there to pick up a cart of cedar shafts for the spearmen under the banner of House Kunagno, and they were passed through with no further questions. For a one-time knight of Sunna trained to beat on shields and knock other men off their horses with a stick, Drystan was developing into an impressive operative of information. Eselt smiled to herself at the thought of his reaction to that idea. He would probably think it absurd. She almost laughed out loud.

Craftsmen and tradesmen of every sort crowded the streets and alleys of the lower ward. Eselt couldn't remember a time when it had been so crowded. Of course, Eriu had never been at war in her lifetime, so it was jarring that the home she thought she knew was almost foreign and unfamiliar. The buildings and streets looked the same, and the sprawling, ivy-covered Tower House elevated above them still held familiar pleasure, but it was something about the masses of people, so serious and driven by their efforts to organize for war, that ruined the exotic delight of the city she knew. She longed for that feeling again, and she lamented that it might never be the same.

The line for the upper ward was far shorter than the one at the lower ward. Only nobles and invited guests would be permitted beyond the inner gates. Eselt maneuvered her mount closer to Drystan. "Give me your charm, love."

"Won't I be recognized?" he asked.

"It will be no matter once we get to that gate," she replied.

He handed over the charm, and she tied it securely around his wrist. "We may need these again soon, and if the guards think it is a worthless trinket then the more likely they will leave you with it."

"Is it still working?"

"I hope not," she laughed. "We need to be recognized for who we are by those guards if we are to go any further." She pulled her necklace from around her neck and quickly tied it around her own wrist.

"Are you ready?" she whispered. "It won't be long now."

"I am with you always, love." Drystan took her hand and kissed it.

She immediately rode to the front of the line, and before they made it half the way, a cry went out from someone nearby. "The princess! It is Princess Eselt! She has returned!"

More people turned to look and gasp at her unexpected appearance. Eselt was sure it was her golden hair that gave her away, like a beacon on the loch, and a crowd began to form and shout for her. Quickly, a pair of the High King's Fianna appeared nearby, looking for the source of the disruption, and they, too, immediately recognized Eselt. One of them blew an alarm from the ram's horn he carried, and within minutes a full contingent of thirty mounted Fianna was pushing through the growing crowd toward them.

Eselt waited patiently surrounded by the thickening crowd with Drystan. All she could do was wave and smile until the Fianna could make their way to them. When they finally broke through, the commander at their head saluted smartly.

"We feared the worst had befallen you, Princess Eselt! Welcome home. My men will see you safely inside." He nodded slightly to Drystan.

Eselt smiled gracefully. "Thank you, Commander. It is good to be home."

The elite knights of the Fianna immediately formed up around them and escorted them out of the crowd and into the upper ward. Once through the gate, there were no crowds, and the pace slowed a little as they ascended the steep hill to the Tower House. One Fiann had ridden ahead at a gallop to announce her arrival, and she knew her father would be aware of her return within minutes. Even if they wanted to abandon their courage now, there would be no turning back, and certainly the Fianna would not allow them any other course than the one they traveled.

Eselt found herself praying to Eriu. Not for herself, but for Drystan. He rode beside her like the regal knight she knew him to be and smiled reassuringly from time to time as if she were the one in grave danger. She decided again, for at least the hundredth time in her head, that she would die before she let anything happen to her lover.

It didn't take more than a dozen minutes to ascend to the final courtyard, and when they arrived, she could see a crowd of people gathered at the forecastle entry to the Tower House. Among them were various nobles, her sisters and their husbands, and her father and mother front and center. Everyone one of them gazed at her from a distance as if she were a ghost.

The Fianna split to the sides of the vast courtyard, leaving Eselt and Drystan to ride the rest of the way on their own. Nearly halfway, Drystan held back and allowed Eselt to move forward alone. He knew how critical this first meeting would be between her and her father. There wasn't a sound in the courtyard other than the natural gait of the horse she rode, and the quiet lent tension to her already heightened anxiety. Then without Eselt's realizing it, the horse stopped of its own accord a span from where the High King stood. Eselt sat upon her mount in somewhat of a daze. Protocol required that she dismount and display a full curtsy before the High King, but she did not move. She could not move. Every emotion was building inside of her, paralyzing her.

Finally, her father hesitantly came forward and walked to stand at the horse's flank, looking up at her. "Eselt?" he spoke softly and uncertain.

She looked down at him from where she perched, determined not to show any weakness, and nervously cleared her throat. "I have come home," she announced in a strong voice that wavered just a little at the end.

If she expected to impress her father, then she sorely miscalculated. No one said a word after she had spoken, there were no cheers, and there were no cries of relief. Stunned disbelief was all she saw, and her strategy changed. Her father saw his little girl, not the travel-weary woman she had become, broken by so many harrowing experiences.

He father looked sad and concerned, his eyes haunted by loss. Had she also underestimated his sincerity to mourn her? He reached up toward her as he had done so many times when she was a little girl.

"Eselt," he said softly once more. "You are home."

She fell into his arms, desperately sobbing while he cradled her close like a small child and slowly sank to his knees. If anything surprised her that day, it was that her father, who she allowed herself to believe only thought of her as a mere pawn in his game of politics, sobbed as desperately as she did.

CHAPTER 24

Reunion

Drystan sat atop his horse under the shadow of the Tower House and watched the royal family reunion in the courtyard. He felt no jealousy or envy. He only wished he could have been a part of it. Eselt was surrounded by her whole family, and they were all crying tears of relief and happiness. He felt a tear crawl down his cheek just to watch it, and he was happy for her.

The approach of a horse's slow gait behind him tugged at his attention, but he kept his eyes on his lover. The minutes might be ticking away that he may never see her again, and he wanted to savor every second of her beauty and joy.

"It's a very touching scene." The man on the horse said when he moved up next to him. Drystan recognized the voice of the man as none other than Teutjorïk, Commander of the Fianna. He remembered the commander of the Fianna from when he was here to retrieve Eselt for the wedding. It seemed like a lifetime ago. Commander Teutjorïk was a good man, as far as he knew, and Drystan expected he would be treated well by him regardless of the eventual outcome.

"It is," replied Drystan.

"Perhaps we should give the family some privacy. They have all suffered so much, and they will need a little time alone together." The commander made it sound like a suggestion, but Drystan knew it for what it was: a politely worded command.

Drystan sighed. "Where to, Commander? The dungeons or the gallows?"

"Why would you say that, Drystan?" Teutjorïk sounded genuinely affronted. "You are our guest and will be treated as such until the High King says differently."

Drystan felt a little ashamed. "Thank you, Commander Teutjorīk. I appreciate your hospitality."

They rode along to the stables on the north side of the Tower House, where he handed the reins to one of the waiting stable boys.

"Will Eselt . . . I mean, Princess Eselt, be back in her old chambers again?" he asked while Commander Teutjorīk led him through the dim corridors of the Tower House.

"I believe she will." The commander stopped and turned to face him. "Drystan, I'm going to need you to be patient. Tensions are running high in the household right now with the prospect of war and now the princess arriving at our doorstep unexpected. There are going to be a lot of questions, and before they are answered to everyone's satisfaction, let's avoid any misunderstandings."

The commander was smiling as he spoke and clearly making an effort to keep the conversation light and friendly. Drystan understood his concern. The last thing he needed was to find Drystan skulking around the princess's chambers—or worse, inside them—before it was determined how much the High King really welcomed him.

"I understand, Commander. You don't have to worry about a thing from me." Drystan said the words, but he wasn't sure how sincere he was about them. If he didn't see Eselt again soon or at least know how she was doing, he knew that he would be compelled to seek her out.

They arrived at a familiar door. It was the same room Drystan stayed in on his last visit, one appropriate for a highly regarded knight or lesser noble. They didn't know he had relinquished his station.

The commander opened the door for him but did not enter. "You are free to go about the Tower House as you please, except for the royal residences. No one will hinder you unless you try to leave the upper ward."

"You have conducted yourself with true honor, Commander. Thank you," Drystan replied.

The commander made a slight bow. "I will look in on you from time to time in case you need anything." He vacated the frame of the door and allowed it to close, leaving Drystan alone in the utter silence of the room.

He sat on the bed and rubbed his tired eyes. He missed her already.

~~~

Eselt was in her old room. She was finally alone after the fervor of the afternoon with her family. They'd assaulted her with an emotional storm of questions, but it was too difficult to talk about anything that had happened to her since the wedding. Fortunately, her father realized that she was overwhelmed and put a stop to it. He suggested that she rest for a while and then he and her mother would speak to her privately.

She had been able to sleep for only a few hours before waking terrified, searching for Drystan, only to realize where she was and that he was not there. It was already late afternoon, and the sun was on its last arc toward the horizon. Her family would be having dinner together, and she was sure they would expect her to join them. She thought about Drystan and what he would be doing. It was a relief that he was in one of the lavish guest chambers and not shoved in a cold dungeon where he might suffer abuse and disease. She wouldn't have stood for it anyway, leading her to confront her father with ultimatums that would have made things much worse than they already were going to be.

Eselt got out of bed and prepared to get dressed. She needed to see her father and explain everything while he was still feeling sympathetic. The sooner he understood that the war was pointless and that Drystan was who she was meant to be with, the better. Some of her old clothes were still in her closet, and she picked out a burgundy gown with green trim that complemented her complexion and accentuated her golden hair.

She dressed, did her hair, and put on makeup on her own before presenting herself to her father. Her recent change in social status had given her the practice she needed to make a fair likeness of her previous reflection.

The last rays of the evening sun were nearly below the horizon when she left her chambers and made her way to the private dining room where her family would gather every night to share the last sup of the day together. When she arrived, they were well into the evening meal, and the jovial conversation they shared reminded her of days long gone. All went quiet when they realized she was there. The laughter, the casual chatter, a story about something funny that had happened during the day to one of her sisters—all ceased. They all watched her entrance in guarded silence.

Eselt stood there smiling as if everything was right with the world, but the awkward lull in conversation was becoming evident when her mother stepped in to right the situation.

"Darling! So good of you to join us." She gestured to an empty chair at the table. "Please take your place among your family. It has been far too long since we were all together."

Immediately, chairs moved as her father and her sisters' husbands stood while she took her seat. Then there were servants surrounding Eselt, offering platters of her favorite delicacies and filling her cup with wine. She wasn't very hungry, and the food she accepted was mostly for the show of it since her nerves had driven hunger from her. She did take the wine. Eselt had a feeling she might need more than a little liquid courage if she were going to make it through the kind of night she anticipated.

"That's such a pretty dress, dear. Did you find it in your closet?" Her mother was an expert at making casual conversation.

Mairwen, her eldest sister, held an unflattering broad grin on her usually serious face. "You look wonderful, Eselt. Who combed your hair?"

Her other two sisters, Gwynn and Braith, also added their overly cheerful observances of her angelic state. Eselt couldn't wait until she had them alone to tell them how ridiculous they all looked. At least the men had the good sense to keep their mouths shut.

"How are you feeling, daughter? Did the rest clear your head?" Finally, her father asked the first pertinent question of the evening.

"Much better now, Father. And you?" Eselt smiled on the inside. He should have expected the question would be turned back on him given his performance when she first arrived at the Tower House.

When she was younger, they played a game where each would remind the other, in very subtle ways, that they were regular people. Her father always said that it was a good exercise in humility and helped endear them to the people they ruled. She played the game now, and her father knew it. If anything, she hoped it would remind him of their relationship before the wedding and make their eventual talk a little easier.

Her father's face reddened around the edges, and he took a long draft of wine to give himself time to recover. When he put down the mug, he stood, and without making eye contact announced that he had a meeting to attend.

"It's good to have you back with us," Eselt's father told her on his way out, touching her shoulder. "When you are ready, we will talk more." The other men made excuses and left with him, leaving Eselt alone with her mother and sisters, almost as if their presence would corrupt whatever moment the women would share together.

Eselt's mother and sisters began a light banter about court politics and society gossip. Soon she was right in the middle of it, laughing with the others while they brought her up to date on the latest scandals and mortifying behaviors of the nobles.

It went on for an hour before her mother stood to retire for the evening. "Eselt, dear, when you speak to your father, remember that he loves you." She had a very serious look on her face that gave Eselt the impression that she was trying to convey something very important. "No matter what he says, and men will say many foolish things without thinking them through, he still loves you."

Her mother leaned down and kissed her on the forehead and then lifted an eyebrow at her sisters. They all immediately stood from their chairs, each stuttering a jumble of excuses about how tired they were.

Mairwen, her oldest sister, lingered just a moment after they all filed out the door. "Go easy on Papa," she told Eselt, and Eselt wasn't sure if the sympathy in her voice was for her or her father. "He was so distraught after word of your trial and even more so when he thought we lost you." Then she was out the door in a hurry to catch up with the others.

Eselt stayed where she was for a short while, just staring at the empty table and running scenarios through her head about how the conversation would go with her father. She wanted more wine, but even the servants had scattered, so she poured for herself. In short order, she was filling her cup again. She felt numb, not drunk, and emboldened. She knew that not just her future, but Drystan's as well, depended on the outcome of this evening. Then it hit her that she was not even sure if her father had called off the war. There had been no talk of it at dinner, and if he still intended to march his troops to Tintagel, then thousands of souls depended on her words tonight.

Eselt gulped down the remaining wine in her cup with the enthusiasm a drunken sailor would have admired and slammed the vessel on the table. It felt good to have even the smallest hint of control. Then she was out of her seat and marching down to her father's chambers. It was time for them to come to an understanding. When she arrived, Eselt found his rooms empty, and one of his scribes informed her that he was meeting with his generals in the war room.

The war room!

The thought angered her. The only reason she and Drystan came here in the first place, with no assurance that it would not affect their lives detrimentally, was to stop this terrible war. The war room was a few long corridors away, and with every step, she became more outraged. The anger must have been obvious on her face, as servants and nobles alike practically fell over themselves to get out of her way. No one dared to inquire what was the matter, no one tried to stop her to find out what was wrong. When she arrived at the door to the war room, she was practically seething.

A lone guard stood staunchly next to the door. She stopped in front of him with the expectation that he would open it for her, but instead, he blocked her way with the shaft of a spear. "His Highness is in conference at the moment and wishes not to be disturbed," he said blandly.

Eselt stepped nearly toe to toe with the guard and looked up at the big man towering over her. Then she held up her tiny fist a hair's breadth away from his face. "I am going to ram my fist up your nose if you don't open the door this instant." She was surprised by the vehement hiss of words that escaped her.

The guard couldn't move without causing incidental contact with her, so only his eyes moved to look down at her uncertainly. He knew who she was and that she only recently returned. He probably also considered under what circumstance he wanted to face the High King—after a brawl with his youngest daughter outside the war room or after he allowed her entry. He reached down and opened the door.

Eselt smiled sweetly, patted him on the massive metal chest plate he wore, and strode through.

Down a long, shadowy stone corridor she went until it ended at the open entrance to a large, well-lit oval room with a high vaulted ceiling. The walls were decorated with numerous shields, heralds, and weapons of every sort and from every house in Eriu mounted along the perimeter. The entire surface of the opposite wall was covered by an enormous diagram of the Western Kingdoms. There, eight men stood with her father, who held a long pointer that he pressed against the map, indicating different points under discussion. Between them and where Eselt stood was the largest table she had ever seen, also covered with various maps with little figures commanding different positions on them.

Men and their toy soldiers, she thought.

They all faced away from her with their attention firmly on the map. None detected her quiet entrance.

"What of King Praeter?" One of the generals was pointing toward a dot identified as Lyonesse City. "If he enters the war after we pass, he can take us from the flank or rear."

The High King moved his pointer to an area near the city with images of an open field lined by a forest. "We will position the cavalry here behind the trenches, barriers, and other defensive formations. Flanking their position will be several companies of archers in the wood on each side. If he fields his army, they will be forced to march into us there, and we can forestall them long enough to move in reinforcements."

"A nasty little surprise," another general chuckled.

"That is the essence of war," the High King agreed.

"There will be no war." Eselt spoke loudly enough that her voice echoed in the great room, immediately gaining their attention.

Every one of them turned and just stared. How odd it must seem, that a diminutive young woman in a burgundy evening gown was standing in this place. Her father walked forward hesitantly to stand in front of the others. "Sweetheart," he began in a soothing tone, "this is not the time or place for this discussion. Let us speak of it on a more proper occasion. We can invite your mother and have tea."

He will not patronize me! Eselt could almost hear an audible pop in her head as the fury overcame her. "There will be no war!" she shrieked.

Her father, the High King of Eriu, Protector of the Liafal, champion of countless tourneys and veteran of a hundred battles, took a step back. Then he addressed his generals. "Leave me," he said in a calm voice.

One of them foolishly began to protest, "Your Highness we have so much—"

"Leave me!" the High King roared. For a second, Eselt was very proud of her father. No one commanded a room like he did.

Eight highly decorated and battle-hardened generals practically ran from the room, not even glancing at Eselt as they passed. She wondered what the guard outside would think about her going in and the generals rushing out. She bet he was glad he didn't tangle with her now.

Her father looked at her in a way she had only seen him look at men who had angered him. It was a dangerous look. Her mother's voice spoke inside her head, *Remember your father loves you.*

"Sit," her father commanded, waving her to a nearby chair.

He stood on the other side of the massive table with both arms locked, palms on its surface. Eselt was glad the table was between them. He never struck her when she was a child, but she had the distinct feeling he wanted to now.

This is not a time to show weakness, she told herself.

Cocking her head defiantly, she looked him boldly in the eyes. "I will not!" Her voice was strong and unwavering, even if her arms were tight by her sides, hands balled tightly to prevent them from trembling.

Her father flinched as if she struck him. She had no doubt that he could have leaped over that massive table and knocked her to the ground if he wanted to. Maybe he did want to, but he was a study of self-control that could have won a prize if there was one to give.

He just stared at her a long time. They stared at each other, like statues from across the room. She would not give in to him, not this time.

She was not a little girl anymore, and she had the lives of thousands on her shoulders and the strength of Drystan in her heart. She couldn't let him down most of all.

Then suddenly he dropped his gaze and stared down at the maps on the table below him. "To look at you is to see the reflection of myself."

This was her moment, she had to press the advantage and win him over. "You have to stop this war!" she shouted with undeniable conviction.

His head came up immediately, anger in his eyes, but not like before. "I don't know if I can!" he shouted back.

"You are the High King, Father. They will do as you say." She lowered her voice but did not allow the forcefulness in it to diminish.

"I know this war is about my pride now. You are standing here and safe. I have only pride to avenge, but there is more than that to consider." He straightened and slowly made his way around the table toward her. "Our family is in grave danger from the powers here in Eriu. Not answering this affront from Duke Maruk would be seen as a sign of weakness, and some might begin to challenge my authority. It could lead to another civil war in Eriu. No one wants that."

"There are other ways, Father. No one in Lyonesse knows that I am safely returned home. Use it to your advantage and gain trade concessions from King Praeter. That will be a win for Eriu. Show them you are a High King that looks after the future of our people. Show them you are strong and benevolent."

He was next to her then and gently took her into his arms, hugging her to his chest like he used to do when she was a child. "I will think on it, daughter. You have good reasoning and wisdom beyond your years. How did I never notice?"

"What about Drystan?" She willed herself to stay strong and pulled away from him a little to look him in the eyes. "I love him, Father. It is real, and it is true. Not even your power can change that."

He sighed. "He will complicate the matter. If I could win the trade concessions and hang the boy, things would be better for us."

"I will agree on the condition that you hang me beside him." There was no jest in her proposal. She needed him to understand how serious Drystan's well-being was to her.

He pulled her close again and kissed the top of her head. "I will speak to him."

Joy raged through her as surely as the fury had earlier, and she thought she might have won. *Did I just beat my father? The feared High*

King of Eriu? She prayed to the Goddess Eriu that it was true.

CHAPTER 25

Treachery

"So here we are again, young knight."

"I am no knight. Not anymore."

The High King raised an eyebrow while he looked Drystan over. "Is that so?"

"It's a fairly simple thing. I stole my father's wife and ran away with her." Drystan was not trying to come off flippant, just matter of fact. He intended to speak plainly to the High King, and where it concerned his daughter it was likely the best way to keep his head.

"You did, at that," the High King agreed while pouring them both a cup of mead. "And managed to start a war at the same time."

"That part you can attribute to my uncle." Drystan gratefully accepted the cup of mead and drank it down quickly to moisten his cotton-laden throat. "His cruelty toward your daughter is the cause of the war."

The High King, not to be outdone, finished his cup and poured them each another. "And what would you do if you found out the one you loved was in love with another? Look the other way? Forgive them?"

"I would be heartbroken."

"Certainly you would be enraged as well, wouldn't you? Maybe do something you might regret later?" The High King was relentless, but Drystan saw through his ploy.

Drystan fixed the High King with the most severe stare he could muster. "If Eselt were in love with another, then I would love her enough to let her go and wish her no ill will."

The High King nodded and refilled their cups. "You know, I knew you were near for the past several weeks. I thought maybe you had come with something of Eselt's or a final message to pass on and were unsure how to approach me."

It was Drystan's turn to nod. "The Liafal Stone. Why didn't you come for me?"

"I knew you would come in your own time, and I was grieving." He briefly patted Drystan's hand resting on the table. "If I know anything about you, it is that you are honorable, even if your honor has a strange way about it."

"Thank you, I think." He wanted to laugh, but he held it in.

"So, about the princess." The High King let out a long breath. "She has informed me that if I hang you, I must hang her with you as well."

Drystan allowed himself a smile. It was good to hear something about her considering he had not laid eyes on his lover since they arrived at the Tower House.

"Yes, you can thank her for your life, for the time being." He turned very serious. "As much as I may like you, Drystan, I would have happily put you at the end of a rope. I still might."

The High King just stared at him a few moments, and Drystan wondered if he was expecting appreciation for sparing his life. The one thing Eselt told him before they decided to come here was to never give in to her father. He was trying hard to follow her advice.

The High King tapped the fingers of one meaty hand on the table. "I have to decide what to do with you both."

This was the opening Drystan had been waiting for. "Princess Eselt and I are joined as closely as any two beings can be. If you value her happiness, then you must allow her to make that choice."

Slamming his fist on the table, the High King leaned in close. "Do you think I am a fool, boy? You two are in love, right? And you can't live without each other? Am I on the right trail?" His face was changing colors of red and purple. "How many times has that story played out? How many times has it ended in sorrow and sadness? Do you think I never felt that way in the years that I have walked the earth?"

Don't back down, Drystan reminded himself. "It's not the same." He met the High King's steely gaze with one of his own while keeping his voice calm and controlled. "I can't explain it, but Princess Eselt and I are destined to be together. No matter what you do, short of killing us both, we will be compelled to be together. If you force me to leave, she will find a way to follow, just as I would do for her."

"Then what do you propose?" the High King huffed with scorn.

"You let her go. Let her decide for herself what she wants as I do."

"How can I have my daughter out in the world unprotected and living the life of a vagabond?" the High King countered.

Drystan felt snubbed, but he held it in check. "I will protect her, and I have enough money to provide well for her."

"The money you have in the Knights Temple?" He must have noticed Drystan's look of surprise. "Yes, I know all about that, and so will the agents for Tintagel, eventually. How long do you think it would take them to track you and Eselt down? A month? A year? When they find you, they would happily kill you both and return your heads to the duke. And we would be right back where we are now, at war, except you would both be dead."

Drystan didn't know what to say about that. He didn't have a defense. He had no idea that his ruse at the Knights Temple was so transparent. He didn't want to give in, so he deflected. "And what ideas do you have, O High King?" It came out almost mocking.

"Don't test me, boy," the High King warned. "Eselt may be your shield for now, but you will need me as a friend if you are going to survive."

Drystan slumped a little in his chair. "You're right. I apologize for the insult."

"Look, we have the same goal in mind, and that is keeping Eselt safe and happy." He shoved another cup of mead toward Drystan. "Now it's time you listened to me."

Drystan took the cup and responded with a nod. Eselt told him that this was going to be the way of the conversation and that whatever her father offered next was going to be based completely on how effective she had been with him. How she could know all this so far in advance, before they even set foot into Teamhrach, was a mystery to him. She had a talent for the strategy of politics and diplomacy that he could never understand. Drystan made a mental note to heed her advice more often.

The High King took a long draft of his mead, and Drystan took the opportunity to drain his cup as well. Grabbing the clay pitcher, the High King attempted to fill Drystan's cup, but the vessel was empty.

"Bah!" The High King spat a curse and threw the pitcher at the door of the chamber, where it shattered into a thousand pieces.

Almost immediately a servant rushed in with another pitcher and filled the cups, leaving the pitcher on the table when he finished.

"Thank you, Langly," the High King called after the retreating servant, who bowed quickly before disappearing through the door.

Drystan's mind was well into fuzzy from all of the mead they had drunk so far, so he wasn't sure whether to be alarmed or amused.

"My daughter has apparently decided that it's worth keeping your neck its current length and that she is determined to be with you no matter what I say." The High King was brooding into his cup while he said it, almost as if he were reminding himself of his own predicament.

He looked up at Drystan, studying him again as if trying to reach a decision. Under normal circumstances, he might have felt awkward or insulted, but the mead was working on him, and he merely smiled back and emptied his cup again. The High King snarled at the unintended challenge and drained his cup as well.

So it went for the next several hours. Drystan had no idea what they discussed, what he might have agreed to or what was decided for him. He had flashes of drinking and singing and arm wrestling with the High King. There was a competition having to do with who could break the pitchers into more shards and the image of them on the ground in a mountain of clay fragments, counting them together. Many other images came to mind that he simply didn't understand and was probably better off never knowing.

What he did know was that he woke up sometime after noon the next day with a splitting headache that was made all the worse by a pounding on the door. Fortunately, he was still completely dressed, so he stood on shaky legs, shoved his face into a bowl of water nearby, and then stumbled to answer the door.

When he opened the door, he was surprised to see the smiling face of Commander Teutjorīk. "Good day, Drystan. How are you feeling?"

With a wave to enter, Drystan stumbled away from the entry and fell into the nearest chair. There was a pitcher of water on the side table that he nearly drained before attempting to speak. "What do you want, Commander Teutjorīk? As you can see, I'm not entirely together yet."

"Yes, I heard about your evening with High King Cadeyrn." The commander had not stopped smiling since he walked in the door, and Drystan found it so irritating that he wanted to punch Teutjorīk right in the mouth. "But I am not here to relive the moments with you. Rather, I have come to escort you to a meeting of sorts."

Drystan peered up at Commander Teutjorīk while vigorously rubbing his temples to relieve his headache. "So, the High King has decided to hang me after all? At least I won't have to worry about my throbbing head. You people really need to rack your mead longer."

"That's probably true, wise sage of fermentation." The commander apparently thought he had a sense of humor. "Be that as it may, I have things to do yet today, so why don't you hurry along your suffering and get dressed?" The commander sat down in a chair near the window. "I'll wait until you are ready."

With a sigh, Drystan forced himself to rise. "What's the occasion?"

The commander turned his head in thought. "I would say casual with a sense of formality."

"Great. You really are going to hang me, aren't you?" Drystan grumbled, drawing a quick laugh from the commander. Then he went about washing up and dressing in a white silk shirt and light wool trousers.

Briefly, he considered strapping on his sword belt, but unless he was allowed to leave the upper ward, he was unlikely to have a need for it. He also doubted that his host would appreciate him bearing arms in the Tower House, as it would be viewed as an insult, implying that he felt unsafe as a guest under their protection.

"Very well, I'm ready," Drystan told Commander Teutjorīk, and they left his chamber in the direction of the feast hall.

A short time later they arrived at a junction in the corridors where one hall led to the royal apartments, and to Drystan's surprise, it was down this hallway that they went. Several guards lined the way, but not one of them so much as flinched to challenge their passing. Drystan knew that had it not been for the commander's presence, he would not have been allowed five paces into the interior.

They didn't travel far before they arrived at an unassuming doorway at which Commander Teutjorīk knocked. Drystan prayed to Sunna that it wasn't the High King summoning him to pick up where they left off the night before. It certainly wouldn't have surprised him, given the High King's reputation for a hefty appetite for drinking, but if Drystan had to so much as smell another cup of mead, he might well empty his stomach right on the spot.

The door was opened by a pretty young ladies maid who curtsied to the commander and left the room without a word.

"This is as far as I go," the commander informed him. "I wish you happiness, Drystan, truly I do."

Drystan was speechless as he watched him walk back down the hallway the way they had come. What did that mean? There was nothing left but to go into the brightly lit room and face whatever was waiting for him.

Inside, the airy high-ceilinged room was crowded with comfortably pillowed chairs, couches, and divans set upon plush carpets. There were also a number of various sized tables, tapestries on the walls depicting royal ceremonies and a fair-sized hearth against the west wall. Surprisingly, not a soul was in attendance. On the other side of the room, there was a door between the tapestries that he almost missed. Before Drystan was halfway into the room, the obscure door opened, and his heart wanted to leap from his chest.

Eselt.

"Drystan!" she squealed and ran to his open arms. They clutched each other tightly, and he kissed her all over her face and lips. He couldn't believe he was holding her in his arms again.

"I missed you," he breathed between kisses. It had only been three days, but it might well have been a lifetime.

Eselt was crying tears of joy and trying to speak between sobs. He kept her close and hushed her reassuringly, although in truth he wanted to join her sobbing, so overwhelmed was he with emotion. If there were ever two people who loved each other the way they did, Drystan had to believe they were touched by the gods, as he and Eselt seemed to be.

"It appears that you have done well with your father."

"We both did, love, I am happy to say." Then she giggled. "I heard about your evening with him."

Drystan exhaled a long sigh. "I'm still feeling the effects of that particular adventure, although I fear what I might have agreed to."

"Don't worry about that." Eselt thumped him playfully on the chest. "I can assure you that he won't remember much of it either."

"How is it we are here together now? Has your father agreed to allow us to leave?" Drystan was hopeful, but he didn't really believe their departure would be a simple thing.

"Not yet," Eselt confirmed his expectation. "My father is trying to negotiate terms in his favor with King Praeter to end the war before he is forced to march his army. As long as word has not gotten out about my return, along with you, he has a better chance to get what he wants."

"What about all the people who saw us enter the upper ward when we first came here? Shouldn't there be rumors all over the city by now?"

Eselt laughed her beautifully melodic laugh. "There was, but Commander Teutjorīk squashed it quickly by putting forth news that it was a cousin of mine with a similar hair color entering the upper ward that confused a grieving public."

"And how did he explain my presence along with your . . . cousin?" Drystan asked.

Eselt couldn't look him in the eyes. "No one noticed you, dear." Then she quickly kissed his cheek and giggled.

Drystan just shook his head and smiled. He couldn't blame anyone for not noticing him when she was around.

"So once your father gets what he wants from Lyonesse, then what?"

"I'm working on that still, but my father will see reason." Drystan could hear the determination in her voice and see the steel in her eyes and felt comforted that there was no better representative on their behalf.

"What of us until then?"

"My father has graciously allowed that we may travel anywhere in the upper ward and the Tower House together, except for my bedchamber." She stood on tiptoes then and tweaked his earlobe with her teeth. "But he didn't say anything about your bedchamber."

Drystan tried hard to avoid the fulsome grin that came over his face and then lost the inhibition altogether when he realized he could never match the one that Eselt was already wearing.

~~~

Three days passed. Three glorious days since she and Drystan had been reunited and they were inseparable during the daylight hours. They found every lonely tower, every arching walkway, every dark corridor, and every secluded garden niche in their travels until there was nowhere they hadn't been at least once. The Tower House was immense, and the upper ward even more so, but three days confined to their boundaries made it feel very small. Not that Eselt minded much, and she didn't think Drystan did either since they were happily together and free to be themselves, or at least who they wanted to be.

They strolled the massive courtyard in the shadow of the Tower House, enjoying the cool breeze of the overcast summer morning. Eselt thought it might rain in the afternoon, but she was unconcerned. That would give her the excuse to cuddle up next to him on a comfortable couch and watch the rain through one of the tall glass windows high up in one of the tower's many sitting rooms.

Few words passed between them on this day. Sometimes they didn't need to. Just being together was enough, and the communication between them found its way through a touch or a squeeze. Today, though, she had news, but she wanted to time it just right and waited. It would happen soon, and when it did, she would tell Drystan without delay. Until then she kept it bottled up inside, nearly bursting from anticipation, hoping she didn't blow it.

"Are you feeling well today, my love?" he asked while giving her shoulders a tight squeeze with his one arm around her.

"Oh, yes. I feel just fine." She tried not to let her voice warble with the laughter she desperately held in. "Why do you ask?"

"I'm sure it's nothing, dear. You just seem anxious, as if you had something on your mind." He was acting oddly casual as they walked toward the wall to look down on the city. "As if you had something very important to tell me. Like the war is over or something along those lines."

Eselt gasped with shock and stopped in mid-stroll. "How did you know?" She laughed while playfully pounding on his wide chest.

Just then bells began to chime all over Teamhrach, and she could hear the voices of thousands in the city below cheering and celebrating the significance of their ring.

"I was waiting for the bells!" She spoke loudly so he could hear over the high-pitched chime.

Drystan laughed and kissed her hard on the lips. "Commander Teutjorīk told me this morning when I was on my way to meet you for breakfast. He and I have formed quite a friendship, it seems, or maybe he just thinks I'm lonely."

"Why would he think that? Surely he has seen us together many times in the last few days."

"He has, but for some reason I cannot fathom, he thinks of me as a warrior, despite my lack of a gold-fringed cloak." Drystan laughed with only a bare hint of humor. "He must suppose that since I am not drunk and singing my lungs out with the Fianna every night, I must be lonely."

Eselt pinched his side, causing him to flinch. "Little does he know how lonely you really are since I am unable to share your bed at night yet."

"I should hope that changes soon," he said.

Eselt noticed a man walking in their direction not far away. He was dressed in a long robe with the cowl pulled up and concealing most of his face.

"It must," she said, somewhat distracted by the approach of the odd figure. The approaching man had a feather dangling on a thong like a Druid might wear, but something about him appeared a little off. "I will speak with Father this afternoon and hopefully gain his permission to leave."

The man was closer, not moving so fast or slow to stand out, but it was a deliberate line he walked that would bring him very close to where they stood when he passed.

"If all else fails, we always have our charms Myrllin made for us!" Drystan laughed.

Eselt could see the bottom half of the man's face more clearly. It must have been a long face. It was covered by reddish-brown whiskers on pale skin, much like many of the men in Eriu. Drystan didn't seem to notice the man, and just when the stranger was about to pass, he suddenly reached out and poked Drystan in the stomach.

"Purin sends his regards," the man growled.

"That was odd," Drystan uttered, turning to watch the man pick up speed until he was sprinting toward the low wall that formed the perimeter of the upper ward above sheer cliffs.

Eselt turned back to look at Drystan. There was blood at the spot where the man poked him.

"Drystan!" Eselt exclaimed, and he followed her gaze down to his midsection. The stain was slowly spreading through the white fabric of his silk tunic.

"I'm not feeling so well all of a sudden." He fell forward and onto his knees.

"Drystan, what is it? Drystan?" She crouched next to him, holding his face in her hands. His skin felt cold—too cold.

She glanced over her shoulder just in time to see the hooded man jump over the wall as if there wasn't a thousand-foot fall on the other side. She felt Drystan leaning heavily on her, and he was sweating profusely.

He tried to speak. "Eselt. Esel . . ." was all he said before collapsing on the ground beside her.

"Drystan!" she shrieked. "Drystan!" She heard the urgent footfalls of heavy boots approaching, but she could not tear her eyes away from his face. She stared in horror at her lover. His breathing grew dangerously shallow, and he began to twitch uncontrollably.

"Drystan!" she wailed holding his head from bouncing off the stone pavers. Men were beside her now, asking questions that she could not understand. It was everything she could do just to hold on to his convulsing body.

Then as quickly as it began, it stopped. Drystan's body went completely limp, and a red froth appeared between his lips. There was no expansion from the bubbles in the foam produced. There was no breath at all.

CHAPTER 26

Running

Darkness. He was surrounded by darkness. There was a door ahead and then a long corridor beyond. He ran. Like a rodent in a maze men would bet on in the market, he ran one way, then another, making quick choices along the way, but there was no light ahead no matter which way he turned. Always there was something that pursued him. He could never see or hear it, but he knew it hunted him and it was coming fast. If he hurried, he could stay ahead of it, and if he faltered, he knew the chase would end.

He ran in fear of what drove him as much as he searched for . . . something. He didn't know what. It went on and on. Sometimes he thought he gained and other times he was sure it was upon him. Either way, his need was desperate, and so he ran on. Through the fear and uncertainty, he realized that he never tired. It was an odd sensation, knowing that he could go on like this for eternity or until he lost his sanity. Maybe he had been running for an eternity already. He couldn't remember.

Somewhere up ahead he thought he saw the faintest flash of light. *Could it be true?* he wondered. *Could light exist here?* He ran harder and faster than he had before. Each time he turned a corner, he was sure the light turned another ahead of him. Still, he ran. No longer did he feel the fear of unseen, silent death from behind. There was something different that replaced it—hope. He felt hope. And it drove him harder than the fear ever had.

Then there was something new, a sound that echoed back to him from the light. He could not understand the words, if they were words at all, but there was a question or calling in the way the sound ended. He had to get closer. Pressing as hard as he could, he sprinted faster and faster, and with each step he gained on the light, death fell a step farther behind.

He was gaining on the light, the sound grew louder, and it repeated slowly over and over every few seconds. A little bit closer and he thought he could make it out.

"Drystan!" it called. Then again.

Drystan? Who was this Drystan? he thought.

He was only a few steps behind, but he was no longer gaining. There were no more turns, and the corridor he ran seemed to never end. The light was calling a name in a voice that was soft and beautiful almost like a song. Somehow, he thought he should recognize it.

A thought came to him that perhaps once he had been called Drystan, and the light seemed to pull him closer. He struggled to remember. And what of that beautiful voice? The name *Eselt* came to him, and the light drew him closer still. He could almost touch it. If he did, he knew he would be saved. He thought hard to understand and remember.

"Come back, Drystan, come back," the voice of Eselt pleaded, and he was filled with desperation.

He struggled to stretch his arm as far as possible. If he could just reach a little farther . . . just a little . . . The tips of his fingers entered the radiance, and he felt love flood through him. Love for life, love for survival, and most of all love for Eselt. The light encompassed and blinded him. He was no longer running or even moving. He was lying flat, and when he opened his eyes, she was there.

"Drystan!" she cried and kissed his face. "You're back, thank Eriu, you're back!" She fell upon him, embracing him tightly, and wept tears of happiness that soaked through the thin linens that covered him. He never felt so happy in his life.

~~~

"You died, young man, and if it wasn't for the particular knowledge of poisons in this man's head," the High King clasped the shoulder of the young druid standing next to him, "you would be in the ground by now."

"I owe you my life then, Druid." Drystan sat up in his bed and stretched his numb limbs. "And I'll give you my firstborn for a cup of water."

The High King gestured, and a servant came forth with a flagon of water that Drystan quickly drained. Handing the vessel back to the servant, he looked around the room in a panic. "Where is Eselt?"

"Fear not, boy, she hasn't abandoned you." The High King smiled. "I sent her to wash and change her clothes. I can't have a daughter of mine smelling like she lives under a dock."

Drystan felt relief. After he initially woke up, he did not remain awake for long before fatigue overtook him. Eselt had been with him then. "How long was I out?"

"About four days, almost five. We didn't expect you to come back after the second day." The High King shrugged and shook his head. "I might have been glad, except that it was the darkest time for Eselt, and I could never wish such misery upon my child."

"Do you feel strong enough to get out of bed?" the druid asked. He was dressed like almost every druid he had ever seen—long dark brown cloak decorated with feathers and shells and, of course, the Druid Stone hanging from a short cord around his neck. He was younger than one would expect, and his skin had fresh tattoos and a cool paleness about it, but if he saved his life, Drystan could care less how old he was or what he looked like.

"I do," Drystan responded. "Surprisingly, ready to get on my feet again."

He put his legs over the side of the bed and attempted to stand on wobbly legs before he was forced to sit down again. He tried again with the assistance of the High King—the man was remarkably strong for his age—and stood longer before he was forced to sit once more.

"You keep working on that, boy. When you are up to it, come see me. There is much to discuss."

Drystan nodded at the High King's back as Cadeyrn walked out of the room, and he briefly worried that their next meeting might involve excessive volumes of mead again.

Drystan was left alone with the young druid and decided he might as well get to know his savior. "What is your name?"

"I am called Odhrán." The druid smiled politely and continued to help Drystan exercise his legs.

"How is it that you know so much about poisons and remedies at your age?" Drystan tried not to sound patronizing, but he wasn't sure he had succeeded.

Odhrán looked at Drystan thoughtfully for a moment, and then his smile returned. "For most of my youth, I mixed poisons for the Arid Fellowship. I was very good at it and learned everything there is to know about poisons and their compositions." He shrugged. "That was how I survived until I was found by the druids."

"Isn't the Arid Fellowship a powerful assassins guild that stretches across the Western Kingdoms?"

"It is."

Drystan was standing on his own now, with Odhrán only a pace away in case he stumbled. He heard that the Druids came from every walk of life, but he never would have imagined one would be found among killers in the most infamous guild in the Western Kingdoms.

He was going to ask the druid more about his past, but that was when Eselt breezed in and the entirety of his thoughts transferred to her. Without pausing for an instant, she immediately embraced him gently, taking care not to cause him any further pain. Her skin carried the fresh scent of lavender and daffodil, an intoxicating combination that filled his senses when he buried his face in her long golden hair.

"Father told me you were up," she said with a smile fairer than the most beautiful sunrise.

"And walking again," added Odhrán.

Eselt turned her smile on the druid. "Thank you, Odhrán. You are truly blessed by Eriu for bringing my Drystan back to life."

"It is my pleasure to serve in the preservation of life." He bowed deeply and made his exit.

"Did you know he was once in the Arid Fellowship?" Drystan asked her after the druid left the room. He sat on the bed again to rest his legs.

Eselt sat next to him and put her head on his shoulder. "Oh yes, he is quite the success story in Eriu."

"I'm surprised the guild didn't have him eliminated after the druids took him away."

Eselt giggled. "They are the ones who informed the druids that he had unusual abilities in the first place."

"Why wouldn't they use him to their advantage?"

"Because the druids would have found out eventually, and that would have been a problem." She stroked his arm that she leaned on while they talked. "Would you want the Druids of Eriu as your adversary?"

"I suppose not," Drystan had to agree. Then he changed the subject. "Your father wishes to speak with me again. I hope he's not planning another long night, I don't think I could survive it!"

Eselt laughed and tickled his side. "Then you better meet with him early in the day. Otherwise, the two of you will be dancing down another rabbit's hole."

"Do you know what it's about?"

"It's about our departure." She was smiling again and looking up at him with her pretty blue eyes. "I don't know the details, but he agrees you're not safe staying here, and I told him whatever he decides, it had better include me."

Drystan felt relief, joy, and concern all at the same time. "Did they find the culprit that stabbed me?"

"Sadly, no. I thought for sure that when the would-be assassin went over the wall, we would find him squashed like a bug from the fall, but he was gone. There was one report of a man in black floating down the east side from the upper ward, so Commander Teutjorīk assumes that it was our man with the aid of some form of sorcery."

"Then he got away." Drystan hoped the assassin was dead or, better, captured so they could find out if he acted alone or if there was a price on Drystan's head for anyone to collect.

"Before he stabbed you, he said he had a message from Purin." Eselt shifted to face him. "How could Captain Purin know that you were here?"

"It was rumored that he had a particular taste for entertaining his lovers somewhere in the seedier section of Tintagel." Drystan shook his head. "I never believed it, but if it were true, then he might have a number of contacts through the guild networks that he could use to buy information and hire assassins."

"More the reason for us to disappear," Eselt reasoned. "I suppose that means that Duke Maruk knows we are alive and under the protection of my father."

"I don't think so." Drystan frowned as he thought through the logic. "For reasons only Purin knows, I believe he has kept the information to himself. If he told my uncle, then surely the duke would have informed King Praeter, and the negotiations with your father would have broken down." He spread his hands apart for emphasis. "But that hasn't happened."

"Captain Purin has become more dangerous than ever to us." She leaned forward, hugging him tightly. "We must be careful, Drystan. Next time there may not be a druid specializing in poisons nearby."

Drystan stroked Eselt's long golden hair reassuringly. "We will, love. Have no fear. I will speak to your father in the morning, and we can be off soon after. To where, I don't know. A place you will be safe."

~~~

"You will have to leave Eriu for a while, years maybe." The High King paced as he spoke and slapped a pair of riding gloves on his thigh periodically. Drystan found him just before his morning ride, sober and irritated. He hoped this meeting would end better than when the High King was drunk and happy.

The High King was none too happy that he was being forced to send his youngest daughter into hiding with a subverted knight just days after she returned to him. He as much as said so. Drystan understood the High King's frustration and reluctance to release his daughter into Drystan's care after everything that had happened, but Eselt had not given anyone much of a choice in the matter. She was going with Drystan even if it meant jumping over the same wall the assassin had to make his escape.

"Where can we go that we will be safe from the Arid Fellowship?" Drystan didn't like the idea of spending the rest of his life hunted.

The High King stopped and turned to face him. "It wasn't an assassin from the Arid Fellowship that attacked you. I can assure you that they are looking for your attacker as hard as we are just to prove it. The last thing they want is this kind of attention."

"That means Captain Purin must have used someone from outside of Eriu to come after me," Drystan speculated. "This would also suggest that there isn't a general guarantee on my head for anyone to collect."

"Very well considered, young man," the High King nodded his approval while he scratched his graying beard. "I don't know how resourceful this Captain Purin is, but he has lost his advantage now that we know his plan."

"I've known Purin my entire life, and he often acts impulsively. I would be surprised if he had a backup plan." Drystan's throat was dry, and he reluctantly took a draught of the mead that the High King had poured him when he first arrived. "Especially considering that whoever he hired was no amateur and must have cost him a small fortune. He would have been confident of success."

"The good news for you is that the assassin and Purin are very likely to believe they have succeeded." The High King wore a sly smile. "We have kept your identity and condition very quiet. In fact, Commander Teutjorīk let a rumor slip out that there was a tragic death in the Tower House, but not the how or the who."

"That should give us the time we need to depart Eriu before the truth gets out anyway." Drystan was glad of the help, but he doubted that Purin would ever give up his search as long as he thought Drystan was alive. He worried more about Eselt than he did himself because he knew that the captain was devious enough to take his rage out on her just to get to Drystan. Wherever they went, it would have to be a place where they would not stand out or draw attention. Myrllin's charms would help with that initially, but Drystan didn't expect to wear them forever.

"Now, I have made some arrangements for you both." The High

King began his pacing again, but his eyes were steady on Drystan. "I will not have my daughter living as a homeless vagabond. Rather, the two of you will be from obscure noble families outside of the city of Kenno, you a knight and Eselt a lady betrothed to you."

"Sounds reasonable"—Drystan took another swig of the mead; it was starting to taste better—"except that I don't deserve the honorific of knighthood and would only bring dishonor to those who have earned it."

There was sincere sympathy in the High King's eyes, and he nodded quietly for a moment. "You forget one thing, boy; we are tied to each other for eternity because of the Liafal Stone." The High King's gaze was intense and held his own without wavering. "I know your heart, and despite the ruin of your uncle's marriage to my daughter, you have more honor in you than anyone I have known."

"That is a generous thing to say, but—" Drystan began before the High King cut him short.

"Listen to me!" he demanded, pointing a thick finger Drystan's way. "This is not a negotiation. You will do as I say, or I swear that I will risk the love of my daughter and remove your head!"

The High King slowly sat in a chair nearby and placed a large meaty hand on Drystan's knee. "If you are minor nobility of Eriu, I can quietly install you and Eselt in houses that will provide you both with a reasonable income. No one will have cause to question, and any that do will be dealt with. I will knight you under Eriu law before you leave Teamhrach, and you will be able to go anywhere that you will not be recognized. You will have also have to adopt new names that will be provided to you."

Drystan said nothing, unsure of whether or not the High King finished with what he meant to say.

He had not.

"Finally, I have spoken to the Arch-Druid of Eriu, Caomh, the one that married Eselt to Maruk, and he has agreed to invalidate the marriage. The druids don't believe in marriage anyway—they see it as unnatural—but to satisfy the laws of Eriu and Lyonesse, he will dissolve it on the grounds of faithlessness prior to the union. He is confident that Filberzh will agree on behalf of Sunna, and I will add my influence to assure a beneficial outcome."

Drystan must have betrayed a briefly panicked look on his face because the High King smiled and said, "Yes, I know. Eselt told me. Do you think I was never young and concupiscent?"

"Of course you were, Your Majesty."

The High King leaned back and picked up his cup of mead. "From now on, when we are alone you call me Cadeyrn."

"As you wish ... Cadeyrn." Drystan was feeling an unexpected kinship with the High King, and he wondered if it wasn't because of their connection through the Liafal. "What will happen once Eselt can marry again?"

The High King nearly spit the mead he just guzzled. "If you are still in love and Eselt remains determined to stay by your side, then I cannot compel her to marry another. Besides, she is of no political use to me now anyway, so she might as well be happy."

Drystan smiled. Inside and out he felt pure joy at the idea of him and Eselt married.

"Now we have to figure a way to get you out of the Tower House unnoticed by anyone who could possibly recognize the two of you." The High King was tapping the table with the knuckles of his fist. "We could cut your hair and change the color of hers . . ."

Drystan interrupted politely, "Cadeyrn, we won't need to do any of that. In fact, we will walk out the front doors, through the city, and out the gates just as we are now, and no one will be the wiser as to our identity."

The High King appeared very surprised. "How will you accomplish this? Are you practiced in the arts of sorcery as well?"

"The next best thing." Drystan held up his wrist with the charm tied around it. "We had a chance meeting with Wodanaz and his brother Myrllin at the camp where I freed Eselt. The wizard gave Eselt and me charms to conceal our identities and allow us to travel unhindered to Teamhrach."

"Ah yes." The High King folded his arms over his chest. "Eselt told me about that meeting. She left the part about the charms out, though." He smiled broadly. "She probably planned to use them to escape me if I did not agree to her plans, clever girl."

Drystan smiled at that too. "So where are you sending us?"

"It will be natural for you to go to Kenno—that is the closest city to your new houses—and from there it is up to you." The High King ran his fingers through his dark, graying hair. "I recommend Ys. It is a large city, and from there you can go to Courth or even Rasna if you choose."

"I agree. How soon should we plan to depart?"

"Tomorrow morning would be best." He had a sad look on his face that betrayed the High King's conflicted thoughts of letting his daughter go again. "Now that the war is over and the tourneys back on schedule for the spring, you will simply be two more travelers in the rush."

"Very well." Drystan stood to go. "It will be tomorrow morning, then."

"One last thing, Drystan." The High King stood and leveled his gaze at Drystan one more time. "If you make my daughter unhappy, the Arid Fellowship will have a target after all if my own blade does not find you first."

"I would just as soon cut my own throat," Drystan replied sincerely.

The High King nodded and embraced him like a son before Drystan walked through the door and into the corridor beyond. He felt the exhilaration of starting a new life with Eselt and hoped that this time it was for real.

CHAPTER 27

The Storm

Purin was pleased that there would be no war. He thought of it as a waste of time, resources, and lives that would not in any way further his goal of retribution upon the man that very nearly took his life. Now, all that was about to change. He just exited a meeting with the duke and a mysterious emissary from Eriu charged with a mission that would right everything in the world again. Purin's world, anyway, and perhaps the duke's to some measure. That's all that really mattered to him.

Only a few days before, he had learned of his hired assassin's failure to eliminate Drystan in Teamhrach. Purin had been infuriated at the news given the cost and reputation of the man he had contracted through the guild intermediary, Tudful. At the risk of losing his source of entertainment, Purin threatened Tudful with an ultimatum—punish the failure or suffer the cost himself. The assassin turned up dead in the street three days later. It was little consolation to Purin, but if nothing else, he cemented his power and influence in the lower city, and everyone knew it.

Purin wasn't sure he would ever have the opportunity to confront Drystan again until the emissary arrived that morning. The emissary revealed that the lovers were in the port city of Kenno a little over a hundred leagues downriver from Teamhrach. They were living under assumed names of obscure rural noble houses and had plans to take a ship south to Ys sometime in the near future. Purin was surprised. He would have expected High King Cadeyrn to surround his daughter with layers of security and keep them locked up inside the Tower House for years. Instead, he cunningly sent them away, south, toward the grand city of Ys. That was weeks ago, but it was music to Purin's ears. He had no plans to set foot into Eriu or send another assassin—that could turn out badly again. Purin would wait until they crossed the border and confront them himself. In the meantime, he would send spies to Kenno to watch the lovers until they departed and assign men to cover every port and inn between the coastal border of Lyonesse and Ys.

"Captain," a voice called to him from the far end of the corridor. It was the duke.

"Yes, Your Grace." Purin quickly retraced his steps to stand before Duke Maruk.

The duke leaned close and spoke in whispered tones, "I want Drystan returned alive, if at all possible."

"I will do everything in my power to make it so, Your Grace."

"Good." Duke Maruk pat Purin on the shoulder and turned to leave. "I know I can count on you."

Purin smiled with gratitude for the duke's benefit with the full knowledge that after what they planned for Eselt occurred, there would be no possibility in hell of taking Drystan alive.

~~~

Early in the morning, Eselt was standing next to Drystan on a shallow-bottomed riverboat traveling west to Kenno on the Elawar River. It was unusually cold that morning, and Eselt was happy that she insisted they wear their heavy cloaks even though Drystan had grumbled about it until they were on the water. The river paralleled the northern slopes of the Kenno-windo Mountain Range, providing them with an endless panorama of beautiful white-capped mountains to the south and heavily forested terrain to the north, which, if she remembered correctly, would last the entirety of their two-day voyage.

Hardly a year passed in her youth when she did not travel to Kenno with her family. They had a palace of sorts near the market district, and she would spend her days with her mother and sisters selecting fabrics for their annual wardrobes. Kenno was the fashion and art center of Eriu, and their dressmakers were fabled artists known throughout the Western Kingdoms for their distinctive craft. She suspected that her father considered the annual trips more of a penance that must be suffered to keep the women in his life happy, but she knew he had his own vices in the city known for more than just beautiful dresses.

This trip to Kenno was very different than any of the others in her past. She endured a tearful parting with her family that morning, which left her feeling melancholy and reflective. She wanted to stay longer among them, but the dangers she and Drystan faced and the urgency to depart before word escaped the Tower House of their presence and current state of health eliminated any excuse for delay. Drystan expressed concern that Captain

Purin would not relent once he discovered the truth, and if that meant going through Eselt and anyone else who got in the way, then he would see them as merely casualties of his objective.

So here they were, on a boat fleeing her home to Kenno and then Ys, where they would start a new life as strangers. Her father provided them with new identities—her name was Lady Esmeth of House Dubhshláine, and Drystan was Sir Lugaid of House Gille Fhaolain. Both were old families with estates that actually existed in remote areas of the wilderness and who had little interaction with the more urban houses in Kenno. It didn't matter to her, since they would probably never visit either of the estates, and she hoped that Captain Purin's spies would never learn of their deception and think to go there either. She couldn't bear the thought of innocents harmed because of her deceit.

They traveled under assumed names and altered appearances, and Eselt decided it couldn't have been more romantic. She loved the idea of running away with her lover, desperately evading danger at every turn and employing sorcery in clandestine practice. *Well, maybe it wasn't as dramatic as that,* she thought. But they did depend on Myrllin's magical trinkets to hide who they were, and her fantasy version might make for a good story one day.

She wondered if it was the same for the heroes of legend. Did their entire life stories hinge on a few dramatic events sandwiched between long intervals of nothing interesting going on at all? What were they like when they were at home with their families and the people they loved? Was it too mundane to warrant adding to the annals of history before they left their homes for adventure? She was sure they must have had far more exciting lives than hers. Eselt was fine with that. She was happiest without all the excitement and danger and worry and anxiety, just next to Drystan—or Lugaid, she reminded herself—watching the landscape roll by.

Ugh, I am never going to get used to Lugaid, she thought irritably. At least the new name her father gave her was vaguely similar to her own. She had a feeling her father chose Lugaid just to aggravate her. It was working.

"Do you suppose we can lead normal, quiet lives now?"

Eselt was startled by Drystan speaking after so long standing together in silence, enjoying the scenery and her own thoughts. "I have certainly had enough adventure for a lifetime," she replied.

"I'm glad to hear it." He put his arm around her waist and gave her a squeeze. "Nothing would please me more than to buy a rural estate, marry you and have a string of children."

Eselt nuzzled up into his thick cloak. "I would like that more than anything." She really would, more than all the titles and balls and witty conversations with self-important nobles or even strings of pearls and emeralds stretching back to Teamhrach. She was content.

~~~

Kenno was a fortress city with a well defended port often subject to raids by the Vikja, especially in the summer months, according to the innkeeper of the upscale inn where they stayed. To keep up appearances, they rented two adjoining suits and planned to dishevel both beds before the chambermaids arrived each morning. Considering that they were not yet married and believed to be nobility, they decided to follow the outward appearance of proper protocol and avoid scandal by the idle gossip of lodgings staff. Behind closed doors, it was a very different story, and except for the time it took to wash and dress, they were inseparable.

Drystan was enjoying his new life, and it was easy to see that Eselt felt the same. The High King provided them with a modest income to live on in addition to the small fortune Drystan was able to retrieve from the forest where he buried it before they departed Teamhrach. He was still irritated by the fact that he could not access the much larger fortune he accumulated and left in the care of the Knights Temple under an assumed name. The High King had warned him that if he did, he would surely be giving himself away. He and Eselt would simply have to live on what they had until they could purchase land and a small estate that could produce an income. It might take years, but he would do it happily as long as Eselt was with him.

They stayed in Kenno through the winter and the following spring. The High King thought it would be best for them to establish their new identities in the social circles of the local nobility. There was never a shortage of their parties, balls, hunt clubs, and competitions to build their social cachet. Drystan was surprised at how quickly they were accepted, and soon they were known as the friendly young nobles from the country. Eselt played her part to perfection and never let her royal blood get the better of her. Drystan was impressed with her humility and command of the role she played. If she weren't a princess, she might have followed a path to the theater.

Eventually, word came through House Gille Fhaolain that they were cleared to leave Kenno, and Drystan booked passage to Ys. He didn't know what the High King was up to behind the scenes, but he had to trust that he knew what he was doing. Drystan assumed the months of delay had something to do with the tourneys that raged through the Western Kingdoms and culminated in the Champions Tourney in Tintagel this year. And with the newly rejoined friendship between Eriu and Lyonesse, the tourneys were expected to be bigger than ever. Besides, the High King's own daughter's life was at stake in his maneuverings, and if Drystan knew anything about the High King, it was that he was an expert at manipulating fortunes in his favor.

Over the next few days, he and Eselt said their farewells to those friends they had made, promising to write and return soon. Although they knew it was a lie, they smiled just the same. Their destiny was far away, and their voyage would begin on a seagoing ship that would take them to the grandest port city in the Western Kingdom and the new life they desperately pursued for so long.

~~~

"Don't you worry, lad," the first mate assured Drystan. "Once we get into open water, no Vikja craft is fast enough to run down this ship!"

"What about the hours we will be on the river until then?" Drystan asked.

The first mate had an answer for that too. "We'll run in a group with other merchants and an escort of warships from Kenno all the way to the Primal Sea. Have no fear, lad—your girl will be safe enough. We've only been nearly boarded two or three times this season!"

"That's just great." Drystan didn't quite share the first mate's enthusiasm.

Down the river they went, accompanied by three merchant ships and escorted by two medium warships from Kenno, all powered under oar with the current. The weather stayed cool and the wind brisk against their faces as Drystan held Eselt around her waist. Looking out at the thick forest to the north and high mountains to the south, the contrast was at the same time striking and awesome in its natural elegance. So far, their lives in the months after leaving Teamhrach was a pleasure, and Drystan could almost forget the misery and suffering they had faced as a way of life in Tintagel. Sometimes, it seemed like a different life when they had skulked through hidden passages just to spend a night together.

The journey to Ys would be five or six days, depending on the weather, and they were eager to reach their destination. Drystan was familiar with Ys and regaled Eselt with fables of its beauty to pass the time. No one would know them there, and with a change of wardrobe they would fit right in. He was unsure how long they would stay there. A short time or forever, it all depended on how they got on with the people and how secure they felt. If they decided to stay, they would find a patch of land not too far outside the city and start their lives. If not, there was always Courth farther to the south.

Early on the second day out from Kenno, a bell rang in the distance from one of the merchant ships ahead of them. It clanged insistently and was soon joined by the clanging of other ships in the line. Drystan and Eselt were already up and enjoying the morning air while they ate some crusty bargina bread provided by the crew.

"Well that's not good," the first mate announced uncertainly. He was standing not far from them, barefoot and wearing a low-cut tunic . . . and buckling on his sword belt.

"What's happening?" Drystan asked urgently.

"Something has been sighted up ahead there near the mouth of the river. Sometimes the Vikja wait there and pick off the slowest merchant before it can hasten to pick up speed in the open waters. There!" he pointed off into the distance. "See that black mast? Looks like two, no, three of them. That's the Vikja. Keep your girl away from the sides. It could get rough, and I wouldn't want her to fall over or get poked by an arrow."

Drystan took Eselt below deck to safety. "Stay out of sight, love. I'm going to see how I can help."

"Drystan, be careful. We haven't come all this way to have you murdered by a marauder's arrow."

He kissed her tender lips and smiled. "I will stay low. By the way, do you know how to swim?"

"I do, why?"

"No reason." He bounded up the ladder before she could ask any more questions.

Drystan crouched under the railing and looked out between the supports. From his vantage point, he could see the two Kenno warships engaging two of the black Vikja ships. He knew those black sails well, and he was familiar with their tactics from the year he had spent in their captivity.

The two ships that engaged the Kenno warships would keep them distracted while the third went for one of the trade vessels. Once the Vikja had one, the other two would disengage from the warships and join the one boarding the merchant. The warships would likely withdraw or move to protect any of the lingering merchant vessels trying to escape. When the Vikja had you, they had you, and only overwhelming force would drive them off a kill.

He watched as his prediction came true and the Vikja chased down a merchant vessel ahead of them and a little north. Had the Vikja been positioned on the south side of the river, it would have been Drystan and Eselt's ship they attacked.

The captain ordered the sails at full, and they tacked around due south with the prevailing wind and away from the embattled merchant vessel.

Drystan watched it being boarded by fur-clad warriors swinging axes or swords. The warriors on the trade vessel would give their best, but they were too few and overmatched by the fury of the Vikja on the sea. When it was done, the Vikja would load anything of value onto their ships and leave the merchant vessel burning at the mouth of the river.

Less than half an hour later, with Eselt standing on the deck again, they could see the black plume of smoke rising in the distance behind them.

"Isn't there any way the merchants can protect themselves from those demons?" Eselt asked.

Drystan shrugged. "They could carry a battle wizard with them, but that's very expensive, and the odds are low that their ship would ever come under attack."

"But the lives of all those men, surely some had families, aren't they worth the cost?"

"Most ship captains are too frugal. Battle wizards would cut into their profits far too much considering the relatively cheap cost to replace a seaman."

From behind he heard a passing *humph* as the captain walked on, having overheard their conversation.

Drystan and Eselt looked at each other and burst out laughing.

Later that evening, when the crew was quiet and the wind was steady, Drystan untied Purin's sword from his travel pack and went to stand by Eselt at the ship's railing.

"What will you defend me from now, my love?" Eselt's beautiful smile glowed in the moonlight reflecting off the diamond-speckled wake that the ship cut through the water. "Have you spied a sea monster? Or the black sails of the Vikja?" He knew she was joking, but that last part was a real possibility given the events earlier in the day.

"This is Purin's sword, the magical one that I told you about the night I found you in the camp." He pulled it out a few inches to show the fine Dvergr steel, and an electrical charge popped between the blade and the metal edge of the sheath that carried it. Eselt's eyes went wide at the sparks, and she backed away a pace. Drystan slammed the vile thing safely back into the protection of the scabbard and threw it overboard.

"Drystan!" Eselt exclaimed. "Why did you do that?"

"I've got scalds and blisters all over from trying to use that thing. The lightning in its blade is a distraction, and just as much a danger to myself as to any opponent I might face with it. It's a shame that the enchantment was placed on such exceptional steel." He leaned close and kissed her gingerly. "Besides, if things go as planned, I'll be wielding tools for farming with little need for a sword from now on."

Eselt threw her arms around his neck and hugged him tightly. "I pray that Eriu grants that dream for both of us."

~~~

The fourth day at sea, the weather was beginning to turn, according to the first mate, far more rapidly than it should.

"'Tis unnatural for the clouds to come in like this so fast. An' comin' from behind us where we been sailin' at that!" He looked out over the water. "We entered the Bay o' Morgens a few hours ago. An' it's a dangerous place t'be in a storm like what's comin'. We got rocks under the water on one side and a rocky shore on the other, an' still a day out from Ys! I better see what the cap'n gonna do."

"We had to travel by boat, didn't we?" Drystan joked nervously.

"Don't worry, love. We will be fine. After all we've been through, I don't think Eriu and Sunna will abandon us to the Morgen."

Drystan almost laughed. He knew Eselt must have been nervous since she only invoked the Sister Goddesses when she was. Although he tried not to show it, he was nervous too.

The first mate came running by. "Cap'n says we gonna anchor in a cove east of us till the storm passes. He will let you off there if you wish so you can go the rest of the way by land. It's gonna get rough on this bucket, and even the most seasoned of us will be stickin' our heads over the side ta' empty our stomachs! An' we may be stuck here for a day or two if it's a hurricane comin' up on us!"

Within an hour the ship sailed into a deep-water cove on the southern coast of Lyonesse and away from the rocks. Drystan had already decided that he was ready to be off the churning water, and Eselt enthusiastically agreed. Neither of them had the sea legs or the digestive fortitude to withstand the tossing that the ship would endure when the storm blew in on it, especially if it lasted for more than a few hours.

"Cap'n says there be a way station you can stay at 'fore it gets dark if you hurry," the first mate offered.

"Thank you for your hospitality," Drystan responded, "and may you weather the storm safely."

The captain had brought the ship close enough to the shallow water for a crewman to row them over. Their tethered horses swam behind them supported by empty barrels strapped to their flanks. Once on shore, they watched the ship move back out to deeper water, where it would anchor safely away from the rocky shallows to weather the coming storm.

Donning the waterproof hooded cloaks they brought with them, Drystan quickly tied all the packs onto the horses and then surveyed their surroundings. He could see the coastal road with the extra height from the back of his horse, and they spurred their mounts up the seagrass-covered slope to follow it south. To their left, the thick forest gave way to rolling hills carpeted with high green grass that curved toward the east from the constant force of the sea breeze. The coastal road skirted the Bay of Morgens, traversing an uneven landscape that sometimes took them high over sheer cliffs pounded by angry waves sending salty spray towering over their heads and other times brought them almost level to sandy beaches populated with boulder-size black rocks and waist-high erosion. Drystan had ridden this way many years before and had forgotten the unusual natural beauty of the region.

By late afternoon the wind picked up, and the rain started to come in slow, thick droplets. Far to the west where the waters of the bay met the horizon, storm clouds, black as coal, promised a far less accommodating torrent upon them. If they didn't find the way station soon, Drystan worried they would have to take shelter in a cave or the forest, neither of which would be very comfortable. Fortunately, the weather held long enough, and they found the inn just before it began to pour. Drystan turned their mounts over to the stable hands, who were busy closing up and tying down everything that the wind might carry away and went inside to rent a room for the night.

After so many days traveling by road and sea, Drystan's beard had grown, and Eselt's undone blonde hair was in desperate need of grooming. Even without the charms concealing their true identities, few could have mistaken them for anything other than simple travelers. Still, they were a little nervous. The trade vessel let them off in a cove only about forty leagues south of Tintagel, and they were still a few leagues north of the River of Mists, which marked the southern border of Lyonesse and the beginning of the territories of Ys.

There were few travelers at the inn, leaving ample space for Drystan and Eselt to dry off in front of the fire of the quiet common room. Drystan noted with some concern that Eselt removed her charm so she could dry her hair without getting tangled in the leather cord. No one seemed to notice except a young man innocently gawking at her beauty. He looked away, embarrassed, and left the room in a hurry when Drystan caught his eye.

The storm was getting worse by the minute. Drystan could hear the boom of waves against the cliffs a league or so to the west, and he worried about the crew of the ship that brought them from Kenno. He wasn't the only one concerned about the gale-force winds. The innkeeper, a lanky man of middle years, paced nervously through the small inn, checking the doors and shutters compulsively.

"Haven't seen a storm like this in years," he was saying. "And never one that came on so strong and so quick."

"It appeared to be heading straight into the bay before nightfall," Eselt said, nervously looking to the creaking shutters as if expecting them to blow open any second. "And there were dozens of ships that fled into the bay to anchor in calmer waters. Now I am concerned about them."

"It sounds like it is right on top of us now," Drystan added. "Although it is too dark to see anything outside, especially the clouds."

"What about Ys?" Eselt asked the innkeeper. "Won't the city be in danger of flooding?"

The innkeeper barked a quick laugh. "Not likely. Not with that massive sea wall they have built around their port. In fact, that's where I would prefer to be right now."

Drystan felt his stomach drop at those words. "Are you suggesting we are in danger staying here?" he demanded.

The innkeeper had a look of shock on his face, and he pat the air in front of him with his hands in an effort to calm Drystan. "No, no. We are perfectly fine. The inn has a solid stone foundation and sturdy cedar timbers. Believe me! This building has been standing strong for over two centuries, and through the worst of storms. There is nothing to fear!" He seemed sincere in his assurances, and Drystan relaxed.

The innkeeper disappeared for a while, and they were soon joined by his wife and daughters serving hot stew with crusty flatbread. Before they finished, the innkeeper returned, and Drystan could tell that he was a little flustered. Whatever his concern, it must have been a minor thing, and soon he joined them at the table. For the remainder of the meal, the innkeeper entertained them with funny stories of some of his most unusual guests to keep them distracted from the tempest brewing outside. Drystan was sure the man had regaled his patrons with these same stories many times over and appeared to enjoy the retelling for them.

"Just this evening we had a strange one." The innkeeper had a perplexed look on his face. "A young man. He had been renting a room for a few weeks. Never seemed to have anything to do but hang around. And he didn't talk much. Then tonight he demanded his horse and rode out of here like fire was on his tail, into the weather. Right after the two of you arrived, in fact. I sure hope that boy is OK out there."

A natural storyteller, Drystan mused, and for a moment he thought of

Wodanaz with his strange brother in tow. He almost laughed out loud when he recalled the peculiar pair. The way they spoke to each other as if the world around them were an abstract curiosity and the respect they commanded from kings and druids. There was something strange and compelling about them, for sure. And what was it Wodanaz had said about a geas when the brothers were leaving? Was he talking about him and Eselt? What sort of geas could he or Eselt have over one or both of them? He wondered if they would ever meet again. He doubted it, but if they did, he would surely ask about it.

The hour grew late, yet the intensity of the storm did not change, and Drystan suggested he and Eselt retire to their room so the innkeeper could finalize his checks before attending to his own family. As bad as the storm was, Drystan was sure they were on the edge of it with the majority of thunder booming loud but distant to the south. Even so, waves of intensity battered the inn throughout the night to the point that it was impossible to sleep with the whistling of the wind through loose boards and the frequent boom of thunder that sent vibrations through the whole of the stone and timber structure. Drystan held Eselt tightly in their bed and whispered quiet assurances that the roof would hold despite several leaks already streaming through narrow cracks throughout the room. Somehow, with the maelstrom raging around them, they fell asleep secure in their embrace.

CHAPTER 28

Ys

SY5491

Elegant twisting spires with delicately carved, soaring walkways between them; lush blooming gardens abundant with fountains; and broad causeways interrupted by graceful arching bridges over rambling rivers. This exceedingly beautiful and vain city is the personification of one of the most remarkably sophisticated women I have known at the height of her form, with a dangerous bite to match. It is the passing of this Grand Dame that I mourn more than any other, and my ballads shall weep for her into eternity.

Wodanaz the Wanderer

Drystan awoke to the first rays of a beautiful morning. The violent wind, rain, and thunder of the storm had passed and took with it the fear that was so real the night before. He tossed back the shutters and looked out the narrow window to see clear blue skies frequented by puffy white clouds that lingered over the grassy hills and shifted only slightly in the mild breeze from the west.

"At least we didn't get soaked," Eselt commented sleepily from the bed. "It looks like we managed to avoid the downpour from the leaky roof."

"The innkeeper's words were true about this being a sturdy building." An urgent thought came to Drystan. "I better check the horses!"

He rushed outside to find the stable intact. The horses were wet from gaps in the roof, but neither animal was injured, to his relief. Drystan checked them over thoroughly just to be sure and instructed the stable boys to brush them down before he returned to join Eselt for breakfast. There was debris in the coral and all around the property from roof tiles and tree branches. He hoped the innkeeper had not sustained too much damage in the ordeal.

When he walked back inside, Eselt was chatting with the innkeeper's wife and enjoying a modest meal of warm porridge topped with cream and fresh crusty bread with honey. Drystan's stomach responded with a groan of hunger, and after dried fish and dates for three days on the ship, this meal looked set for a king.

"Sometimes the road gets flooded or blocked by fallen trees after a storm like what we had last night," the innkeeper said when he walked in, "and out here in the country, it might be a few days getting it cleared away. But if it's not too bad, you should arrive in Ys by tomorrow afternoon."

"How has your inn fared in the storm?" Drystan asked. "I see the stables have lost much of their cover."

The innkeeper ran a hand through his thinning hair. "My boys will be spending the next few weeks patching holes in all our structures, but I'm not complaining. They're still standing, and none of my family or guests were injured."

"We can all thank Sunna for that," Drystan agreed. "Any word on conditions south of us?"

"Other than the fallen trees and flooding, not much word has come in yet, but what I've seen so far is mostly superficial." He paused as if considering whether or not to add more. "I wish I could say the same for those ships that took refuge in the bay last night. I don't think they fared so well."

"What makes you so sure?" Drystan asked.

"Just like you mentioned last night, dozens were dotting the waters up and down the shore as far as you could see at anchor to ride out the storm." He shook his head sadly. "This morning my grounds man reported that he could see less than a handful still upright when the sun came up, and wreckage from the less fortunate was already littering the beaches."

Drystan looked to Eselt with unspoken concern for the first mate and crew of the ship that brought them from Kenno. Drystan made a mental note to check with the docks after they arrived in Ys. He knew Eselt was likely just as worried.

They finished their breakfast with light conversation and no more talk about the storm. Drystan had a sinking feeling that they would encounter more devastation farther south that day, but kept those thoughts to himself. There was no reason to upset Eselt unnecessarily before they were sure about anything and he fervently hoped his intuition was wrong, at least in this case.

"Could we trouble you for a lunch pack for our journey?" Eselt asked when she rose to return to their room.

"After putting up with my leaky roof last night, it's the least I can do for you," the innkeeper replied happily.

Drystan paid him well for the accommodations, such as they were, and the innkeeper seemed to be doing everything he could to keep them happy. He even sent his daughters to prepare a bath for Eselt and to comb out her hair before they departed.

Sitting in the quiet common room near the warmth of the large fireplace, Drystan had time to consider the direction their lives were taking and the hope they shared for the future. So many things changed for them after their latest departure from Teamhrach. They had, for the first time, begun to make friends. The kind of friends that they would write and keep up with, go to visit when they were near and do things together as couples or groups. First, the people they met in Kenno, then the first mate of the ship that took them away from that city, and most recently the innkeeper and his family—good people who cared about Drystan and Eselt. It was an odd feeling knowing others in that way. He never had friends growing up in Valiant Keep, and then later he squired to a knight there was no time for any. Even after he earned his gold-fringed cloak, he never made real friends. There were the other knights he drank with, the girls he spent time with, and his family, but friendship was new and strange to him. He wondered if it was the same for Eselt. Both of them had been children of politics and governing, kept separate from the rest of the world, insulated and protected. Most of the kindness he received from common folk he just assumed was due to his station. He had to admit to himself that view was a flaw in the character of today's nobility and maybe, just maybe, there was more genuine kindness in the world that he ever suspected.

In a real way, Myrllin and the High King changed more than the couple's names and appearances; they gave the pair new identities. And Drystan actually liked who he was now: Sir Lugaid of House Gille Fhaolain, Knight of Eriu. He had to laugh. Never would he have imagined the course his life would take. He was at peace.

He knew it was Eselt who entered the common room before he saw her. The fresh scent of lily of the valley preceded her entrance, and when he turned to greet her, he wasn't disappointed. Her golden hair hung tightly braided almost to her waist, and she wore a tailored black riding dress that she must have brought with her from Kenno. He had never seen it before that occasion, and it made him pause to catch his breath at how beautiful she looked. He wondered if everyone else saw her in the same way as he did, even with the charms they wore. Was she as stunning to look at to them? In a rare moment of jealousy, he hoped not.

Their packs were already strapped to their mounts by the time they said their goodbyes to the innkeeper and his happy family. They promised to stay again when they traveled north one day, and Drystan genuinely believed that they would when the High King sent for them. *That will be a good day,* he thought, *the day I go back to Kenno to marry Eselt.*

As they rode south from the way station, Drystan couldn't resist making the observation, "You know, we would probably be in Ys by now if we had stayed with the ship."

"I wish that to be true, my love," Eselt agreed, "and that the men on that ship came through the storm intact. But can you imagine what last night would have been like rolling around in the water? Besides, look what a beautiful morning it is."

It was beautiful, Drystan had to agree. For a while they trotted at a good pace along the coastal road. Then in the afternoon, their pace slowed to almost a crawl, and they were forced to make detours around flooded valleys where the road was submerged. They even stopped once along the way to assist a farmer with removing an overturned tree from the road so he could get his cart by. Oddly enough, they did not pass a single soul coming from the opposite direction. There were local farmers, tradesmen, and even a few merchants going in the same direction as they were, but no one came from the direction of Ys.

~~~

It was raining hard. The heavy drops thumped like small stones on the soft ground on the other side of the tree line. It was unusual to set up camp in the forest, but Purin was glad that they did. The wind and rain might have ripped their tents apart if not for the cover of the trees. As it was, he stood outside his tent facing a young man desperately trying to catch his breath. He had ridden his horse to death a league or so south and run the rest of the way. Even with the thick canopy above them, Purin was quickly soaked, but he hardly noticed. Before he nearly passed out from exhaustion, the young man managed to get out that he had news of Princess Eselt. Purin waited patiently until the man could speak, although his patience was wearing thin.

One of his men brought wine, and the young man coughed and sputtered while he drank until, finally, he recovered enough to tell his tale. "I have news about the princess, my lord."

"Yes, Yes. I got that part. What's the rest of it?" Purin was growing seriously agitated and resisted the impulse to throttle the young man on the spot.

"She is at a way station just north of the River of Mist." It was an obvious effort to speak the whole sentence without pausing, and he gasped for breath, throwing up the wine he just drunk. A soldier standing next to Purin handed the young man another cup.

"Are you sure?"

Draining the cup of wine, the young man visibly calmed. "It was strange. At first, I did not notice her, and then she began to dry her hair near the fire, and it was suddenly clear to me who she was."

Purin moved a step closer and almost whispered, "Was anyone with her?"

The young man nodded. "A man in fine clothing. He's probably her escort or guard. He was so plain I don't remember what he looked like."

"Then it wasn't Drystan?"

"No, my lord." The young man looked confused. "Didn't he die when he jumped over the edge of the upper ward escaping the guards?"

Purin ignored the question and asked his own. "What names did they travel under?"

"I don't know, my lo—"

Purin backhanded the young man across the face, and he fell to his knees stunned. "Don't you think that might have been important?" he screamed at the young man.

His mouth full of blood; the young man couldn't immediately respond. Purin didn't need to hear his excuses anyway, he left the young man where he was and began barking orders. "Prepare your mounts, but leave the camp as it is! We are leaving now!"

"What about the weather, Captain?" one of his soldiers asked.

Purin rounded on the man as if he might strike him as well. "The storm is moving south fast. Pray we can move just as swiftly, for your sake."

~~~

Drystan set camp in a small glade just off the road. It was only midafternoon, but they weren't in a hurry, and Eselt was showing fatigue from the little sleep they had gotten during the storm the night before. Ys was, at most, half a day's ride south, which should put them in the city by about noon the next day. That would give them more than enough time to find a proper inn at which to stay before they began the adventure of exploring the city over the next few weeks.

Drystan dismounted and took hold of Eselt's mount while she climbed down from the sable mare she rode. Her father picked out the beautiful horse from the royal stables before they departed Teamhrach and presented it to her as a parting gift. He hobbled the horses nearby and brushed them down while Eselt foraged in the forest for herbs and roots to add to the dried vegetables and salted meats that the innkeeper provided. He even gave her a quick lesson on how to prepare camp stew before they left. Drystan wasn't sure if he looked forward to the results of that effort or not, but it didn't matter. They were together and free. They were beginning the time of their lives that they would tell their children about one day, and funny stories about their mother's camp stew might just be among the tales.

He and Eselt had not spoken much about it, but they both wanted a family, and as far as Drystan was concerned, the more the better. He could imagine a farm estate where they would live, growing whatever people grew where they lived, with his sons farming their land and his daughters making dresses. He was sure it was a naively simplistic fantasy that he harbored; anyway, it was his dream.

His ears perked up at a sound, and he turned to see Eselt emerging from the forest with the folded front of her skirt full of the treasures of her search. She stopped and smiled at him. Drystan smiled back, and for a brief moment in time their eyes were locked in the perfection of the moment that only those blessed by Sunna must be fortunate enough to experience. He loved Eselt with every fiber of his being, and somehow, he knew that she returned his love just as unconditionally. He wanted this moment to last forever, frozen in time like the memory it would soon become, a memory that he would remember in every detail for the rest of his life.

Vaguely, he thought he heard an odd *thunk*, like someone hitting a tree trunk with a rotten branch, and then Eselt's eyes opened wide with shock. Another *thunk* and Drystan looked down to see an arrow protruding from the ground next to him. He didn't have time to concern himself with that. Eselt was falling forward, stumbling toward him, dropping the roots and herbs she collected for their dinner.

Sprinting to the other side of the glade, Drystan barely managed to catch her before she hit the ground. Quickly he backed toward the horses, desperately scanning the forest for their assailant. He had Eselt in one arm and his sword out protectively with the other. Nothing moved. He located the arrow protruding from her back. It was near her spine, and surprisingly not lodged very deep. He was able to remove it without causing further damage, and it bled very little. Even still, Eselt was acting extremely lethargic.

Drystan held her close and sank to the ground. "Eselt! Eselt, can you hear me?" He feared the arrow had been poisoned.

"Drystan?" she spoke weakly. "I can't see anything."

"Don't worry, love, we will escape and get help." She didn't respond, and he shook her a little to try and wake her. Nothing. She was unconscious.

Lifting her as he stood, Drystan prepared to hoist her onto one of the horses and make their getaway.

"Let her be, Drystan. You're not going anywhere." He recognized that voice.

Still holding Eselt, Drystan sprang to his feet, thrusting his sword in the direction of the speaker. Several paces in front of him stood Captain Purin with at least twenty men. Half of them wore the coat of arms bearing the likeness of a boar from Duke Maruk's guard, and the other half wore the brown-and-green regalia of High King Cadeyrn.

"If you don't let these men tend to her," Purin waved his own sword toward the High King's men, "then she will die right here in this glade. You don't want that, do you, Drystan?"

Drystan was confused by what was happening. What were the Duke's Guard and the High King's men doing together, here of all places? They didn't look like the Fianna. Was this some kind of trick? And how could they have found them in the first place?

"Is there an antidote?" Drystan screamed like an animal. "Give it to me if you have one! You cannot let her die!"

Purin was not smiling. His expression was unemotional, if anything, and deadly serious when he spoke. "She will die, Drystan. Leave her on the ground and move away from her. Time is running out fast."

Drystan held Eselt tight to his chest and kissed her forehead. Tears were streaming down his face; frustration and anger coursed through his body. What could he do? He was so helpless to save her. How many times had he failed her? What was his life worth if he couldn't protect her?

"Drystan . . ." Purin cautioned softly.

He had no choice if she had a chance to live. Drystan gently placed her on the ground and kissed her soft lips. Then he backed away to the edge of the clearing.

Quickly, the High King's men rushed in and dragged her to the forest on the other side of the glade. Drystan took a step forward to pursue, but the Duke's Guard moved forward to put themselves between him and his lover.

"See? That wasn't so hard, now was it?" Purin was smiling broadly now.

"How did you find us, Purin? How do you recognize me now?" Drystan wondered if the charms had failed.

"Sunna knows, it wasn't easy." Purin his head. "Lugaid, is it? It's hard to look at you and not see someone else." He spread his hands apart innocently. "But isn't it obvious?"

Drystan was pacing back and forth in front of Purin and the line of guards still with him. Ten men. The others, the supposed High King's men, had disappeared into the forest with Eselt. "What's so obvious, Purin?"

"You have been betrayed." The statement was made so matter-of-factly that it did seem obvious. "Do you really believe that the High King would allow his daughter, a Princess of Eriu, to run away with a fallen Temple Knight?"

"Then why did he allow me to leave Teamhrach with Eselt to begin with?"

Purin laughed. "It wasn't about you, Drystan. It never was. The only way the High King could ever hope to separate you from his daughter was if you went back to Tintagel or if you were dead."

"Do you think to drag me back to Valiant Keep for my father?" Drystan spat defiantly. "You will not take me alive."

"Excellent news! I was counting on that. Your father has been feeling sentimental since you escaped, and if I brought you back alive, he might eventually forgive you. I could never allow that, could I? Especially now that I have the full trust and confidence of the duke."

Drystan stopped pacing. Instead of fury and adrenaline flowing through him like he had experienced with Sir Murhalt, he felt pure calm. He fixed Purin with a steady gaze. "Captain, I'm going to kill you and all here with you. Then I'm going to retrieve Eselt from those men you call the High King's. This is a ruse. I've spent enough time in Eriu to know what they look like."

"Look at you, Drystan. So confident and proud. You don't have your armor nor even a shield, and there are ten of us against you. It's over for you." Purin was obviously in no hurry to kill him. He was enjoying his moment too much to end it quickly. Drystan was in a hurry, however, if he was ever going to catch the men who abducted Eselt.

He was just about ready to ruin Purin's moment for good. "I'm not the man you knew once, Purin. I don't need my armor or a shield." Drystan casually walked up to the nearest guard. "All I need is this man's sword."

The guard's expression was one of astonishment. "I'm not gonna give . . ." Drystan's blade interrupted the man's remaining words in his throat, and he adeptly caught the guard's sword as it left his limp hand.

Then it began.

His own blade in one hand and the dead man's blade in the other,

Drystan waded into the line of the Duke's Guard with one purpose: kill them all. Whirling steel met steel, and he pivoted. One edge found a leg, and a sharp point discovered an eye socket. Three dead or maimed. Knocking away the raised swords of the next two, he impaled one in the chest and carved through the neck of another. Five out of the fight. Startled and confused, the others grouped together instead of surrounding him. He shattered one's collarbone with a brutal downward strike and gutted the nearest underneath the breastplate he wore. Seven out.

Drystan paused and retreated a few paces. He was covered with the blood of the guardsmen, and not one of them had managed to land a single blow. Purin's face was livid. He shouted at his remaining pair of guardsmen to attack. They hesitated and then ran into the forest. Nine away. Only Purin remained.

"I thought I killed you in the Valiant Keep," Drystan taunted.

"I thought I killed you in Teamhrach," Purin countered.

"Yet here we both stand. Just you and me. Let's end this." Drystan took a step forward.

Purin backed away. "I'll find you again." He turned and ran for the cover of the forest.

Two blades left Drystan's hands and sprouted in Purin's back. Pushed forward by the impact, he stumbled and fell to the ground. Drystan walked over and pulled the swords from Purin's back. This was not how he wanted Purin to die. Blood gushed from the open wounds and flowed onto the green grass of the glade, spoiling its romantic setting. Drystan rolled Purin onto his back with the toe of his boot and let the blades fall to the ground beside him.

The captain looked up at him defiantly. "I thought you were a knight."

Drystan straddled Purin and bent in close, nearly nose to nose. "Not anymore."

Slowly, he wrapped his hands around the captain's neck, squeezing tightly, deliberately. Purin struggled weakly, he had no strength left from the loss of blood. "This time, I will make sure you are dead."

Drystan took his time. He wanted Purin to experience every moment of his end.

Then it was done.

The adrenaline faded, and Drystan realized something was wrong, there was a sharp pain in his abdomen. He rolled himself off of Purin and just managed to get to his knees. Blood poured from a deep wound inflicted by a needlelike dagger in Purin's now dead hand. Drystan hadn't noticed it earlier. He pressed hard to stop the bleeding while his eyes flickered across the glade for any further threats. The guardsman with the injured leg had crawled quite a distance before his severed artery bled out, leaving a long crimson trail in the grass behind him. Another guard, the one with the punctured eye, lay twitching on the edge of the forest. Drystan's blade must have penetrated his brain enough to disable him for the remainder of his short life. No one else moved, and he doubted the two who got away would stop running until they reached Tintagel.

Exhaustion flooded through him, and he fell over to lie on the soft grass. He had to find Eselt. The remains of the small campfire he started earlier smoldered from neglect. He crawled over to it, pulled his long dagger from his belt, and shoved its tip into the crackling embers. Drystan prayed it would be hot enough. Rolling over on his back, he released his belt and pulled free the now ruined white tunic from his trousers exposing the wound to the air. Pulling the dagger out of the campfire, he tried to steady his shaky hand, then very deliberately thrust the flat of the blade against the wound. His scream rent the silence of the newly recovered serenity of the forest around him. He held the blade to his flesh for as long as he could—the acrid smell of burned blood and skin was sickening—and then he let the dagger fall to his side. He could barely move from fatigue, and his eyelids felt so heavy. Maybe just a quick nap . . .

Epilogue

Drystan opened his eyes to a chilly morning with the sunlight reflecting off the light frost that collected on the ground during the night. He lay motionless looking up at the clear sky still showing lines of oranges and reds as it pushed the darkness away, and his first thought was to take care not to wake Eselt. His contentment lasted only a moment before a tidal wave of pain and memories crashed down upon him.

He bolted upright, wincing at the burning ache in his abdomen, and looked around. Drystan was in the glade still, but not as he remembered it with Eselt. Nearby, on the crimson-stained grass of the once picturesque clearing, lay seven bodies of men he did not know, and one that he knew well—Purin. None of them moved, nor would any of them ever move again. Somehow he survived with the wound that must have festered during the night given its inflammation, but at least he had succeeded in cauterizing it. Drystan was grateful to be alive with only one objective that consumed him: pursue the men who had Eselt. He suspected that they were taking her back to Teamhrach with the expectation of collecting a hefty reward or ransom. Either way, High King Cadeyrn would most likely stretch their necks just for putting his daughter's life in danger.

Drystan hoped he could catch up with them before it ever came to that. Regrettably, the wound did not heal much during the night, and now they had several hours head start on him. That left him with only one reasonable choice: proceed to Ys and find a ship sailing north back to Kenno. If he was lucky, Drystan could get ahead of the men with Eselt and ambush them before they came anywhere near Teamhrach.

He stood up on wobbly legs and slowly made his way over to his horse. His head was swimming, and his stomach churned like the winds that rocked the way station two nights previous. Drystan realized then that he felt desperately sick and would need to find a healer when he reached Ys. In the meantime, he would do his best to stay alert and steady on his horse. As quickly as he could, he packed his and Eselt's possessions and tied her horse to his. This was going to be a long day for him, and if he survived his injury, worry over Eselt might be the death of him yet.

~~~

It was late afternoon when Drystan crested a rise and spied multiple plumes of black smoke that rose above the hills a league or two ahead of him. At first, Drystan was not sure what they were. There were so many that together they formed a dry, black cloud in the distance.

"It looks like the smoke is coming from Ys," Drystan commented to himself dubiously. "They must be burning debris from the storm the other night."

He had been on his horse all day, and he was nearly out of water. His injury was playing hell on his system, and he feared that it must be severely infected. Drystan was getting to the point that he wasn't sure if what he was seeing was real. Delirium was creeping up on him, and it was all he could do to keep his mount pointed in the right direction.

As he surmounted the last hill, his senses were nearly overwhelmed by the stench of cremation and the sights of devastation clear even from his distant view of Ys. He stopped and stared in stunned disbelief. It was a scene one would expect from an unimaginable nightmare conjured by the most depraved of demons. Drystan sat on his mount and took it all in silently, unable to wrap his mind around the madness his eyes revealed to him. For a while, he struggled to believe what he saw, but the scene never shifted, never changed. The horror was real.

Entirely half the city, from the port westward, was flooded with water-choked debris from ships, carts, and wooden structures. The port itself was so thick with the ruined remains of vessels that it might have been possible to walk from one end to the other without touching the water. The only structures left standing near the port were the granite walls that enclosed the inner harbor. Even the massive reinforced sea gates that once hung solidly between the walls were splintered and useless, floating freely against the walls.

The remnants of fires were everywhere blackening the beautiful white stone towers and catwalks farther away from the harbor. Outside the elegant white stone walls that protected the land side of Ys, enormous blazing pyres were erected to burn the dead and stave off disease; even at this hour, there were still many yet to put to the flame. Drystan had been to Ys only once in his life and remembered it as a beautiful, vibrant city, ancient and proud. What he witnessed now was not recognizable as the city that he knew many years before.

The entire world was going mad.

Drystan truly believed it was so. Every time he and Eselt were free to do as they pleased, something terrible would occur in their lives that would change their direction entirely. First, there was the night they planned their departure from Tintagel when they were captured by the dwarf's magic. Then they escaped and fled to Teamhrach only to be confronted by war and the poisoned blade of an assassin. Now here he was, facing a ruined city where they had thought to start a new life together. Worse than all of that, Eselt had been taken far away in the opposite direction. His heart sank when he looked back at the harbor. There would be no ships leaving for Kenno. Not today. Maybe not for many days.

The strange storm that he and Eselt endured that night at the way station must have barely touched them compared to the destruction that it visited upon Ys. That was two days ago, and from the looks of the damage, the population was still trying to crawl out from under the rubble. In a strange way, he was glad Eselt was not here to bear witness to the sadness. She would have been heartbroken.

He rode down the hill toward Ys, slowly taking in the whole of the devastation with no particular destination in mind. And then Drystan realized something wonderful, even beautiful was happening that gave him a measure of hope—the people of Ys were coming together to take back their city. Sun reflected off the shiny metal armor of the Temple Knights patrolling the streets of Ys on their equally brilliant armored mounts, keeping the looters at bay. Then there were the Atlantean wizards pushing the floating debris into the sea by expertly controlling the wind and water. The city guard had set up temporary kitchens and tents in dry areas around Ys to feed those in need, and the priests manned triage stations to heal the injured and provide comfort to the ones beyond their powers. There was even a small company of Dwarfs clearing heavy stone from fallen walls and crumbling houses.

Nudging his tired mount the rest of the way down to the city, he dismounted at the enormous gates. No guards were present to challenge his entry, and few people were going in and out of Ys unless they carried bodies by hand or cart to the fires. Most of the remains were covered by linen or a blanket. Still, the covering did not hide the tragedy that many of the deceased had died too young.

On the other side of the gates, the crowds were thin, and he was able to locate an inn that was converted to an infirmary. Inside, there were dozens of injured lined on tables and floors, anywhere space could be found, some in worse shape than others.

~~~

"Are you injured, sir?"

Drystan opened his eyes to look up at a young priest kneeling next to him. It took Drystan a moment to comprehend the words the man spoke. His head was swimming again, and he thought he might throw up. "I am not well. I have a wound that's become gravely infected."

The priest's expression turned to alarm, "Stay still, and I will bring you some water before I take a look at you."

Drystan nodded. "Bring a bucket if you have one. Please hurry."

The priest returned just in time for Drystan to empty what little he had in his stomach into the wooden bucket that was provided. The priest waited patiently for him to finish and then handed him a water skin.

The cool liquid felt magical spilling down his throat despite the pain he endured to drink it.

The priest crouched down next to him again. "My name is Gilber. Now tell me, where are you hurt?"

For the first time since he had regained consciousness, Drystan realized that he lay in a cart path on the low side of a hill. His gaze darted in every direction to find some semblance of recognition – the last thing he remembered was walking through what remained of the city gates to Ys. There was death, so much death, and ruin unimaginable.

Above him, at the top of the hill, his horse stood impassively munching on the long green grass. There was no smoke, the air was clear and fresh like any country morning.

"Where are you hurt?" Gilber repeated.

"Here." Drystan pulled back his long cloak, revealing the injury to his abdomen. The wound was an angry red around the black dagger-shaped scorch he applied, and the stench of burned flesh caused even the priest to recoil a little.

"This is beyond my power," Gilber admitted. "We need to get you to Ys where an associate of mine can fix you up."

"Ys," Drystan grabbed the priest's arm and held tightly. "What has happened in Ys?"

Confusion crossed Gilber's features. "Whatever do you mean? Other than the antics of Princess Ahes, not much has changed in Ys."

Drystan felt relieved. He had dreamt it all, suffered massive delusions or both. He pulled his cloak back over his abdomen to smother the foul odor and tried to relax. Once he felt better, he would buy a half dozen horses and ride as fast as he could north. If he changed mounts often and rested them three or four times a day, he could make up some of the time he had lost. He closed his eyes to control the desperation he felt. Even on the fastest horse that would never tire, he doubted that he could catch up with Eselt's captors before they reached Tintagel. And that was assuming they were going to Tintagel. Maybe Purin spoke the truth, and they were taking her to Teamhrach. Drystan wanted to weep, but he held it in. They were just as likely to be taking her to the Leprechauns again.

Gilber stood and thrust his hand out to help Drystan to his feet. "You can ride in my cart. There is no way you're getting on a horse in your condition."

He took the offer and slowly followed the priest to his cart. Drystan wasn't about to argue. He could barely stand, let alone climb onto his saddle. Moments later, the priest snapped the reins to motivate the pair of mules pulling his cart to clamber up the muddy road to the top of the hill where Drystan's horse stood.

Gilber brought the cart to a stop when they got there, jumped out and secured Drystan's horse to the side-board. Drystan hardly noticed. He was staring in relief and wonder at the vision of Ys a league or so in the distance.

Impossibly tall towers with arching walkways between them sparkled in the afternoon sun above high crenelated walls that stretched around the whole of the city and embraced a massive port far into the ocean. There, two sets of massive double doors stood open to allow maritime traffic to flow freely in and out on the smooth waters. Everywhere, trees, gardens and fountains integrated seamlessly with the architecture lending the impression that the stone structures were designed around the natural areas. There were even plants on top of most of the buildings or crawling up the towers at impractical angles that defied what little he knew about nature. Drystan was astounded at the beauty of the Ys. Not even Lyon's Gate could compete against her raw beauty.

The sudden jerk of the cart moving forward caused a jolt of pain to streak through his body that nearly made him scream. He held it stoically, refusing to submit to the agony inflicted by each bump in the road. Nearly more than he could bear, Drystan focused his mind on what his love, Eselt, must be enduring in her own reluctant journey in the opposite direction. It was only the excruciating pain deep in his abdomen that kept him from chasing after her captors immediately and the weakness in body, if not spirit, and the rolling of the cart, that eventually settled him into a deep slumber.

~~~

Drystan was startled awake by Gilber gently shaking his shoulder. He didn't know if he passed out from the pain or fallen asleep from exhaustion – probably a combination of both as he didn't even realize the cart had stopped. Bleary-eyed and feeling more than a little disoriented, Drystan vaguely realized they had entered the city as Gilber helped him from the cart to stumble through a set of doors into the shade of a darkened room.

Struggling to clear the haze from his eyes, Drystan first noticed a sweet floral scent heavy in the room. Then the soft glow of a light globe abruptly appeared causing him to shy back and squint from the illumination.

Gilber moved out of the shadow of a man looming over his shoulder. "I'm sorry to startle you, but I have brought the specialist that I believe can help you. This is High Priest Surthian of Atlantis."

Drystan's eyes were glued to the man standing next to Gilber from the moment he opened them. The high priest Gilber introduced as Surthian was an Exceptional One. Of course, Drystan had seen them before in Tintagel and other places where he traveled and even met one briefly many years ago in Valiant Keep. It was said that they were called Exceptional Ones because of their highly adept skill with magic. Drystan was sure it had something to do with their very 'exceptional' appearance as well. This one wore blue robes several shades darker than his blue-tinted skin, with long white hair that came to his shoulders and unnerving large almond-shaped eyes that didn't blink often enough. Just like all the others Drystan had seen, Surthian was very lean, with a broad chest and long thin limbs. He wasn't young, but he wasn't elderly either—probably late-middle-aged by their standards.

"What is your name?" Surthian spoke in a medium timbre that was soothing to the ear, and his face held a smile that compelled trust. Drystan didn't think it was a trick of magic. The Exceptional Ones seemed to have a way with others that laid the souls of those they met bare.

"Drys . . . Lugaid, honored one." Even here, with this Atlantean, Drystan needed to keep his secrets to himself.

Surthian's smile broadened just a little. "Very well, Lugaid. Shall I have a look at you, then?"

Drystan slowly pulled back his cloak and was immediately aware of the terrible stench. Gilber was kind enough not to comment, but the man's nose twitched involuntarily, and he appeared on the verge of gaging. Not so for the Exceptional One. He seemed not to notice the stink at all and moved closer to have a better look at Drystan's injury.

"Your wound is very deep and infected. Were you struck by an arrow or dagger?"

Drystan was surprised. Surthian knew wounds very well. "It was a dagger."

Surthian poked gently around the edges of the wound with a small metal rod he produced from his robe. "This wound has festered badly and infected some of your internal organs." He cocked his head to look into Drystan's eyes. "You cauterized it poorly almost a day ago. I am surprised that you survived the night without proper attention." To Drystan's relief, there was no question in Surthian's statement, and he didn't have to think of another lie.

The Exceptional One rubbed a dry yellow powder onto the wound and then pressed his hand against it. Drystan felt his skin grow very warm, almost hot, and then very cold. An intense blue glow radiated eerily between the cracks of Surthian's fingers. Drystan's first instinct was to pull away and bring a halt to the procedure. With what he was sure was superhuman resolve, he kept at it, and just when he was sure he could bear it no more, it ended. When the Exceptional One finally pulled his hand away, Drystan's abdomen appeared fully mended.

"That's incredible," Drystan muttered.

"The area where the wound used to be will be sore for several days. Try not to exert yourself too much if you don't have to. And the infection is gone." Surthian placed his hands on Drystan's head and pressed firmly. "If you will indulge me, I'm going to check to make sure that you have no other internal infections. This will not take long."

Drystan nodded.

A few moments went by and then a few more. Drystan began to worry and wondered if Eselt's cure had been any more comfortable. Purin said they had the antidote and there was no benefit to that madman if she died. Besides, he could still feel her presence inside of him, and he knew in the depths of his heart that she was among the living.

Surthian finally spoke up. "There is a presence of magic that blankets your consciousness like a shroud. It is unclear what its purpose is, except that I am sure it is not harming you. In any case, I am going to remove it just to be safe. It's called a geas and is usually cast upon someone to gain control or influence over them."

This was a surprise. He remembered that Wodanaz used that same word when the minstrel and Myrllin were leaving the camp where Drystan had rescued Eselt. Whatever it was, it didn't sound good. "What is the purpose of this geas?"

Surian shrugged. "It's hard to tell. After I remove it, you may feel like you are missing something or have forgotten something you are supposed to do. Hold still. This might become . . . uncomfortable."

At first, Drystan felt a subtle pulling, as if all the hairs on his head were being wrenched at one time. It only intensified, and in short order, Drystan was screaming at the top of his lungs. Gilber did his best to hold him down in his chair, but it wasn't enough to stop Dryustan's arms and legs from flailing about. Surthian also applied pressure at the top of his head, his exceptional strength serving to keep Drystan planted in one spot. As it was, Drystan was certain that his brain was being plucked out through the pores in his scalp. When the Exceptional One released him, Drystan practically collapsed from exhaustion. He felt himself being carried and then laid gently on a hard surface with blankets. There were voices above him, but he was too tired to make an effort to understand the words. All he wanted to do was sleep. Not even the desperation to find Eselt could keep his eyes open.

Eselt.

For reasons he could not have explained, Drystan felt different when he thought about her now, and he wondered if he had ever really been in love with her. Maybe he hadn't. Maybe it had been nothing more than infatuation. Sleep called to him, and even through his delirium, he knew that he was somehow his old self again.

~~~

A cold gloom pervaded the darkness of the stone chamber where Eselt spent most of her life growing up in the Tower House that was her home in Teamhrach. Never had her room felt so devoid of life and happiness. The wooden dolls with painted faces and pretty dresses that lined the shelves on one wall reflected sad, mocking smiles in the pale moonlight that spilled through the open balcony window. No candles were lit; there were no light globes activated to bring warmth back to the room. Eselt couldn't bear it. She needed to be alone and in the dark, in a place where her despair could find comfort.

She awoke fully less than an hour ago for the first time in more days than she could know, and immediately she felt something missing. Her scream echoed through the halls and chambers of the Tower House, disrupting the quiet slumber of the early hours, sending those that tended to her recovery scrambling to her side.

Eselt's mother appeared and shooed them all away, allowing Eselt the privacy to sob freely in her mother's arms like she had rarely done when she was a child. The warmth of her mother's embrace and soothing coos calmed her. But with the calm came the memories.

She was in Drystan's arms the last time they were together, right after she had been bitten in her back by something sharp. Within the span of a few short moments, she could barely keep her eyes open, and Drystan had held her, terrified, calling her name. After that, the memories were a blur.

Men had taken her, forced water and food into her mouth, cleaned her and restrained her with chains inside a wagon covered with a thick fabric. There was no clarity. They must have kept her drugged the entire journey back to Teamhrach until she was dumped at the gates of the upper ward inside a heavy sack.

"Mother," Eselt sobbed. "I don't think I can go on."

"Nonsense, child, you are home with your family, and I have no doubt that your brave young knight will soon be breaking down the walls to be with you again."

"Not this time, Mother. I don't feel him anymore. Drystan is dead."

GLOSSARY AND CAST

Arid Fellowship - A professional guild of assassins based in Eriu.

Atiod-bherto - Cult of Druids defeated in the one-hundred-year Oak Wars by the combined forces of the Druids of Sunna and Eriu and the allied cities in both Eriu and Lyonesse. The Atiod were infamous for ritual sacrifice of holy animals and humans on stone altars or burned alive in large wooden effigies. Their stone circles are identified by the center recumbent stone and flankers used for astronomy, ritual, and sacrifice. The Atiod were chiefly located in the extreme north and south of Eriu with a few enclaves scattered around the fringes of Lyonesse.

Aja - Once a benevolent healer, she is possessed by a Chaos Demon and begins a killing streak across the Western Kingdoms.

Bargina - Sweet bread from Eriu.

Caomh the Enlightened - The Arch-Druid of Eriu.

Captain Purin - Captain of the Duke's Guard in Tintagel.

Commander Teutjorīk - Commander of the Fianna, elite guardians of the High King of Eriu.

Drystan - Adopted son of Duke Maruk, Temple Knight of Sunna, and Eselt's lover. AKA Sir Lugaid of House Gille Fhaolain, Knight of Eriu.

Duke Maruk - Ruler of Tintagel, adoptive father of Drystan, and Eselt's husband.

Earl Fineas Eckert - Lord of Stoddenferry Castle in Lyonesse, husband to Lady Rhoswen, and father of Sir Reginald and Perault.

Eselt - Youngest daughter of the High King of Eriu and Drystan's lover. AKA Lady Esmeth of House Dubhshláine

Fianna (singular Fiann) - High King of Eriu's elite knights.

Filberzh the Risen - The Arch-Druid of Sunna.

Greallán - Druid of Sunna who helped heal Purin.

High King Cadeyrn - High King of Eriu and father of Eselt.

Hydruntin Ass - An ass common throughout the Western Kingdoms, Hella, and the Capsians.

Isaro - Stable boy at the inn outside of Teamhrach where Drystan and Eselt stayed.

Kenno-windo - The "white-headed" mountain range in southern Eiru.

King Praeter Eldorath and Queen Penelope Eldorath - Rulers of Lyonesse.

Lady Fedelmid - Lady-in-waiting to Princess Eselt.

Liafal - The Stone of Destiny where the High Kings of Eriu are coroneted.

Loch Angu - *Angu* meaning snake.

Lochlann - An arrogant young Druid who attempted to heal Moina, one of Aja's victims.

Lunula - A crescent-shaped jewelry traditionally worn as a necklace in Eriu.

Mairwen, Gwynn, and Braith - Eselt's older sisters.

Miniver fur - Soft white fur from the underbelly of the red squirrel's winter coat.

Moina - The baker infected by Aja's poison.

Morgen - Community of Merpeople who live in the depths of the Bay of Morgens.

Myrllin - The Mad Bard, the Prophet, the Sage, the Steward of Hy Brasil. He has the ability to foresee the future with varying degrees of clarity. He is a powerful wizard with an obscure past. Myrllin lives in a castle on the mystical island of Hy Brasil, which is not always visible. When he is not needed, he has the ability to hibernate without aging for hundreds of years at a time. Son of the legendary Tuatha De hero Dhroghan and a Nymph, and a twin brother, Wodanaz, whom he is older than by one minute.

Odhrán - Eriu Druid specializing in cures for poisons who saved Drystan's life.

Ourea - Massive volcano in the Atlas Mountains on the Island of Atlantis.

Perault - Squire and youngest son of Earl Fineas Eckert, Lord of Stoddenferry Castle, and Lady Rhoswen.

Reskalin Arlth - Master Assassin and second to the FatMan.

Salik - Herb originating from the bark of a willow that has the healing properties of an anti-inflammatory, usually mixed with warm tea.

Sione - Master thief andDaughter of the FatMan.

Sir Blevin - Knight Commander of the Temple Knights in Tintagel.

Sir Clavemore of Bours - The knight that Drystan was apprenticed to.

Sir Wilhem - Duke Maruk's closest advisor.

Spearmen of House Kunagno - From Dunon in Eriu, considered the finest spearmen in all of the Western Kingdoms.

The FatMan - Guild Master of the Seven Stars Brotherhood, Master of the Sewer Rats, and Benefactor of the Sassy Ladies.

Triskele - A symbol with three spirals radiating from a common center.

Tuatha De - A mysterious, magical race of people who reside in a kingdom of four cities far to the north.

Tuatha De Blood - The pure race of Tuatha De that comprises the leadership, scholars, and wizard class of their people.

Tudful - Guild facilitator in the lower city of Tintagel.

Valiant Keep - Home of Duke Maruk in Tintagel.

Vuro Menjo - "Cold mountains," the most northern mountain range in the Western Kingdoms.

Wodanaz – The Wanderer, Famed Poet and Minstrel, Seeker of Wisdom, Chronicler of the Fourth Age, Son of legendary Tuatha De Dhroghan and a Nymph, and brother of Myrllin.

About the Author

Born in Homestead, Florida, Ravek Hunter grew up in the United States and Belgium. He earned a bachelor's degree in marketing from Florida International University and went on to become a sporting goods executive. He currently serves as a consultant in the same industry and occasionally assists his wife of fifteen years at her floral design company. The proud father of two boys, Ravek counts reading, exercising, and family travel among his leisure hobbies.

Over the past thirty-five years, Ravek's passion has been researching ancient civilizations with a focus on the origin stories behind their mythology. His writing style attempts to immerse the reader into the story by bringing to life historically accurate and rich details of the culture that frames the narrative of the time period in which the novel is based.

Inspired by classic fantasy authors like Robert Jordan, Terry Goodkind, and R. A. Salvatore, Ravek writes to entertain and provoke his readers, who, he hopes, share his fondness for mythology.

CONNECT WITH RAVEK HUNTER

Thank you for choosing this work of blood, sweat and tears by *Ravek Hunter*! If you enjoyed reading this novel, please consider posting a review, telling me what you think on one of the social media platforms listed below or reach out via my direct email:

Friend me on Facebook:

https://www.facebook.com/Ravek-Hunter-Literary-LLC-238417183579740/

Follow me on Twitter:

https://twitter.com/RavekHunter

Subscribe to my blog:

https://www.goodreads.com/author/show/17885196.Ravek_Hunter

Visit my website:

https://www.WorldsofAtlantis.com

Email: Ravekhunter@gmail.com

www.ingramcontent.com/pod-product-compliance
Lightning Source LLC
Chambersburg PA
CBHW031939010726
47493CB00007B/1995